TITLES BY JULIA LONDON

THE PRINCES OF TEXAS NOVELS

The Charmer in Chaps
The Devil in the Saddle
The Billionaire in Boots

STAND-ALONE NOVELS

You Lucky Dog

JOVE
New York

You
Lucky
Dog

Julia London

A JOVE BOOK
Published by Berkley
An imprint of Penguin Random House LLC
penguinrandomhouse.com

Library of Congress Cataloging-in-Publication Data

Names: London, Julia, author.
Title: You lucky dog / Julia London.
Description: First edition. | New York: Jove, 2020. | Series: Lucky dog
Identifiers: LCCN 2020014148 (print) | LCCN 2020014149 (ebook) |
ISBN 9780593100387 (trade paperback) | ISBN 9780593100394 (ebook)
Subjects: GSAFD: Love stories.
Classification: LCC PS3562.O48745 Y68 2020 (print) |
LCC PS3562.O48745 (ebook) | DDC 813/.54—dc23
LC record available at https://lccn.loc.gov/2020014148
LC ebook record available at https://lccn.loc.gov/2020014149

First Edition: August 2020

Printed in the United States of America
1   3   5   7   9   10   8   6   4   2

Cover design and illustration by Colleen Reinhart
Title spread art: Basset hound silhouette © oorka / Shutterstock
Book design by Laura K. Corless

This book is dedicated with love to the dogs that have shaped my life:

Punkin, Nibbles, Pepper, Junior, Junior-Junior (JJ),
Bessie, Emmett, Ug, Sam, Sadie, Cissy, Charlie,
Hugo, Maude, Sonny, and Moose

One Day in Austin, Texas

In a central part of town, a man with demonstrably limited ambition (one only needs to see how much time he spends playing video games), collects the dogs he walks three times weekly. There are seven altogether—two basset hounds, a lab, two medium-sized dogs of questionable heritage, a beagle mix, and a dachshund that struggles to keep up. The man—Brant—loads the dogs into the back of his ten-year-old Toyota 4X4, drives down to the shores of Lady Bird Lake, leashes up the dogs, and walks them on the heavily trafficked Butler Hike-and-Bike Trail. He likes this particular route because there are other dogs and access points for the big dogs to swim (the dachshund is afraid of water). Also, there is a spot just under the Pfluger Pedestrian Bridge where Brant usually can sell enough weed to get through the week.

He's noticed a new guy hanging around his business location on their last couple of outings, and today the new guy saunters over. When Brant asks what's up, the new guy says, "I'm visiting in town and looking for a friend." Brant doesn't want to ask what that means because he feels like he ought to know. "Cool, cool," he says. But then another thought occurs to him, an unsavory thought, and he takes a step backward and says, "What *kind* of friend?"

"Depends," the new guy says. "What have you got?"

Ah. That kind of friend. Still, Brant is mildly confused, because he is not a grocery store and people generally know what they want. But he's relaxed, because he had a little toke earlier, and this is Austin and everybody smokes weed and everyone is cool with everyone . . .

Well, except the new guy, turns out. New guy is a cop, which Brant discovers after he makes a pretty good sale and what he thinks is a really funny joke about dogs and weed. That's when two squad cars roll up and the dogs start barking, and the new guy reads him his Miranda rights. "Come on, man," Brant complains to the officer who cuffs him. "At least let me call my buddy to take the dogs home."

In old West Austin, just east of Tarrytown, a woman in a blue sedan in desperate need of an oil change rockets down the gravel drive to a cottage tucked behind a much larger house. The cottage was once a carriage house, then it was occupied by a coven of witches or hippies or maybe even Matthew McConaughey—it depends on who you talk to—and then renovated into sleek urban sophistication by the Californians who bought the property and now rent it out for an outrageous amount.

Carly has been stuck in traffic and really must avail herself of the facilities. She bangs through the door, leaves her key dangling from the lock, and abandons her overstuffed tote bag in the entry. She is trying desperately to untie the strange but fashionable wraparound jumpsuit with the billowing sleeves she is wearing, but in her rush she draws up short and stares into the living area. She doesn't comprehend what she is seeing. Her eyes simply cannot reconcile the sight of the dog on the couch with her brain. It's not that she doesn't have a dog—she does. It's not that she doesn't have a basset hound—she does. But she doesn't have *that* basset hound.

That is an imposter basset hound.

An imposter so miscast in its role that it is on her couch eating one of her expensive throw pillows without an ounce of remorse, as telegraphed by the enthusiastic banging of its tail against the cushions.

That dog is a mystery, but in that moment, Carly must make a necessary decision. She dashes off to answer the call of nature.

Hours later, on a leafy street a couple of blocks from the woman's house, in another old West Austin home that has withstood the onslaught of modernization and McMansioning that is going on around town, a university professor bangs through the side entrance with his arms around another university professor he's had a few drinks with tonight. Though his thoughts have turned to a slushy, boozy mess, he does notice that his dog is in the mudroom with her head pressed in the corner where the walls meet. He notes that her food bowl has not been touched and her favorite chew toy—the longhorn with the two missing horns—is on the other side of the room. This is strange behavior for his otherwise enthusiastic and friendly dog, but Max assumes she is pouting because he is home late. Well, sue him. He watches out for his dad and his brother on top of a full-time teaching job and two massive research projects, and sometimes, a person develops an itch that needs to be scratched.

One

Austin, Texas

What a peculiar phenomenon it is to see something that the brain cannot comprehend. Not something that simply doesn't make sense in the moment—like that time you saw your mother tiptoeing out of the neighbor's house in the early morning hours half-dressed and giggling. Or that time your boss handed you a pink slip after you'd helped him reorganize the staff, and you smiled with delight because you didn't get that you had efficiently organized yourself right out of a good job.

No, this was different. This was like a weird ministroke, but without a headache or heart palpitation. Carly felt perfectly fine. And yet she could not comprehend how the dog stretched out on her couch could look *exactly* like her dog and not *be* her dog.

It was a basset hound, just like her dog, with a black and brown coat with patches of white, long floppy ears, and ginormous paws and eyes that could look happy and sad at the same time.

"You're not my dog," she informed the imposter. "Where is Baxter?"

The dog had no answer for her other than a tail that thumped a happy beat against the pillows it had destroyed.

Actually, *technically*, Baxter was not her dog. He was her sister's dog. Except that *technically* Baxter was not Mia's dog, either. He was a dog her mother had tried to give one of Mia's kids for his birthday, but of course things had gotten out of hand, because they always did where her mother was concerned. It was a long, complicated story, and, frankly, when you got right down to it, Carly's entire family was complicated, and their lives were muddied together, and anyway, that's how she and Baxter the Dog had ended up in each other's company.

Carly had not wanted the responsibility of a dog. Carly was very busy. Carly was going to move to New York City as soon as she found a job there. A dog required attention and care and food, all of which Carly did not have. Nevertheless, she and Baxter had been going along with this arrangement since a tearful Mia had pushed the listless dog like a big sack of flour across her kitchen's tile floor to Carly's feet. That was Carly's first glimpse into life with a basset hound: they were disinclined to cooperate.

But Carly had pitied the poor creature and had taken him just to spare him the chaos that was erupting around him in Mia's house. And Baxter did seem to appreciate the rescue. Carly had never had a dog before, so in addition to a dog bed and water bowl, she bought a manual, something like, *The Care and Feeding of Your New Best Friend*. She read it cover to cover, and was happy to report to no one that in their monthlong acquaintance, Baxter had never once gotten on her beautiful cream West Elm couch. He liked to keep to his corner of her kitchen, near the back door. He liked to press his head to the wall, as if he thought if he couldn't see anyone, no one could see him. Carly didn't have the heart to tell him she could still plainly see him.

He seemed to be okay with her tiny backyard. He liked to sleep a lot, too, and he liked to chew on giant bones. Occasionally, he'd go outside and bark at something only he could see, but then he'd trot back in, mission accomplished. Sometimes, when Carly was sitting cross-legged on the floor next to the coffee table, listening to Megan Monroe, the host of her favorite podcast, *Big Girl Panties*, give tips for how to navigate life when it was pummeling you with lemons, Baxter would come and sit next to her, his butt pressed against her leg, facing away. Carly would absently caress his back while Megan convinced her that she *could* have it all. Megan said she could have the perfect boyfriend (she would need a boy for that), the perfect home (if she could scrape up the rent), the perfect job (if someone would just hire her already), and still be *her*. Given the current state of Carly's life—a complete and utter mess—she felt compelled to listen to every single episode, sometimes taking notes, while Baxter dozed beside her.

Yep, they'd had the perfect working relationship, and Baxter had never once branched out of his territory and onto a couch, much less taken up pillow eating. Which made him much more desirable than this imposter.

"Maybe I'm being punked," Carly mused, and quickly rifled through her mental catalogue of friends in search of the jokester who would pull a stunt like this. But her close friends—Karma, who had just gotten married and was in the honeymoon phase and was *never* free, and Lydia, an ER nurse working night shifts and never awake— didn't have the comedic chops to pull this off. No disrespect to her friends.

Was she in the wrong house? She'd been in desperate need of a bathroom, and a lot of the houses around here looked sort of the same. She'd rushed in without really looking at anything but the dark hole of her tote bag where her keys were swimming. She did a quick scan of the room, her eyes flicking over the built-in bookcases that framed the fireplace, the hand-scraped wide-plank pine floors, the pale blue rug, the cream-colored couch, and the floral armchairs.

Definitely the right house. Definitely the wrong dog.

Speaking of which, the dog apparently grew bored of waiting for her to figure it out. It stood up on its stumpy legs on the couch, paused for a good and long downward dog, then slid off, landing with a thud, before confidently trotting over to sniff her legs and lick her shoe.

"Listen, I don't know who you are or how you got here but I want Baxter back." She leaned down to scratch him behind his long ears.

The dog allowed it and sat to give her a moment to reconsider, its tail swishing hard against the floor and knocking around the balls of synthetic white stuffing that had previously occupied her throw pillow.

"You're super cute, but I'm not keeping you. I want you to go home. Who are you? Why aren't you wearing tags?"

The dog's tail wagged harder. It slid down to the floor, rolled onto its back, presenting for a belly rub. That's when Carly had visual confirmation that this most certainly was *not* Baxter. This dog was female.

"Okay, we've got to get this situation fixed," she said, making a circular motion at the dog's head, "before wrong bassets start showing up at regular intervals around here." But she did reach down and rub the dog's belly to demonstrate she could be hospitable, even in the face of disaster.

From the bowels of her overstuffed tote bag, still on its side in the entry, the contents partially disgorged, her phone sounded a cheery little notice of a text. "Stay," she said to the dog.

Of course the dog didn't stay. She hopped up and trotted into the kitchen like she lived here and helped herself to big, loud laps of water from Baxter's bowl.

The text was from Phil, the photographer Carly had coerced into doing a shoot for her. It said simply, Meet me at five.

Meet him at *five*? First of all, five was the worst possible time to meet anyone anywhere. And second, their shoot was tomorrow. *Tuesday*. Wait a minute . . . Carly looked at her watch. *Shit*. Today was Tuesday.

Don't be late, he added.

"I'm already late! I'm like a day late!" she shouted at her phone.

Carly and Phil had worked together at the big advertising firm of Dalworth, Bartle and Simmons. Phil had been an art creator at DBS and had been made redundant in the reorganization, too. With his photography skills and his contacts, he'd quickly transitioned into a professional photography career specializing in headshots and weddings. Carly knew this because she and Phil, and some of the others who'd been laid off, met occasionally for drinks and to complain about the unfairness of it all. (Megan would not approve. *Time spent complaining or feeling sorry for yourself is time you could have spent creating your new reality.* But as Carly was still struggling to create her new reality, she was up for a little whining from time to time.)

Carly's new reality was a tiny little one-woman marketing and public relations shop with a grand total of two clients. *Temporary* clients, just until she got a full-time position with a firm. Unfortunately, temporary clients willing to take her on between jobs were not the kind to spend a lot of money, and life had become a struggle. Carly knew that Phil felt sorry for her, so borrowing another page from *Big Girl Panties*, she had used that to her advantage and had asked him for a huge favor.

How the hell had she gotten her days mixed up? How could it be Tuesday? She thought it was Monday. Where did Monday go? How did a person forget a Monday . . . unless, maybe, you were working every day, including weekends. The last time she and Lydia spoke, Lydia had insisted Carly was the one with the scheduling problem. "You work *all* the *time*," she'd complained.

Wait—Tuesday was also the day her dog walker took Baxter on his walk. "You have got to be kidding me," she muttered as the imposter dog padded out of the kitchen, water dripping from her jowls and leaving a trail across Carly's hardwood floors.

She texted Phil back, said she'd see him at the studio at five, which was impossible, then squatted down and started shoving things back into her tote bag. She had schedules to keep. Deadlines to meet. These photos of a young fashion designer's collection were going to Ramona McNeil, the influential creative director at *Couture* magazine. *Couture* was one of the premier fashion magazines in the country, and it was the holy grail for someone like her client Victor Allen.

It was the holy grail for her, too. Carly currently had two applications submitted for vacant positions at the magazine. One, in marketing and publicity. One, in the creative department. In the meantime, she'd worked her ass off to get Victor noticed, and considered it a feather in her cap that she'd succeeded.

Carly needed these photos and she was not going to be derailed by an imposter dog. She shoved her bag onto her shoulder and ran down the hall to find the dog, grabbing a leash off a peg in the entry on her way.

She found the basset hound in the bathroom with one of Carly's very expensive shoes between her paws. Carly cried out with alarm. She dove for the shoe as the dog's tail wagged. "Are you crazy? You must have a death wish," she said, and tossed the shoe onto her bathroom counter. "Come on. You're riding along. I obviously can't leave you here alone and, by the way, you owe me a couch pillow," she said as she hooked up the leash on the dog's collar. "An *expensive* couch pillow, too, because I bought that one when I had a job." She rubbed the dog's head and caressed its back a moment. "We have to get out of here before you eat my house."

The dog responded with excited tail wagging as she trotted alongside Carly on their way down the hall. "If you're wondering who is responsible for this disaster? It's Brant, your former dog walker." She opened her front door. "Just so you know, he's a dead man walking, so FYI, you may not be romping around Lady Bird Lake next week. He's dead just as soon as I get Baxter back." The dog gazed up at her with adoration. "No offense, Bubbles."

Judging by the wag of her tail, it didn't appear that any offense was taken.

❧

On the way to the studio, Carly cautioned Little Miss Sunshine in the back seat to be on her best behavior when they arrived. Her client, the youthful and phenomenal fashion designer Victor Allen, was doing some different and colorful things with his hair these days and, on occasion, he appeared to be dressed for Halloween.

"So no barking," Carly said. "I have only two clients and I can't afford to lose either of them. Got it?" She looked in the rearview mirror, but all she could see was the back half of the dog and that furiously wagging tail. Bubbles had her head out the window.

"Victor is going to be huge in the fashion world *if* I can get him through the New Designer Showcase without killing him. And, yes, that is why I am wearing this mess," she said as they inched across town in heavy traffic. "Don't judge."

Bubbles surged forward to lick her face. "Yeah, okay," Carly said. She pushed the dog back before she wiped her cheek of her slobbery kiss. "I still can't believe this happened, can you? I mean, having the wrong day, the wrong dog . . ." She sighed. "Well, whatever, it happened, and, like Megan says, I don't have time to dwell on it because I am dwelling on solutions." She glanced in the rearview mirror to see if the dog bought any of that. Bubbles was sitting in the middle of the seat now. Her tongue was hanging from one side of her mouth. She was panting as she stared out the front windshield like she hadn't heard a word.

For what it was worth, Carly didn't buy it, either.

The light turned green, but the cars stacked up at the light in front of her didn't move. Carly instructed her car to call Brant. Not surprisingly, given the magnitude of his screwup, the call rolled to his voice mail.

"Brant! This is Carly Kennedy. You know, the one with the depressed basset hound? Well, guess what? You put a *happy* basset hound in my house! I want my depressed hound back! How could you

do that? Where is Baxter? Whose dog is this? Call me back immediately!"

She ended the call and muttered her opinion of Brant the Dog
Walker. The line of cars began to move, and she shot forward. In the
back seat, Bubbles had stuffed her nose into a crack between the two
back seats, snorting loudly. But then something outside caught her
attention and she surged to the window and released a deep, baying
howl of joy.

When they reached the studio, Carly grabbed her tote bag, the
dog's leash, and dashed inside.

She didn't know what she expected—probably Victor and Phil
pacing around each other, the models antsy . . . but no. Victor, with
his rainbow hair and hand-painted jeans, was on a skateboard, slowly
moving around the two models who were sitting on plastic chairs,
their gazes on their phones. Phil was sprawled on his back on the
beat-up earth brown couch that looked as if it had been picked up off
the street.

"I made it!" Carly shouted, as if she'd just swum across the English
Channel to get here.

"Great." Phil slowly rolled up to a sitting position. He yawned.

Victor stopped skating and maneuvered his board around to face
her. He looked her up and down and shook his head. "That's not how
you're supposed to wear that." He hopped off his board and strode
across the room to her. He forced her arms into a T and began pulling
and tugging at the weird wraparound jumpsuit thingy she was wearing.

Victor was twenty years to her twenty-eight, but sometimes the age
gap felt much greater. He was still at that young and dumb age about
so many things in life. The sole exception was fashion, and in that he
had the talent to lead the charge into fashion-forward designs like a
boy king. He was a creative genius, and that was not hyperbole.

"Hey, Bax," Victor said to the very interested basset who was
sniffing around his sneakers.

"That's not Baxter," Carly said as Victor jerked her around so that her back was to him. She had to drop the leash so as not to get tangled in it.

Victor snorted. "Yeah, it is. I'm looking right at him."

"So funny thing," Carly said. "This dog *looks* like Baxter, but it's—"

Victor put his hands on her waist and made her twist again.

"But it's not Baxter. There was a mix-up with the dog walker and somehow I—"

"Hey, are we going to do this, or are we going to talk about dogs?" Phil asked, and unfolded his lanky self from the couch.

"Yeah," Victor said. He stood back and examined her for a moment, then gave a nod of approval. "But listen. I'm hungry."

Carly waited for him to finish his thought. That apparently was the entirety of his thought.

"Hungry for what?" Phil asked.

Victor shrugged. "Whataburger?"

"I'd be down for that," Phil said.

Victor looked at the models. "How about you ladies?"

"Fries," one of them said without looking up from her phone. The other one held up two fingers to indicate two orders.

"What . . . you mean like *now*?" Carly asked, looking around at her assortment of fashion people.

"Now," Phil said.

"You told me you'd give me thirty minutes," she reminded him. "You said not a minute longer."

"I'll give you an hour if there is a Whataburger in my future," Phil said, and crouched down to pet Bubbles.

"*Car*-ly." Victor often said her name like that, as if he'd just remembered who she was. "I'm like, *so* hungry."

He couldn't have told her this on her way in? He had to wait until everyone was assembled and Phil was donating his free time to decide he wanted a burger? This was the thing that drove her crazy about Victor and his rainbow hair—he could be so creative and yet act like an impetuous teen.

Sometimes Carly couldn't help but wonder how he had managed to accomplish what he had. Victor was an Austin phenom. When he was eight, he was creating looks in the family's game room. When he was fifteen, he was working on a team to design juvenile looks for Gucci. At the age of eighteen, he'd become the youngest contestant to ever win *Project Runway*. He'd designed a red-carpet look for a popular television actress that had garnered a lot of national attention. But that attention came with a price—Victor couldn't handle the fame. He'd been caught drinking underage at a bar in Nashville. He'd made a comment that some mistook as body shaming. His response to media inquiries about his behavior was to threaten to punch people. He gained a reputation for not showing up when he was supposed to, for not delivering on his designs when he'd given his commitment. And then, he'd just disappeared.

Now, at twenty, he was ready to make a comeback. He was going to have his first solo show at the New Designer Showcase in the run-up to New York Fashion Week in February. It was by invitation only, and Victor had been asked to participate because his work was on fire.

One would think that Victor would have had a publicist in place after all his early success. Someone to help guide him. But he didn't until Carly came along.

She was still working at DBS when she came across Victor's pop-up shop on South Congress Avenue. She'd thought his aesthetic was very interesting and had googled him out of curiosity. That's when she'd learned about his antics outside the fashion world. "Wow," she'd muttered as she'd perused the Google listings about him one rainy evening. "Way to blow it, dude."

It wasn't long after seeing his pop-up that Carly was laid off. At first, she'd been shocked. Then incredibly pissed. And then she'd skipped over a few steps of the grieving process and gone straight to determined to make it, thanks to the encouragement of her former college roommate, Naomi Burrows.

At Naomi's insistence, Carly had flown to New York to hang out with her for a couple of weeks. "You can't mope," Naomi had advised her. "You can't walk around like the little match girl, all downtrodden and shit. You've got to get out of your own head. What you need is a change of pace and a change of location."

Carly knew better than to argue. Naomi was used to telling people what to do. She was the assistant to a big-time literary agent, and she worked with authors, which, Naomi said, turned a person into a boss. "It's amazing," she'd once told Carly, "these people write such incredible books, but can't put a schedule together. You have to take them by the hand and lead them."

Carly didn't know what that meant exactly, but Naomi loved her job and she was always talking about publisher parties and book launches, and she was good at taking people by the hand and leading them. So Carly took Naomi's advice and flew to New York.

She'd only ever been to New York for quick work-related trips, but until she stayed with Naomi and her roommates in Manhattan, she had never really *been* to New York. For those two glorious weeks, Carly lived more, partied more, slept more, and genuinely laughed more than she had in her whole life. She felt like she was living inside a *Sex and the City* episode. She was Carrie Bradshaw! Well, maybe Miranda . . . but still.

Naomi and her roommates went out every night, and every night, there were guys around, flirting and teasing and, wow, Carly had never been around so many eligible men. Naomi and her friends did not seem to care that they were crammed into a two-bedroom apartment where they'd converted a dining alcove into a third bedroom. Carly spent the entire two weeks sharing a bed with Naomi.

But it was worth it. Carly accompanied Naomi to a book launch at a swank hotel that made her feel like she'd hit some jackpot. She attended a book signing at the Strand with a famous author and felt very cosmopolitan. While Naomi worked, Carly took in all the tourist sights and visited museums, and even stopped in at the Ritz-Carlton for a thirty-dollar cocktail.

Naomi was right—Carly had needed the change of scenery. She began to believe her mistake was limiting her life to Austin, whereas in New York, she could see endless possibilities stretching before her. What did she have holding her at home besides a crazy family? And, frankly, a break from them would be good for everyone.

By the time Carly returned from that two-week sabbatical, she knew what she wanted. She was going to get a job in New York and live entirely on her own. She was going to go out every night and visit museums, and read lots of books and go to book signings and art openings. She was going to dine out and order in and laugh with colleagues about how she didn't even own a frying pan. She was going to work out and look great and wear the latest fashions so that when she dashed across the street, people would stop and look and wonder *Who is that girl?*

Carly had marched into this new vision for herself with a lot of optimism and this-was-meant-to-be chutzpah. Back in Austin, in her eagerness to get on with it, she'd discovered *Big Girl Panties*. After glomming the podcast backlist, her enthusiasm for New York and the unlimited possibilities for a woman her age with her skill set only grew.

Unfortunately, she wasn't having much luck on the job front. She scoured the job listings every day in search of a good fit. Hell, she'd even take a mediocre fit. All she needed was a foot in the door. But until she could insert that foot into some door, she was going to need a source of income. Megan said one should never underestimate her own power. Maybe, Carly thought, she could build some sort of portfolio to help her on the job front. Gain more experience to attach to her résumé. She would have to create this experience, she realized, and thought maybe she could pick up a couple of local clients, and . . .

And the idea of Victor just popped into her head. If anyone had ever needed expertise in public relations and marketing, it was that young diamond in the rough. So armed with her determination and those episodes of *Big Girl Panties,* Carly had hunted him down and had convinced him to hire her.

Actually, she'd convinced Victor's mother to hire her.

June Allen was slender and statuesque. She was always impeccably dressed in tailored clothes, the polar opposite of her son's aesthetic. She'd been a lawyer, but when Victor's career had begun to develop, she'd stopped practicing to manage him. Victor's parents were divorced, and his father lived in Boca Raton. Carly didn't have the impression that Victor had much contact with him. The only thing he'd ever said was that his dad "didn't get him."

But his mother got him, and Carly convinced June to take the meeting where she made her well-rehearsed pitch: Victor needed help with his press and his public image. He needed great publicity for his fashion show. He *needed* Carly Kennedy Public Relations, and she'd laid out all the reasons why.

Victor had sat on the brown couch in the studio, his long legs spread insouciantly, surrounded by his creations in various stages of construction. He kept twirling his ball cap on the edge of his forefinger. He seemed at times to be somewhere else. But June was intent on everything Carly had said that day. She'd agreed that Victor needed help. She'd urged her son to give Carly a shot.

Victor said nothing to all of it, and, honestly, Carly thought it was a bust. She told herself she'd given it her best shot. *No one can ask more from you than you do your best*, Megan had whispered in her ear. But then, Victor raised his arms overhead in something of a stretch, pushed himself up to sit straighter, and asked one question, "Can I dress you?"

Carly's heart had begun to pound with excitement. He *had* heard her. "Are you kidding? I would *insist*."

And that was why Carly was wearing Victor Allen right now. She wore it every chance she could. Victor was so talented! He would be a huge success! It was her job to promote him wherever she went! But . . .

But.

His clothes were not her style. Lord, not even close. She'd thought his aesthetic was interesting, but she'd never wanted to actually *wear* it. He was an avant-garde designer, a Betsey Johnson on steroids with his giant shoulders and superlong sleeves. Nonetheless, Carly wore his clothes. She worked hard for Victor.

Carly really did love the challenge of getting a talented person noticed for the right reasons, and Victor definitely was a challenge. It had taken her exhaustive hours to get his image rehabilitated. She'd booked magazine interviews, blog tours, appearances on regional morning talk shows. She'd talked June into paying for a website and had negotiated a rock-bottom price for a top-dollar design of it. She'd gotten him in front of YouTube vloggers and Instagram influencers and written so many press releases for so many different channels of publicity that she felt she'd given birth to him herself. And the cherry on the top of her sundae, she had the invitation to share his designs with Ramona McNeil.

With only a few weeks to go to the showcase, Victor was being heralded as the next great designer. *Thank you, Carly Kennedy!* She'd almost single-handedly elevated his image, for very little money, and she was very proud of that, particularly because Victor had been absolutely no help. To this day, after months of working together, he still didn't see the difference between a publicist and a lackey.

"So . . . you're going to get burgers, right?" Victor asked.

"You really want me to go get burgers?" It was less a question than a statement.

"Maybe you could have them delivered," one of the models suggested.

"Nah, she can go. It's just a mile or so down the road," Victor said. He hopped on his skateboard and began to move around the studio. Bubbles thought that was super exciting and began to bark and romp alongside him.

"As much as I'd love to dash down and order burgers, I've got the dog," Carly said with an apologetic wince. Bubbles lost interest in the skateboard and trotted into the kitchenette, her leash trailing behind.

"Bax can stay with us," Victor said, and went shooting across the concrete floor.

"That's not Baxter. Come on, guys," Carly said. "We have the shoot, and Phil has a very limited schedule—"

"We really don't need you here to do the shoot," Phil said. He lifted his camera and snapped Carly. "I can take it from here."

"You gotta go, Carly," Victor said as he swooshed by her. "I can't focus without something to eat, man!"

Bubbles reappeared from the kitchenette. As Victor skated by her, she began to bark again. Phil whistled, and Bubbles changed course, trotting directly into Victor's path. "*Whoa*," Victor said, hopping off his board and flipping it up to his hand just before he might have collided with the dog.

"Got him," Phil said. He leaned down and hauled Bubbles onto his lap. "What are you feeding this dog? He's heavy."

"See?" Victor said, waving at Bubbles as he looked at Carly. "We've got it under control."

Carly knew when she was defeated. "Yeah, okay, I'm only your publicist, but whatever," she said.

When Carly returned a half hour later with two bags full of burgers, Phil showed her the photos. Every one of them featured a basset hound. The photos of Victor's designs with Bubbles were adorable.

As the others ate the food she'd bought *with her personal money*, she called Brant again. Still no answer.

She was really worried about her own photogenic dog. Where was Baxter?

Two

Dr. Tobias Maxwell Sheffington III was a tenure-track professor of neuroscience at the University of Texas. One would think that the holder of an advanced science degree might have some basic common sense, but that clearly was not true, because if Max had any, he would have known it was not a good idea to go out drinking the night before a big presentation to his department. He would have remembered that he was the kind of guy who could have a couple of beers, but any more than that was guaranteed to make him blotto, which was how he'd earned the moniker of Lightweight in college. And he would surely have considered that it was *never* a good idea to sleep with another professor in the department.

It had all been so spur-of-the-moment, an impromptu goodbye party of sorts. For a dog.

Max was conducting a study on how the human bond with canines affects the release of oxytocin and elevates levels of dopamine in the brains of dog lovers and in dogs and, specifically, how the relationship of social behavior and the oxytocin system in canines could lead to a better understanding of the same relationship in the autistic brain. It was a mouthful, but the work had a lot of potential in the study of autism.

Part of his research included overseeing an undergraduate lab where the students assisted with some of the work he was doing. The presence of dogs made his lab extremely popular.

In particular, he had a blockheaded yellow Labrador who was single-handedly increasing the dopamine levels of everyone who came into contact with him. Clarence had not shown the aptitude to be a service animal, nor was he particularly good at learning the commands necessary to work effectively in a research lab. But he was aces when it came to hauling his enormous body onto laps and demanding to be petted.

Tuesday was Clarence's last day. He was on loan from the Austin Canine Coalition—otherwise known as the ACC—but had been recently adopted from the rescue organization. Clarence seemed pretty happy about his change in fortune—or maybe it had been the paper ball one of the graduate subjects had tossed his way—but everyone in the lab was heartbroken.

Max explained to the students and the two volunteer research subjects that they'd have a replacement dog next week. He'd already arranged it with the ACC—a three-legged Australian shepherd named Bonnie.

The ACC was a joint, citywide consortium combining the forces of several local dog rescue organizations. The rescue groups took dogs they couldn't place or couldn't house to the ACC. The ACC then attempted to train those dogs as companions and therapy dogs, as comfort buddies to soldiers, to kids who had to testify in courts, autistic youth, and to medical and senior centers. The dogs that flunked out of the ACC training program were put up for adoption, but while waiting for that happy day, they could be loaned out for projects, such as the one Max was conducting.

The ACC occupied fifteen acres right in the heart of some prime

Austin real estate, where dogs romped under grand old live oaks. Max had learned about the consortium and the work they did when his little brother, Jamie, got a job there. Jamie was twenty-seven, and had autism spectrum disorder. He particularly had difficulty understanding social cues and was not functionally verbal, which severely limited his employment opportunities. But Jamie could express himself in other ways. Like in his art. To Max's untrained eye, Jamie was a brilliant impressionist artist, painting familiar landscapes and people through a hazy, soft pastel lens. His artwork hung on the walls of his room in the family home, the sunroom his dad had converted into a studio for Jamie, and the den. Max had a few at his house, too. He liked them. He thought there was something entirely relatable and familiar about the scenes his brother painted, but at the same time, something hauntingly distant.

But Jamie's artistic abilities were not enough to compensate for his inability to verbally communicate or consistently behave in a manner deemed socially acceptable to the world at large.

A couple of years ago, Jamie's doctor had recommended behavioral therapy to help with social situations. In the course of learning how to integrate with society, Jamie had been introduced to dogs at the ACC and had fallen into obsessive love with them. He wanted to know all about them. He ordered books on the different breeds and read them all. He drew pictures of all sizes of dogs.

Max had been fascinated with this. Their mother had been extremely allergic to pet dander, which had ruled out any chance of having a dog at home. And in his memory, a younger Jamie had been suspicious and nervous of animals. Maybe Max had imagined that, because the adult Jamie was changed by that trip to the dog campus. He was not affectionate and didn't like to be touched—but a dog could lay its head on his arm or lap, and Jamie seemed not to mind. A dog could crawl in his lap, and Jamie would hug him. Dogs seemed to understand Jamie and would press their bodies against him when he was nervous or anxious.

When the opportunity for part-time work came up at the ACC, Max and his dad had helped Jamie apply. His job was to clean the kennels and walk and feed the dogs. He had never missed a day he was scheduled to work.

Max began to wonder if a dog companion would make it possible for Jamie to live in a group home. His father wasn't ready to think about Jamie living somewhere without him, but Max believed Jamie would thrive in one. His brother wasn't stupid and, in fact, he was brilliant in some aspects. He just needed some extra help, and maybe a dog was the answer to that. As Max continued to notice the subtle changes in his brother's behavior—such as his willingness to be touched by a dog and how the presence of a dog seemed to soothe him when he was agitated—Max began to think more about the interaction between dogs and humans and brain chemistry, particularly as it related to autism. There was not a lot of research that employed both qualitative and quantitative methods to determine if dogs were an effective social intervention and how it compared to other techniques used to help adults on the spectrum.

So he developed a research proposal around this idea. His department was on board with it. So was the ACC. If Max's research could inform their special-needs training, they were happy to supply the dogs.

Through Jamie's social skills program, Max was able to find two adults on the spectrum willing to participate in his study. Clarence was the first dog to come on board and had begun his weekly lab rotations two months ago. For Clarence, that meant a happy adventure where he sought out treats. The ACC reported to Max that Clarence had gained four pounds since he'd begun his weekly lab rotations, the result of treats being snuck under the table to him.

Yesterday, on what was Clarence's last day, the students threw him a goodbye party. Clarence slept through most of it. The guests had included Dr. Alanna Friedman. Like Max, she was a professor in the department and had asked Max if she might audit his lab. Dr. Friedman was cute in a sciencey sort of way with her turquoise and purple framed glasses and the messy bun of dark auburn hair at her nape. She was doing some amazing research into the effects of narcotics on the brain that Max admired. And she had a sultry little smile that he really liked, too, so he'd said yes.

It was Alanna who suggested that the lab students go for drinks after Clarence trotted off with the ACC volunteer to start his new life as a family dog. Predictably, many of the graduate students were down for that. At first, Max had hesitated. He'd had some papers to grade and some analyses to run, but it had been a while since he'd hung out with a pretty woman. It sounded like fun.

Last night happened as those nights tend to do—one drink too many, one touch too intimate—and the next thing Max knew, he was giggling like a little kid with Alanna as they slipped in through the side door of his house.

He was drunk, he was horny, and while he noticed that Hazel had not eaten her food, he was not concerned. He figured she was mad at him for coming home so late.

This morning, Max and Alanna had said an awkward goodbye, both of them clearly questioning themselves in the light of day. Max took his splitting headache and blurry vision into the kitchen in search of coffee. He padded past the utility room in his boxers and said, "Good morning, Hazel." Generally, that would cause his dog to launch her sausage-like body across the floor, enthusiastically slipping and sliding her way to him for petting and whatever food he might offer. But this morning, Hazel didn't move.

Max paused. She was in the same spot she'd been when he'd come in last night. Something was wrong. Was she sick? He backed up a step and changed course. He went into the utility room where she was, but as he got closer, Hazel tried to shove her body into the corner. "Whoa," Max said.

He rubbed his eyes. He looked again. *Hey.* That was not Hazel.

He carefully inched down onto the floor beside the basset hound who was not Hazel. This one had the same coloring as his dog, but the markings were different, now that he looked at her ... wait. At *him*.

He knew instantly what had happened—Brant had probably been high and brought the wrong dog home. That's what Max got for hiring a pothead dog walker, even one who'd come recommended, notwithstanding his perpetual state of stoned. *Fucking Brant.* Max's neighbor had vouched for him! "Yeah, sure, he walks my dog every day. Sits with him when I'm out of town," he'd said. "Just an old Austin hippie who has a dog-walking gig to get by."

At the time, that had seemed entirely plausible to Max. He'd lived in Austin his whole life and had known his fair share of hippies. In fact, the current occupant of the Hoffman Chair of Neurophysics lived in a tiny house off the electric grid. And Hazel did seem happy and tired on the days Brant walked her.

Still, this was unbelievable—you couldn't call yourself a dog walker and return the wrong dog.

"Hey, buddy, it's okay," he murmured, and attempted to stroke the dog's head, but the dog pressed harder into the corner, as if he thought he was hiding. So Max turned around and sat next to the dog, carefully petting him until the dog finally melted down and pushed his head against Max's leg with a heavy sigh.

"I get it," Max said. "I've definitely had those days. Frankly, all signs point to me having one today. For what it's worth, I'm going to personally kill Brant for doing this to you."

The dog sighed again and rolled into Max's thigh.

"But first, I'm going to need, like, a bucket of coffee. I'm pretty sure this situation is going to require some cognitive function, and I don't have any just yet."

The dog lifted his soulful eyes up to Max.

"Here's some free advice, buddy—don't ever let anyone talk you into drinking boilermakers." Max scratched the dog beneath his chin before he hauled himself up and carried on into the kitchen for that much-needed coffee.

After he'd slugged some down, Max located his phone and looked for the calls he was sure would be there, all from Brant, all offering profuse apologies for the mix-up. But there were no such apologies on his phone. There were no calls from Brant. Neither did Brant answer his phone nor pick up his messages, because his voice mail was full.

Yep, he was definitely going to kill Brant in some horrifying manner. Right after work.

He dressed. Then, he tried to get the dog to eat, but he wouldn't even look at his food. So Max put a lead on him and told him to come on. The dog stubbornly refused to move from the corner of the mudroom at first. But with a few tugs and stern words, Max eventually convinced him to get up and get in the car. He had to. He couldn't very well leave the dog at home—if Brant called him, Max would have to duck out between classes to take this one back and exchange him for Hazel.

Where the hell *was* Hazel? He was worried about his Very Good Dog, a fourteen on a scale of ten on any damn day. He hoped whoever had ended up with her was taking good care of her. Hazel liked to watch Dog TV and lie on the couch with her front paws hanging off the edge. She wouldn't understand if there was no couch. Max's eyes got a little wet imagining Hazel trying to figure out where the couch was.

He rolled down the back seat window for the dog, and the old boy perked up at that. When they started moving, he pushed his head out the window and let his long ears fly. He even wagged his tail a little.

Max called Brant again on the way to work. He called from his office where the dog had taken up residence in another corner. He called during his advisory period. He called between classes and in the middle of grading papers.

By the end of the day, Max had reached a new level of anxiety. He was ramped up from debating whether to drag the dog around with him or leave him in his office. He opted for the latter, and during his presentation on his research progress to the department chairs, he winced every time he heard the distinctive bay of a hound down the hall. Dog's howl was full of displeasure. He was probably alarmed by the plastic brain with the removable parts Max kept on the windowsill.

As the day wore on, he grew increasingly worried that something had happened to Hazel. He even worried about Brant. Where the hell was he? Max pictured him strung out in some alley, high on something more potent than pot.

Moreover, Brant was supposed to have been Hazel's dog-sitter this weekend. In just two days, Max was taking Jamie on a long-planned weekend trip to Chicago to see a big regional dog show. He was accomplishing two things at once with this trip—treating his brother to a slice of dog heaven because Max was convinced Jamie could handle it, and giving his dad a well-deserved and much-needed break as Jamie's caregiver. The old man had planned a big fishing trip with his buddies for the weekend. He'd gone out and bought himself a new reel and rod, for Chrissakes.

Max had invested a considerable amount of money and effort into this weekend, and if Brant wasn't going to be around to dog-sit like he'd promised, then Max was in an even bigger bind.

By the next afternoon, Thursday, there was still no word from Brant, and Max was starting to panic. He tried *not* to panic—he was well aware that while his sympathetic nervous system had geared up, his parasympathetic nervous system would soon enter the picture and bring his anxiety down, because he did not have, insofar as he knew, a panic disorder.

But he sure might develop one if he didn't find Brant or Hazel soon. He hadn't had much time to look, honestly—he had a major research article due to his faculty adviser, two tests from two different classes to grade, and he'd agreed to sub for another professor whose mother had died. But he did manage to swing by the ACC after work

yesterday, hoping Hazel might have shown up there, taken by whoever had gotten her instead of Dog.

The dogs were out for group play. There were at least two dozen
of them, some of them lounging on preschool play sets, some engaged
in a serious game of chase. But no Hazel. When Max walked by the
field on his way to the office, all of the dogs raced to the fence to greet
him, save a bulldog in the back who didn't seem inclined to give up his
space on the play set bench.

In the office, a young woman with pink hair and heavily tattooed
arms said, "I'm sorry, sir. We haven't received any bassets this week.
But I've got a coon hound mix if you're interested. He's very friendly.
But I would not advise leaving leather boots lying around."

"Thanks," Max said. "But I'm just looking for my dog."

"Good luck!" she said.

Thursday morning rolled around, and Max took Dog to work
with him again on the slim chance that Brant might call and announce
where he and Hazel had gone. But instead of leaving him in his office,
Max had decided his classroom students could deal and Dog would
be happier, so he'd brought him to the lecture hall. At first, Dog had
stuck to a corner of the room, his head pressed to the wall. But he'd
warmed up to the class, and, let's be honest, the number of new smells
a dog could not overlook or ignore, even the most depressed of basset
hounds. Dog had wandered around as Max tried to instruct the students on the nervous system, plunging his nose into backpacks and
crotches at will. The students were delighted, but also distracted by
Dog, which was okay with Max, given the circumstances.

But he hadn't counted on a visit from Dr. O'Malley, the department head.

O'Malley's face set into a dark frown as Dog lumbered around the
classroom. As if he thought dogs only belonged in the lab, and not in
the auditorium. Dr. O'Malley generally frowned about a lot of things,
but Max didn't want him to frown in his class, especially since he'd
just found out that he was not the only candidate being considered for

tenure this year; he was apparently one of two. And only one would be allowed to go forward through the university process. Max was well aware that what O'Malley thought of either candidate would definitely factor into the decision.

And still, surprisingly, tenure—the thing he'd worked so long and so hard toward—was the least of his problems this week. Max had discovered that he couldn't board a nameless dog without vaccination records and at least a name. He didn't have a pet sitter, either, and couldn't find one on such short notice.

He'd considered asking one of his students. But he'd looked at the bunch of budding neuroscientists, half of whom were too much in their own heads, and the other half he wouldn't trust not to experiment on a chunky sad-sack dog, and had passed on that idea with a hard no.

As a last resort, he decided to worry his father with this problem on the chance he might know of a buddy who could take Dog for the weekend.

Max stopped by his dad's house on his way home from work, Dog in tow.

Tobias Sheffington II, otherwise known as Toby to his friends, lived with Jamie just around the corner from Max, in the same house where Max had grown up. The same house that had belonged to his grandparents. It was a comfortable ranch that had seen better days, sitting in a prime location. So prime that his father fielded a few requests to sell every year. When Max was a kid, the entire street had been made up of similar comfortable ranch homes that had seen better days, but most of them had been added to or reconfigured, or razed altogether so that houses that hardly fit on the lot could be built in their place. Next to those houses, the Sheffington family home looked like it had blown into town on a tornado with a girl and her little black dog.

His father was in the garage at a workbench, the door raised. When Max and Jamie were kids, his father had dressed in a suit every

morning and strode off to work carrying a heavy briefcase. But when
Max's mother had died six years ago from a sudden heart attack, his
father had retired from his career as a financial adviser. Now he wore
ball caps and chinos.

Dad had a line of fishing poles propped against the wall and was
bent over an open tackle box on his workbench.

"Hey, Max." He held up a yellow and green feather lure. "What
do you think? Got it down at a little convenience store next to the
river."

"Looks spectacular."

"Got some for the boys, too. We like to have a little contest when
we fish. So, hey, when are you picking up Jamie tomorrow?" He put
his lure down. "Me and the guys want to get an early start."

"Yeah . . ." Max shoved his hands in his pockets. "I've got a small
problem." Actually, it was a pretty big problem. "I have—" He was
distracted by Dog's sudden barking at a plastic bag ghost dancing
across the garage floor on a breeze.

"Hazel!" his dad said sternly. "Stop that barking. It's just a plastic bag."

"That's the small problem," Max said. "That's not Hazel."

Dad laughed. "Funny. C'mere, Hazel," he said.

Dog, still concerned with the plastic bag, which had come to a halt
next to the lawn mower, cowered behind Max. Max went down on
his haunches to vigorously rub the dog's back. Dog immediately
melted onto the floor and presented his belly for attention. "*Oh*," his
dad said. "Well, look at that. I could have sworn that was Hazel. Hey,
wait a minute, there—where's Hazel?"

"That's the million-dollar question." Max filled his dad in on the
mix-up. He was just getting around to the part of needing someone to
look after Dog when the door to the house suddenly opened and Jamie walked out. "Dog show," he said. Then he glanced down. "Who?"
he asked, pointing at Dog. He knew immediately that it wasn't Hazel.

Jamie was as tall as Max, maybe a half inch taller, two or three inches over six feet. Where Max had dark brown hair, Jamie's was more of a golden brown. Their aunt had always said they both had their mother's green eyes, but that was wishful thinking on her part— Max's were really gray. Regrettably, his mother's eyes were fading from Max's memory. "This is a friend," Max said to Jamie.

Jamie looked at the dog, then at Max. "Come on," he said, gesturing to the door.

"Give me a minute to—"

"Come on, come on, come on, come *on*," Jamie insisted, flapping one hand.

"Go," his dad said. "I'll be here with . . . what'd you say his name was?"

"Dog," Max said.

"Dog show!" Jamie shouted, pointing at Dog.

"Okay, okay," Max said. He followed Jamie inside.

They walked through the kitchen, through the family room where every wall held one of Jamie's paintings, and past the view of a lush green backyard filled with birdhouses and fountains and wind sculptures—also created by Jamie—and down the hall to where Jamie's room looked out over the backyard.

Jamie wanted to show him his preparation for the trip to Chicago. He'd laid out three pairs of jeans, neatly folded. Next to that were two pairs of identical Adidas white sneakers, cleaned and polished. A stack of folded black T-shirts, and four pairs of boxers, all gray. At the foot of his bed, he had his favorite dog books—an encyclopedia of breeds, one on dog training, and one that peeked into a dog's mind. Next to the books was an open sketchbook, and Max could see a pencil drawing of the dogs in the open field at the ACC.

"This is great, Jamie," Max said as he picked up the sketchbook.

"Dog show," Jamie reminded him.

"That's right," Max said. "We're leaving tomorrow." Somehow, some way, they were getting on a plane tomorrow and flying to Chicago for the Midwestern Regional Dog Show Competition. Jamie had been looking forward to this for weeks. He asked about it every time Max stopped by. And his dad was obviously looking forward to his fishing trip with just as much anticipation.

Max spent a little time with Jamie looking at his breed book, then went back out to the garage. Dog had crawled under his dad's workbench and was stretched out on his side, snoozing.

"So, Dad, do you know anyone who could keep this dog over the weekend?" Max asked, gesturing at the slumbering basset.

"Not off the top of my head, but I'll ask around," his father said as he studied his lures. "Hey, Max, remember that red tail lure I had? Can't find it. Could catch anything with that lure." He launched into a rather long-winded tale of the time he'd caught a striped bass with that lure.

Yeah, Max was definitely on his own.

Eventually, he made an excuse about needing to feed the dog, and went home to think about who he could beg to take this dog for three days. And what to do if, by some miracle, Hazel came home while he was away.

Max lived in another old family house. It had belonged to his aunt and uncle, but his uncle had left his aunt for a coworker several years ago, and his aunt had moved to San Antonio to be close to her daughter. No one in the family had wanted to lose that prime piece of real estate, and everyone wanted Max to be close to his father and Jamie. So Max had bought it from his aunt far below the going rate around here, because Max couldn't afford the going rate on an assistant professor's salary. It was a blessing. The house was perfect for him, and it was close to campus, too.

In contrast to his father's house, Max's was more of a Spanish style, with some interesting curves and angles that he liked. The floor was Saltillo tile and wood, the ceilings lower than what was fashionable. Dog had certainly settled into the accommodations. He'd discovered Hazel's favorite hangouts—the couch and Max's bed. But the dog was still reluctant to eat and, in fact, hadn't eaten anything today. Max couldn't figure it out. He tried to coax him into the kitchen, but Dog seemed afraid to leave the couch, as if he'd miss an episode of Dog TV.

The couch is where they ended up that late afternoon, Dog watching fellow canines on TV romp in a field of green, and Max scrolling through his contacts, trying to find anyone who would save him from this mess. He made a few calls to old friends of his, but no one was buying what he was selling. "Buddy, you know I'd help you out, but I'm headed to the Oklahoma State versus Texas game." And, "I would, you know I would, but my dog hates other dogs."

He even called Aunt Jean, his mother's sister, who was as deathly allergic to pet dander as his mother had been. "Maxey, you know I'd do anything for you boys. Except this. I'd look like a blowfish for a week."

Max was down to his very last idea, and it was a bad idea. His bad idea was Alanna Friedman.

The thing was, he didn't know Alanna that well, really. Besides auditing his class, he'd only seen her at a couple of departmental functions. What he knew was her research, which had been cited in several addiction studies done by the U.S. government. She was cute, and they'd had a very fun evening. Probably because she'd leaned forward, sloshed beer out of her glass, and said, "Let's try not to be such *scientists*. Let's just have some fun for once." And then she'd kissed him.

It was the "scientist" remark that had struck a chord in Max. He knew what Alanna meant, and, frankly, he'd heard something similar from a couple of women he'd casually dated in the last few years—he didn't emote properly because he was "such a scientist."

What could he say? He was down for having some fun. A lot of fun. Why not?

But things got interesting the next morning, because the mood was sheepish, and Max had the distinct impression Alanna was sorry she'd let her hair down. And while he'd very much enjoyed the activity, he was hungover and not thinking clearly.

"This was great," she'd said as she turned her back to him and put on her bra. "But I don't think it's a good idea if we . . . you know. I mean, we're in the same department."

"Umm . . ." Max had to pause to have an internal debate of what to say, because as usual, his ability to think fast on his feet where a woman was concerned was severely compromised. He didn't know if he should agree immediately, or if that would make him look like a dick who was trying to get rid of her. There it was, the big shameful secret about Dr. Sheffington, brain scientist: he didn't entirely understand women. He was no ladies' man. He was the sort of guy who meant what he said and assumed everyone around him would likewise say what they meant. In his experience, men did, for the most part, if they spoke up at all. Women did sometimes, but sometimes they did not, and somehow, he was supposed to know the difference.

"I mean, I'm up for tenure this year, and I've got a lot of work to do," she added as she pulled her shirt over her head. "I shouldn't get distracted from that."

Did she just say she was up for tenure? Max stared at her, trying to make sense of that. She had noticed him staring and said, "What? You didn't know?"

"Ah . . . no." He dragged his fingers through his hair. "So am I."

Alanna gasped. "*You?*" she said, her voice suddenly quite high.

"Me," he said. "I thought I was the only one in the running this year."

"Me, too!"

They'd both been at a loss for words.

But Alanna snapped out of it first. "Well?" she said, her hands finding her hips.

"Well?" he echoed.

"I mean . . . we obviously can never do *this* again," she said, gesturing between the two of them. "We're in *competition.*"

"Right," Max said. That much, he definitely understood.

"So?"

"So . . . ?"

She sighed with exasperation. "I don't think you get it."

"No, I get it. We can never do this again. We're . . . we're scientists." The moment the words came out of his mouth, he pummeled himself mentally. What a dumb thing to say. It was amazing to him that a man who had studied psychiatry and neuroscience and could communicate complex concepts could be so bad at communicating.

"Yes, we are," she said, swiping up her purse. "Like . . . you really didn't know?"

"I really didn't know, Alanna." He didn't add that he'd thought for several weeks now that at long last, it was his year. That he'd been working so hard for tenure, and he'd done all the necessary work to get it, only to find out that someone whose research into addiction was cutting-edge and didn't involve dogs was in the running, too.

"Well . . . okay," she said. "Just as long as we're clear."

He wasn't clear about anything. "We're clear. Can I drive—"

"I'll call a Lyft." She looked like the car couldn't arrive quickly enough.

Needless to say, Max had been terribly flummoxed on a number of levels for a couple of days now, and asking her to dog-sit was just about the dumbest thing he could consider. But he also knew that she was single and lived close by (they'd had a brief discussion about where to go when they left the bar that night) and liked dogs (she'd said it when she'd seen Dog in the corner). Maybe, he thought, he could use this as a way to say he was sorry for . . . well, he wasn't sure what for, but he'd say it all the same. Maybe they could establish a friendship.

A friendship. Oh, man, he was more desperate than he'd thought.

He stared at her number that she'd typed into his phone at the bar and tried to guess just how desperate he was. But then he thought about Jamie's stack of clothes waiting to go into a suitcase, and his dog books all lined up, ready to be consulted, and he suddenly didn't care if he was being a dick or not. He was out of options. His thumb hovered over the little phone icon.

But he hesitated. And then Dog's stomach growled.

Max put his phone down, her contact information still on his screen. "Come on, buddy, let's eat something," he said.

Dog responded by laying his head down between his paws.

Max sighed. He got up and went into the kitchen. He poured some kibble into a bowl, then opened the fridge, pulled out some leftover mac and cheese he and Jamie had made one night, and heaped a big helping of it on the dog food.

He called the dog, but he would not come off that couch. Max absently scratched his head, wondering how he would get the dog into the kitchen to eat, when he was startled by someone knocking on his door. Not knocking, exactly, but slapping it. Like someone was slapping the palm of their hand against the door. It was a strange way to knock.

Dog lifted his head. His ears perked in that direction. But then he turned back to Dog TV.

The person slapped his door again.

No one knocked like that unless maybe they were drunk or high, and . . . *Brant!* That bastard, it had to be him. That dumbass had come out of his fog and had come to get this dog and give Hazel back. Max walked into the living room, set the bowl of food down on the floor near the couch, and strode to the door, all dialed up to give Brant a good what for.

Three

Max jerked the door open and prepared to launch . . . but it wasn't Brant standing on the other side with Hazel. It was a woman. And she didn't have a dog.

The woman was quite attractive, which knocked him off-balance for a beat too long, because attractive women did not frequently appear at his door. As in never. He had to think a minute—his brain needed to posit some theories to him about why this woman might be standing at his door. Unfortunately, Max couldn't think very well because he was completely distracted by the black hair that hung in a silky sheet down her chest and back. And unusually blue eyes, big and thickly lashed, beneath a perfect line of dark bangs. Her face was a lovely oval shape, and her dark brows were arched very expressively—she was as surprised as he was. But the thing that really stood out to him, that really tied his thoughts up in a knot, was what she was wearing.

What *was* she wearing? He'd never seen anything like it. Was it a dress? Pants? The garment had oversized shoulders and sleeves too long for her arms. Her pant legs were so wide that they looked like some futuristic antebellum gown. He couldn't see her hands and, in fact, she had to push a sleeve back to reach into her tote bag.

"What's the matter? Haven't you ever seen high fashion before?"

"What?" If that was high fashion, he had some questions.

She yanked her hand free of her bag. She was clutching a piece of paper.

Was it a costume, maybe? Maybe one of those singing telegrams? Once, Dr. Fridlington, a professor in his department, had received a singing telegram. But that costume had been a poop emoji. Turned out, the telegram was from his wife, and the singing telegram was to inform him that she was divorcing him. This was clearly not that. But what *was* it?

She looked up from the paper. Her eyes narrowed suspiciously. "Tobias Sheffington?"

No one called him by his first name but his late grandfather. And his grandfather had never called him Tobias in such an accusatory tone. Max's distraction suddenly turned in a completely different direction, one in which his amygdala started firing limbic neurons filled with consternation. Was she about to accuse him of something?

"Tobias Sheffington?" she repeated, a little louder, as if he hadn't heard her.

"No. I mean, yes, that is my name. But I go by Max. Max Sheffington."

Her eyes flicked the length of him. "Your name is Tobias and you go by Max? *Okay*," she said, as if she thought he was trying to pull a fast one on her.

He was not. Tobias was so damn stuffy that he went by Max. "It's my middle name. Okay?" he repeated uncertainly. Was she a former student? Surely he wouldn't forget that he'd taught a woman who looked like her. Not to mention he'd never done anything to a former student to warrant any sort of accusation . . . *that he knew of.* Oh God—he'd never done anything that he *thought* might warrant an accusation. Had he done something offensive and hadn't known it?

Wait—could this have something to do with Alanna? She'd seemed so annoyed the morning she left. But surely this was not that. Surely he wasn't so obtuse that he misread a woman's intent to sue him. So why was this woman at his door staring at him like that? "Excuse me—I'm not sure what's going on here, but is there something I can do for you?"

"You bet there is something you can do for me, Mr. Sheffington. You can give—" The woman suddenly gasped and her eyes lit with delight in such a stunning change of pace that it jolted him. "Baxter!" she cried, throwing her arms so wide that one of her sleeves slapped Max in the shoulder.

Max looked back as Dog gallumphed to the front door.

"Oh my God, you're alive!" she cried, and went down on her knees, wrapping her weird sleeves around the dog's neck.

Well, then. He would not have guessed she was here for a dog. "I take it he is yours?" he asked dryly as Baxter's happy tail banged against his leg.

"I have been so *worried* about you," the woman said to the dog, and buried her face in his fur. "Are you okay, Baxter?" Dog responded with a sloppy lick of her cheek. She rubbed Baxter's sides vigorously with both hands, but Baxter wiggled out of her embrace and hurried back inside.

"Well," Max said as he watched him go. "That's the most energetic I've seen him. He's been kind of mopey."

"He has some issues, and of course this little stunt hasn't helped matters."

"Okay, for the record, I didn't do the stunt," Max said, holding up both hands. She was trying to gain her feet, but she couldn't find her hands. "Do you need some help?"

"No, thank you. If you can't do for yourself in high fashion, then you shouldn't *wear* high fashion."

He didn't know what kind of fashion she was wearing but he could definitely agree with high, because whoever had come up with that costume had been as high as a kite.

She managed to come to her feet, and when she did, she spent a moment trying to do right all that was wrong with those gargantuan sleeves, then said, "I can't believe I found him!" And she smiled with delight, and the effect was very confusing and *very* pleasing. For one, Max didn't fear being punched in the face anymore. And two, she was really pretty. He preferred pretty. He was much more on board with the idea that a pretty woman had shown up to claim her dog, because it was a damn sight better than looking at Brant's mug.

Max stuck out his hand. "Can we start over? I'm Max."

"Hi, Max. I'm Carly. Sorry about all that, but it says Tobias on the list, and, honestly, who can you trust these days?" She pushed the sleeve back and took his hand with a surprisingly strong grip and gave him a couple of firm shakes as she looked him in the eye.

"Hello, Carly. I think I speak for both Dog and myself when I say we are very glad you found us. Just how did you find us, anyway?"

"Well *that's* a story." She folded her arms, and those weird sleeves bunched up in the crooks of her arms. "I have spent the last two days tracking down one Mr. Brant Reynolds, with whom I believe you are acquainted?"

"Unfortunately."

"Guess where he is?"

"If I knew that, I'd have killed him by now."

"No, seriously—guess."

"Well, I thought maybe a—"

"Jail!" she shouted, and threw open her arms, hitting him in the shoulder with a sleeve again. "He's in *jail*!"

Jail. Huh. That hadn't actually occurred to Max for some reason. He'd imagined Brant getting himself killed or hospitalized . . . but not jailed. But as Brant didn't seem like the most upstanding citizen in town, it did not come as much of a surprise. "What did he do? Wait—where is *my* dog?"

"I've got her. What happened to Baxter?" she asked, trying to see past him into his house.

"I think he headed back to the couch."

Carly with the blue eyes blinked.

"He's watching a little Dog TV," Max said, jerking his thumb over his shoulder.

She laughed. "I don't think so."

"Yeah," Max said with a shrug. "He likes it. Have you never had it on?"

"I've never even *heard* of it. I don't know TV. Baxter and I don't have time to watch. What is Dog TV?"

Max was always very suspicious of people who said they didn't watch TV. Generally, they said it like they were so much busier than anyone else, like they were too busy solving world hunger or designing an affordable health care system to kick back and watch a little tube. "You don't watch TV?" he asked dubiously.

"Nope."

"Nothing?"

Carly shook her head. "Too busy."

Uh-huh. "Do you *have* a TV?" he asked curiously.

She blinked. She shrugged a little. "I *have* one. But I don't watch it. I have no time to watch TV." She shook her head, as if that was a given.

Oh yeah, she watched TV. Maybe even a lot of it. "But if you don't watch—"

"So, like, what is Dog TV?" she said, interrupting him before he could make his totally logical argument.

He gave her a smile with the teeniest tiniest bit of smugness to it. "Come in. I'll show you."

He led her down the hall to the living room, where Baxter had resumed his place on the couch and was busy licking his paws. On the TV, two French bulldogs were romping in a field. Off-screen, a child laughed and intermittently whistled to the dogs or whispered, "I love you" or gaily called, "Come!" to the dogs.

Carly stared at her dog and then the TV. "That's it? That's Dog TV?"

"That is it," Max confirmed. He felt bad for Baxter, deprived of something so basic.

Carly turned those lovely blue eyes to him, and her brows dipped, and she said, "You have to be kidding me."

"Don't take this the wrong way, but maybe you shouldn't be too judgy since it's clear your dog is very happy with it." He gestured to said dog, who looked very comfortable in lounge mode.

"I *am* judgy," she agreed, and folded her sleeves. "Because dogs don't watch TV. It's a scam." She looked back at her dog and pointed a sleeve at him. "Also, what is he doing on the couch?"

Max didn't understand the question. Baxter was lying there, his head propped on the armrest now that he'd finished licking his paws. What did *any* dog do on the couch? She didn't know Dog TV, she didn't know about couches? Maybe she really didn't know dogs. "Dogs like being up high—"

"No." She shook her head.

"Yes," he said, feeling slightly irritated. "It's a proven fact. It's like an observation point."

She stared at him. "Are you seriously explaining dogs to me right now?"

"Well?" he said. "You're asking dog questions."

"My question was obviously rhetorical."

Her question was obviously not rhetorical.

"Baxter, get down," she said. Baxter didn't move. "*Down*, Baxter." Baxter thumped his tail a time or two to indicate he'd heard her, but he did not move. He was comfortable.

"Oh my God, what has happened to my dog? He's not allowed on couches!"

She said this as if Max had done something really vile, like chained her dog to a tree. It felt a little as if she was taking aim at his dog skills, and he didn't like it. He knew how to handle dogs, for fuck's sake. "There is nothing wrong with dogs on couches," he said defensively. "And there is nothing wrong with Dog TV. Why do I feel like I'm being pressed to defend my very good care of your dog before I even get to know where my dog is? I am happy to talk about couch philosophy, if you could just—"

"Baxter, get down from there!" she commanded again.

Baxter shifted his gaze to her as if he'd just noticed her, found her uninteresting, and then shifted his gaze back to the TV.

She lunged forward as if she intended to drag the dog off the couch. But then she stopped and made a sound of alarm so loud that had Max not been standing there, he would have thought she'd accidentally run into a pitchfork.

She was staring down at the dog food bowl, which Baxter had cleaned out. Mostly. She gasped again, this one more of a whimper, then squatted down and peered into the bowl. "Is that . . . *was* that *mac* and *cheese*?" she asked almost weepily, pointing at the telltale remnants that Baxter had left around the bowl.

Max briefly debated claiming the bowl was his, but wisely opted for silence.

She slowly rose up and pinned him with a look. "You fed my dog mac and cheese? And before you deny it, I know what the unnaturally orange remains of *boxed* mac and cheese look like."

She said it like she'd discovered arsenic in the dog's food. Like she was Columbo and had worked out the attempted murder in her head. Max put his hands on his hips. "Just so I have this straight . . . your main complaint is that the mac and cheese came out of a box? Or that it's unnaturally orange?"

"My *complaint* is that mac and cheese is not good for a dog. It's *horrible* for a dog. The manual says dogs metabolize food completely differently than we do, and besides, processed food isn't good for anyone."

Okay, that was it. Max didn't know what manual she was talking about, but he'd taken *very* good care of her dog. "Yes, Carly, it is mac and cheese. You know why? Because your dog wouldn't eat. But he has now, thanks to the mac and cheese, and you are welcome. Now if you don't mind, I'd like to know where is *my* dog?"

"At a photo shoot," she said, folding her arms.

Whatever Max was going to say flew out of his head—the words *photo shoot* walked up to a counter in his brain and banged on the bell for attention. "Wait, what? What does that even mean?"

"It means someone is taking photos. Can we just back up here to the moment before you got upset?" she asked, making a whirring motion with her finger.

"*I'm* upset?"

"Do I have this right? You come home to an imposter basset hound," she said, holding up one finger, "and instead of taking him to the vet to have his chip read, you invite him to eat *that* in the *living room*," she said, pointing at the bowl, then holding up another finger. "While he *couch surfs*, and watches *Dog TV*," she said, holding up two more fingers. "Yes?"

"Couch surfing and Dog TV are the same thing," Max shot back. "But, yes, you have it *exactly* right. What have you been feeding *my* dog, if I may ask?"

"Organic kangaroo and lentils like the manual says!" she nearly shouted, as if that was some written rule of what you were supposed to feed a strange dog that showed up in your house. It also sounded outrageously trendy and expensive. She'd spoiled his dog. And then, in a moment of sheer irony, she said, "Oh my God, let's everyone calm down here." As if she were the sane one in this room begging for cooler heads. She held out her arms in a way that he thought signaled to calm down, but he wasn't sure with those sleeves. "I just need to absorb what has happened."

"What has happened is that I've made sure your dog was comfortable. And frankly I think I've helped him come out of his shell, because that is one depressed dog," he said, pointing accusingly at Baxter, who gave them a couple of thumps of his tail in acknowledgment before carrying on with the cleaning of his face.

"Why didn't you get his chip read? I've been worried *sick* about him."

Well, she had him there. "Because I didn't think of it, okay?" Max said, tossing his arms out in the universal mea culpa. "And before you complain about that and Baxter's improved personality, where is *my* dog?"

"I told you." She was looking at his kitchen now, her nose wrinkled with disapproval. Okay, all right, he wasn't a great housekeeper, and he shifted so that he blocked her view of it. She looked up at him. "Photo shoot."

"So when you say *photo shoot*, what exactly does that mean?"

"You don't have to say it like she's been forced into hard labor. She's at a photo shoot where a photographer takes many pictures. I'd be there, too, but Brant's *friend*," she said, putting air quotes around the word, "finally called me back. Like, where is the sense of urgency with these people? You just toss a strange dog into someone's house and think you don't have to answer your phone?" She leaned around him and looked at his kitchen another moment, then pressed her palms to her cheeks. "I guess you can't blame Brant for not answering, given he's in jail. I don't know, I honestly don't know anything because I'm kind of in shock."

Max still couldn't figure out the photo shoot thing. And she was making it sound as if Brant had murdered someone. "What did he *do*?"

"What?" She dropped her hands. She stared at him. Then her brows dipped. "I mean, I'm in shock because my perfectly behaved dog is on the furniture and eating his dinner in the living room like some sort of animal. And that bandanna!"

Baxter was wearing one of Hazel's pink bandannas with yellow ducks on it.

"Baxter doesn't like bandannas," she said mournfully, as if something terrible had happened to her dog.

Baxter thumped his tail.

"Okay, all right," Max said impatiently. "Will you please fill me in with what is going on? With my dog or Brant—either would work at the moment."

Carly planted the giant sleeve cones on her hips. "Oh, I'm going to tell you, all right. But first, you would not believe how long it took me to figure it out. And it's not like I have the time to go chasing after stoned dog walkers, you know. I have a life. A very busy *life*."

Right. World peace and lobbying-for-equal-pay kind of busy life, he had no doubt. He gestured for her to continue.

"Anyway, when I came home and found an imposter dog in my house who had destroyed my couch pillows . . ." She paused here for the dramatic effect and to give him a look that suggested she thought he had purposely trained Hazel to do that.

Max held up a hand. "I will replace your couch pillows." Because it was true that Hazel would, from time to time, let her separation anxiety be known.

"*Thank* you," she said pertly. "They were not cheap pillows."

"Fine."

"Anyway, I did some digging. First, I took your dog to a vet to have *her* chip scanned, which would have cleared this all up right away, but guess what?"

"Yeah," he muttered.

"Your dog doesn't have a chip! How can you not have chipped your dog?"

Max glanced guiltily at the floor. He'd meant to do that, but he hadn't had time. He was busy, too. "Well? Your dog doesn't have a tag on his collar," he said, as if that evened things out.

She folded her sleeves again. "No, he doesn't. Because he's *chipped*."

"Nevertheless, I would recommend tags."

"*Your* dog didn't have tags."

Okay, obviously he was not going to win this game. He let dogs on couches and he didn't get them chipped on day one, and it hadn't occurred to him to check if Baxter had one. He cast an accusatory look at that dog, as if he should have reminded Max to have him scanned for a chip.

"*Nevertheless*," Carly continued, "I kept at it. I called the morgue; I called the hospitals; and finally, at long last, I located that chucklehead in the county jail. I got a copy of the police report and, by the by," she said, holding up a finger, "if you ever need a police report, I know how to get one. Anyway, I found out that Brant has been selling bags of marijuana under the Pfluger Bridge." She paused, leaned forward and said gravely, "*On the dog walks.*"

"Wow."

"It's really disturbing, isn't it? I keep trying to picture it. He just takes our dogs on a walk, then stops off and sets up shop under the shadow of Stevie Ray Vaughan and sells bags of weed? And then what, just moseys on home?"

She gestured in a direction Max assumed in her head was Lady Bird Lake, but was the wrong direction. As Stevie Ray Vaughan was dead, Max also assumed she was talking about the statue erected to the former Austinite at Auditorium Shores. "I agree," he said. "That is disturbing. I'm actually surprised that Brant has the mental acuity to pursue a criminal enterprise of any size. He doesn't seem to have the sort of ambition I would think that would require."

"Agree one thousand percent," she said. "Anyway, Brant got himself locked up for a few days, and I finally got hold of the cop who arrested him. He'd allowed Brant to call a friend to come get the dogs. He pulled up his phone log and gave me the number."

Wow. She *had* done a lot of detective work. He was grudgingly impressed and ashamed that he hadn't thought to do half of what she'd done.

"His name is Kai."

"The cop?"

"The friend. His name is Kai and he is Brant's yogi. He teaches Brant yoga."

"Huh. Wouldn't have guessed that, either," Max said thoughtfully.

"Same," she said, nodding.

"What about my dog?"

"I'm getting there," she said in the sort of voice a parent might use on an impatient child. "So. Kai went down to the park to get the dogs, and he got Brant's list of the dogs and owners, and he delivered the dogs to their homes. But he mixed up Baxter and Bubbles, because, if you haven't noticed, they look exactly alike."

"What?" Max asked, trying to follow. Who the hell was Bubbles? "But where is Hazel?"

"*Hazel?*" Carly scrunched her pert nose and clearly fought a smile. "No offense, but I think *Bubbles* better reflects your dog's awesome personality."

Bubbles sounded like someone who danced on poles for a living, but he kept that to himself.

"Anyway, she's at a photo shoot with a friend of mine. So I'll just take Baxter and bring her home when she's done—"

"No way," Max said instantly. "And what is this business about a photo shoot? On the surface, it sounds a little exploitative."

"Oh, sure, making your dog a star is exploitative. You should thank me."

He imagined Hazel dressed in something like what Carly was wearing and suppressed a shudder. "I'm not going to thank you for something that makes no sense and before I see that she is okay. Why didn't you just bring her with you?"

"Are you crazy? What if you were a dognapper or some other kind of perv? You can't be too careful these days."

He looked aghast at her.

"Hey, I just lost one dog. I wasn't about to lose another one. Which is the real joke here, because Baxter's not even my dog. I mean he *is* my dog, but technically he's . . ." She stopped and shook her head. "Never mind. It's a long and complicated story that no one has time for, especially me. Do you have a leash I could borrow?"

"Nope. Not taking him. Maybe *you're* the perv."

She snorted. "As if."

"Look, even trade. I'll give you Baxter when you deliver Hazel."

Carly frowned. She clearly did not approve of this idea, because every emotion seemed to end up on that pretty face of hers. But she studied him a long moment and finally gave him a curt nod. "Fine. I'll be back by seven. You better be here when I get back. No running off with my dog."

"Again, not a dognapper or a perv."

"Yeah, well, that's exactly what a dognapper or a perv would say." She walked past him to the couch to where Baxter was now snoozing. She rubbed his head, and her dark hair spilled over her shoulder in one long cascade when she leaned over the dog. "You poor thing," she cooed.

"He's fine," Max said, trying not to be offended. "He's better than fine. He's *great*."

"Sure, if you think losing all sense of discipline is great," she said as she headed to the door. "Okay, don't move, Tobias. I'll be back."

"It's *Max*," he said adamantly and followed her to the door and watched her jog very slowly and awkwardly down the brick steps to her car on very high heels. When she'd backed her car down the drive, Max closed the door. He turned around to see Baxter sitting behind him, looking bewildered. "Don't worry, she's coming back," he said. "I think." He crouched down in front of the dog. "Looks like you're going home, buddy. And Hazel is coming home, too."

Baxter wagged his tail.

Max was relieved to have found his dog. Carly was right—Hazel had an awesome personality and he'd missed having her around. At least he could relax now that he knew she was safe. But he still had the issue of the next few days.

He was looking at Baxter when a thought occurred to him.

It was a silly thought. It made no sense. It was in the realm of fantasy, really. But . . . what if Hazel came home, and they were reunited, but then she spent three days with Baxter?

Baxter nudged his arm with his nose, reminding Max to pet him. Max absently scratched his head. "It's a certifiably insane idea. Well, not insane *certifiably*, as that would necessitate some sort of dysfunction in the neural pathways and a release of chemicals into my brain, not to mention a psychiatrist to properly diagnose it. But more in the category of crazy pants."

The idea wasn't more crazy pants than asking Alanna. He didn't even *know* this woman, and his impression was that she was nutty and maybe bossy and pretty intense and she dressed so weird one could reasonably guess she belonged to a cult. He did not get the vibe she was the type to jump on the opportunity to do him a favor, either.

Yep, this idea could be filed under Worst Idea Ever.

But in science, you learned to test various hypotheses. What if he did ask Carly with the sleeves? What if she said yes? What if, assuming Hazel was in good health and spirits and no worse for the wear, that he could make this crazy idea work?

"Nope," he said aloud, scoffing at himself. "Don't be an idiot, Sheffington."

Baxter rolled onto his back.

Max obliged his silent request for a belly rub. "But . . . she cared enough about *you* to go the extra mile to find you, right? And seems like severely and overly concerned about what you're eating, which means she wouldn't feed Hazel cat food. And really, we're talking only three days. Not a month or a lifetime." He rose to his feet. "What's the worst that could happen? The worst that could happen is that she would say no."

Baxter, sensing the personal attention had come to an end, waddled back to the couch. "You didn't answer the question," Max said.

Seriously, if she said no, he'd go with plan B, which was Alanna. He was leaving tomorrow—there was no time to get him into a kennel, assuming there was any room at the inn. Neither idea was great, but plan B was the worse option.

He was about fifty percent certain.

Four

It was true that Carly was in a foul mood when she'd arrived at Tobias Sheffington's doorstep. But who wouldn't be after going through what she'd gone through to find her dog, all the while experiencing how incredibly uncomfortable a true Victor Allen design could be.

Not to mention humiliating.

She'd discovered that when she'd stopped off at a Wag-a-Bag for some mints and couldn't grasp her wallet from her purse while several construction workers stood impatiently behind her until one of them tossed a couple of dollars onto the counter. And if that wasn't enough, she'd been so stressed today that she hadn't been able to think of a single thing to tweet, Instagram, or post on Facebook, which was essential when one was in the business of publicity. She was desperate for content, but she would *not* post a picture of herself in this . . . this *thing*.

She was going to have to rethink her strategy of wearing Victor's designs.

Nevertheless, she could have been nicer to Mr. Tobias Sheffington. With a name like that, she'd been expecting a senior citizen in a bow tie, and she'd been taken aback to find such a young man at the door. She certainly hadn't expected him to be hot, either. He was tall and muscular, like a baseball player. And he had these lovely gray eyes framed with very dark lashes.

And then again, that physique might have all been an optical illusion, because the man was swimming in *so much denim*. A denim collared shirt over a white T-shirt over denim jeans. He was dressed like he was going to have to excuse himself so he could step out back and quickly chop some wood before they discussed the dog issue. Carly could picture Victor holding out the edges of that denim shirt and shaking his head as he worked out what he could possibly do with the look.

But the other thing that set her off was that when she understood Tobias Sheffington was not a doddering retiree but a living, breathing handsome man presumably with all his faculties, she couldn't believe he hadn't had Baxter's chip scanned. It was like chapter one in her dog manual. Responsible Pet Ownership.

Okay, well, maybe she could apologize to him when she returned Bubbles to him. And then again, maybe not. Megan said she shouldn't be apologizing all the time. *Women say "I'm sorry" far too often. Men never say it.*

She pulled into the parking lot at the Umlauf Sculpture Garden and went in search of Phil and his bridesmaids. She had agreed to let him take Bubbles because she'd had to find Baxter.

She found them soon enough, and discovered she wasn't nearly as confused about the overuse of denim on Max Sheffington as she was about discovering Phil had dressed Bubbles in a glittery white tutu. "Why?" Carly asked, gesturing to the offending garment.

"One could ask the same of you," he said, giving her the once-over.

"Okay, fair question, but I have a *client* who asks me to wear these things, remember? What's your excuse?"

"Also a client." With a sharp jerk of his head, Phil indicated a bride and twelve bridesmaids gathered around a sculpture of a man and woman kissing. The bridesmaids wore identical white crop pants and black T-shirts that said Bride Tribe in cursive. The bride wore a gray T-shirt that said Bride over slim white jeans. They were all blond, save one.

"Isn't this the cutest puppy?" one of the bridesmaids gushed.

"Yes," Carly agreed, tilting her head to one side. Bubbles—or, as she was known in the land of denim, Hazel—was an adorable dog, and she had to admit, especially in a tutu. Why not? She pulled out her phone and snapped a couple of pictures to post on her social media later. That would be two problems solved today: finding Baxter and finding something to post. Megan Monroe would say that made this day better than the last day but not as good as tomorrow could be.

"They wanted him to look like he was part of the bridal party," Phil explained.

"Her," Carly corrected.

Phil snorted as he set up the camera. "If it's a her, why'd you name her Baxter? Okay, ladies, if you would, please lean in," he said. "Someone hold the dog."

Hazel happily sat in the middle of them, her long pink tongue hanging out the side of her mouth for the camera.

Denim Man with the arresting gray eyes and photogenic dog named Hazel was a curious man. She wondered what else was curious about him. Probably loads. Probably everything he did was curious. He was probably a mess in general, because, come on, feeding a dog in the living room?

"Lean in a little more and look here," Phil instructed, holding his hand up above his head.

To be fair, Carly had had it in for Tobias Sheffington III the moment Kai had handed her the list of Brant's clients. Standing in a dingy apartment near campus, he'd handed her an even dingier sheet of paper, onto which someone had written their names, their addresses, and their dogs. Carly had scanned the list:

Mr. Alvarez—beagle.
Tammy Pachenko—2 pit bull/lab/kitchen-sink types.
Molly Davis—Labrador, yellow.
Justin Carmine—dachshund, old.
Carly Kennedy—basset, fat.
Tobias Sheffington III—basset, skinny.

Carly had gasped with indignation on Baxter's behalf. "My dog is not *fat*," she'd said to Kai. "He's big-boned."

Kai had shrugged and coughed, and suddenly everything smelled like stale pot.

Carly had stewed about Brant's list all the way to the Sheffington house. Forget that Baxter probably had been tossed into an overgrown backyard and told to fend for himself while she'd provided all the comforts of home to Bubbles—Brant thought Baxter was the fat basset. Well, Hazel wasn't missing any meals, that was certain.

Mr. Sheffington had a dark scruff of beard, too. Like he'd had to dash out to the denim store to make a bulk purchase and hadn't had time to shave. And the knit cap he was wearing looked like he'd gotten it out of a bargain bin about fifteen years ago and worn it every day since. He'd stood in his doorway with an expression of confusion, and then surprise, and then, he'd had the nerve to let his gaze travel the length of her. His brows sort of dipped into confusion, and she knew without a single word from him that he did not understand haute couture. Yes, she was wearing an oddity that looked like a futuristic space suit, but *still*, she should have been afforded the benefit of the doubt.

Except that no one afforded her the benefit of the doubt when she was wearing Victor Allen, she'd noticed.

Well, anyway, Tobias Sheffington III, who was really Max, didn't have to look at her like she'd just walked out of a big silver pod that had bounced into his yard after falling from the sky. There was something about him that was seriously cute, and when she met seriously cute men, she liked to think—

"*Earth to Carly!*"

Carly jumped.

Phil was staring at her. "Will you hand me that lens?" he asked, gesturing to a round black thing on top of his camera bag.

Carly handed it to him. "Sorry to be a party pooper, but I have to take the dog and go. I found Baxter!"

"What are you talking about?" Phil muttered as he squinted into the camera sight.

Carly rolled her eyes. "Should I just leave the tutu on a rock or something?"

"Oh, that's from me!" the bride said. "I didn't want him to feel left out."

How did all these adults fail to recognize that was not a male dog?

The bride leaned over and scratched Hazel behind the ears. "You can keep it! Thank you for letting us use him!"

"Come on, Hazel!"

The dog, who had been completely absorbed in the bride, jerked around so hard at the sound of her name that her ears flew out like helicopter blades and she practically levitated to her feet. She sprinted toward Carly at full tilt, her tutu flapping in time with her ears. Just when it looked like she would plow into Carly's shins, the dog veered to the right and loped over to Phil's camera bag to have a good sniff of it.

"Ladies, hold that pose!" Phil shouted. He lunged for his camera bag, tossed out a biscuit to Hazel and her leash to Carly. "Hey, can I borrow him again next week? I'm doing a shoot for the Austin Film Festival."

"It's a *her*!" Carly said crossly. And then it occurred to her that Baxter would be just as good at this. "Maybe. Call me later." She hooked the leash up to Hazel's collar and the two of them started for the parking lot.

"*Byyyeeee!*" the Bride Tribe shouted after her in unison.

Carly responded with a wave overhead.

It took Hazel two attempts to actually get in the car, but she made it. Carly thought about removing her tutu but decided that Tobias Sheffington III should see that dogs had fun with her, too, all without ruining furniture or destroying discipline.

A minute or two later, Carly and Hazel were on their way across town to do the dog swap, doing the inchworm through Austin traffic again. Hazel had her head out the window and, Carly noticed, had gotten a couple of honks with her winsome grin.

How many hours of her life did she waste sitting in traffic? Too many. Naomi didn't lose one-third of her life to sitting in a car because she walked everywhere. Carly picked up the phone and called Naomi.

Naomi answered on the fifth ring. "Hey!" she shouted brightly. She sounded like she was in a hole.

"Please tell me you are doing something fun because I am stuck in traffic for like the fourth time today," Carly said.

"We're at a club!" Naomi shouted into the phone. "I met this guy at the Starbucks around the corner. We got stuck behind a massive Frappuccino order and hit it off, and he had friends, and I had friends, and you have to come to this club, Carly! It's awesome!"

"I wish!" Carly shouted back at her.

"I hope you're calling to tell me you got a job and you're moving to New York," Naomi shouted over the din.

"I wish that, too! I haven't had any luck with—"

"Are you following up?" Naomi quickly interjected. "You have to follow up."

"I'm following up," Carly assured her. She was following up so much she was making a nuisance of herself.

"You need to come and pound the pavement. You can stay with me and Tandy and Juliette until you find a place."

"I'll be there in a few weeks for the New Designer Showcase. We can meet up and I—"

"What? I can't hear you! Carly, wait." There was a muffled sound, and Naomi said suddenly, "You didn't. You *did*?" That was followed by a squeal. "I *love* champagne cocktails!"

"I love champagne cocktails too," Carly said wistfully.

"Carly, I have to go. Dan got me a champagne cocktail, and it's delicious and he's cute—yes," she said, laughing, "I just said you are cute. Carly, I have to go. Call me!"

"Bye," Carly said, but Naomi had already clicked off.

Damn it. Carly never went to clubs anymore. With Karma and Lydia married and working odd hours, she didn't have a crew. When she'd worked at DBS, they would hit happy hour at places around town, but now that she was on her own, her relationships with her former coworkers had sort of faded away, and the opportunities were few and far between.

She glanced in the rearview mirror at Hazel's tutu-clad butt and wagging tail. Was this the moment, then? Was this the day, the hour, the second she finally admitted her life was not going to plan?

Every day, Megan Monroe posted a #motivation tweet to remind her followers that all they had to do with lemons was make lemonade. But sometimes that wasn't as easy as it sounded in a tweet or on a podcast. Carly felt as if she had spent the last year digging her life's river channel with her bare hands, but her life was not running along in that channel like it was supposed to. It was breaking its banks and flowing in so many different directions that stuff was floating away from her.

She would soon be thirty years old.

In the life plan she'd made for herself when she was sixteen—she still had the spiral notebook with the sparkly stickers and colorful page decorations—she was supposed to be successful and maybe even married by now. She was supposed to live in a house with a deep backyard, with a dog or two and maybe even kids. She was supposed to be a member of giving circles and organizations that mattered, to champion causes like climate protection and humane immigration policies, and somewhere along the line have turned into a gourmet cook and be a highly sought-after doubles partner at the tennis club. She was supposed to be at the top of her professional game, maybe even being considered for partner at DBS.

But the reality was that in spite of her hard work, last year she'd been organized out of a job, her boyfriend of six months had decided he wanted to date other people—maybe all the people, she wasn't clear on that, but specifically not her—her parents had split up and divorced and dragged their grown children down that path with them, and her sister was melting down a little more each day with her young kids and her chronically absent husband.

The truth was that Carly was beginning to flounder. She'd be eating out of dumpsters if it weren't for Victor and her other client, Gordon; but, make no mistake, neither of them were paying her enough to cover her expenses and sometimes working for Victor felt like a full-time babysitting job. Her applications for positions in New York firms seemed to be disappearing into black holes.

If she allowed herself to dwell on it, she would plainly see that not only was she in the middle of a lot of family drama, but she was living a lifestyle she really couldn't maintain any longer. She was on the verge of losing everything, and if that wasn't enough stress, she was desperate for a day where she had nothing to do.

A single day.

A day of solitude during which she never changed out of her pajamas and lay in bed, flipping back and forth between Bravo and HGTV and Hallmark—she *did* watch TV when she had nothing else to do— while she ate from a giant plate of nachos, and someone would come by and quietly do her laundry and mop her floors and clean her toilets, then slip away like a sprite. When could she have *that* day?

Her life was running a little short of desperate. Like today, she'd had a game plan: follow up with two publications she was hoping would feature Victor's work; follow up on two job applications she'd submitted last month and submit at least two more job applications; find an art show for Gordon to attend; and, oh, while she was at it—find her dog. But there was never a moment of solitude. Every hour was interrupted.

In the middle of a phone call with a magazine, her sister, Mia, had beeped her. Not once but several times, distracting Carly so much that she wasn't sure what she'd said to the magazine in the end. When she finally answered Mia's call, it was with a curt "*What?*"

"Don't yell at me! I'm having a horrible day and I can't find Mom, Carly. I'm afraid something awful has happened."

It sounded like something awful was happening in Mia's house. Carly could hear her niece and nephews screaming in the background. Early on, Mia and her husband, Will, had adopted the free-range parenting style, which meant, Mia had explained when she was pregnant with her oldest, that they wanted their children to do and be what came naturally to them and without intervention. Mia had worked for the state Department of Education before she'd married and started having kids, and had read all the studies about effective parenting techniques. But after one particularly bad Saturday that ended with all three kids breaking out in poison ivy rashes, Mia had tearfully confessed to Carly that those theories didn't really work in the real world. Unfortunately, it was hard to put the genie back in the bottle.

"What do you mean, something awful has happened?" Carly asked loudly, so that Mia could hear her over the shouting. "Did you go to her house?" She rifled through her bag looking for a pen.

"No, but I've called her twice and she hasn't responded, and she had a date last night, and you know how she's going out with anyone who slides into her DMs."

Carly stopped looking through her bag because she could not reconcile the phrase *sliding into her DMs* with her fifty-eight-year-old mother. Second, her mother had been on *another* date? That meant her mother had been on half a dozen more dates in the last three months than Carly had had in a year. There was no reality where that was remotely fair.

"Either that, or she is with Dad and doesn't want us to know."

"Dad! What is wrong with you, Mia? They hate each other. She's fine," Carly had said impatiently. "Hold on a minute." She'd put Mia on hold and called her mother.

Her mother answered on the first ring and sounded groggy. "Mom? Is everything okay?"

"Well of course! Why wouldn't it be?"

"Mia tried to get hold of you and you didn't answer. She's worried."

"Oh, I'm *fine*, Carly. I slept in, that's all. What time is it?" There was a pause. "Oh no! Is it *eleven*?" Her mother had giggled like a schoolgirl. "I was out pretty late last night, *if* you know what I mean."

She did know what her mother meant, and she didn't want to know any details. Not a single one. "Okay, Mom, as long as you are okay—"

"I have to say, I really like this new sexual liberation you young women have embraced. I wish we'd had more of it back in the day. Like I told your father, I might not have married him if I knew then what I know now."

"Mom!" Carly said quickly and desperately. "I'm begging you, don't talk about sexual liberation. It's disconcerting and a little frightening. I mean, do you even *know* these men?"

"Guess it depends on what you mean by *know*," she'd said, and chortled gleefully.

Carly had squeezed the bridge of her nose to stave off a tension headache she could feel coming. "Will you please call Mia? You know how she gets."

"Well, do you blame her? Her husband is gone half the time and she—"

"Gotta go," Carly said.

That disturbing call with her mother had been followed with a call from Carly's dad. Because why not call his daughter during a workday just to shoot the breeze? "Hey, Peach! How's my girl? Did you find Mia's dog? What happened there, did you leave the gate open?"

Where had he gotten that idea? But Carly was not about to stop what she was doing and explain the entire, convoluted basset mix-up situation to her father, and tried very hard to get him off the phone, but he tended to ask a lot of questions and he indeed proceeded to ask a lot of questions, and she ended up explaining most of it. To which he said, "Well if that isn't the most millennial thing ever, hiring someone to walk a dog. When I was a kid, we walked our own dogs."

"Oh my God, that is not what any of this is about," she said with a sigh.

"You need to speak to your mother about this dog business anyway. You know, I don't want to talk bad about Evelyn to you kids, but she never showed so much interest in dogs until the divorce. And now suddenly she's the Austin Canine Coalition ambassador to all of Austin—"

"Dad? I really have to go," Carly said, before he could launch into his litany of all the things her mother did wrong now that they were divorced.

"Wait, wait, before you hang up," he said. "Have you had a chance to look at the information I sent you? It's a really good deal, Carly." He'd begun to rattle through his sales pitch about the benefits of a time-share on South Padre Island. His postdivorce plan was to sell time-shares.

It was official—*both* of her parents had gone off the rails since they'd divorced.

"Think how often you could get down to the coast and take a break from that kid you work for," he said, wrapping up his sales pitch.

"Victor is not a kid," she'd said defensively, and then thought the better of defending that statement. "Anyway, I can't get into the advantages of youth when it comes to creative genius, because I really have to run."

She'd ended the call from her dad, had managed to return one single email when she got a call from her other client, Gordon Romero.

Gordon was the son of an old Austin family who had made a name in oil and land development. At the age of seventy-two, he'd come into a vast fortune. He'd quit his law practice and had grabbed on to his hobby with both hands—specifically, hand-carved wooden objets d'art that he was interested in promoting and selling. Except that his objets were really just large and funky circles of wood, carved and polished to a high sheen.

Like Victor, Gordon was great at making his art but terrible at getting the art into the world. Gordon was convinced that a hand-carved bit of wood that was not quite a perfect circle and not quite an oval had a wide market in the United States. He believed that he would make a small fortune if he could get his circles in front of the right people. The only problem was, Gordon didn't want to go out of his way to make that happen. He just expected it. Felt a little entitled to it, truth be known.

Carly wished she had half his confidence. Or the confidence of any old guy who had always gotten his way and rarely had been told no, if ever.

One of her former coworkers at DBS had told Carly about him and his desire for some publicity. "He's too small for us," Alexis had said. "Maybe you could pick him up. He's shopping around for a publicist now."

Carly had done a lot of research into the art world and had discovered there was not a vast market for hand-carved wood art, and none for circles that she could find—but nevertheless, she'd put together a great plan for exposure and had submitted it. Gordon had called her in for an interview. At the interview, she'd handed him another copy of her proposal, of course, along with her résumé, both of which he'd promptly set aside and said, "If you think you can do it, I'll give you a shot."

Carly had been astounded. "Really?" She'd felt herself puff up a little. *She'd done it.* She'd studied the problem and had put together a kick-ass proposal, one that he could not possibly turn down, and she'd won this job with her creativity and assertiveness, just like Megan said she would. She was *good* at this. She could *do* this on her own! She was badass, and she had on her big girl panties, and she was going to get a plum job in New York. This man, this *artist*, had seen her talent and recognized genius, and so would someone in New York. "That's . . . that's amazing!"

"Yeah," he had said with a flick of his wrist. "You're the only applicant I had and I need the help. I'm willing to give you a shot."

She had deflated, the air leaving her so quickly it was a wonder she didn't fly all over that nicely appointed study like a punctured balloon.

Nevertheless, she'd taken that job to build her portfolio. Turned out, it was a much greater challenge than she could have anticipated, because good ol' Gordon liked to second-guess her at every turn. That, and he had the computer skills of a Neanderthal.

"How in the *fuck* do I get into this damn blog?" he shouted at her on the phone earlier.

It had been Carly's suggestion that he start a blog, nothing more than one entry per week, just talking a little bit about what he was doing and showing his work in various stages of creation. Well, actually, her original suggestion had been Instagram, which she thought would be much less work for him, but he'd scoffed at that. "I'm not some teenager looking for followings," he'd said.

Followers, she'd corrected him in her head.

As she suspected, Gordon had once again confused his username with his password when trying to get into his blog. She had to hold the phone away from her ear as Gordon launched into a profane tirade of opinions about computers and technology. Carly had promised to drop by as soon as she could and fix it for him, and she would probably end up writing the blog for him while she was there, and then she would do what she always did, which was stick a Post-it on his computer with his username and password and beg his dumpy, sour-faced housekeeper, Alvira, not to throw it away. Alvira was delightful—she grunted at Carly when she came around and glared at Gordon when he asked for a drink.

"Well, okay," Gordon said reluctantly when she'd offered to swing by today or tomorrow. "But can you please wear something normal, for God's sake? Those clothes you like will have my neighbors thinking a hazmat team had been called out. You could cause a mass panic around here."

"Very funny," Carly had said. At the time, however, she did think she would love to put on something a little less constricting.

She was thinking that now. She was so close to her house—what would it add, another fifteen minutes to this impossible day? She glanced at the clock. It was already a quarter past six and traffic was still crawling. This dog exchange had thrown a huge wrench in her plans.

Carly picked up her phone to text Gordon and let him know she'd come by tomorrow in regular clothes. She hated making him wait, but this was the overextended life she'd been living for a little over a year, since she'd walked out of the door of DBS carrying her cardboard box of personal belongings and had to create her own livelihood.

Nevertheless, Carly remained optimistic. She just refused to look at her savings account until she absolutely had to.

Megan said to always look forward.

Five

Max was beginning to fear she'd ditched him. Maybe she'd decided Hazel was a better dog than Baxter, and who could blame her? Baxter was great, but Hazel was amazing. Why the hell hadn't he gotten Carly's full name? At the very least, her number? Why hadn't he asked more questions? Why hadn't he gone with her? What was the matter with him?

He could be so naïve at times, so distracted by a pair of pretty eyes. He was like a seven-year-old kid in a toy store.

It was half past seven when he finally saw the sweep of car lights into the drive. He stalked to the front door and threw it open, prepared to give her a piece of his mind. But that piece of his mind crumbled into ash when Carly got out of her car. She'd changed out of her costume and was wearing yoga pants that fit her very well, a zip-up hoodie over a T-shirt that said *Back in my day we had nine planets*. She'd pulled her sleek dark hair into a ponytail at her crown and he guessed the thing that startled him the most was that not only did she look normal, she looked delightfully curvy. *Curvy in all the best ways*, his testosterone receptors whispered.

No wonder it had taken her so long. She probably needed a team of people to extract her from the contraption she'd been wearing.

She gave him a wave from the drive and then opened the back door of her car. Hazel leapt out with the agility of a show dog and raced to the front door.

"Hazel!" Max exclaimed and went down on one knee to accept the lash of her tongue and to hug her for a long moment. "I missed you, girl," he said, scratching her behind the ears. That's when his brain registered the fact that Hazel was wearing a tutu. He stood up and frowned as Carly strolled up the walk.

She grinned, her eyes sparkling. "Cute, right?"

Cute was not the word that came to mind. "Umm . . ."

"It's a tutu."

"I noticed. Is it a joke?"

"A joke! Ha! Of course not. They make clothes for dogs other than bandannas, you know."

"Yeah, but why is—"

From somewhere in the house, Baxter let out a deep bay that startled them both. That was followed by the sound of Baxter running. Not just running—racing at full bore.

"Baxter!" Carly went down on one knee, prepared to accept the eager greeting of her dog. But Baxter didn't race for her, he raced for Hazel. He ran so fast that he couldn't stop himself on the slick Saltillo tile floors and crashed into Hazel. The two basset hounds spilled out into the yard, tumbling over and around each other, running together in the grass with Hazel in that ridiculous tutu.

Carly and Max watched a moment in mutual stunned silence as the two mounds of black and brown and white fur tumbled over each other before righting themselves and racing again. "*Wow,*" Carly murmured. "I didn't know Baxter had a turbospeed."

"Same here," Max said. "I guess they're friends?"

"I guess? I didn't know he had those sorts of feelings about . . . *anything*."

"Same again."

Hazel raced in a circle and headed toward the front door, Baxter in hot pursuit.

Carly and Max hopped out of the way just before they were bowled over by the dogs. "Curious . . . what is the deal with that tutu?" Max asked as the two dogs blundered past them and into the house.

"She was a bridesmaid."

Max shifted his gaze from the dogs to Carly and caught her looking at his hair. "A what?" He self-consciously put his hand on the top of his head on the chance that his hair was sticking up after removing his knit cap.

"A *bridesmaid*. At a prewedding photo shoot." Her gaze flicked down his body. Max looked down. He'd changed his shirt for a sweater and had removed his contacts—he really needed to get his prescription checked—and had put on glasses.

Carly lifted her gaze again, and the corner of her mouth curled up in a strange little smile.

What the hell? Did he look weird? Did he have pizza sauce on his face? "I'm sorry—is something wrong?"

"Nope." She pressed her lips together, caught her ponytail, and flicked it over her shoulder.

"Why are you looking at me like that?" he asked.

"Like what? I'm not even looking at you. Everything is *fabulous*. I found my dog, I saved the day for Bubbles—excuse me, *Hazel*—and, yes, I've had a very productive day. Thank you for asking."

"That's great," he said, his gaze locked on her. "I didn't know I'd asked."

"Well," she said, her gaze locked on him, too, "you looked like you were about to."

There seemed to be some weird energy flowing around them that

Max couldn't quite decipher. But before he could, she said, "I'm just going to, ah . . . go get my dog." She pointed to the interior of the house.

"Right," he said and with a bend of his head, indicated she should come in.

Carly walked into his living room where Hazel had Baxter pinned to the floor by his neck. Carly didn't seem to notice. She shoved her hands into her hoodie and her gaze flicked quickly over him again. "You have a cute house. I really didn't notice the first time. I like the Spanish style. You don't see so many of them around town anymore. You know . . . the tech millionaires." She glanced away from him.

The tech millionaires. Was that supposed to mean something? Had he missed some innuendo, some social cue, maybe even part of a conversation? Was he crazy, or had the mood done a definite shift into a weird, dithery space? She had those blue eyes that sort of pulled you in, and maybe he'd been pulled in for a moment too long and had shot past something vital. "I don't . . . not following," he said.

"You know . . . buying all the houses and turning them into mansions." Carly pushed a bit of hair behind her ear. Only there wasn't any hair to push back, and he wasn't certain she even realized it. What had happened? Earlier, she'd been ready to bust his balls for having failed to have Baxter's chip scanned. And now she seemed almost nervous. It made him feel uneasy, too, and they stood there for a very awkward moment, their gazes locked again, the air around them bubbling hot like dry ice in warm water. But Max didn't like the awkward standoff, and in an effort to end it, to sound completely unaffected by the strange vibe, he said breezily, "Oh, hey, looks like you lost the sleeves."

She looked down at one of her sleeves. Then at him. "What?"

"The, ah . . . the costume you were wearing with the sleeves," he said, gesturing to his own arm. "What sort of costume was it, anyway?"

Carly's mouth dropped open. And then closed. Well, then. If he wanted to dissipate the strange little spell between them, he'd done it, and but good. She cocked her weight on one hip in a manner that had irked female written all over it and Max didn't know how, or what, but he realized he'd said something horribly, terribly wrong. "I'm sorry," she said with false airiness. "Did you say *costume*?"

"I mean . . . wasn't it?"

She folded her arms. "For your information, I was wearing an *original* Victor Allen."

He had no idea who or what that was, but he could plainly see he'd tripped a wire and blown up a mine. "Oh. I didn't know—"

"You'd pay *thousands* for that ensemble in New York or Los Angeles," she said, clearly gathering some steam.

An inadvertent chuckle of disbelief escaped him. "Why?"

She gasped. Her eyes rounded.

"Okay," Max said, and held up his hand. "I sort of live under a rock—"

"Yes, you do!" She made a sound like a shout and gasp of air at once. "I don't even know where to begin! I mean, you *obviously* have never heard of Victor Allen—"

"True—"

"But he just happens to be one of the nation's most exciting young fashion designers and he's from Austin."

"Cool," Max said.

"He won *Project Runway*."

He was beginning to feel like a visitor to a strange land. "I didn't know that." *Should* he know it? Was that a thing—to know fashion designers and what they'd won? He shoved his hands into his pockets and fisted them in a vain attempt to keep from exploding into full nerd and asking exactly that question.

"You don't know what that is, do you?"

He winced. "I'm sorry, I really don't."

"You really don't know anything about fashion?"

For her information, he owned a leather jacket that he thought was pretty awesome. "I guess I just know what looks good," he offered. But the minute the words were out of his mouth, he realized how they must sound to her, and if he had any doubt, Carly's expression confirmed it.

"That . . . *costume*, as you call it, is an avant-garde piece. It's art. It's not supposed to look good, it's supposed to promote brand awareness and make you think. The theme of his collection is futuristic space diva."

Max was flummoxed. He had never thought about clothes past what went with what. He couldn't name a brand of any clothes he wore. Nope, he just put on his pants and a shirt and went to work.

"I mean, I'm not surprised," she said with a dismissive flick of her wrist, "you're a guy, so . . ." She glanced away.

Curiously, her tone suggested that she was repulsed by *guys* and at the same time, thought she was being magnanimous by naming him one. He didn't know how he felt about that. He was a guy, but he wasn't a complete idiot. He was a scientist—surely that counted for something. Surely he shouldn't be expected to know fashion labels, too. "So?" he pressed her.

"And . . . no offense, but most guys don't get fashion. At least not the ones I seem to run into." Her gaze flicked over him, as he apparently was one she'd run into. "You should really check out Victor Allen online. He's insanely talented."

That was not the technically correct meaning of *insane*, but Max thought the better of pointing that out.

"I'm his publicist, so I wear his designs."

Aha. Mystery solved. He wondered if that meant she had to wear that . . . art . . . all the time. If so, it was a bit of a buzzkill.

"What? What is that look?" she asked, making a whirling motion with her finger in the direction of his face.

"What look?"

"One of your brows just shot up."

"Nope. Didn't shoot up."

"Yes, it did. I know what you're thinking. You're thinking just like my brother-in-law, who said that jumpsuit looked stupid, and, by the way, this from a man who is in sweats and T-shirts most of the time when I see him."

Max laughed with surprise. "It was a *jumpsuit*? Wow . . . I did not have jumpsuit on my list of possibilities."

"Okay, all right," she said, nodding as if she'd just figured him out. "You just proved my point—you're such a guy. I don't expect most people to understand haute couture any more than you probably expect me to understand accounting or whatever it is you do, and yet, I can stand here and see that your eyes are really gray, and not green like I first thought, and I can also see that high fashion is art."

"What?"

"*Whew* boy," she said, as if she'd just jogged her way into this conversation. She put her hands on her hips. "That was rough." She blew out her cheeks, looked around him and into the hall. "Okay, well, now that we covered that, I guess I should get my dog and get—"

The sound of a crash startled them. Carly jumped. "What was that?"

Max groaned. "I think it might have been a pizza." He turned toward the kitchen. "Hazel, that better not have been you!"

On the other side of the kitchen bar he found Baxter with his head hung low, prepared to be guilty even if he hadn't done anything wrong, and an unrepentant Hazel munching away at what was left of the pizza Max had put aside when he'd begun to suspect Carly wasn't coming back and had begun to worry in earnest. "Seriously?" he demanded of the two of them. "How could either one of you possibly get up that high? It defies all known properties of gravity," he said, gesturing to the counter. He dipped down, pushed Hazel away from the box, and picked up what was left of the pizza. He placed the mangled pieces of pizza on the bar and looked at his fingers, covered in pizza sauce. The dogs, divested of the rest of the pizza and probably sensing there would be no dire consequences, were wrestling each other again.

"Oh no."

Max jerked toward the sound of Carly's voice. She'd followed him into the kitchen and saw the remains of pizza on the floor. "That's a mess."

"Understatement," he muttered, and grabbed a roll of paper towels.

"I have never seen Baxter like this. I really think he and Bubbles are *friends*."

"Hazel," he reminded her. He turned on the faucet to wash his hands. "I don't see Hazel like this very often, either, to be honest. And I've never seen her in a tutu. I appreciate the gesture, but I'm going to take it off."

"It's adorable, but if you want to be a killjoy . . ." She smiled pertly.

"I want to be a killjoy," he said. Bandannas were one thing. Tutus were quite another. He turned off the tap and dried his hands. Then he stepped in between the wrestling dogs, lifted Hazel up by the back end, and yanked the tutu free of her body. He opened one of the French doors and flipped on an outside light. "Take it outside, you two," he commanded.

The two dogs frolicked their way out the door.

Carly moved to stand beside him at the door and peered out into the yard. Max had done a little landscaping last year. He'd made a small firepit and had installed a Buddha in the flower bed. "Nice," Carly said. "I worried that Baxter was tied up in someone's bare backyard." She turned to face him. "Did you worry about Hazel?"

"Of course. But I think I worried more that Hazel would make herself too comfortable."

Carly laughed at that, and Max was surprised by the sound of it—her laugh was lovely. She'd come in so hot that any laugh was unexpected, and especially one like that.

And then, just as suddenly, her smile faded a little, and she was looking at him again in that strange way that made Max feel self-conscious. He didn't like it. He brushed his hand across his cheek just in case.

Carly abruptly pirouetted away from the door and into his living area. "I think we've learned a valuable lesson here, don't you?"

A lesson? What lesson? "We have?"

"Sure! We've learned that crazy things happen when dogs are involved. Like, your name is Max? Because Brant had you down as Tobias Sheffington III, and he is definitely the type to pounce on a shortcut like Max."

"One hundred percent," Max agreed.

She smiled, and that strange vibe rushed through him again.

"I should get Baxter and go. Busy, *busy* day tomorrow. I have to swing by someone's house and log them on to a computer. Need to rest up for that."

"You have to do what?"

She shook her head as she looked at her watch. "I'm kidding. Well, I'm *not* kidding, but it's a long, boring story, so I'll save that for someone I don't like." She glanced up and smiled. "Lucky you."

Did that mean she liked him? Was this the time to ask for his favor?

"Well, Mr. Sheffington, this has been a week! May you and Hazel find a new dog walker who is not selling pot on the side. I may skip the dog walker for the time being. I've got some super serious trust issues now." She made a flourish with her hand and bowed, then walked to the French doors and peered out. "Oh."

The dogs had a dog rope between them and were engaged in a fierce tug-of-war. "They *really* like each other, don't they?" Max said.

"I'm not gonna lie—Baxter has been so depressed since I got him."

"Yeah? He was really down in the beginning here, too, but he perked up for me after a day."

"Why?" She peeked up at him. "Are you a dog whisperer or something?"

"I let him on the couch." He smiled.

Carly snorted. "He's probably ruined for life, so thanks for that. Hazel looks pretty happy, too. She's a real people person."

He resisted the urge to point out that she was mixing species. "How long have you had Baxter?"

"A few weeks. How long have you had Hazel?"

"Not quite a year," he said. "You seem to like Hazel, at least."

"I *love* Hazel. I love all dogs. Dogs are the best."

"Even the ones that eat your pillows?"

She gave him a wry smile. "I'm sure she didn't mean it."

Max was relieved to hear it, because he was about to ask her the most outrageous favor, and it helped if she wasn't holding a grudge against his dog. "I'm more than happy to reimburse you." He shoved a hand through his hair and knocked some of it loose over his brow. He resisted the urge to brush it back like a nervous Nellie, but what he was doing suddenly seemed ridiculously absurd. So absurd that he almost talked himself out of it. But then Jamie's face flashed across his mind's eye.

"Carly, I need to, ah . . ." *Get hold of yourself, man.* "I would like to ask you a favor." There, he'd said it.

And just as he suspected, Carly instantly frowned with suspicion. "That doesn't sound good. What *sort* of favor?"

"So here's the deal. I am taking my brother to the Midwest Regional Dog Show in Chicago tomorrow. It's a special gift for him, and we've had tickets for a long time."

Carly said nothing, but her brows sank deeper into a frown.

"Brant was supposed to dog-sit for me."

"*Eew.*" She wrinkled her nose.

"That plan is definitely dead," he said with a sweep of his hand. "But as everything happened last minute, and I didn't have the right dog, and . . . well, I can't find anyone who can take Hazel at a moment's notice."

Carly stared at him. Her brows went from a deep vee to arching high over her eyes as understanding dawned in her lovely eyes. "No way."

"Hear me out," he begged her.

"I rescue your dog for you and now you want me to *keep* her for you? I don't even *know* you. I'm still getting over the fact that your name isn't Tobias."

"Well, it is Tobias, but it's also Max, and if you think about it, you actually know all of my names—"

"You aren't going to ask me to take your dog this weekend, are you? You aren't *really* going to do that."

"I get it," he said, holding up both hands. "I know this is the last thing you expected when you saved the day, and I swear to God, I would never ask if I didn't find myself in such a bind."

"This is crazy!" she said with a disbelieving laugh. She stacked her hands on top of her head and twirled in a circle. "You want me to *dog-sit*?"

"I'll pay you," he said. "And you can stay here if you want. Baxter, too, of course."

"Well, that's not going to happen—I would never stay in a house with a kitchen in that state," she said, pointing to the mess in his kitchen. "I'd need search and rescue just to find the fridge."

"Fair point," he said. "It's been a long week . . ." He decided not to delve into the reasons behind his haphazard housekeeping. "I'll clean it—"

"Max! For all you know, I could be an ax murderer."

"Oh," he said with an inadvertent chuckle, "I think I know you're not an ax murderer."

"How?" she demanded. "How could you possibly know?"

"I have a pretty good feeling that someone who is into high fashion and calls it art is not going to get blood on her clothes."

She considered that for a minute. "True. Okay, fine, I'm not an ax murderer, but you know what I'm saying, and, besides, isn't it a rule of thumb that you're supposed to wait until you've at least had dinner with someone before you ask for a favor?"

"There's a rule?" he asked, surprised by this.

"If there's not, there ought to be. I can't believe you are *asking* me this."

"Carly, I know—it's beyond," he said apologetically. "It's an audacious and gross abuse of our very meager acquaintance. And I wouldn't ask, but this is so important to my brother, and my dad is going fishing—"

"Come on—*surely* you've got someone else. What about your mother? Another sibling? A friend? You've got to have one or two of those lying around. You're a good-looking guy. You must have some girlfriends who would do it."

He would save his pleasure at being called good-looking for later. "My mother is dead, my aunt is allergic to pet dander, and my dad desperately needs a break because my brother, the one I am taking to the dog show, is profoundly autistic and has to have someone with him all the time." He strode across the room and picked up a picture from the mantel of his dad and Jamie. His dad was grinning, leaning against an old car he'd refurbished. Jamie was standing close by, unsmiling, his gaze on something to the side.

He held the picture out to Carly. She looked at it.

"My dad needs a break. My brother needs a break. We've been planning this a really long time and then Brant ruined everything for these two guys and they don't even know him. I've tried to find a dogsitter at such short notice, or even a kennel, but I can't find anyone."

She looked at the picture again.

Max stepped closer. "Jamie has already packed his bags. He has his dog books on the bed. He's obsessed with dogs. Dogs are the only thing he really responds to, and that's why I got Hazel in the first place, so he could have a dog around. How am I going to tell him he can't go to a dog show because of a dog? How ironic is that?"

"Oh my God," Carly whispered to the ceiling. "That's ridiculously ironic."

"My neighbor used Brant a couple of times and said everything worked out fine. I assumed it would for me, too." Max shifted even closer. "Listen, Carly, were it not for my brother, I would never dream of asking you. Look at them," he said, swinging around to the French doors again. "Baxter obviously loves Hazel and she loves him. *Look* at them."

Carly turned her head and looked out. The dogs were romping like puppies.

"Come on," Max said softly. "Have you ever seen Baxter so happy?"

"Unfair," she said weakly. "You know I haven't. But two dogs is a *lot*."

"They will be a piece of cake. They will keep each other company and because they have each other, they will stay out of trouble. It will feel like they're not even there."

She looked dubious.

"It's obvious you care about dogs, and you've been hanging out with Hazel for a couple of days now. You even took her to someone's wedding."

"I didn't take her to a wedding—"

"Jamie loves dogs, and this means so much to him. He has a job at the Austin Canine Coalition now, did I mention that? It's the first job he's managed to hold on to. He doesn't talk much, but in his job, he doesn't have to because he gets dogs and they get him."

She stared out the window at the dogs, her lips pressed together as she considered it.

"You would not believe how much progress my brother has made since he started working there. He's so eager to get there that he started taking the bus by himself once a week. He didn't have any social life before this job, but he's actually gone for ice cream with some of the other workers. His entire world is home and the ACC, and he has been looking forward to this since I booked it. Every time I see him, he says *dog show*. Look." He walked to the wall near the fireplace and lifted a canvas from a hook. He brought it back to show her. It was a painting of a floppy-eared dog. "Jamie painted this. He even *paints* dogs."

"That's a really good painting," she said softly. She closed her eyes and drew a long breath. "Okay." She opened them again. "How can I disappoint your brother? Or Baxter? Or Hazel? Oh my *God*," she said with a dramatic, backward drop of her head.

Max understood, but he couldn't help but sigh with relief. "Thank you so much, Carly. I will never be able to convey to you how much I appreciate this. I'll be back before you know it, and I swear, I'll return the favor. Anytime you need to get out of town, you let me know. A week, a month, whatever you need. Baxter always has a home here."

She snorted. "You think I'm going to let Baxter stay here with you, eating mac and cheese and lounging on the couch? It's going to take forever to undo that damage as it is."

"I appreciate it so much. This has been weighing on me—I thought I was going to have to resort to drastic measures."

"Well, news flash, Max—asking a total stranger to take your dog for a few days is a drastic measure."

"Yeah . . . but there are worse options," he said with a bitter laugh. "I mean . . . no offense." He clasped his hands together in prayer pose. "You're a good person, Carly . . . What is your last name?"

"Kennedy. Carly Kennedy Public Relations."

"You're a good person, Carly Kennedy Public Relations. I've got a few things," he said, and walked across the living area to a box on the floor near the kitchen. "Hazel's things. Her favorite toy, some treats," he said, rummaging through it. "Plenty of food, too."

Carly stared at the box in disbelief. "You were really hoping this worked out, weren't you?"

"I really was." He carried the box under his arm and went to the back door, opened it, and whistled. Both dogs came running.

"I am taking them *now*?" she asked incredulously.

"Our flight is at seven in the morning. I thought it would be easier this way. I could drop her off in the morning if you like."

She covered her face with both hands, her red nail polish stark against her fair skin. "How do I get myself into these things?" She dropped her hands. "Well, all right, then, if we're going to do this, let's do it."

A bubble of maniacal relief was building in Max's chest, but he pushed it down before it escaped into a deranged laugh, then walked to the front door. When he opened it, Hazel shot past him and out onto the flagstones. Baxter ran behind her. He actually looked like he was grinning.

Max followed Carly to her car and put Hazel's things in the back, stuffing the box down between yards of fabric and what looked like two carved wooden circles. He loaded the dogs in the back seat and asked for her phone. "I'll enter my contact number. Text me or call me if you have any problems."

"Don't think I won't."

He entered his number, then rang his number with her phone so that he'd have her contact as well. "I promise I'll make it up to you."

"Don't you even want to know where I live?" she asked curiously. "I could live in a rusted-out bus next to the highway. You really have no idea where you're sending your dog."

"I considered the rusted-out bus theory, but since you and I had the same dog walker, I'm going to go out on a limb and guess that you don't. I think you probably live around here somewhere."

"On the other side of Mopac," she said, pointing in the direction of a highway that ran north and south on the west side of town.

"See? You can tell me exactly where when I get back from Chicago. I'll text you from the airport."

She opened the driver door.

"Carly?"

She paused and looked back to him.

Inexplicably, his gaze went to her mouth. For a single breath he had the wildly inappropriate thought of kissing her goodbye. It was such a wayward thought, popping up like a weed between all the logistical thoughts in his head, that it shook him a little, and he reached around her and opened the car door a little wider. "Seriously. Thank you so much."

"Okay, stop thanking me. It's starting to get weird." She got in, pushed two overeager dogs off the console between her seats and to the back. As she backed out of the drive, she paused and through her open window shouted, "I can't believe you talked me into this!" then rocketed out of his drive onto the main road.

Max couldn't believe it either. And for the first time in days, he could actually breathe a sigh of relief.

But as he walked back in his house on that wave of relief, that weed of a thought, the idea of kissing her, wouldn't wither away like it was supposed to.

Six

Carly told the dogs on their way home that she was an idiot. "This is what happens when a handsome guy asks me for a favor—I end up with you two. I mean, let's be real. Everyone in this car knows that if Brant had asked me, I would have laughed in his face."

The dogs surged forward to lick her with agreement.

"It was that business with the brother that did it," she muttered as she pushed the dogs back. *Note to self: invest in a car harness for the dogs. Dog.* "He's handsome and he's taking his brother to a dog show. You can't even find that guy in a romance novel, am I right?"

They had reached the gate to her house. She pulled through and turned down the long drive to the cottage in back.

She loved her quaint little two-bedroom cottage with its front porch and red chimney. She loved the location, too—it was almost exactly smack-dab in the middle of town. She'd stalked the cottage for months before it was available, and when the FOR RENT sign had finally gone up, she was the first one at the gate. It was her sanctuary, tucked in beneath some pecan trees and away from the road.

The slap of a happy dog's tongue across her cheek startled her back to the present. Carly ducked to one side. "*Stop* that, Hazel. It tickles." Hazel panted in her ear a moment, then went back to her window, crowding Baxter out for the prime spot.

"Don't take that lying down, Bax," she advised her dog.

Baxter responded by lying down on the seat.

As she was coasting down to the cottage, she spotted her landlord, Conrad Rutherford. He was in his drive, illuminated by floodlights. She tapped the horn in greeting.

Conrad and his wife, Petra, had moved here a few years ago after retiring from some tech job in Silicon Valley. In spite of having a name that sounded like a round, monocled man in an old dime-store detective novel, Conrad was actually a young, rich hipster. He'd once tried to explain what he'd done in California, but Carly's thoughts had taken a mental trip to Italy in the middle of his long-winded explanation. Whatever the job was, it had paid them enough to tear down one mansion and build another, then renovate the cottage on their property. As far as Carly knew, the only thing Conrad and Petra did now was grow herbs and tomatoes and flowers and talk a lot about climate change.

Conrad jerked upright when she honked, then he waved at her. Both hands, high overhead. "I think he wants me to stop?" Carly mused. She slowed.

He had on wide-legged shorts that hung to midcalf and a bandanna tied around his forehead. At his crown was the impressive man bun he'd been cultivating for a few months now. Petra was a former dancer, and sometimes in the very early morning, Carly would see her in the yard moving through a sun salutation. She was so graceful that she could make a simple yoga practice look like a performance. Occasionally, Conrad and Petra would invite Carly to the big house for supper, and they would regale her with tales of California over a plant-based meal featuring microgreens.

Conrad waved again but with some urgency, even though Carly had rolled to a stop. He began to lope across the drive, his lanky frame making it look like he had too much leg to run properly. "Hi, Conrad!" Carly said when he reached her.

"*So* glad I saw you," he said breathlessly. He paused to bend over and press his hands to his knees and wheeze a moment. She rolled down the window so the dogs could say hello.

"Hey," Conrad said, and reached inside to pet them both. "Am I seeing double?" He laughed. He continued to pet them as he said, "So, listen, we need to have a chat about the rent."

The abrupt transition from dog to rent startled Carly. "Come again?"

"Yep, 'fraid so," he said with a bit of a casual shrug. "You're on a month to month, you know."

Well, yes, of course she knew. Her heart started to jackhammer. She did not want to hear what he was going to say. No good news ever came after *We need to have a chat about the rent*. Her life was in enough of a shambles—

"Looks like we're going to have to go up on the rent, and we'll probably want to sign you up for a year or so. Petra wants a two-year lease, but I don't know if we need to push that idea just yet."

She could only gape at him as her brain cells scrambled together, trying to get in working formation.

"Hey, don't look so surprised. It's just business."

"How so?" It was remarkable she could speak at all, given how high up into her throat her heart had just climbed.

"Well, our property taxes have gone up, and we've got that hospital district that's taxing now, so . . ." He shrugged again. And then smiled at the dogs and called one of them a *good* dog.

"How much more?" she made herself ask.

"Two hundred."

Lord help her, it was all she could do to keep from fainting dead away behind the wheel. She'd thought maybe, *maybe*, he'd ding her for another seventy-five a month. "*Two hundred* dollars?" she repeated, her voice almost a whimper.

"That's still under market rate, you know," Conrad said. "I could get four grand for this place, easy, so you're getting a bargain, Carly. And you know, Petra and I like you. We don't want to push you out."

Didn't they? Because raising her rent two hundred a month and forcing her to sign a year's lease would probably push her out, and she suspected they had to know that.

"Hey! Want some crookneck yellow squash? That stuff is still growing, can you believe it? Wait right here and I'll get you some." Conrad turned and loped back up his drive.

Carly sank back against her seat. Baxter nudged her shoulder with his snout. "I know," she muttered. "I'm freaking out, too."

Conrad returned with an armload of squash, and she took it, piling it into the front passenger seat, assuring him that she understood the rent situation all the while. Then she drove down to the cottage with squash rolling around in her seat and onto the floorboard.

She did not sleep well that night for two reasons—one, because of the rent, obviously. And two, because two dogs crawled onto the bed with her during the night, which, in the beginning, had been kind of nice and comforting, but by morning, they'd spread themselves out, leaving her just a patch of her own bed.

She woke up with a crick in her neck and a sixth-sense type of dread that things were about to go south. How could they not when you added another dog to the mix of dogs that you already hadn't asked for? How could they not when you'd just heard about a two-hundred-dollar-a-month rent hike when you didn't have a full-time job? It was just the laws of the universe—stuff was bound to happen.

Her first business of the day was to log Gordon into his blog. But with no dog walker—she wouldn't be able to afford one now, for sure—and no place to park her two matching beasts, Carly had to take the dogs along with her. She parked in Gordon's drive, took the dogs out of the car, and leashed them to a magnolia tree, where they lay side by side in a cool breeze, apparently a-okay with hanging out in the shade for a time with the water bowl she set up for them.

Gordon wasn't home, but his housekeeper, the evil Alvira, was. Alvira wasn't appreciative of the dogs, but Carly just smiled and went into Gordon's office and logged him in to his blog. He hadn't written anything but the initial blog post she had helped him with, and that was two weeks ago. So her plan was working beautifully! *Not.* She would need to rethink her five-point publicity proposal.

From there, she took the dogs with her to run a dozen errands—no way was she leaving Hazel with any pillows in the house, her brand-new subscription to Dog TV notwithstanding, which, if she was being honest, was pretty soothing for people, too. That was as much TV as she'd watched in weeks.

She took the dogs to her sister's house when Mia called on the verge of tears, as she often did. "It's Finn," she said, referring to her oldest child, a five-year-old. "He's the devil, Carly. Satan has inhabited his body, and you can't convince me otherwise."

"Why? What'd he do?"

"He tried to flush his brother's bear down the toilet. But it wouldn't go down, so he got a stick to help it along. My bathroom is flooded, and the toilet is probably ruined, and Will called and said he had to extend his trip by two days. *Two days!*"

Mia did not handle stress well. Once, when Mia was pregnant with Millie, Carly had pointed out that she didn't handle stress well, and Mia had almost come across the table for Carly's throat. Thereby, Carly had further pointed out, proving her point.

"It's too much, Carly. I can't take another thing today. What am I supposed to do?" Mia cried into the phone. "Just tell me, *What. Am. I. Supposed. To. Do?*"

"I'll be over," Carly said. When Mia got like this, what she really needed was contact with an adult, and Carly was always the one on speed dial.

She showed up with Baxter and Hazel in tow. Mia took one look at the dogs, then at Carly, and shrieked, "What are you *doing*? Why do you have *two* dogs? Why are they *in* my *house*?"

"I told you the whole mix-up story. The second dog is the basset I found in my house. And, of course, you know Baxter." Baxter wagged his tail. "I'm dog-sitting."

Mia stared at her. Somewhere upstairs in this beautiful, modern home, a child screamed. Mia glared at Carly. "Carly? I can't deal with your dog sitch right now. I am having a meltdown and can*not* add anything else to it."

"You are not adding anything to your meltdown, Mia. This problem," she said, gesturing at both dogs, "is not a problem. Think of it as a playdate."

Another shriek and a loud thud made both of them wince.

"Mommy! *Mommy!*" Bo screamed, and came running down the stairs. "Finn *hit* me!"

"No, I didn't!" Finn shouted, running down the stairs behind his brother. At the top of the stairs, little Millie had to stop and turn around so she could crawl backward down the stairs.

"Finn. Stop hitting your brother!" Mia shouted.

Finn instantly burst into tears and ran off in the direction of the kitchen. But the rush of shouting children had stirred up the dogs, and they began to bark. The barking only excited the children more, and as Bo and Millie ran from the dogs, Hazel thought it was an invitation to play, and went chasing after them. Baxter followed, barking loudly and often, then running back to make sure Carly hadn't deserted him.

Finn reappeared, still sobbing. "I don't like you, Mommy!" he shouted, and ran up the stairs.

"I know why mothers eat their young," Mia said tearfully. "I totally get it. They never sleep. They eat like animals. They won't mind me."

Carly noticed then that Mia's hair, as light as Carly's was dark, was standing on end. She had a mysterious stain on her shirt, and her chinos were worn at the knees. "Where is your nanny?" Carly asked.

"Oh, didn't I tell you? She left! Got a job in West Lake Hills that paid better. Second nanny this year to find a better job in West Lake Hills, and we are paying top dollar."

"Let's fix your plumbing problem," Carly suggested evenly.

Mia pointed toward the guest bath.

Crammed together into the small room, they stared down at the toilet and the bear leg, the only part of the bear that was visible. "What are we going to do?" Mia asked.

"Dig it out," Carly said.

"I don't know what I'd do without you, Carly. You always know what to do," Mia said. "You're always there for me and my hellions."

"I don't know what to do, but it seems like the only solution. And I don't know what I'd do without you, either. You were there for me when I got laid off. And when Blake broke up with me."

Mia thought about it a moment, and nodded. "You're right. So it's like you practically owe me this." She smiled.

Carly laughed.

It took fifteen minutes to dig the bear out of the toilet. Carly did the digging. Mia stood over her, too close, watching and offering her opinion about how it should be done. But somewhere in the middle she said, "Do you think Mom and Dad are getting back together?"

"What?" Carly yanked on a soggy paw. "Why would you even say that? They are *divorced*. The ink is dry on that deal. It's over."

"I don't know," Mia said. "Don't let it drip on the floor!"

"Then could I have a plastic bag, please?" Carly asked.

Mia moved to dig a plastic bag out of a bigger plastic bag, and when she did, Hazel suddenly appeared. She chomped down on the wet teddy that Carly was holding between two fingers, yanked it free, and raced away with it, leaving a trail of toilet water down the hall. Somewhere close by, Baxter barked.

"Why did you let that dog have it?" Mia exclaimed.

"I didn't let her! She took it," Carly said. They hurried out of the bathroom and down the hall after Hazel. The dogs were nowhere to be seen, but standing in the living room was Finn. He was clutching marigolds. His face and shirt were smeared with dirt.

Mia blinked. "Where are your brother and sister?"

"Outside," Finn said, and sniffed back tears. "Mommy? I'm sorry." He held out the clutch of marigolds.

"*Aww*," Carly said.

"Oh, Finny," Mia said, and went down on one knee. "C'mere." She opened her arms to her son. Finn ran to her, and Mia hugged him and kissed his dirty cheeks, and as she pushed his hair back from his eyes, she said, "Where did you get the flowers, sweetie?"

"Out there," Finn said, pointing to the backyard.

A tiny little red flag reluctantly presented itself in Carly's brain. She sidestepped her sister and walked to the windows that overlooked the backyard . . . and stifled a scream, lest she upset Mia even more.

From that distance, she couldn't say which of those bad dogs was at the fence, digging to the core of the earth. She couldn't say which one of them had scattered the marigolds all over the backyard, either. She couldn't even guess which one had knocked Millie to the ground and then romped off to chew the garden hose left on the patio to bits as the child ate dirt. Or which one it was who had torn the bear apart and scattered stuffing across the lawn like so many snowballs—although she'd put her bets on Hazel for that one.

Mia suddenly appeared beside her holding Finn. Carly heard her sister's breath catch, and she said, "Where's Bo?"

"Bo?" Carly immediately yanked the door open and walked out, following a trail of cotton stuffing to the edge of the yard, where Bo was trying to fit himself through a narrow and freshly dug hole beneath the fence.

There was a lot of shouting and scolding, a lot of tears and apologies as Carly rounded up the dogs and the cotton stuffing and the bits of chewed hose. She left the marigolds on the ground and made Millie go in the house. Mia was dragging Bo by one hand, Finn on her hip.

"This is why I didn't want a dog," Mia said. "Does everyone understand now?"

"I do," Carly assured her. "I totally do."

Mia stepped inside and yanked her kids in after her. "Thank you, Carly. Call me later," she said, and shut the door.

Carly looked down at her two mutts. They looked utterly exhausted from all their hard work and both would need baths. "Great. *Juuuust* great. Which one of us is going to call Mr. Sheffington and let him know this is not a piece of cake after all?" To ensure that he did indeed understand what a cakewalk this was not, Carly sent him a picture of the backyard carnage, complete with one she'd snapped of Millie and the dogs just before Mia had come roaring out of the house. Millie and the dogs were covered head to toe in dirt in the middle of those unrepentant bassets. All three beings were smiling.

Carly received a single text in response:

Ugh.

> Ugh? That's it? That's all I get for the destroyed garden and two dogs that now need to be bathed?

Sorry.

That was the sum of his concern? He'd gone off and left his dog with a stranger, and his dog was wreaking havoc in spite of his assurances to the contrary, and his sole comments were *ugh* and *sorry*. She pictured him in a restaurant somewhere with his brother, having a great lunch and maybe even a cocktail since it was the weekend, maybe even a *champagne* cocktail, because apparently, the whole world got to have one while she dog-sat. He was probably checking out the girls as they went by, and swiping right, and he didn't have time to engage with Chump Carly in Austin who was taking up space on his phone.

She took the dogs home and bathed them in the backyard, which delighted them to no end, and managed to soak herself in the process.

But things calmed down that evening after she cleaned out her car and showered off the drool and dirt and dirty soapy water they'd flung on her when they shook their coats. The dogs were exhausted and curled up, back to back, on one of the dog beds. They snored while she indulged in a medicinal glass of wine and a review of the pictures she'd taken—it would be funny if it wasn't so horrible—and Carly could look at the two mutts and think, *this isn't really so bad.* Maybe the obliteration of Mia's garden was just a one-off. Maybe the dogs had been overexcited because the kids were running around, and really, didn't Finn start it by picking the marigolds? That was just an invitation to a pair of dogs.

Maybe, she thought, after she'd had a second glass of medicinal wine and the evening seemed a little rosier, she needed a couple of bassets in her life. Maybe she'd be happier. She didn't have a boyfriend. Her friends were fading away into their own schedules and demands on their time. And hadn't she read somewhere that dogs added years to their owners' lives? Something like that. She didn't know how she would work out the dogs in New York, but it wasn't impossible. Apparently people did it all the time. It would require a mindset adjustment, but she could do it.

Somehow, Carly snookered herself in those lovely hours of Friday evening to the point that she was actually toying with the idea of getting Baxter a companion once Hazel had gone home. He was undeniably a different dog in Hazel's company—he hadn't once pressed his head to a corner since she'd arrived. Carly pictured herself heading over to the ACC to find a rescue, another basset who would adore poor old Baxter the way he adored Hazel. She imagined walking them on the streets of New York, and people would stop her to tell her how cute her dogs were, and her dogs would be perfectly behaved because of course she'd have them professionally trained, as the manual strongly recommended. She would look like the women on the cover of the books she saw in Target—cute and carefree and walking a dog down a tree-lined street. She'd meet guys who loved dogs, rich businessmen also walking down the street in snazzy French suits who would stop and speak to her dogs, then to her.

She imagined having a dog-friendly office somewhere, and Baxter and his puppy sibling would sit on the window seat and gaze out the window, attracting people to come in. People would come for the adorable dogs and stay for the public relations, or . . . or whatever her job ended up being. She would build some lucky company an entire client base on the backs of two adorable dogs.

She envisioned all that into a dreamy slumber.

The next morning, Carly woke up to the smell of something fishy. She lifted her head from the pillow and hissed with the pain that the sudden movement put in her neck. "Damn it," she said, and rubbed her neck. Well, no wonder—she was on the very edge of the bed again, having been pushed aside by two basset hounds who had taken up almost the entire bed. "I don't get it," she said hoarsely to her slumbering companions. "It's not even possible to get up here on those stumpy legs."

Baxter lifted his head and looked at her. Or maybe that was Hazel. Whichever one it was sighed and resumed sleeping. The other one slid off the bed and onto the floor. With a grunt of dissatisfaction, Carly sat up, pushed her tangled hair from her face, and grimaced at the sound of her laptop sliding off and clattering on the wood floor. She'd fallen asleep with it.

She got out of bed. She felt groggy from the lack of sleep and stretched her arms overhead on a big yawn. And then, scratching her side, she took one step toward the bathroom door. Her bare foot landed in something cold and oily and slipped out from under her. She caught herself on the bed before she fell, but a muscle pulled in the back of her leg and she let out a grunt of pain. When she'd righted herself, she looked down to see what she'd stepped in.

She was still trying to work out which one of them had gotten into the fish oil when she heard the unmistakable sound of a dog retching. It was coming from the direction of her closet. "*No*," she whispered as the worst sort of horror struck her. She dove across her bed, half sliding and falling across the foot of it just as the dog retched. By the time she made it to the closet, she very nearly combusted. Baxter had just vomited on her expensive, special-night-out, silk and beaded Jimmy Choos. "*No!*" she screeched. They were insanely expensive, even in spite of her having purchased them from a consignment store.

Baxter made a run for it, slipping and sliding out of her room in his haste to put some distance between himself and the remnants of the fish oil he'd eaten. Hazel, still at her slumber, lifted her head and looked curiously at Carly. That's when Carly noticed an empty fish oil capsule stuck to the bottom of one of her paws.

And then she noticed the trail of oily paw prints the size of personal pizzas across her floor and on her bedspread. "Oh my *God!*" she shouted.

Hazel slid off the bed and trotted out of the room.

"That just makes you look guilty!" Carly shouted after her. She grabbed her phone, shoved her hair from her face, and FaceTimed Mr. Tobias Sheffington III.

After a couple of rings, his face appeared in the square. He was wearing his glasses, and his stubble had disappeared. He looked like he was in a hotel room. He squinted at the screen and said, "Oh," as if he hadn't known who it was. "Hi, Carly." He leaned closer, squinting. "Oh, wow . . . has something happened?"

"Oh," she said, nodding hard, "something has happened." She pointed the phone at the fish oil catastrophe, and then to her ruined shoe, then turned the phone back to her. "Did you see it?"

"See what?"

"The fish oil! The dog barf!" she exclaimed, gesturing to the mess on the floor, probably with a hand he could not see.

"The what?"

"Those two ate an entire bottle of fish oil supplements! And not the cheap kind, the good kind! And then Baxter barfed on one of my Jimmy Choos!"

"Okay," he said slowly, like he thought he was going to have to call security from a thousand miles away. "Are you okay?"

She blinked. She glanced down at herself, and the old, oversized T-shirt that had belonged to a boyfriend. At the thick tangle of hair draped over one eye. "Are you . . . are you judging the way I look right now?"

"No," he said, rather unconvincingly. "But you look . . . different."

"Well maybe it's because those beasts give me like one inch of my very own bed, like I'm supposed to get any sleep like that. And they had fish oil on their paws and my bedspread is . . . What are you look-ing at?"

Max was looking over his shoulder. "Umm . . ." He turned back. "Is there something I can do for you from here? Someone you need me to call, or . . ."

Or what. That's what he was wondering—*or what*. Either he'd forgotten that he'd told her to call him, or he never meant it. "Nope. Nothing. Just thought you'd like to see how it's going with this giant favor I am doing for you that you said would be a piece of cake."

"I'm sorry. It definitely looks like you have your hands full." He glanced over his shoulder again. "I will replace anything you've lost, and I hate to do this, but I've really got to go."

He was in an awfully big hurry. Antsy, really. Wait a minute . . . Did he have a woman in there? Had he given her some sad story about his brother so he could actually go off with a *woman*? For heaven's sake, was she *that* gullible? "What's going on?" she demanded.

"What, here? Just getting ready to go to the dog show," he said. "Would you mind if I call you back?"

She was such an idiot. Of *course* that was what he was doing. "Fine. Whatever," she said. "Go and have a grand time." She clicked off in a huff and looked down at the mess again. She couldn't believe that jackass, off on some romantic weekend with a woman while she dog-sat. She was so stupid sometimes.

This was her fault, really—she'd forgotten the fish oil was on the edge of her dresser. She'd been so tired lately, so scattered. It was one thing to be busy, but add money worries to it, and things like where she put the fish oil were the first to fly out of her head.

She had to throw her shoes out—they were ruined—and clean up the mess. She was washing up the last of the oil when someone pounded on her front door. She sat back on her heels and looked at the clock. It was ten o'clock on a Saturday morning. Who was it? No one should pound on anyone's door at ten on a Saturday unless the plague and locusts were coming through the neighborhood.

One of the dogs gave a half-assed bark. They were exhausted, too.

Carly hopped up, pulled on some shorts under the T-shirt she'd slept in, and hurried down the hall to the door, pausing only to cast a withering look at Baxter and Hazel, who'd made themselves at home on the couch, their crimes apparently forgotten, and clearly not inclined this morning to ward off intruders.

She carried on to the door and peered out the peephole.

Victor was standing on her porch, his head down, one hand braced against the jamb. He lifted his hand, apparently to bang again. Carly opened the door before he could. He took a step back. His gaze flicked the full length of her. "Wow," he said, shaking his head. "Didn't know you had this side to you. Did you go out last night? Tie one on?"

"Ha ha, Victor. It's Saturday morning. I wasn't expecting visitors."

"Seriously? You always look like this?"

She sighed with impatience. "What do you want?"

"Don't get me wrong. I kind of dig it," he said, gesturing to her T-shirt and shorts. "Like you've been on a deserted island with nothing but a volleyball."

Okay. Carly was willing to walk the talk, but she should be able to wear the loungewear of her choosing in the privacy of her own home without being critiqued. "Again—what do you want?"

Victor's face suddenly lit. "Hey! Did you clone Baxter?" The dogs had apparently decided to investigate and had ambled into the entry. Victor squatted down as they crowded in beside her, Hazel actually going between her legs, snorting and sniffing at Victor, their tails wagging.

"There was a mix-up with the dog walker, remember?"

"So, what, you found two dogs and kept them both or something? Man, it's cool that you walk around and pick up stray dogs."

"What? No. No, it's nothing like that. I don't do that." Did anyone ever listen to her? "Anyway . . . you were just about to tell me why you have stopped by this lovely sunny morning, right?"

"Oof," Victor said, wrinkling his nose. He stepped around her and crowded in through the door with the dogs, then walked into her house. "Smells like fish in here."

Apparently, Victor had come to take her patience out for a spin. Carly took a steadying breath and slowly shut the door, then followed Victor into her house. He'd already made himself at home on the couch, and one of the dogs had crawled up on his lap. She realized it was Baxter, who was clearly on a mission to prove her theory that Max had ruined everything.

"So you know the red pieces in my collection, right?" Victor asked.

"Sure." They were the signature pieces of his show. They were the dresses that Phil had shot for them, pictures she'd Fed-Exed to Ramona McNeil yesterday. She was so grateful that Victor hadn't made her wear one yet—whereas the white pieces featured oversized shoulders and long sleeves, the red pieces featured oversized hips.

"Yeah, I'm not feeling it. I'm pulling them out."

Carly waited for the punch line. When she realized none was coming, she panicked a little. "Victor, you can't do that. Not the *red* pieces. They're your finale. The showstopper!"

"Not feeling it," he said again. He dumped Baxter onto the floor and stood up and walked into her kitchen.

Carly's heart began to pound at a clip that was far too fast. She'd talked Phil into shooting those pieces for free. She'd begged her way into Ramona McNeil's email. She'd arranged a podcast for Victor that would focus on those red pieces. "Victor . . . that's crazy. You *know* that's crazy, right? We've been teasing those dresses. People are coming to your show just to see the red pieces."

He winced, as if considering that, then shook his head. "Nah. I don't want them." He opened the fridge.

"But . . ." She darted to the end of the bar, hopping over the two dogs who were curious to see what was going on in the kitchen. "But they want to send a photographer from *Couture* to shoot them. And the only reason is because the creative director wants to see if those pieces are as editorial as she thinks they are. The design is *so* innovative."

Victor turned around to her. "Look, Carly, I mean, I get it. But that's why I dropped by. I was talking to Mom this morning and she . . . she said I should let you know so you can cancel that interview." He turned back to the fridge and pulled out a pan of leftover lasagna.

Carly felt herself either on the edge of a complete nervous breakdown or murder. How interesting that those two distinct impulses could feel so similar. "Okay," she said, trying to change tack. "If you don't have the red pieces, how will you end your show?"

He shrugged. "I'll make something else. I've got a few weeks." He started opening drawers, and finally found one with the utensils. He pulled out a fork and took a giant bite of lasagna from the pan. "Man, I need a colonic. I'm feeling all kinds of backed up. You know that feeling?"

Carly stared at him.

"Can you do that?"

"Do what?"

He glanced up from the lasagna, confused. "Like . . . get me a colonic. Mom used to schedule them, but she's kind of pissed at me right now."

"You're going to have to find someone else to schedule your colonic, Victor." This was a teachable moment where she should explain to him that scheduling colonics was not part of a publicist's duties, nor should he pay her going rate for that task. But she was too worried about the red pieces and Victor had proven so far to be pretty unteachable. She sank onto a stool at the bar. "You've just thrown a wrench into all my plans. I'm going to have to redo everything, and your colonic is the last thing I'm going to deal with."

"You know what? You should really get one," he suggested, pointing a fork at her. "You seem a little uptight and, trust me, a colonic will clear you out in more ways than one."

"*Eew*," Carly said, wrinkling her nose. "I really don't want to have this—"

"*Hel-looh!*"

Carly froze, midsentence. *Please, no.*

Hazel and Baxter began to bark and raced to the front door to confront this intruder. For the life of her, Carly didn't understand their logic.

"Mind if I heat this up?" Victor asked, oblivious to the intruder. He'd already put the dish in the microwave. She wouldn't be completely surprised if he tossed a salad next.

"Carly! Why are there *two* basset hounds?" her mother called before appearing in the living area, sailing in with the dogs trotting on either side of her. She was dressed in tennis togs, which seemed an odd choice for a woman who didn't play tennis. But that was typical of Carly's mother—she liked to assume personae she didn't actually inhabit in real life. And she always managed to get away with it.

Evelyn Kennedy was a pretty and petite woman, with hair still a buttery shade of blond, and a figure that looked like she couldn't possibly have given birth to three children more than twenty-five years ago. She had the same blue eyes as Carly, but that was where the simi-larities ended between mother and daughter, both in physical features and in personality. Carly was four inches taller and had a figure her mother had once said was good for childbearing. Carly also had big ambitions in life and didn't care who knew—she was very direct in her approach to her goals. Her mother had ambitions, too, but took a more passive-aggressive route to achieving them.

Her mother bent down to pet the dogs, then walked up to the kitchen bar and spread her hands wide, leaning forward. "Isn't any-one going to introduce me to the nice young man in your kitchen?" she trilled.

Oh no. Carly wanted to die—her mother had met Victor before. "Mom!" Carly said with a nervous giggle. "You remember Victor Al-len. You met him, remember? He's my fashion designer client."

"Oh!" Her mother laughed. "Is *that* who you are."

Victor closed the door to the microwave. "That's okay, Ms. Ken-nedy. Fashion designers all look alike." He turned around to get his fork.

Carly took the opportunity to shoot her mother a dark look. Pre-dictably, her mother didn't see it. "Well, I'm not surprised I didn't recognize you, Victor—your hair is many different colors and much bigger than the last time we met."

"That's because I put some product in it to make it stand up," Vic-tor said. He pressed the start button to heat the lasagna. Carly's mother looked at her, raised her eyebrows, and not so subtly jerked her chin in Victor's direction, as if she was the one who was offended.

"So!" Carly said brightly. "What brings you here, Mom?"

"Do I need a reason to see my daughter? I wanted to make sure you were all right. I haven't seen much of you lately, and, by the look of things, I arrived not a moment too soon. What has happened to your hair, sweetie?"

"I haven't dressed yet," Carly said through gritted teeth. "And I never see you because you are hardly ever home, remember?"

"You know, that's true. I've been *terribly* busy these last few weeks. It's amazing how emancipating divorce can be."

She wasn't kidding—after forty years of marriage, Mom was sowing some major oats. As in, doing the walk of shame fairly regularly and bragging about it afterward to her friends and daughters.

Evelyn Kennedy had announced one day to Carly, Mia, and their brother, Trace, that she was not going to wait for life to come to her, she was going to go find it. "I've watched the three of you grow into confident people who go after what they want. Well, I'm going to do the same." And she'd begun in earnest, joining all kinds of meetup groups and getting involved with volunteer organizations. Her latest obsession was volunteering her time at the ACC. "That's where you meet the hottest men," she'd said to Carly at happy hour once. She'd waggled her brows before sipping her skinny margarita. "You should try it, sweetie."

The thought of taking advice from her mother about where to find a date and, even worse, the thought of checking out single men *with* her mother was enough to make Carly never want to date again.

Obviously, the ACC was where her mother had gotten the idea of picking up a depressed basset hound and dumping it on one of her kids. Carly's mother was famous for pulling shit like that when everyone was least expecting it, for deciding what was best for her children without consulting them. When her parents were married, her father provided the ballast. Without him, her mother was all over the place. How she could have thought Mia could handle an untrained basset hound was beyond Carly's ability to imagine. Mia's husband, Will, was in tech. He was Asian-American, spoke Mandarin fluently and flew to China at least once a month for his job, leaving her with three kids under the age of five for a week to two weeks at a time. It was hard enough for Mia with three small kids, and then here came Mom, all happy and excited to add a mopey basset hound to the mix.

Her mother had actually gone through the entire adoption process, then had shown up at Mia's house and presented the dog to the same three kids who had terrorized a cat so far into crazy town that the cat rarely came out of hiding.

Predictably, Mia had lost her mind and had threatened to have a full nervous breakdown in the middle of the street so that her entire neighborhood would know how dysfunctional her family was. Carly had stepped in to save a nuclear fallout between her mother and sister. And the dog.

Since then, her mother hadn't seen much of her because Carly had the problem of Baxter, which meant that she had to rush home to let him out instead of stopping off to see her mother or father or anyone else at the end of her day. And what really annoyed Carly was that her mother seemed to think it was all perfectly fine now—no harm, no foul.

One of the dogs had wandered over to get a good sniff of her mother's bare leg. "Goodness, here is one of them again. *Two* basset hounds, Carly? I thought you were against dogs." She leaned down to pet Hazel. "Aren't *you* a cutie," she said.

"I'm not *against* dogs. I love dogs. I'm against irresponsible pet ownership. I don't have time in my life to pay proper attention to a dog."

"Then why on earth did you get two?"

"I wondered the same thing," Victor said.

Seriously, Carly was beginning to think that when she talked, the sound was disappearing into a void. "I *didn't* get two. One, I rescued from my sister before something awful happened." She paused to look meaningfully at her mother. "The other is the result of a mix-up with the dog walker, and somehow I got talked into dog-sitting while this guy flitted off to Chicago."

"I've always admired how helpful you are, sweetie. Well, I hope the rest of your week has gone well," her mother said cheerfully.

"That's not . . ." Carly shook her head. There was no point—her mother wasn't listening. She'd walked into Carly's kitchen, crowding in next to Victor as he took his dish from the microwave. Her mother opened the refrigerator door and stared at the contents. She finally picked up a carton of blueberries and came back to her seat. "Well I've had the most *delightful* week," she said, and popped a blueberry into her mouth.

"Oh yeah?" Victor asked.

Her mother cast a golden smile at both of them. "I may have met someone." She waggled her brows.

"Like, who?" Victor asked.

"I'm not ready to say just yet. I don't want to jinx it. Everything is very new, and we're taking it slow to see if this is a thing or not."

Carly was confused. "But . . . but you weren't taking it so slow a couple of days ago." She was referring, of course, to the phone call with her mother where she'd proclaimed her joy at having been sexually liberated.

"What?" Her mother looked thoughtful for a moment. "Oh, that was Bob," she said with a flick of her wrist.

Her mother had *two* boyfriends? It was inconceivable! What the hell was Carly doing wrong? "Mom! Are you dating two men at the same time?"

Her mother laughed. "Well, look at you, keeping track of your dear old mother."

"I'm not keeping track, I'm confused."

"I told you, it's called sexual liberation, my love," her mother cheerfully announced.

"Hell, yeah," Victor said, and held up his hand for a fist bump.

Her mother completely missed the gesture and popped a berry into her mouth. "Your father and I couldn't fulfill each other—"

"Mom!"

Her mother glanced up, saw Carly's expression, and popped two more berries into her mouth. "Sorry. So what are you two doing this morning?"

"I'm taking the red pieces out of my show," Victor blithely announced.

"Thinking about it," Carly amended.

"Doing it," Victor countered.

"Pieces of what?" her mother asked.

"Pieces of fashion. Pieces of fashion from his big show in New York in a few weeks."

"Well, I have to admit, red is not my favorite color in a garment," her mother opined.

"Exactly," Victor said, and looking at Carly, pointed his fork at her mother. "She understands."

"She doesn't understand."

"What do I not understand?" her mother asked.

"The red pieces are the big finale of his show, Mom. I've had photos made to tease them and lined up media who are interested in his work. *Couture* magazine wants to do an article about them! There is a lot of interest in his designs, the red pieces in particular, and everyone is waiting for the big reveal. Which I've arranged."

"Well, listen to you! That sounds so clever, honey."

Carly pressed her lips together at that backhanded compliment to keep from saying something she'd regret. "But we really need to work this out, Mom, so maybe you could come back later?"

"Are you dismissing me?" she asked brightly. "That's all right. I'm going over to the ACC to walk some dogs."

"You could walk these two," Carly suggested.

"No, thank you. I'm dressed for success and would prefer to be seen." She laughed. "Don't frown, sweetie. I read that is the number one cause of wrinkles around the lips. I never frown anymore. Goodbye, Victor! Don't let her talk you into the red dresses!"

"I won't," Victor promised as her mother walked to the front door.

Carly heard the front door open.

"Carly, you might want to get that shoe away from whichever dog it is!" her mother called as she went out the door.

"What?" In her haste to rush into the hallway, Carly kicked a stool, and probably broke a toe, but she didn't stop. Hazel was in the hallway with one of Carly's good shoes between her paws. "No, no, *no*," she cried, and lunged for the shoe. "Is one ruined pair not enough this morning?"

Hazel looked terribly pleased with herself, thumping her tail against the floor. Carly looked at the mangled heel on the shoe and sighed wearily. She was going to have to figure out how to close the door on her overstuffed closet and lock it. She glanced up and noticed the front door standing open. "Baxter?" She looked around her. No Baxter. "Victor, is Baxter in there?"

"Nope."

"*Baxter!*" She dashed outside just in time to see Baxter's tail disappearing over the hill and headed for Conrad's garden. She raced after him. Hazel raced after her.

She did not reach Baxter in time to keep him from trampling through Conrad's herb garden, but she managed to right some of the plants so it wasn't obvious. She hoped. By the time she'd trotted Baxter and Hazel back to her house, and had put all of her shoes out of dogs' reach, and had finished silently cursing her mother, who'd left the door open, and Victor, who had polished off the lasagna she'd made, Victor was ready to go.

"Man, you need, like, some help," Victor said as he walked out the door.

"Wait, wait, *wait*, Victor! What about the red pieces? We should talk about this!"

"Listen, Carly. I know you're, like, totally into the red. But I've made up my mind." He walked out the door and got in his car and with a nonchalant wave he drove away, as if he hadn't just brought her carefully crafted publicity plan crashing to the ground.

Carly had a very bad feeling about this. It felt like the tip of the proverbial iceberg, and she was the *Titanic*, sailing right into it. When she turned around to retreat into her house, she tripped over Hazel, who was standing right behind her. "Seriously?" she muttered, stepped around the dog, and went back inside with the dogs following her. She picked up her slobbered shoe and took a selfie with it. She texted it to Max. She thought the photo spoke for itself.

Max did not answer. He was probably too busy taking a postcoital bubble bath with his girlfriend, that lucky bastard.

Seven

Max didn't answer Carly's texts or take on the responsibility for the fish oil debacle—which may or may not have been Hazel, let's be honest, as there were two dogs in that house—because he was living his own personal shit show.

The weekend in Chicago? The one that was supposed to be a joyous occasion for his brother that would eclipse all other memories? It turned out to be one of the hardest things Max had ever done. Oh, but his dad had warned him when Max had first floated the idea. He'd scratched his chin as he'd considered it, then had slowly begun to shake his head. "I don't think that's a good idea, Son. I don't think Jamie can handle all that excitement."

"Sure he can," Max had said with all the confidence of a neuroscientist who thought he knew everything there was to know about anything. He studied brains for a living. He taught budding young scientists the intricate wonders of the central nervous system. He was an expert on neurodevelopmental disorders. He knew what medications Jamie took to manage the aggression and self-harm he sometimes exhibited; and he knew all the behavioral, sensory integrations, and occupational therapies that Jamie had been exposed to so that he could better navigate this world. He knew everything like a thirteen-year-old knew everything.

"Look how well he's been doing," he'd pointed out to his father, as if his father might not have noticed.

"Because he's got a routine," his dad had countered. "We do the same thing every day, and every day, he knows what to expect. But when we step out of that routine, he gets flustered. An airplane? A new city? I don't know about that, Max."

"Dad." Max had spoken with the patience and compassion a brilliant neuroscientist would have for an addled father, and had even put his hand on his father's shoulder and squeezed it in a reassuring way. "I know what I'm doing."

Well, the verdict was in, and he did not know what he was doing.

In the space of three days, he'd proved once again that all the study in the world could not substitute for actual experience in the field, in the lab, or in life. He wanted to kick his own ass for assuming that it could. Jamie wasn't a lab subject, he was his brother, and Max had prepped for this weekend like it was a lab experiment. He had all the necessary ingredients in place, and all he had to do was set the wheels in motion, watch Jamie enjoy the event of a lifetime, and record the results. An event Max had designed with all his brain science.

Stupid asshole.

The trip had gotten off to a fairly good start, maybe better than Max had hoped, and he'd been smugly pleased with himself. He'd prepared for the flight, had a new copy of *Dogster* magazine just in case Jamie didn't take to the flight well. But Jamie had been enthralled and had spent most of the flight with his face glued to the window, his unintelligible grunts a sign of his pleasure at what he was seeing.

There was a small hiccup in Atlanta when they had to catch a connecting flight. Jamie had not understood the need for that. He'd tried to pull Max toward the exit. "Dog show," he'd said impatiently, pointing at the exit sign. Max had finally convinced him by showing him the boarding passes, and they'd carried on to Chicago.

But Chicago, with the cacophony of sounds and lights and the crush of people in the streets, was too much for Jamie. It began at the airport. When Max hailed a cab, Jamie refused to get in until Max lied and told him it was the only way to get to the dog show. At their hotel, Jamie kept putting his hands over his ears at the sounds of traffic and the grind of a garbage truck making its rounds.

His first outburst had occurred on the street. Max had thought it would be a good idea to get something to eat. The concierge had suggested a diner down the street. So off they'd gone, crowding in with everyone else at a street corner, waiting for the light to turn green. The crowding had unsettled Jamie, and he'd begun to rock back and forth on his feet, one hand flapping. But when the light turned green, and the stream of people began to move across the street, brushing past Jamie, it had startled him so badly that he wouldn't move. Max had tried to urge him on, but Jamie would not step off that curb. His reluctance prompted some jerk to yell at him, and that was it—Jamie began to melt down.

Max was familiar with Jamie's outbursts and was not alarmed. He knew what to do. But when a grown man—a big man at that—began to frantically flap his hands and make strange, loud noises that sounded like a distressed animal, mothers grabbed their children and men moved out of the way.

Fortunately, they'd been close to the hotel and Max had steered Jamie back to their room and talked him through his panic, employing the skills Jamie had learned to calm himself. And then he ordered room service. They spent the evening cooped up in a hotel room, Jamie poring over his dog books, and Max staring out the window or flipping channels.

But when Saturday dawned—as in, the sun was hardly up—Jamie shook Max awake. He was dressed. "Dog show," he said.

"Jesus, Jamie, it's seven in the morning," Max had complained.

He'd rolled away from his brother and had tried to go back to sleep, but Jamie just walked to the other side of the bed and said, "Dog show," and thrust a piece of paper into Max's face. It was a schedule his dad had printed for Jamie, and Jamie had circled *hounds and herding groups*. The start time was ten.

"We've got plenty of time," Max said, and rolled the other way.

Jamie came around the bed and shoved his shoulder. "Dog show." Max got up.

Jamie grew increasingly anxious as the clock slowly ticked toward ten o'clock. He wanted to go. When Max told him he'd have to wait, that the dog show hadn't started, Jamie punched his fists against the wall and bed.

Carly had FaceTimed him in the middle of Jamie's frustration. Max had had exactly two thoughts: one, that she looked incredibly sexy and hungover. Her hair was a tangled mess around her face, her eyes luminous in the natural light wherever she was. And two, he did not want her to see Jamie's meltdown. He didn't know why, exactly, but he didn't. He wanted to stay on the line and talk to her, but Jamie was getting agitated, and he'd had to cut the call short.

He and Jamie arrived at the arena at nine thirty. Jamie hadn't even allowed Max to stop for a cup of coffee.

The Midwest Regional Dog Show was a benched show, which meant they could walk through where the dogs were being groomed and talk to handlers. Or rather, Max talked while Jamie stared at the dogs. From there, they attended the agility trials, and then the best in breed. Jamie sat on the edge of his seat, and when he saw a dog he liked, he'd say, "Good dog."

By the time they reached the evening judging rounds, Max was running out of steam. He wanted a gin and tonic. And/or a burger. Whichever came first, whichever he could get his hands on. But Jamie made it clear he wasn't going anywhere until the last dog was shown.

Still, they passed the day without incident and returned to the hotel and spent another evening with room service, Jamie poring over his books, Max restless and wishing he could have a very stiff drink.

Sunday began much the same way as Saturday. Max woke with a start, and there Jamie sat, not two feet from him, dressed and ready to go. "For fuck's sake, Jamie," Max said, blinking back the sleep. "You have to stop acting like some weird stalker."

"Dog show."

"Yeah, I know," Max said wearily. "Believe me, I know." Max was a dog guy, but this was a *lot* of dog.

He got up and showered. The trouble started when he packed up their things to store with the concierge. They were leaving on a seven o'clock flight back to Austin. Jamie didn't want to store their things. He began to rock back and forth, flapping his hands, growling. Max tried to explain to him why it was necessary—they had to check out, had to leave their bags someplace safe. Jamie whirled around and pushed the desk chair across the room. It crashed into a floor lamp, which fell over, taking a small glass coffee table with it. Max had to physically restrain his brother before he did some damage.

Jamie finally agreed to let the concierge hold their bags, and they made their way to the dog show, but Jamie never fully settled. And it seemed to Max as if there were twice as many dogs on Sunday. The arena was filled with confusing smells and crowds, and Jamie had rocked in his seat, chewing the cuticle on his thumb, and moaning that he wanted to go home. It wasn't until the herding group entered the ring that Jamie's attention snapped to the dogs. "Beauceron," he said.

Max didn't understand him.

"*Beauceron*," Jamie said hotly.

"Do you need a bathroom?" Max asked dumbly.

Jamie opened up his program and jabbed his finger several times on a page. Max looked down. Beauceron, as it turned out, was a type of dog.

"Never heard of it," Max snapped back.

By the time best in show rolled around, Jamie was better. He wanted the whippet to win and kept whispering *whippet* under his breath. The French bulldog took the grand prize, and Max steeled himself for another outburst, but Jamie surprised him. He surged to his feet, clapping louder than anyone.

They stopped by a booth on the way out of the arena and Max ordered digital disks of previous National Dog Show broadcasts. They went back to the hotel, and Max collected their bags from the concierge, had to physically push Jamie into a cab, and they headed to the airport.

They arrived in Austin at 9:45. Max spent much of the flight exhausted by the weekend and his arrogance. His guilt weighed heavily on him—he kept thinking how many times he'd assured his dad that everything would be okay. Of the many times he'd left his dad's house secure in his belief that his father and brother were fine, just fine, without him there. He'd been acting the part of an egotistic professor and thought he knew more than his father who lived with and cared for Jamie every day. Max was ashamed of himself.

But one thing was becoming clear to Max. Jamie really needed to be in a supervised group home, living with other adults. He needed to be with peers, to learn how to navigate life better than he was learning at home. His routine was isolating him from real-world experiences. His dad needed his own life, too. Max was convinced that if Jamie had a comfort dog, and experiences outside his routine, he would learn how to cope better than he'd coped in Chicago.

He wearily drove his brother home, then texted Carly. Too late to pick up the beast?

She responded simply, No. That was followed by a picture of something orange. He had to zoom in to see it. It looked like it might have been a pillow. He didn't know what had happened to the stuffing but could probably assume it was either inside a dog or a trash can.

Your dog's handiwork, she texted.

Max frowned. Had Hazel's separation anxiety kicked in? Was Carly really so certain the culprit was Hazel? She seemed to think Baxter could do no wrong. Max hadn't seen Baxter do anything wrong, but, come on. He texted back, asking for her address.

Ten minutes later, he pulled through the gate at Carly's house—at first mistaking the modern mansion as hers, then seeing the wooden sign that pointed to her address near the back of the property. He parked his car in the drive of a cute little cottage that reminded him of his childhood, when bungalows were what covered the central part of Austin. The little house was set among some towering pecan trees. It was white with green shutters. There was a semicircle of brick steps that led up to a small covered porch.

Max walked up to the black door with the three transom windows and looked around for a doorbell. When he didn't find one, he knocked. Somewhere deep in the house, one of the dogs bayed.

A moment later, the door swung open.

Carly looked harried. Her hair was tied up at her nape, but a few tendrils wafted around her face. There was a slash of something like dirt on her cheek. She was wearing a hoodie and no shoes, and stood with one hand on her hip and the other on the door. But it was her hip that caught his attention—or rather, the skirt. It looked like two small boxes had been glued on the inside of a red silk skirt, and from there, it tapered down to a tight circle just above her knees. She was basically wearing an inverted triangle with a hoodie. It confused Max, and he didn't realize he was staring before it was too late.

"Let me guess," she said. "You don't know what kind of costume this is."

"I am . . . I really don't get it," he answered honestly.

She pushed the door open all the way. He could see behind her into a living area. Directly in his line of sight was a white couch, which he immediately considered the worst choice if one had a dog. On the arm of that couch, two bassets had perched their heads, side by side, lazily watching the door. Some guard dogs they were.

"You didn't answer my texts," she said.

He was a bit confused by this. "I didn't?" He'd answered some of them. He thought back. "I guess there were a couple . . . but I didn't think a response was necessary?"

Her gaze narrowed. "You didn't think a response is necessary when someone texts you? Like, that's the whole point of texting."

"Not always. The picture of the orange thing—"

"My last good pillow—"

"Came without a question. It looked more like an observation. And the one in the garden bed? Wasn't sure what the takeaway was and didn't have the luxury of time to inquire."

"Really? You didn't get the takeaway? How about this? Your dog dug up my sister's yard."

He tilted his head to one side. He would really love to know how her brain worked, both professionally and personally speaking. "Do you know for a fact it was Hazel? Because there were two muddy dogs in that photo, and, incidentally, a little girl. She was grinning, so I thought maybe she'd done it."

Carly's eyes widened. "*She* didn't do it."

"I don't know," he said with a shrug. "She was covered from head to toe in mud, just like the dogs. Could have been any of them."

She glared at him. "For the record, I will admit it's entirely possible it was Millie because, God knows, those kids are out of control. But you're missing the point here—generally, people answer their texts unless they are otherwise *engaged*."

"Engaged," he repeated. "May I ask exactly what bee has climbed into your bonnet? Because I am not understanding. Like, at all," he said with a wave of his hand.

"Okay, I'll just throw it out there. Did you go to Chicago with a woman? Did you make me feel bad about your brother so you could . . ." Her gaze swept over him. "Get freaky?"

"Get *freaky*?" He couldn't stop a bark of incredulous laughter. "Are you hanging out at a high school in your spare time? Where the hell would you even get that idea?" He pulled out his phone. "Look," he said, and showed her a couple of pictures of him and Jamie in front of the Midwestern Regional Dog Show sign. Max, smiling at the camera. Jamie, looking somewhere else.

She squinted. She put her hand on his, her fingers light, and pulled his hand and the phone closer. He swiped through a couple more. In the arena. The two of them with a German shepherd. "Adorable," she murmured, and glanced up. "Okay." She sounded only slightly contrite.

"Okay? Is that all you're going to say after accusing me of lying?"

"Okay, *sorry*," she said. "But do you blame me? I don't know you, and you were so weird when I FaceTimed you. You looked nervous, like you were afraid of getting caught."

"*I* was weird? You were the one who looked like you'd been on a bender."

"Ha! Believe me, I wish I had," she said. "All right, all right, I am truly sorry for accusing you. I get a little wound up when I think someone has chumped me."

"Chumped you?"

"You know, when you become a chump because you're naïve or too trusting or whatever."

"I didn't chump you, Carly. I'm sorry I wasn't more responsive, but it was a long weekend. My brother needs a lot of attention. And are you going to keep holding my hand, or can I put my phone away?"

She jerked her hand away from his like she'd been bit and then nervously tried to smooth the strange panniers of her skirt. "Stop staring at my skirt," she said.

He looked up. "I can't."

"Well, neither can I, and that's a problem." She whirled around and stalked into her house. Or rather, she moved like she was doing a sort of quickstep dance move, because her skirt was so tight.

This woman was as confusing as she was pretty. She left him standing there, and after a beat or two, Max decided he was supposed to follow. He walked down the entry hall toward the couch. He couldn't see Carly anywhere, but Hazel excitedly wagged her tail. She looked very much at home.

Carly suddenly appeared in front of him and held a shoe up in front of his face.

Max recognized that shoe. She'd sent him a selfie picture with this shoe in another text this weekend. What he remembered about that text was her. He'd noticed the tiny smattering of freckles, and how pink her lips were. "I've seen that before."

"Yes, you have. You didn't respond to that text, either."

He looked at the shoe. He would like to see her in that shoe, actually. "It was just a picture."

"I sent it for a reason."

"What was the reason? It's sexy."

"Of course it's sexy. But you can see the problem, right?"

"With the shoe?"

"Yes, Max, the shoe." She lifted the shoe higher. "Look at the heel."

Max shifted his gaze to the shoe and looked at the heel. That's when he saw the heel had been chewed up. "Ah, I get it," he said, nodding. "Are you implicating Hazel in this crime, too?"

"Well, there was no little girl here at the time, and Baxter has never chewed anything. Not even his tail." She dropped her arm. "Plus, I caught her red-handed with the evidence. *Your* dog definitely did this to my shoe. But *my* dog did this." She stooped down and picked up half of an orange pillow.

Another chuckle escaped Max in the form of a snorting cough.

"Was that a laugh? That better not have been a laugh."

"So not a laugh," he lied, grinning.

"It must be hilarious to you that Baxter is now a changed man. I knew you'd ruined my dog."

"I wouldn't go so far as *hilarious*," he said, but he couldn't wipe the smile off his face. "Sort of funny, though." He was a little distracted by how bright her eyes were, shining with ire. The effect was strangely arousing. "And by the way, Baxter is a dog, and dogs are pretty predictable in their behaviors. Two, I didn't *ruin* your dog, because one of those predictable behaviors is that dogs chew things. They do it to combat boredom and frustration. And it keeps their teeth clean."

"Are you seriously explaining why dogs chew right now? I *know* they chew. But Baxter didn't chew my pillows before *you* let him on your couch and fed him mac and cheese. How can you not see the correlation?"

He couldn't stop grinning. He knew she was serious, but she was so damn pretty and weird and interesting right now. "I don't see any correlation, but I am very sorry for it all the same. I will reimburse you for the pillow."

"*You* said it would be a piece of cake. *You* said the two of them would keep each other out of trouble."

"I honestly thought that they would."

She groaned and tossed the shoe and the pillow carcass into a basket on the floor. "You wouldn't believe the weekend I've had. Sure, it wasn't all bad dog behavior—there was plenty of bad people behavior, too—but still, Baxter won't stay off my couch now, which is all on you," she said, pointing at him, "and now I have to humiliate myself and ask you a favor."

"It humiliates you to ask for a favor?"

"It humiliates me to ask *you* for this particular favor. It's not a favor I want to ask of anyone. I am *very* self-sufficient."

"I have no doubt."

She eyed him suspiciously. "It's just that what I need you to help me with ranks right up there with volunteering for a root canal."

"Wow. Okay," he said, nodding. "So apparently, there's nothing more reprehensible than asking me for a favor. Got it. What is this horrible awful favor?"

She sighed. She tucked her hair behind her ear. She looked away from him and said, "It would seem that I'm stuck in this adorable little number." She gestured with a flourish to her skirt.

"Stuck. In what way?" he asked, looking at the skirt.

"In the *stuck* way. As in, the zipper is stuck, and it's so tight I can't shimmy out of it. I called my mother, but of course she is never there and her phone rolls to voice mail. And my sister? Forget it. She would have to get three kids in the car. So I am asking you to return the favor of pet-sitting your very bad dog and get me out of this . . . *thing.*"

Max blinked. And then he was laughing. Oh, but he laughed. He put one hand on his belly he was laughing so hard.

"That's just mean," Carly said.

"*This* is hilarious. How the hell did you get stuck?"

"A long story, but the short of it is, I had an idea about a problem I'm having with my job, which includes this piece of fashion, among others. But my idea to save the day is not going to work and now I just want it *off*," she said with a bit of a shimmy.

"Okay," Max said. "Happy to help. Where is the zipper?"

Carly reluctantly turned around and presented her back to him. The zipper ran down the center of the skirt. *All* the way down. It was so tight she'd not been able to zip it all the way up to her waist, and the zipper had stuck just above *her* center line. Max stared at that zipper. He had a couple of thoughts about whether or not he ought to be doing this. "That thing is on here good and tight, isn't it?" he asked, looking at the roll of her flesh spilling over the skirt's waist. "Looks like if you took a big breath you could pop right on out of there."

"I tried that. And I am aware of how tight it is," she said impatiently. "Victor does not design for a silhouette as . . . robust as mine. Will you just do it already?" She tried to look over her shoulder at him.

The term *robust* was clanging in his head. He had a sudden urge to put his hands on her robust hips and her robust waist and her robust breasts. "I'm studying it."

"You don't need to study it, just unstick it!"

"All right," Max said. "I'm going to touch you now—"

"For the love of Pete, I *know* you're going to touch me, I asked you to touch me. Can you just get on with it?"

Max bent down to have a closer look. He could see a patch of pale pink fabric had been caught in the zipper's teeth. "It looks stuck on fabric or something." He leaned closer. "Oh."

"*Oh?* Oh what?"

"I think it might be your panties."

"Yes, Max, those are my panties, thank you for pointing that out. But you don't have to announce what you're finding like an archaeologist. Just please do it."

"Right." When he thought of pink silk panties, something waved through him. He tried to carefully manipulate the zipper loose, but the skirt was pulled too tightly. "Can you maybe pull the skirt around a little and give me some slack?"

She sighed. "Max? If I could give you some slack I would have given *myself* some slack and turned the damn thing around and fixed it!"

"Okay, okay," he said. He had to slide his fingers into the skirt to get a grip, and they brushed against the warm, firm flesh of her butt.

"Well?"

Well . . . he was having a moment. "Carly, calm down—"

"*What?* Did you really just tell me to calm down? Do you not see that I'm *stuck* in a skirt and I'm having to ask a complete stranger to get me out and he's taking his own sweet time and telling me to calm down?"

"Stranger! I don't think you can say I'm a complete stranger anymore. I mean, *especially* now."

"Oh my God! How do you expect me to be calm? Would *you* be calm?"

"I'm not saying to *calm down*, not like that," he said as he worked the bit of silky panty. "I was going to suggest it's not good for your heart to get so agitated. You're releasing catecholamines into your bloodstream left and right and you don't want your blood pressure to get too high."

"What the . . ." She tried to look over her shoulder at him.

"You're moving around too much," he said, and with one hand, pushed her shoulder forward.

"What is wrong with you, Max? Seriously, what is *wrong* with you?"

"Nothing that I'm aware of. But you, on the other hand, are letting an inconsequential observation get under your skin." He almost had the bit free. His fingers were pressed into her hip, and he was terribly distracted by it. He could imagine the feel of her in his hand, could imagine how it would feel if he squeezed. "I'm a scientist and I was just explaining the biological reaction to anxiety."

"Right," she said with a snort.

He pulled a little more of her panty free. "A neuroscientist," he clarified. "I study brains for a living."

Carly snorted. "Uh-huh. And I'm a supermodel."

He knew she was not a supermodel, but Max was attracted to women who had curves, and he was discovering that Carly had some of the most enticing curves he'd seen in a very long time. He managed to get a bit of the zipper undone and discovered she was wearing a thong. "Seriously. I am," he muttered absently, absurdly transfixed by that thong and imagining all the places it went on her body.

"Please hurry. This is so awkward."

"What is awkward? Me being a scientist? Or the zipper?" He managed to free the thong and unzipped the zipper.

She whipped around. "Thank you!" She reached behind her to the zipper.

"I wouldn't do that if I were you. That thing is, like, way too tight."

She glared at him with her flushed cheeks and sparkling blue eyes and with the memory of her hip still on his fingers, he was, once again, slightly aroused.

"Max?"

"Yes?"

"Thank you for freeing me. But I've had a really long day. *Really* long. Being stuck in this skirt and having to ask you to free me is just the icing on the cake. My sister is having her fourth meltdown of the week because her children are demons and she is a pushover. These dogs are eating all my nice things and one of them is stinking up the place, and I had to throw out my Jimmy Choos. Victor is questioning the show lineup, and I haven't had even a *moment* to go to the store and get the jug of wine that I so richly deserve, so if you would be so kind as to take your dog and go and let me wallow in my self-pity, I would appreciate it."

A number of responses flitted through Max's brain. A number of questions, too. But she looked at the door, and it was late, and it was clear he needed to go. "Can I reimburse you—"

"Nope." She sighed. And then she smiled a little. He would even say it was a warm smile. "Thank you for the offer. Really. But it's not necessary. I was just making a point."

So this was it, then. He looked around her to the dogs on the couch. "Hazel, come."

Hazel obediently crawled off the couch. Baxter followed, trotting after her.

"Here are her things," Carly said, gesturing to the box he'd sent home with her.

Max picked them up and started for the door. The two dogs trotted ahead.

"Baxter," Carly said wearily. "The last thing I need is for him to get in the herb garden again." She went around Max to the door to grab Baxter.

Max opened the door, and Hazel trotted out without a single look back. Baxter tried to go, too, but Carly held on to his collar. Baxter's tail began to wag pretty hard. He whimpered. Max dipped down and rubbed Baxter's nape. "You're a good dog, Baxter. Don't let anyone tell you otherwise. And you come see me if you ever need a couch."

"Dogs do not belong on couches. Baxter knows that," Carly said, and got down on her knees next to him to hold him from racing after Hazel.

Max stepped out onto the porch. He paused there and turned around. "Carly, I do want to thank you again for your help. Sincerely. I don't know what I would have done."

She softened and smiled again. She had an adorable smile. "Don't mention it," she said. "I really like your dumb dog."

"I think she likes you, too." He glanced at his car where Hazel was patiently waiting. And still, he couldn't make himself go. He turned back once more.

Carly was still smiling. "Sorry for biting your head off," she said. "I've been pretty stressed lately."

"Apology accepted. Sorry for explaining anxiety to you."

She laughed a little. "Apology accepted. I did need to calm down because I was on the verge of one helluva panic attack. I was imagining having to call the fire department. *That* would be humiliating."

Max smiled. He walked off the porch. He could hear Baxter whimpering and trying to scamper behind them. He turned back.

"Take care of yourself," Carly said, and shut the door.

Max walked on to his car. He opened the door to the back seat and Hazel climbed in. He hooked her up to the dog harness, then slid the box of her things onto the seat next to her. As he got into the driver's seat, he could hear Baxter's howls. "I hear you, Baxter," he muttered.

He felt strangely unsettled. This was clearly the end of his brief and strange acquaintance with Carly Kennedy, she of the weird clothes and short temper. He liked her in spite of that short temper, because on some level it amused him. And he was truly sorry he wouldn't see her again.

He was sorry he wouldn't see Baxter again for that matter. He glanced in the rearview mirror at his dog in the back seat. What Hazel felt would remain a mystery, because she didn't look like she cared who she would or wouldn't see and was perfectly content to go with the flow.

Eight

Carly woke up with a start the next day because the image of handsome Max Sheffington was dancing in her dreams—a literal dream in which he'd been dancing on an arena stage wearing a Victor Allen design, only the shoulders were much larger than normal. Carly was trying to hold the two dogs as people around them went wild.

She sat up and blinked. "*Jesus*," she muttered.

She slowly lay back down and closed her eyes. She tried to banish the current image of Max from her brain, the one of him as he'd appeared last night in the black Henley and slim chinos. She'd been mortified that he should look so hot when she was stuck in a skirt.

She'd been mortified and strangely disappointed, too, because in that moment, she thought he'd spent the weekend with a woman. But then her mortification had ratcheted up when she understood he was *not* in Chicago having crazy sex. He was hot and apparently unattached, and Megan Monroe said, *Put your best foot forward, every day in every way.* She had not put her best foot forward. He thought she was nutty. And she'd been stuck in that damn skirt.

It was all Victor's fault.

They were due to meet with the *Couture* photographer this week. This was the chance she'd worked so hard to get for Victor. They wanted the red pieces, and after his visit on Saturday, she'd worried and fretted and finally called him that evening with the hope of getting him to see reason. To make him "feel it."

Victor's response was curt. "I've made up my mind, Carly. That's it. None of the red." He'd hung up.

Anybody else might have taken that as the last word, but Carly knew Victor pretty well. Nothing was ever "it" with him. His ideas turned and morphed into something new and better every day.

Her job was to get those red pieces in front of *Couture*. She'd come up with a hastily put together and ridiculous plan B and had called Victor back Sunday morning and asked if she could borrow the red suit. Her totally crazy plan was to wear one of the red outfits herself to meet the *Couture* guy when he flew into town. She would pretend Victor had been stuck in traffic, and then at least *show* him one of the red pieces. She'd say, "Oh, I just happen to be wearing one," and she'd stand up and do a slow turn. Carly was no model, but she was desperate. This kind of exposure for Victor was worth its weight in gold, and while he might have cold feet, she was not going to let him squander this opportunity.

He answered on the fourth ring and sounded groggy. "Before you hang up," she said quickly, "can I at least borrow one of the red pieces?"

Victor didn't even ask why. "Take it, I don't care. Keep it. Wear it, make a tablecloth from it, shred it. Whatever."

She'd hung up. "*Whatever* my ass, Victor," she'd muttered and had looked at the dogs. "Saddle up, boys. We're going for a ride." Hazel had launched herself at the door, clearly familiar with the word *ride*. Carly wasn't sure if Baxter understood anything. But wherever Hazel led, he would follow.

A half hour later, with the leashes in one hand, and a key in the other, Carly unlocked the door to Victor's darkened studio and stepped inside.

The place smelled musty, like someone hadn't taken out the trash. She flipped on the lights and dropped the leashes, and the dogs headed straight for the kitchenette. Victor's studio was small and cluttered with bolts of fabric. On one wall there was wire shelving that he'd had attached to hold his notions and thread, scissors and fabric tape, and different trims. Discarded pieces of fabric and pattern paper always littered the floor. In the center of the room was a long table for patterning and cutting. Against one wall were two sewing machines. Carly had never understood the differences between the two or why two were needed. There were also two naked dress forms on rollers that moved around the studio as necessary. Usually, the forms wore garments in various stages of construction. Victor hung his finished pieces along the back wall.

Carly thought the red pieces would be hanging where she'd seen them last, but those wall bolts were empty. She'd walked around looking for them and gasped with alarm when she found them, carelessly piled in a heap in the corner of the studio.

She rescued them from the floor. "Why would he do this?" she'd said aloud when Hazel came to sniff the pile.

She'd draped the pieces across the back of that disgusting couch and decided she had the best chance of fitting into the jacket and skirt. She hung up the rest of the red collection, took the jacket and skirt, and summoned her hounds.

Those two red pieces were hanging on the door of her closet and staring at her now, disturbing the sanctity of her bedroom.

Her bedroom was her haven. It was small and quaint, and she'd covered her bed with a chenille bedspread her grandmother had used. She'd overstuffed the built-in bookcase with books, because Carly was a devoted bookworm . . . although she hadn't had as much time to read or even stream Netflix in the last six months as she would have liked.

She had a vanity that she'd picked up at an estate sale. She'd spent the winter after she was laid off refinishing it and painting it a very soothing pale green. On the top of her vanity were the brushes and palettes of her cosmetics, lotions and creams, and her jewelry in a cloisonné box. The floors could get cold in the winter, so she'd put down a large, fluffy blue rug that felt delightful year-round beneath her feet.

The room's windows were covered in sheer white drapery panels that gave her some privacy—not that she needed it this far back on the lot—but also allowed for natural light. Her walk-in closet with the crystal doorknobs was a great find for a house this old, because closets had been tiny midcentury. Hers was absolutely bursting with clothes and too many shoes and accessories, and—her dirty little secret—her handbag obsession.

"Ugh," she said. "I need coffee." She looked around for the dogs, and remembered that Hazel had gone home with Max. "Baxter?" She climbed out of bed and went into the kitchen. Baxter had returned to his corner, his head pressed against the seam. "Poor puppy," she cooed to him, leaning over to stroke him. "I know you miss her. I miss her, too. Which I never thought I'd say, but there you go. I kind of miss him, too, you know. I mean, I hardly know the dude. But . . . I kind of miss him."

She thought about Max as she made her coffee. She was grateful he hadn't arrived while she was trying to peel the jacket off, cursing how *tight* the arms were. But once she'd managed to shove her enormous hams through the sleeves, she discovered that she could hardly pull the jacket around her ribs, much less her boobs. So she'd shrugged out of that and tossed it aside, and pulled on a hoodie and had decided it didn't matter, that the skirt with the modern panniers was the interesting piece anyway.

But, as she and Max both knew, the skirt did not fit, and if there had been a fire, she would have surely perished, because she could hardly walk across the room in it. "Why is the fashion industry so hell-bent on a size zero?" she asked a sulking Baxter.

That she was nowhere near a size zero was the pickle she'd found herself in when Max had finally shown up. And of course he'd shown up looking all virile and manly in his formfitting Henley and his tortoiseshell rectangular frames that made his gray eyes stand out and made him look sexy and smart. He couldn't be some regular guy who held no appeal for her whatsoever—he had to be hot. And Carly was just curvy enough that the tight skirt had created a giant muffin top situation, which of course she'd refused to believe existed as she'd tried to zip that damn red skirt, and then had to reveal to him in order to get out of same damn red skirt.

She'd had to suffer the feel of his fingers on her flesh in this most humbling way instead of the way she would like to feel them. Those fingers of his were like fire starters, sending little waves of sparkles through her. And then she'd had to endure that sly smile of his, the one that was a mix of amusement and surprise at her misfortune and, even worse, his unnecessary explanation of the body's reaction to anxiety. *Why, thank you, Dr. Sheffington.*

Dr. Sheffington.

"Stop it," she said to herself, and picked up her coffee cup. "Get to work. You need a plan C pronto and there is no time for this." She padded back to her room, intending to dress.

But he was a *neuroscientist*? For real?

She hauled her laptop up onto her bed and settled in against her pillows with her coffee. She opened her laptop again and googled Max Sheffington.

Wow.

It was true.

Dr. Max Sheffington was a professor of neuroscience at the University of Texas, which meant he was legitimately a brain scientist and not, as she had mistakenly assumed, a giant smart-ass. There were two pictures of him—one, a professional picture on the university's faculty website along with a description of his area of study, which was incomprehensible to her: Discovering cellular and circuit mechanisms of cognitive

dysfunction in neurodevelopmental disorders and understanding the neurobio-
logical basis for individual preference and the effect on neural networks.

"*What?*" she whispered to herself.

The university website listed him as a tenure-track professor.

There was another picture of him, too. This one appeared under the heading of Campus Life. He was standing at a lectern in one of the university auditoriums before a class that was so large it had to be entry level. He was wearing a long-sleeved T-shirt over low-slung trousers, a jacket, that awful knit cap, and what looked like high-top sneakers that did not go with the rest of his outfit. And, at the time of the picture, he'd had a full beard.

He was a sexy hipster in that photo. He looked smart and accomplished and masculine, but also like someone who cared about children and animals and important things like straws littering the oceans and parks for all abilities. How had she ever thought he wore too much denim?

Carly slammed her laptop shut. She refused to fantasize about this guy. This strange dog mix-up was over, and he'd taken Hazel and gone back to his world, and she had Baxter and her world. She had problems to fix, mountains to climb, monsters to slay. She would go back to the problem of Victor, and Max would go back to neural whatevers. Which was clearly for the best because she had no idea what that was. This was one of those things that happened in someone's life, and one day she'd be at a dinner party in some tony New York apartment and she'd say, *Hey, did I ever tell you about the time the dog walker mixed up two bassets?*

All was right with the world again.

All was right with the world until exactly two hours later, after Carly had called the photographer to cancel his trip to Austin and with it, the exposure she'd worked so hard to get. She was very surprised when Ramona McNeil herself called her back.

"Why?" Ramona demanded curtly. "This is a big opportunity for a young designer. Why would you pull the rug out from under it?"

Carly chafed at the idea that she, a public relations professional, would have any hand in *pulling the rug out from under it.* "Victor is changing directions and is not ready to present his work just yet."

"Oh, he's not ready, poor thing," Ramona said, her voice dripping with sarcasm. "Well, that's just great, Carly . . . what did you say your last name was?"

Carly winced. "Kennedy." She would have hoped Ramona had seen it on one of the applications she'd submitted.

"All I can say is that I hope his new direction works out for both of you. But now *I* have to fill a hole. A hole you convinced me to create, you may recall. Just so you know, since I think you're pretty new to this business, it's not cool to cancel a publication at this late date."

"I'm actually not that new," Carly said. "If you have a chance to look at my résumé, you'll see that I have a lot of experience."

"Are you talking while I'm talking?"

Carly pressed her lips together.

"Maybe you don't know, but we have lead times for a reason, and I pushed those lead times all the way to the crash point because *you* would not leave me alone. You begged and cajoled and promised me something pretty fucking amazing, and now you're pulling him?"

This was possibly the worst moment of Carly's life. Ramona McNeil was dressing her down and was clearly never going to look at her résumé. Megan would say to pull on her big girl panties and seize the moment. Naomi would say to go for it. Carly didn't know how to do any of that. "I'm very sorry, Ms. McNeil. I would sew those pieces myself if I could. But he's an artist and he's made it plain that he doesn't want to show the red pieces."

"Don't give me that sensitive artist crap," Ramona shot back.

"What if we photograph the finished white pieces?" Carly suggested. She tried not to sound desperate. She tried to sound like a problem solver.

"The *white* is not editorial. We *emailed* about this. We need a very editorial look and the red is where it's at." There was silence on the line, and for a moment, Carly thought she'd hung up. "What else has he got?" Ramona asked curtly.

Carly perked up. The door had not been completely slammed in her face. "He is in the process of creating a new look," she said quickly. If he wasn't, he damn sure better be by the end of the day. "I can let you know when he's going to have something to show. I know it will be quick, and I know it will be amazing."

"Lord," Ramona muttered. "Okay, listen up. You've got me in a real bind here. You have two weeks to come up with something new. And you can tell your *client* that the likelihood of him getting another shot like this is nil, and the next time he books this kind of exposure, he better be ready to roll. *You* better be ready to roll. Have a good day." She clicked off the phone.

Only then did Carly realize she wasn't breathing and took a dramatic breath, like she'd just burst through the surface of the ocean.

She couldn't disagree with Ramona—Victor was a fool. Even worse, he was making her look bad after working so hard for him.

Carly was so mad about it that she did not dress in a Victor Allen design that day. She dressed in regular clothes that she'd bought right off the rack and that happened to look pretty damn good on her, *thank you very much*, and went in search of Victor.

She found him at his studio. But he wasn't working. He was on his skateboard, slowly circling around the tables and dress forms. He looked weirdly despondent. "Is everything okay?" Carly asked.

"Yeah. Why?" Victor asked. He allowed his skateboard to do a slow crash into the couch and collapsed onto it.

"I have some great news, Victor! I've been on the phone with Ramona McNeil herself. They get that you don't want to showcase the red pieces but are happy to look at something else."

Victor shrugged and rolled onto his side, facing the back of the couch. "Yeah, I don't know. I'm not feeling the whole *Couture* vibe. It feels too fancy."

Too *fancy*? "It's the best fashion magazine there is," Carly said.

"And you're a fashion designer. Every fashion designer wants their designs in that magazine."

"*Am* I a fashion designer? Or am I just someone who sews? I don't know anymore."

Well, this was new from a kid who was overconfident on his worst day. Carly exchanged a look with his mother. She did not like the look of worry on June's face. "This is *Couture*, Victor," Carly said.

He slowly sat up. He looked Carly directly in the eye. "I don't mean this to come off as rude, but I'm not feeling it."

"Okay," Carly said, nodding. "Okay, then. No *Couture*." For now. She had to think of a way to finesse this. If she didn't call Ramona back in the next two weeks, that magazine would never book her clients again. Assuming there were any more clients after Victor. And she definitely wouldn't be getting a job there.

"What do you mean, no *Couture*?" June asked.

Carly lifted her hands, palms up. "They have deadlines. But listen! I have two blog features lined up for you, and they are *very* excited about you. The New Designer Showcase is a big deal for the fashion blogs."

Victor sighed and looked at his hands. "Yeah, maybe." He pushed himself off the couch and walked into the kitchenette.

Carly looked at June. "What is happening?" she whispered.

"He gets depressed sometimes," June said softly, her gaze darting toward the kitchenette. They could hear Victor putting something into the microwave. "He's having some confidence issues."

"But why?" Carly asked with alarm. "Why now? Why at all? He won *Project Runway*!"

"Social media," June muttered. "People are so cruel."

Carly felt sick. She posted content on his social media channels, and of course she kept an eye on his mentions and user comments. She hadn't seen anything to give her concern—most of the comments were positive. But then again, she'd been wrapped up in dog issues over the weekend. "Which account?"

"Instagram." June frowned darkly.

"Mom, we're out of ketchup!" Victor called.

Carly grabbed her phone and pulled up Instagram.

"Look in the cabinet," June called back.

Carly began to scroll through the posts.

"I can't find it!" Victor shouted.

"Look in the cabinet!" June walked into the kitchenette to help him find it.

Carly didn't see anything to alarm her at first. She had posted a lot of pictures of his completed work, pictures of Victor hard at work, mentions of him in the press. Victor had posted some of his sketches, too, all of which she'd seen and thought were great content. But there was a post from last Thursday, a sketch of an evening gown that featured his signature shoulders and hips. Someone had panned the design and called it a second grade art project featuring Minecraft characters.

That was the sort of comment Carly would have paid no heed to at all and would advise Victor, or anyone else, to ignore. That was the problem with social media—there were people in the world who seemingly existed just to tear other people down, but you couldn't give them any oxygen. You couldn't let them steal your mojo. And the best way to keep your mojo intact was to stay off social media and allow your publicist to post for you and monitor comments.

Unfortunately, Victor hadn't done any of that. He'd fired back at the comment, calling the female a wannabe who was obviously jealous of his success and probably, judging from her comment, lacking talent. Others had begun to pile on. They'd called him names, said he was overrated, that they hated him on *Project Runway*.

Victor had responded to each and every comment.

That's when the worst trolls began to suggest that he was such a talentless hack that maybe he ought to kill himself.

"Oh my God," Carly breathed when June returned. She deleted the post.

"And there is this one," June said, and held out her phone to Carly.

It was a fashion blog site called *Felicity's Fashions*. The header was an illustration of a smartly dressed woman dashing across a street with a poodle on a lead, oversized sunglasses, and wearing a polka-dot dress.

"What about her?" Carly asked.

"Oh, she ranked all the designers who are showing in the New Designer Showcase." June glanced back at the kitchenette and whispered, "She ranked Victor last. She said his designs looked like someone took a surplus army tent and cut holes for the arms and legs."

"Don't let him see that," Carly said, pushing June's phone back to her. "Delete it."

"He's the one who showed me. And then said he didn't take advice from someone with so much side boob."

Carly gasped. She grabbed June's phone and scrolled through the comments. They were just as awful on the blog as they were on Instagram, but here an argument had erupted on the blogger's post. Some defended Victor. Some suggested that others who defended a young upstart designer who hadn't sold any clothes to the masses ought to sit down and shut up. Others took umbrage with the word *upstart* and its culturally negative connotations, and especially those with tattoos and rainbow hair and suggested that it was homophobic.

"No, no, *no*," Carly groaned.

"You need to turn this around, Carly," June said. "That's why we hired you."

"I will do my best," Carly promised. "But I can't do that if Victor is going to come in behind me and make these comments. He needs to stay off social media."

"I am doing my best, too," June said. "But he gets like this. He gets all in his head. His dad suffers from depression, too." She glanced back at the kitchenette. "I'm worried."

Carly was, too.

She left them and headed to a coffee shop to craft plan C.

She bought a latte and took a seat at the bar facing the street. She stared into space for a good half hour before she finally admitted to herself that she didn't have a plan C. She didn't know what to do with this side of Victor. Social media was such a trap.

She sipped her coffee. She picked up her phone, pulled up Instagram, and in the search box, typed, Dr. Max Sheffington. The search results came up empty. She tried Tobias Sheffington III. *Bingo.* There weren't many posts, but there were a couple of very cute pictures of a Labrador in goggles. And a diagram of the human brain with the caption The human brain is awesome. And a cartoon from the *New Yorker* that showed two surgeons leaning over a man with half his head sawed off. "It's a no-brainer," one said to the other.

She quietly giggled.

She was supposed to be crafting plan C, but she went to Facebook. She found a public page for Max's courses. There were tabs for class notes and a meme with a mad scientist with googly eyes staring at an overflowing test tube, and a post from Max. "I get it. Axons are tough. Just wait until we get to the endoplasmic reticulum. Neuroscience humor! Are you ready for your axon guidance exam? Come see me if questions."

She was smiling at the post when her phone suddenly vibrated awake. It was Gordon.

"Hi!" she said cheerfully. "How are—"

"Need you to come by this afternoon," Gordon said gruffly, without greeting.

Carly suppressed a groan. "Ah . . . sure," she said, her eye on her clock. She had some cold calls to make to Los Angeles this afternoon to drum up support for Victor. "Could it wait until tomorrow?"

"No, it cannot wait until tomorrow."

She grimaced. "Can you give me a couple of hours? I've got a thing I've got to take care of."

"Fine."

"Can you give me a heads-up?" she asked.

"We'll talk when you get here," Gordon said, with all the charm of a rock.

"Okeydoke," she chirped. So much for developing a plan C. Carly took one last look at Max's Facebook page, then slid her phone into her bag.

She went home to let Baxter out, then headed over to Gordon's lush, riverfront home. When she arrived, no one answered the front door. Carly went around to the side door, through which she often entered, and tapped on that door, peering into the massive kitchen. There was no sign of mean Alvira. But Alvira's little Ford Fiesta was in the drive, and through the garage windows, she could see Gordon's Maserati.

She figured they were probably out back. She stepped into the house. "Alvira? Gordon?"

No one responded.

Carly walked into the kitchen and put her bag on the kitchen bar, took out her phone, and texted Gordon to let him know she was here. There was no answer. A thought occurred to her—what if there had been an intruder? What if they were tied up or murdered or kidnapped? Because it didn't make sense that both cars would be here, the doors open, and no one answering her or her text.

She walked into the living room. Huge picture windows overlooked the backyard, the pool, and the river below. Nothing out there but a giant yellow ducky float skimming along the surface of the pool, turning its strange pirouettes with the breeze.

As she stood there, peering out, she heard a sound from down the hall. "Of course," she muttered. They were in his office and hadn't heard her come in. With a laugh at her wild imagination, Carly walked across the carpeted living room and up the two marble steps to the entry. She turned into the long corridor that led to Gordon's office when Gordon suddenly stepped out of a room. He was looking back over his shoulder, and paused to say something to someone in that room. He was laughing. And he was completely and utterly naked. Carly was so shocked she could not tear her eyes from the flabby paunch and penis dangling from a thatch of overgrown gray hair. She must have cried out with alarm, or maybe Gordon was the first to screech, because he did, and dove back into the room.

"Oh my God," Carly said. "Oh my God, oh my God, oh my *God*." She whirled around and ran, not even sure where she was going. She ran out the side door, all the way to her car, and then remembered her tote, and ran back inside to grab it.

"Carly!" Gordon had donned a dressing gown and was striding across the kitchen toward her.

She grabbed her tote. "I am so sorry, Gordon," she said, pressing a hand to her heart. "I am so, *so*, sorry, but the door was open and your cars were here and I thought something had happened and I am . . . I am *mortified* and I can't apologize enough."

"Come into my office," he said, gesturing her forward. "Come on. It's just a body, for fuck's sake. Stop acting like you've seen the devil himself."

Carly *had* seen the devil himself. She did not want to go inside. She did not want to go to his office. She did not want to look at him. But Gordon gestured impatiently again, so she clutched her tote to her chest and followed him through the living room and to his office.

On their way, Alvira passed them. She did not make eye contact with Carly, but her hair was standing almost straight up and her sweater was on inside out. Carly's breath caught in her throat. *That* was a pairing she would never have guessed. Damn it, even sour-faced Alvira was seeing someone.

In his office, Gordon stomped around to his big leather chair, picked up a cigar that appeared to be still lit (what, had the mood struck them and they'd started ripping clothes off?). He sat heavily, then propped one bare foot on the edge of his desk. Carly had to keep her head down, lest his robe fall open and she was treated to that indelible image again.

"So, Carly—"

"I'm so sorry."

He waved her off with a thick hand. "Listen, let me put this to you straight. I hired you because no one else really wanted the job. But I want sales. I don't want this blog business—"

"I hear you, Gordon. That was one idea. If you don't like it, we'll do something else."

"I think you've got this all wrong. You need to get out there and hustle for me."

"I *do* hustle for you. I have a call into the *Woodworker's Journal*—"

"No, I mean something like setting up a booth at the Pecan Street Festival," he suggested.

Carly stared at him. He wanted her to attend one of Austin's longest-running art festivals and hawk his stupid circles?

"There's probably something like it in San Antonio, too. You need to check into that."

"You mean you want me to put in the paperwork so you can go."

He looked at her like she was crazy. "*I'm* not going to go. *You* need to do that."

Carly needed this job. She really did. But she had her limits. She was in public relations—not sales. And who the hell did he think he was to know her job better than she did? "Gordon, I—"

"Wait, I'm not finished. That's what you *need* to do. But it seems to me you don't have that kind of drive."

Her mouth fell open. Well, now he'd gone and pissed her off.

He suddenly sat up and planted his arms on his desk. "I'm going to give you a piece of friendly advice, Carly. People who succeed work their asses off. They do everything it takes to make a project work. You have to have the burn in your gut—you know what I mean? You've got to want it."

Something snapped in Carly. Maybe it was the accumulation of stress over the last several months. Maybe it was the realization that no matter how hard she tried, no matter how hard she worked, there would always be men like Gordon Romero. Maybe it was something as simple as her day had really, really sucked so far. Whatever, she slowly stood. She thought about her rent increase. She thought about her résumé. She thought about all those job applications that were not being answered. She thought about being a good girl and letting him tell her what she needed to do. The client was always right, after all. But what she said was, "I think you should find someone else." She hitched her tote bag onto her shoulder. "And for the record, I *do* work my ass off. But sometimes, you get a client who thinks he knows everything, and maybe he knows a lot, but then you figure out that the one thing he doesn't know is that no one wants a damn circle of wood."

Gordon squinted. He pointed his cigar at her, and said, "You're fired."

"Nope. Sorry. I just quit. Beat you to it."

"No, I *fired* you," he insisted as she walked out the door.

"Nope! I quit first!" she shouted back at him.

Alvira was in the kitchen when Carly walked past the marble bar and chuckled as Carly walked out.

Carly wanted desperately to tell Alvira she was the rudest person she'd ever met, but she couldn't, because she was too busy fighting back hot tears of frustration. *If you can avoid it, never cry in public, because the world will use it against you*, Megan whispered.

How could her life have gone to shit so completely and so quickly? Because Carly's week did not improve from there. Victor did a vanishing act on her for two days. Naomi texted her and asked if she would be there by the holidays, because they were getting tickets to the new Broadway Christmas show. She was going to be living with her mother by Christmas at the rate things were going. Baxter lost interest in Dog TV and had gone back to his little corner in the kitchen. He didn't want to eat much. When he did go out in the yard, he wandered aimlessly about, then dragged himself back inside.

He missed Hazel. The poor dog was breaking her heart. Everything was breaking her heart.

Thursday afternoon, Carly finally gave in, made a box of mac and cheese, and spooned half of it on top of Baxter's super organic, super nutritious dog food. Baxter sighed as if it were a chore. But he ate it.

"I feel you," Carly said, and with her back to the wall, slid down to sit next to Baxter's bed in the kitchen. "What I wouldn't give to plant my face in a bowl of carbs right now."

When he finished, Baxter lay down beside her and put his head on her leg. She stroked his crown and his ears. Her thoughts wandered to Hazel . . .

Well. To Max, really. She imagined them having a grand old time over there with Dog TV and some strange new food defiantly added to the bowl in spite of the guarantee of an evening of dog flatulence. She thought about Max's gray eyes, and the curious little smile he had when he looked at her, like he couldn't quite figure her out. She thought about the yards of denim he'd worn. She wouldn't mind burying her face in some of that, too. She wouldn't mind the feel of a man's strong arm around her about now. Not because she couldn't take care of herself. But wouldn't it be nice, on occasion, to just let go and let someone else do all the worrying for her? Wouldn't it be nice to have someone to tell all the ridiculous things that happened in a day?

Carly looked at Baxter. She picked up her phone.

Hey, it's me, Carly Kennedy. Hope I'm not bothering you, but I need some advice from a scientist.

The text showed delivered. And there it sat. The minutes ticked by. Whole minutes, each one longer than the last, each one piling up so that she was cringing, wishing she could pull that text back. But then three dots popped up.

Hello, Carly Kennedy. The scientist is in.

Carly grinned. Baxter lifted his head and she showed him the screen. "See? He didn't even bring up the fact that I didn't believe he was a scientist. I think he might be a really good guy, Bax. Cute, too." She texted back:

Baxter is depressed again. Any suggestions?

Ah. Dog problems. Did you kick him off the couch?

I did not. He removed himself. My theory is that it didn't hold the same appeal without Hazel.

The scientist in me is dying to tell you that you are anthropomorphizing Baxter, but you may be on to something. Did you make him go back to organic food like the manual says?

Of course I did. But I may or may not have given him some mac and cheese tonight because he wouldn't eat.

That should have triggered the reward centers in his brain and released some doggie dopamine. Dog TV?

Had it on all day.

Dog toys?

A veterinarian-approved chew toy. The manual says it's supposed to help keep his teeth clean.

Hmm . . . this is a tough case. Did you tell him you love him?

Carly looked at Baxter. "I love you, Bax," she said. And gave him a good belly rub.

Yes I did! AND I rubbed his belly. I'm not a demon.

This all should have done the trick for my old pal Baxter. My professional opinion is that there is only one thing that can be done at this point. You probably won't like it.

Don't keep me in suspense. What will save my dog, doctor?

The only thing that will save your dog is if you and he meet me and Hazel at a dog park near you, and SOON. I think this is too serious to discuss in a text, but let's just say there are only so many remedies for a canine's broken heart, and you need to do something before it gets worse.

Carly smiled. She couldn't have Baxter's broken heart on her conscience. She texted Max to find out when and where. And then she smiled for the first time in what felt like days.

Nine

Carly's text could not have come at a better time.

Max and his good friend and faculty adviser, Dr. Drake Silverman, were sitting outside the College of Natural Sciences, watching a television broadcast crew pack up. A student passing by told them they'd been on campus to interview Dr. Alanna Friedman about her important work in the neurobiology of addiction and her isolation of certain receptors in the brain as it related to addiction. Max knew about her work. It was promising, something that could lead to new modalities of treatment and even pharmacological interventions.

They'd stumbled on the interview quite by accident—Max had asked Drake to do a beta read of his research paper and findings, as well as his proposal for further study into the translational aspects of the behavioral and endocrine phenotypes of dogs and the presentation of autistic behaviors in humans.

"So basically you're saying that our understanding of autism in the human brain can be learned from studying similar behaviors in the canine brain," Drake said.

"That's what I'm saying," Max said.

Drake grinned. "I think you like having dogs in the classroom."

"Who doesn't?" Max asked. "Except for O'Malley. He didn't seem too thrilled."

Drake waved a hand. "He doesn't like anything. I think this is good to go, Max. I made notes for a couple of suggested tweaks, but you're ready to present."

The paper Drake had reviewed was the last bit of research Max would submit as part of his dossier, which included all the research and published articles he wanted to be considered in his quest for tenure, as well as proposed articles and his future research goals. The departmental tenure committee would review his work and his plan. If that committee deemed his body of work and the latest research to be sufficient to move him forward, his dossier would be sent to the college dean. If Dean Goldbart reviewed his research and deemed it worthy, he would be moved on to the campus tenure committee. If *that* committee found him worthy, they would recommend him to the provost. If the provost decided to grant him tenure, Max would move from assistant professor to associate professor with tenure, with a chance to compete for endowments and license to continue his study of neurodevelopmental issues and, specifically, autism. Oh, and there would be a nice pay raise.

It was a long, complicated process and there were a lot of scientists to please along the way. It was little wonder the tenure track took years. In addition, the department had a policy of submitting no more than one candidate each year. That meant all tenure-track professors had to compete for one annual slot. Max had believed that this was his year. He'd been before the committee twice before and had never moved forward. But his body of work was more robust now, and his publication schedule was great. He thought that, for once, he was a lock. Which was why, when he and Drake noticed the TV crew, his belly dropped.

Alanna was doing some excellent work. Most people chuckled at Max with his dogs, like he'd chosen his field of study to hang out with them. "This does not bode well," Max said to Drake as they watched a guy in a photographer's jacket close the van door and hop into the passenger seat.

"Don't sweat it," Drake said. But Max noticed he avoided eye contact. Well, Max was sweating it, and he had a tendency to slide into a hole when he was worried about something. So when his phone pinged in his pocket, he was glad for the distraction.

"CNN," Drake said as the van drove by them. "That's a big deal."

Yeah. A Very Big Deal. Max sighed and looked at his phone. He felt a smile curling his lips. Was this a text from Carly Kennedy? It damn sure was. Nothing at that moment could have been better for him.

"I better get back," Drake said, and stood up. He looked at Max. "Everything okay?"

"Hmmm?" Max looked up from his phone. "You're taking off? Hey, thanks, Drake. As always, thanks for being my mentor."

"Dude," Drake said and, grinning, flicked his wrist at him. "Come on, let's get out of here."

"Umm . . . I need to take care of this," Max said, holding up his phone.

Drake nodded, said he'd see him later, and walked on.

Max zipped his jacket against a north wind and responded to Carly's texts. They agreed to meet tomorrow after work. He was smiling when he stood up, the CNN van forgotten. Everything was forgotten. Whatever worry and angst that had begun to build had been effectively tucked aside, shoved into a back pocket in his brain. He was thinking only of Carly as he walked back to his office. He'd been thinking about her for days.

When Max arrived at West Austin Neighborhood Dog Park the following afternoon, he heard Baxter before he saw the hound—his deep baying bark was rather distinctive. Hazel heard it, too, and began to prance excitedly at the gate, answering with a couple of barks of her own. Max opened the gate; Hazel charged in the direction of a picnic table at a speed that did not seem physically possible given her girth and the length of her legs, and just when Max thought she would crash into the concrete table, she leapt at Baxter, knocking him off-balance. The two of them rolled once, then took off, nipping at each other in a game of chase.

That's when he noticed Carly standing behind the picnic table. She waved.

Max waved back. He was privately relieved that she was not wearing one of the weird outfits. Not that he minded what she wore—he thought she probably looked good in anything—but more that he didn't know what to say about them. Today she was dressed in tights and boots, a long-sleeved T-shirt and puffy vest, and a knit cap with a fluffy white ball at the crown. Her long black hair was braided and hung over her shoulder. An image of that braid wrapped around his fist popped up in his mind's eye, and he felt a bit of a flutter in his chest, a telltale sign that the hormone norepinephrine was coming together with the rest of him to brighten his day.

She smiled as he walked across the park to reach her. Max would swear to the gods of men that he could see her blue eyes from this distance. She was attractive to him in a way that slipped into his blood and spread, turning each and every molecule pleasantly warm. He noted, as he quickened his pace, that he didn't normally have thoughts like this. But he was definitely attracted to her, and by the time he reached the picnic table, he'd lost all sight of his dog and didn't care.

"Hey!" she said cheerily. "Did you hear Baxter? He has it so bad for Hazel."

He hadn't noticed anything but her.

She turned her head, and her braid swung a little. "Look at them."

Max watched her watch the dogs a moment. Then she looked back at him, smiling with such delight that the skin around her eyes crinkled. "The difference in him is *amazing*. They're so cute!"

"So cute," he agreed. But he was looking at Carly.

She gestured to a thermal bag on the table. "Guess what? I come bearing gifts."

"You do?" He was surprised by this. Carly had not seemed the type to bear gifts. So far, she'd presented as the type to knock your block off if necessary. He sincerely hoped it would never be necessary.

"I do, of course I do. I have manners, sir. You don't ask a gentleman and his dog to save your dog from the depths of doggie depression and show up empty-handed." She slanted a look at him as she unzipped the bag. "Also, I owe you an apology for not believing you were a scientist. I thought you were making a joke because you got busted for telling me to calm down."

Max smiled. "For the record, I totally believed you were a supermodel."

She laughed with surprise. "With *that* muffin top? Wait—don't answer that." She pulled out a plaid thermos and held it up to him. "It's hot chocolate. Do you like hot chocolate? I mean, you don't have any weird allergies to chocolate or anything, do you? It would crush Baxter if I had to cancel this rescue because you totally ruined everything by being allergic to chocolate."

He pressed a hand to his heart as if he'd been mortally offended. "I would never ruin this for Baxter. I *do* like hot chocolate and I have no weird allergies. And if I did, I wouldn't admit to them because that," he said, pointing with two fingers at the two dogs, "is a match made in heaven."

"Exactly," Carly said with a grin. "We should all be such lucky dogs." She pulled out two paper cups, opened the thermos, and poured. She handed one to Max, then picked the other one up and tapped it against his. "Thank you again. Seriously. He's been *so* depressed."

Max looked into her eyes. He wanted to speak, but words had drifted out of his mind, almost as if he had frontotemporal degeneration. Which he did not.

"Cheers!" she said and tapped her cup to his.

"Cheers." Max sipped. The taste of rich, warm chocolate hit his tongue and a hint of his childhood came rushing back at him. Which was quickly followed by a hint of his college years, because this hot chocolate was laced with alcohol, and he coughed, then looked at Carly with surprise.

She burst into laughter and sat on the picnic bench. "It's Friday! And there's a nip in the air. I'm actually doing you another favor by keeping you warm."

"I like the way you think, Carly Kennedy. This was a favor I didn't even know I needed." He sat next to her.

"That's high praise coming from an actual *brain scientist*."

"All right, get it out of your system," he said, gesturing. "You don't have to say *brain scientist* like I'm creating Frankenstein's monster in my backyard."

Carly laughed.

"What made you believe me, anyway? It couldn't have been my analytical calculation of how to get you out of that skirt."

"Definitely not that," she agreed. "Google made me believe it."

Max sputtered another sip of his hot chocolate.

"What? Are you surprised? Don't you google people?"

"No! I mean, sure, professionally speaking I have googled people. But nonacademics?" He shook his head.

"You should! You need to know who you're dealing with. Seriously!" she said to his dubious smile. "I wasn't kidding—you could have been a legit dognapper."

"You googled me before you met me?"

"No, but I *should* have, and that's the point," she said. "At the time I was too flustered to think."

"Your theory is that if I'd been a legit dognapper, I would have posted it on the Internet?"

"My theory is that your long rap sheet of dognappings and social media posts about dognappings or other awful behavior would have given you away."

He laughed. "Social media posts about awful behavior? What does that mean?"

"It means, if I googled you, and checked out your social media accounts, and found out you were a big game hunter, *eew*, or liked some racist posts, I mean, come on, I couldn't hang out with you in a dog park."

"Aha, I get it now." He sipped. "Just out of curiosity . . . what did you find?"

"That you really like dogs and brains."

"That's it?"

"That's it."

He smiled. "There's a flaw in your theory, you know. I'm rarely on social media, so there is very little information about me."

She squinted a moment as she considered that. "You're right. You could still be a dognapper. I guess I'll have to go about this the old-fashioned way and interrogate you."

"Great!" Max grinned. "Nothing I like better than a good interrogation. Hey, did you ever google Brant?"

"Now you're getting it! And you just proved my point—we *both* should have googled Brant. I didn't, because he had a card and everything, and, frankly, I was a little desperate. But I learned from my mistake, Max. So when a guy unzipping my skirt randomly announced he was a brain scientist, I knew immediately it was worth a google."

Max laughed. "When you put it like that, I guess so. Did I really randomly announce it? I usually wait for someone to ask." What he remembered about that night was the feel of her skin. Soft and pliant, warm and—

"Anyway, I read your profile on the university website."

"Oh." It felt a little weird, knowing she'd googled him. "What did you, ah . . ." He hesitated, not wanting to ask in case he didn't like the answer.

"Think about it?" she finished for him.

He wanted to know if she liked it, if she was impressed. If by chance his profile had magically separated him from all the other men who sought her attention. "I think that's what I'm trying to ask, yes."

"I thought that there is no way in a million years I could understand what you do, and hats off to you for being so smart."

"I'm not so smart. I just know the science lingo. We brain scientists are a small group, relatively speaking. We have to have our own language so we can stick together."

"Oh, it's a secret club thing?"

"Something like that."

She grinned. She traced her finger around the edge of her cup. "What made you decide on neuroscience? Were you that kid in sixth grade who took the science experiments a step too far? I'm kind of fascinated, because when I was in the sixth grade, Johnny Grakowski threw a dead cricket at me and that effectively ended any interest I might have had in anything remotely scientific."

"A cricket?"

"They're so gross, Max. What about you?"

He couldn't quite make the connection between crickets and science, but that was okay. "My interest in science didn't happen until I was in high school. In sixth grade, I was noticing girls and all senses were pointed in that direction. In high school, my senses had expanded into additional interests. I was good at math and science, but I never really thought about it as a career. It had more to do with my brother, Jamie, really. His disorder fascinated me. Like, how things were so different for the two of us, how our brains could work so differently."

"How so?" she asked.

Max thought about that for a minute. "Aside from his inability to really speak, he's a bright guy. And he's extremely artistic. Remember the drawing of the dog I showed you?"

She nodded.

"I remember in first grade his special ed teacher was sending home the drawings Jamie had made with notes about how advanced he was. So advanced in some ways, but so delayed in other ways. When I figured out I liked science well enough, I wanted to study more about autism and neurological disorders in general. I wanted to figure out ways to make things easier for him and people like him." He smiled a little. "And there you have it."

She smiled, too. "What a lucky guy Jamie is to have you for a brother."

He thought maybe he was the lucky one. "What about you? Are you really a publicist?" he asked.

"Ish," she said.

"Excuse me?"

"Publicity adjacent." She giggled. "I mean, I *am* a publicist, but right now, I'm a little insecure about my skills. I lost a client this week."

"Oh, wow, sorry to hear that. Not the fashion guy, I hope. I was getting used to your, ah . . ." He searched for a word.

Carly smiled, one brow rising above the other. She didn't offer the appropriate word for him—she was going to make him say it.

"The designs," he said at last.

"The designs!" she said gleefully.

"Fine," he said with a lopsided grin. "The costume things."

"The costume things?" She laughed. "Fortunately, I didn't lose him. I lost another guy who—brace yourself—created something even more baffling than giant shoulders and long sleeves."

Max shifted around to face her. "Well, now I'm dying of curiosity. What could possibly be more baffling than that?"

"The other guy made wooden circles."

"He made what?"

She sketched a circle in the air with her hands.

He shook his head. "Not getting it."

"Exactly! Who can get that? I have yet to find anyone who under-stands the circle thing." She pulled out her phone, swiped up and down and all around the screen, then leaned lightly against him to show him a picture. It was a circle, all right. A highly polished round of wood.

"That's . . . definitely a wooden circle." He looked at Carly just in case she was teasing him, then at the screen again. She leaned a little harder against him, holding up her phone. Max liked the feel of her touching him. He did not like the circles. "I'm sorry, I don't get it."

"*Thank* you!" she exclaimed, and swayed away from him. "All this time I thought I was missing some art appreciation gene, but it turns out this dude is just making stupid circles. Some fat, some skinny, some really big, and some really small. But they are all *circles*."

"Let's see it again," Max suggested, and not because he needed to see that dumb circle, but because he wanted to feel her shoulder pressed against his arm again.

They bent over her phone and looked at the pictures of circles as she swiped through. Her scent tickled his nose, reminding him vaguely of rain-soaked air.

"I tried everything. Instagram, blogging, art publications—you name it. And they were all like, never heard of this guy, and, seriously, what is this? Once, I asked Gordon what the circles represented to him and he got mad at me."

"He got *mad*?"

"Furious! He said it was *art* and he shouldn't have to explain art to anyone, including the woman he'd hired to promote his work."

"Ouch," Max said on her behalf.

"I didn't take it personally. He's just an asshole." She smiled at him, her eyes twinkling with amusement.

Max slipped his hand under hers and lifted it so he could see the picture on her phone again. "If I may offer the opinion of a brain sci-entist?"

"Please! I *need* the opinion of a brain scientist."

"That," he said, pointing at the screen, "is just a wooden circle." He kept his hand under hers and grinned. "You are right."

"How delightful! That's not something I hear with enough regularity. Anyway, I quit him. What he wanted was a salesclerk to sit in a booth at the Pecan Street Festival. I wanted at least a *little* cooperation from him. But he wouldn't give me any at all. So I quit."

"Sounds like you made the right call."

"No kidding," she said. "He was so mad. And I haven't told you the worst of it. Just before I quit, he . . ." She paused and looked sidelong at him, her blue eyes dancing with laughter. She was stifling a giggle.

He smiled. "He what?"

"I can't believe I'm going to tell you this."

Her giggle was infectious. He was chuckling, too. "Tell me what?"

"I walked in on him while he was diddling his housekeeper." She slapped a hand over her mouth in pretend shock.

Max laughed. "No way!"

She nodded furiously, then told him the story, regaling him as if she were recounting a horror film she'd seen. "It was like Big Bird and his beak standing there," she said with a shudder.

Max doubled over with laughter.

"Oh sure, yuk it up," she said, laughing, too. "I can never unsee that, you know."

"Sounds like you and Baxter have had quite a week." In fact, the dogs, exhausted from racing around, had wandered back to the picnic table and were stretched out beneath it.

"We sure have. Right, Bax?" she asked, leaning over to look down at the dogs.

Her cheeks were rosy and the tip of her nose red, and a warm flush erupted in the center of Max's chest and slid down to his groin. He realized he was staring at her mouth. His amygdala was tossing out dopamine willy-nilly into the wrong neurons, because his idea of kissing her would be an impulsive thing to do. He was spared from possibly embarrassing himself when a woman with bright red, unkempt hair and wearing a leaf green coat walked by with a pug. The pug barked at Baxter and Hazel, neither of whom were concerned enough to even bark back.

The woman jerked hard on the pug's leash. "Stop that!" she hissed. "How many times have I told you that it's rude to bark like that? They aren't doing anything to you," she said as she and the pug continued walking. "You have to stop barking at every dog you see. It's rude."

Max looked at Carly. She was struggling to keep from laughing. "Do you think her dog speaks English?" she whispered.

"I was just wondering the same thing," he whispered back. "A talking dog, you think? But am I crazy? She reminds me of someone," Max said. "Know what I mean? Animated character with the wild red hair."

Carly gasped. "I know *exactly* who she looks like!" she whispered excitedly. "Poison—"

"*Ivy!*" he finished with her. "That's it!" They both burst into laughter and high-fived each other. Max held on to her hand, and Carly fell into his shoulder again with a squeal of delight. Their laughter prompted Baxter and Hazel to crawl out from under the table and jump up, tails wagging, wanting in on the joke.

Carly caught her breath and wiped a tiny tear from under her eye. She had to lean down and physically keep Baxter from trying to climb on the table. When she did, she scooched away from Max. "More hot chocolate?" she asked.

The opportunity to kiss her had slipped past. He'd blown it. "I would love some, but if I have more, I won't be able to drive. What did you put in that, anyway?"

"Kahlúa, of course. And maybe a little bit of vodka," she said, holding up thumb and forefinger to indicate just how little.

He grinned. "This was great, Carly. Thanks for texting me. But I should get going—I promised my brother I'd come by."

"Yep. I've got loads to do myself," she said, looking down. "I guess we're all on ye olde hamster wheel."

Max rounded up the dogs and leashed them while she put her

thermos and cups into her bag and zipped it. The four of them walked to the gate and stepped out of the park.

In the parking lot, Max paused and smiled at Carly. He wasn't ready for this to end. But as usual, he couldn't think on his feet quite fast enough.

It felt a little like she might have suspected as much. She gave him a charmingly lopsided smile and said, "On behalf of Baxter, I thank you from the bottom of his heart."

"My pleasure, Baxter," he said, without taking his eyes from her.

"Well," Carly said.

"Well," Max said.

Neither of them moved. Hazel sat. Baxter lay down and rolled onto his back, paws in the air.

Max and Carly kept staring at each other as attraction and general horniness swelled in Max again.

"Okay, this is ridiculous," Carly said at last. She suddenly stretched one arm out wide and stepped forward. "Bring it in, big guy."

"Oh." He was caught off guard—she meant to hug him. He leaned into that hug, his arm going around her waist.

She put her arm around his shoulders and rose up on her toes. "Thank you," she said again, gave him a couple of hearty pats on the back, then stepped away from him.

Before she took another step, before she escaped, Max blurted, "Maybe we should meet Sunday at the Yard Bar. I mean, if Baxter is free." Because he didn't know what else to say, and he didn't want that hug to be the end, and he was looking in her eyes now and her pupils had dilated and his serotonin was mixing with his norepinephrine, and Baxter was looking up at him so ruefully.

Carly's dilated pupils sparked with delight, and once upon a time Max may have known the biology behind that, too, but he didn't care, because the effect on him was to release a truckload of dopamine into his blood. A primal, copulatory smile spread across his face. It shone all through him. He couldn't help it.

"Heck, yeah!" she said cheerfully. "Baxter would love that place! You and Hazel are so kind to think of him."

He wasn't kind. He was one hundred percent male and he was thrilled and filled with anticipation, and once they'd arranged a time and had gone their separate ways, he understood that he could hardly wait until Sunday afternoon and the Yard Bar. He felt like Jamie felt about the dog show. *Yard Bar.*

Ten

Well that was a grandma move if ever she'd seen one—Carly had hugged Max. She'd put her arm around him, had felt how hard his body was next to hers, and before she buried her face in his collar to inhale his scent, before she'd nibbled his earlobe, she'd patted him on the back like some long-lost cousin. She'd hugged him because her palms felt sweaty and she felt sort of light-headed, and what the hell had just happened?

She drove away with Baxter panting happily behind her, thinking about how good Max had felt, how strong and thick and hard his body was against hers, and, damn it, she *liked* Max. If ever there was a case of mistaken first impressions, this was it, because once he'd shed a little denim, and had come back from Chicago without lying to her, he was a really nice guy. He was kind. He was obviously compassionate. And he was ridiculously handsome.

Lord, she'd laughed at every little thing he'd said today, just tittering away. She'd found reasons to lean against him, too—in short, she'd reverted to her seventeen-year-old self. But in her defense, it had been a long time since she'd been so attracted to a man.

She could not *wait* until Sunday.

Unfortunately, Saturday arrived first to obliterate her most excellent mood created Friday evening.

On Saturday, she had two depressed puppies on her hands. One was Baxter, of course, who fell into a state of despondency on Friday night when he was not with Hazel. This morning, he was lying curled up in a ball with his back to the world, his snout in the corner of the kitchen.

Her other depressed pup was Victor. June had called Saturday morning and asked Carly to come to the studio and help her try and talk some sense into her son. Carly was beginning to hate that damned brown couch in his studio, because Victor had taken to lying on it, and did so almost all of Saturday. He had fallen into a funk and hardly spoke, and when he did, it was to tear himself down. He questioned his talent. "There wasn't that much competition on *Project Runway*, not really." He would not listen to arguments to the contrary.

He stared off into space with his sad puppy dog eyes. At least Baxter closed his eyes and pretended to be asleep.

Carly and June had tried to give Victor a pep talk. Or rather, Carly did. Like any mother would be, June was both alarmed and disappointed, and in her helplessness, she couldn't help snapping at him. Carly couldn't imagine what it was like to watch an insanely talented son piss away all that he'd accomplished.

When rational talk didn't work, June turned to shouting. "Get up off that couch, Victor Daniel Allen! You don't know how lucky you are, you don't appreciate the opportunity God has given you! You ought to be on your knees right now, thanking the Good Lord for steering you to this point."

"Don't shout at me," Victor said. "I'm sorry, Mom, I really am. I know you sacrificed so much for me, but I just can't do this right now." He covered his head with a pillow until his mother yanked it out of his hand.

Carly tried a more positive approach. "All great artists have moments of self-doubt, Victor, and you're a great artist, and you're having your moment. You just need to give yourself a little time to refill the well. Take a break if that's what you need," she'd urged him, ignoring June's murderous stare. "Just a couple of days. I know that if you take a couple of days and think it through, you'll come out of that break stronger and more motivated than ever before."

Honestly, Carly didn't know what she was saying. She was throwing out platitudes and words of encouragement hoping that something would stick. In all her years at public relations, no one had ever told her what to do with a client who didn't want his work to be promoted. No one had ever told her how to deal with someone who was depressed.

"You're the one who keeps saying I don't have time," Victor said accusingly to Carly, and he was not wrong about that. "You keep saying that I have to come up with something because we're going to lose opportunities."

"Yes," Carly agreed. "I did say that. But now I have a better idea! That's what I do." She said that brightly, as if she were confident in what she was doing. She was not confident—she could see everything crumbling before her. She'd already screwed things up with *Couture*. Ramona was not going to give her another chance if she flunked this one.

She desperately sought her memory banks for any motivating gems she'd picked up from *Big Girl Panties*.

"You guys don't get it," Victor said, and rolled onto his back, staring up at the water-stained ceiling and exposed ductwork. "All it takes is one bad design, one bad moment, and that's it. No one will want my designs then. I've seen it happen. So, like, it doesn't matter how much time I take. What matters is what I put out there, and I keep thinking about that, and I keep thinking that these looks are not the right thing."

"But, Victor, you loved these pieces," his mother said. "You can't please everyone."

"That's right," Carly agreed. "The only person you can truly please is yourself. That's what you've been doing and look where it got you! So many people want your clothes. So many people follow you. Everyone wants to see what else you've got."

"You have to at least try, Victor," June said. "If you don't at least try, you're going to burn everything down."

Carly winced. She was afraid June was right, and Victor would burn everything down, because he'd bought some shiny aquamarine fabric and at some point had made a signature blouse, complete with the oversized shoulders and long sleeves and a new twist—enormous, cartoon-like buttons. His innovative design suddenly looked like a Copacabana dance costume on steroids.

June didn't have the guts to tell Victor the aquamarine piece was hideous, probably because she was so desperate to get him off the couch and creating again. Carly knew that June was going to push her to do it, and she would have to do it. It wasn't just her opinion—she'd snapped a picture and run it by a fashion blogger she'd become friendly with while Victor and June were arguing. She'd sent the picture to Carlos, asking for the strictest confidentiality and a simple question: Reaction?

Girl, ugh, was his response. Hard pass.

"Seriously, Victor, why don't you take a little time off? Go to the skate park and try not to think about fashion."

"That's impossible," he'd muttered. "I can't *not* think about fashion." And then he'd rolled up to sitting, looked at Carly, and said, "But I can't think about it right now. I feel sick." He got up and went into the bathroom.

There was no talking to Victor. Carly left there and went to Mia's, hoping for a glass of wine and a sympathetic ear so she could vent about Victor. But Mia had shooed her out the door because Will had come home last night.

"Where are the kids?"

"With Grandma," Mia said, pushing Carly to the exit. "I mean the responsible Grandma, and not our mother, who has not been heard from in two days. You should call her."

"But I . . ."

"Bye, Carly!" Mia had said cheerfully, and her tall, handsome husband waved at her from the living room.

So Carly had gone home to Sad Bax without a glass of wine and none at home. While Baxter lay at her feet, Carly went through her finances to see how long she could hang on in her little house. She figured she could cover five full months of rent and bills. Had it not been for the impulsive purchase of the Louis Vuitton Neverfull bag from her favorite online consignment shop, she might have squeaked out six. Either way, she had about three months to either get a job in New York or bring in at least another client. *Something.*

She was going to need help if she didn't get something really soon.

She checked the status of the applications she'd submitted for jobs in New York. Two positions—one at a fashion website start-up, the other as an assistant to the digital marketing department head at Bergdorf Goodman—had been filled. Another application was for a position that was still open, and another application was "in process." Whatever that meant.

Carly had to get up the nerve to check *Couture.* She thought she shouldn't even bother, and expected to see big red *X*'s drawn through her application status, signed personally by Ramona McNeil. But amazingly, both applications were listed as "pending." Well then. Carly had listened to enough episodes of *Big Girl Panties* to interpret that as a good sign—it meant she wasn't yet out of the running. At least in theory.

She spent the rest of Saturday scouring the job listings on ZipRecruiter, Monster, Indeed, and Glassdoor. She submitted two applications at two different companies for copywriter positions. Copywriting was not her favorite thing, but the jobs were in New York, and they paid enough to at least allow her to perhaps rent a room from someone.

After that, she turned on her TV and scrolled through the listings. She hadn't watched TV in so long that she didn't know what she was looking for. She landed on an episode of *Below Deck*, but even the idea of gliding around the Mediterranean on a luxury yacht couldn't keep the restlessness from her. She turned off the TV and tried to sleep, but really just thrashed around on her bed, kicking her feet and pummeling her fists into a pillow that said Love Yourself, and the Rest Will Follow—an impulse buy after hearing one of Megan's podcasts.

Carly was not one to participate in pity parties. She really wasn't. But sometimes she had to wonder why this was happening to her. She'd done everything right. She'd gotten good grades in school, had gotten a good job, and had worked hard. She'd been a decent daughter, a better sister. She didn't do drugs or drink much. *She'd done everything right.* It was not supposed to be this way. She was supposed to have it all by now, not be worrying about how to pay her rent.

She groaned and rolled over onto her belly, burying her face in her pillow, her arms splayed wide. Man down. Baxter managed to haul himself up on the bed and licked her arm until she finally sank her fingers into his flesh and petted him.

This was a Saturday night when really good sex would come in handy. She thought of sex with Max, which was probably amazing, but that seemed like a pretty far-fetched possibility, and if she didn't stop thinking about it, she was going to make herself crazy.

She rolled over and sat up, and on a whim, she texted Naomi. What are you doing?

Three dots appeared on the bottom of her screen and danced around for a few moments, then disappeared. Naomi was doing something fun, she guessed. Probably having really good sex like most of the world on a Saturday night, and she did not have time to entertain her broke friend in Texas.

Baxter pressed the length of his body against her leg and sighed loudly.

"You know what, Baxie?" she asked, stroking his back. "If this was a rom-com, my application would land in the in-box of a handsome executive who would send it back with a gruff demand to submit the application again but with the correct information, and I would take issue with his tone and demand my application back, which of course he would not give me because he would realize he needed someone as spunky as me in his company, and then, of course, in his life."

Baxter lifted his head down by her feet and looked back at her.

"But this ain't no rom-com, kid. I'm in serious trouble. I might have to get a job at the barbeque place on the corner." She shuddered.

Baxter lay his head across her shin.

"I know," Carly whispered. "Not ideal." Unshed tears blurred her vision.

Eventually, she did fall asleep, because the next thing she knew, sunlight was streaming into her room. Baxter was gone, probably having retreated to his corner. She sat up and pushed hair from her face. She looked at the window and the dappled shadow of leaves dancing across her wall. And then she remembered.

Today was *Sunday*. Today was the *Yard Bar*.

She hopped out of bed with a squeal, her good spirits returned to her. "Baxter!" she shouted. "Let's go see Hazel today!"

She heard Baxter scramble to his feet and heard him racing down the hall. He tried to leap on her bed but couldn't get enough lift and fell backward before popping back up and prancing around, panting with delight.

So what if her life was falling apart? Carly was almost as excited as Baxter.

Eleven

Carly was the first to arrive at the Yard Bar that afternoon. She paid the daily fee, stepped inside the gate, and set Baxter free. He took off, his nose to the ground and tail high. He stopped to investigate a woman who was setting up to play guitar. She politely ignored him, and Baxter moved on to more interesting smells.

Carly headed to the bar.

An older woman, with a round face and gray hair cropped so short that it stood up on her head, and a glittery gold nose ring, stood in the window of the food trailer. "Hi!" Carly said brightly. "I would like something to drink that is sunny and fun after a very bad Saturday. What do you recommend?"

"The Rescue Me," the lady said. She leaned over the counter window and pointed at a chalkboard. The Rescue Me boasted vodka with ginger beer and spices and flavorings.

"That looks so sunny I might get sunburned," Carly said.

"That looks like a good Sunday to me," the woman opined.

Carly looked at the ingredients again. "Okay!" she said. "Let's do it."

"Make it two."

Carly turned around with a smile so wide she could feel her cheeks cramping with it. "Well, hello, Professor Brainiac."

Max smiled with his snowy white teeth and his dimples and his dark scruff, and Carly felt very fluttery. Max opened his mouth to reply, but before he could utter a word, the baying of a hound interrupted them. She and Max burst into laughter at the same moment and turned to see Baxter and Hazel in the middle of the yard, wrestling each other to the ground. Hazel broke free and took off on a new scent trail, and Baxter trotted besottedly behind her. They were joined today by a small brown mutt desperate to gain the bassets' attention, but Baxter only had eyes for Hazel, and Hazel only had eyes for possible food sources.

"I think Baxter is going to ask Hazel to marry him," Carly said.

"Ya think? If they get married, who will have custody?" Max wondered aloud.

"Obviously you," Carly said.

"Funny you should say that." He smiled down at her, his gaze moving over her face. "I thought obviously *you*."

The fluttery feeling turned to pure delight, and Carly giggled. The seventeen-year-old was back and inhabiting her body again.

"Here's your drinks," the woman at the counter said.

Max reached for a wallet in his back pocket. "Want something to eat?" he asked Carly.

She always wanted something to eat, unless she had flutters in her belly like she did now. "Oh, I—"

"Yeah, you do," he said with a wink. "Let's have the hummus plate," he said, squinting at the chalkboard, and looked at Carly for approval. She nodded. "And some of those lucky puppies. Oh, and throw in some of those weenie bites for the dogs."

"Oh, I—"

"I know, it's not in the manual," Max said. "But it's the weekend."

She couldn't argue with that.

"Coming right up," the lady said.

Max opened his wallet and took out some bills. "How's your weekend so far?"

Oh, but her weekend had sucked until this very moment. "Busy! My fashion guy is depressed." She tasted her drink. It was delicious. She was beginning to feel rescued and sunny and happy again.

"Oh yeah?" Max tossed the money onto the counter. "What's wrong with Calvin Klein?"

"Ooh," she said, nodding appreciatively. "Points for knowing the name of your underwear designer. To answer your question, Calvin has had his confidence shaken by some unkind comments on social media," she said. "And now he won't get off the couch." She paused. "Like, *literally* won't get off the couch. He won't work and he's tossed out everything he's been working on. He's in the throes of a major funk."

"That's not good," Max agreed.

"I'll bring the food out to you," the lady said, waving them on.

Max gestured to a nearby picnic table with an umbrella. They sat side by side on the bench, using the table as a seat back, facing the small concession. They sipped their drinks for a few moments, listening to the young woman sing. Her style was bluesy and melodic, her voice raspy.

"She's really good," Carly said.

"She is." Max sipped his drink. "Sorry to hear about fashion guy. Does this mean you won't be wearing any more . . . high fashion?"

She slanted him a look. "How dare you. I will *never* quit wearing high fashion . . . at least as long as I have a designer for a client."

Max laughed. "What's going to happen with him, do you think?"

"Good question. My father warned me I would deeply regret dropping psychology my freshman year. I think it would come in handy

right about now because I don't know how to deal with him. Have you
ever been in a major funk?"

Max shook his head. "Nothing more than garden variety, I guess.
What does his funk mean for you? I know you're his publicist, but I
don't know what that means, exactly, especially if he's not making
things for you to publicize." He paused and looked at her. "What do
you do, anyway?"

"I try and get him noticed. And that's the thing. I had a spot for
him in front of the creative director at *Couture* magazine. She could
really make his career, you know, but Victor is choking."

"Tell me," he said.

Carly told him everything. About the work she'd done to get Victor back in the fashion conversation. The blogs, the interviews, the
photo shoots. She told Max how Victor was to be featured in the New
Designer Showcase, but was removing pieces and replacing them with
things that looked bad to her untrained eye. How she feared he would
lose all his confidence and, horror of horrors, not show at all.

"Wow," Max said. "That doesn't sound good."

"Nope. If Victor bows out of that show, it will be a huge blow to
me. I obviously can't afford to lose another client right now."

Max frowned. "So what will you do?"

"Hopefully, what I've planned to do all along," she said. "I've been
applying for public relations jobs in New York."

The woman with the guitar began to play a folksy number.

Max paused with his cup halfway to his mouth and looked at her.
"You're moving to New York?"

"Well," she said airily, "that's the plan. I have to get a job first, and
so far, I haven't had much luck in that department, either. But it's
what I've been working toward for a while. I have this dream of getting a job in publicity or marketing, preferably in the fashion industry,
and living my best life in the city that never sleeps."

"Ah." Max smiled thinly. He put a hand on her knee and squeezed
it. "Would I be a terrible friend if I wished you continued to have no

luck in that department? I mean, Baxter and Hazel have quite a thing going."

"Yes, you would be a terrible friend," she said, smiling. "You have to wish me all the luck, because Baxter is accustomed to eating kangaroo and sleeping on fluffy dog beds."

"Fair enough," he conceded. "Then I wish you all the luck, Carly."

They sat in silence a long moment, listening to the music. Carly said, "You know, when I move to New York, you could come visit me and Baxter."

"I might have to," Max said. "Just to assure myself that Baxter has access to a couch. And it looks like I might have the time after all."

"Really?" she asked, perking up. "Why?"

"Oh," he said, and flicked his wrist. "That was a poor joke. It's just that I thought I'd be getting tenure and starting a new research project, maybe getting a fat endowment in the process. But now I'm not so sure."

She wanted to know more about that, but the lady appeared with red plastic baskets of food for them. Baxter and Hazel raced to the table to see if there was anything for them, and while Carly protested, Max tossed them each a weenie bite.

"You're going to make them fat," she laughingly accused him.

"Don't look now, Carly, but Baxter was already fat when Hazel and I met him. Look me in the eye and tell me you aren't feeding him mac and cheese every now and again."

"I'm not telling you anything," she said, and stuffed a carrot into her mouth. "Your turn . . . Why do you think you're not getting tenure now?"

"Because I found out that another professor is in the running. Our department puts forward only one candidate a year for tenure, and sometimes none at all. Alanna is doing some amazing work around drug addiction. She's gotten a lot of well-deserved media attention for it." He smiled ruefully. "My work is not very sexy. But it's important."

"True confessions—I've been dying to ask what your work is,

Max, but I'm afraid I won't be able to follow. Like I said, a cricket trauma shut down my scientific education."

He laughed. "It's really simple. I'm studying the oxytocin system in dogs to better understand the neurohormonal basis of cognitive abilities."

Carly laughed. "Dammit! My fears have been realized with only one sentence! I have no idea what you just said."

He shifted around to face her. "There have been some studies conducted that suggest that some dogs have similar aspects of autistic behaviors that are found in humans."

"You're kidding," Carly said.

"I'm not. For example, one study looked at bull terriers who chase their tails, right? Round and round they go," he said, making a circle with his finger. "That behavior is similar to behavior in humans on the spectrum, like trancing and social withdrawal. It's very OCD."

"Yeah, okay," she said.

"I'm finishing up a study on how autistic humans interact with dogs and how the human oxytocin system is affected. There is a cognitive reward system for both dog and human there that I've documented, especially as it relates to social behaviors. The second phase of my research is studying the canine oxytocin system. I'm hoping to discover some parallels in that reward system that are translational and that will inform either education modalities or even pharmacological interventions in autistic humans."

He hadn't completely lost her yet, Carly was pleased to see, but she had questions. "What is oxy . . ."

"Oxytocin," he said. "It's the hormone that has the most to do with social bonding."

Carly couldn't begin to imagine how he did that sort of work.

Hazel and Baxter raced by at that moment, in pursuit of a terrier. The woman with the guitar ended one song and then began to play an acoustic variation of a song Carly had heard many times on the radio. It was lovely.

"Are you studying Hazel?" Carly asked.

Max laughed. "No. But I'm studying my brother. I found out yes-terday he's getting a dog from the ACC ."

"How fun! What's he getting?"

"A Labrador."

Carly grinned. "We had one growing up. That dog was a lunkhead—he actually ate the mortar from between the bricks on the back porch, and my dad had to replace it. But I loved that big black dog. Why doesn't your brother already have a dog? I mean, given how much he loves them."

He reached for a hush puppy. "My dad's been against it, really. He has a lot on his plate as it is with Jamie's care and didn't want to add a dog to the mix. Jamie . . . he's okay for the most part, but he does require supervision in a lot of things. At least that's always been the reason. But it would appear my dad has changed his mind."

He said something else, but Carly missed it. She found herself mes-merized by his handsome face. He had prominent cheekbones, which made his face appear lean. He had a very masculine face, she decided, all chiseled and perfectly proportioned and—

"Hello?"

Carly blinked.

"I was talking about my dad?"

"Yes! You were telling me . . ." A blush crept into her cheeks.

"That my aunt is the one who told me," Max said. "Yesterday when I stopped by, my dad wasn't even home. My aunt was there and said he'd gone out with friends." He cocked one brow high above the other, glanced around them, and said low, "*That* was also new. My mom has been gone six years, but my dad never goes out with friends, at least not when Jamie is home. I'm wondering what's up."

He had tucked his collar-length dark hair behind his ears. What was it about men with longer hair that was so sexy? It was very *Game of Thrones*-y to Carly.

"I mean, it would be great if he did find someone to share his life with," Max continued. "But I didn't think it would ever be in the cards for him."

Carly forced herself to stop ogling him. "Why not?"

"Well, you know . . . Jamie," he said with a slight shrug. "He and Jamie are kind of a package deal. Personally, I would love to see my brother in a group home for adults. But my dad is very protective of him. Doesn't want him out of his sight, you know? I think it's a big step forward that Dad's agreed to a dog."

Carly couldn't imagine what it would be like to have a severely autistic adult in the house. She could hardly deal with her family as it was, and none of them needed supervision. Or rather, they *needed* supervision but would not accept it. "I meant to ask you if your brother enjoyed the dog show. I was so desperate to get out of that skirt I completely forgot."

His gaze flicked down the length of her. "That was some skirt. And that is a favor I won't soon forget."

"You and me both," Carly murmured. The blush in her cheeks was spreading. "The dog show?"

"It was interesting."

"Fun?"

He gave a half-hearted wince. "I don't know if I would say it was fun." He smiled sheepishly, and the effect was incredibly charming.

"So what happened?"

He laughed a little self-consciously. "I don't want you to think I'm a bad scientist."

"How could I think that from a dog show?"

"You know, I haven't told anyone about that weekend. Not even my dad." He snorted. "*Especially* not Dad."

"Okay, now you have to tell me," she insisted. She propped one elbow on the table, her head in her hand. "I'm all ears."

"The truth is, that weekend was a huge drag."

"Impossible. It was a weekend filled with dogs."

"I know, right? Good dogs, too—it should have been amazing. But

it sucked. My entire professional career has been about cognitive dys-
functions and neurodevelopmental disorders, and the reason I even
went into that field was because of Jamie. I grew up with him. I think
I know him better than anyone, except my dad."

"You don't?"

"You would think. But . . . I could hardly handle him. I was terrible with my own brother, who has a neurodevelopmental disorder,
the very thing I study and teach and research. I was a total fish out of
water one-on-one with him."

Carly was surprised by his admission. "You're exaggerating."

"I wish I was. I'm ashamed, and honestly I don't know why I am
telling you this, because this is no way to impress a woman. I guess I
need to get it off my chest. I figured out that while I study this for a
living, what I know is the brain. And what I got was the personality.
I got really frustrated with him. And he got frustrated with me,
too." He laughed sheepishly. "We practically came to blows in the
airport."

Carly sat up. "You didn't."

"We didn't," he hastened to assure her. He closed his eyes and
shook his head. "Great. You probably think I'm a jerk, ragging on my
autistic brother."

"No! I think you're honest and human and . . . and do you know
how many times I've wanted to haul off and punch my sister? What's
Jamie like?"

Max glanced down at his hand. "Well, he's got a big heart. He's
an artist, like I told you. Loves dogs—you know that, too. He loves
Dad and he gets really anxious when Dad isn't around. And . . . and I
think he loves me, too. The bottom line is that he's so much more than
his disability allows anyone to see."

He put down his drink and told her about a man who collected
oddly shaped rocks, who never missed a day of work, and was obsessed with his clothes. "They have to be pristine," he said. He told
her about Jamie's paintings, and how unique and interesting they

were, a bit like peeking into Jamie's head. He told her it was just Jamie and his dad, that his mother had died a few years ago from a heart attack. And that he lived close by so he could be there quickly if anything ever happened. He told her how, for the most part, things were good, but that there were times when Jamie couldn't communicate the way he wanted to and would grow frustrated and act out. "Those times are relatively rare because he has such a steady routine. Jamie seems content to live in his own head and with dogs."

He told her how he'd been trying to get his father to agree to supervised living for Jamie so that he could be on his own. "I've been trying to convince my dad for a couple of years now. Jamie is twenty-seven. With the right setting, he could do it, he could thrive, maybe learn how to navigate the world a bit better—especially if he has a trained dog to help him. And my dad would have some time to himself."

"Why doesn't your dad like this idea?" Carly asked. "It sounds amazing to me."

"I think what he doesn't like is letting go. He's protective. But who knows? Like I said, he was out last night, so maybe he's coming around to it. But, having said that, the weekend at the dog show made me realize that I don't know what my dad goes through on a daily basis." Max sighed, rubbed his nape. "I've been pretty arrogant about it, I think."

She smiled. "You're being too hard on yourself." She squeezed his arm. "Would you like my expert public relations opinion?"

"I am dying for an expert public relations opinion."

"It's hard to see family objectively, at least in my experience. But how wonderful that you took him at all. How wonderful that Jamie has people around him who care as much as you and your father do."

He smiled gratefully. "Thank you for that. And thank you for listening." He cast his gaze skyward and laughed. "I can't believe I just dumped all my problems on a new friend."

"If that's all your problems, you're living a pretty sweet life, my friend."

"Oh, I've got more, trust me. But I think I'll save them for the next time. What about you? What's your family like?"

"Super dysfunctional. But I love them."

"Come on, give me something. I don't want to be the only one who spent Baxter and Hazel's second date spilling my guts."

Carly groaned theatrically. "I don't know, Max. There's a huge difference between your family and mine—if I start, I will never get to the end of the story because they are all so *extra*. Every single one of them. Completely bonkers, the whole lot."

"Give me an example."

"Okay, here goes. I have a brother who lives in Dallas and steers clear of us except at mandatory holidays like Thanksgiving and Christmas. My sister is very high-strung, always has been, and she's got three small kids who are all over the place. Her husband travels for work to China every month for about ten days and she's alone with them and nearly loses her mind each time. Oh, and my parents? Recently divorced after forty years of marriage. My dad has taken up selling time-shares in South Padre. My mother says one of the reasons she divorced him was because he made terrible decisions, like buying into time-shares. My mother, on the other hand, is playing the field. Incidentally, my dad says one of the reasons he divorced her was because she was always looking for a party. Well, she's found a few. She's dating anything with two legs and a wallet."

Max laughed.

"Oh, you think I'm kidding," she said, pointing a carrot at him. "I'll just leave you with this—when I'm dating someone, I have to date him at least six months before I even *think* of mentioning him to the gang."

"That's just good date management," he said with a laugh. "But it does beg the question—are you dating anyone?"

The question landed with a thud in her head. "Nope." She sipped her drink, then peered into the empty cup. "I've been crazy busy." Which sounded like a practiced excuse. Which it was. She made herself look up and smile like it didn't affect her. "And I'm also not that great at meeting people. I tried the online thing, but when I filled out the form, I sounded so *boring*. I couldn't think of a single cute username. The only decent photo I have of me is half in shadow. And when I tried to take a selfie, they all make me look so insane. So, for right now, it's just me and Baxter. And even he kind of appeared on the scene by accident."

"I see," Max said.

Carly feared he did see, and with twenty-twenty vision. "You?" she asked. "Fighting off the girls? I bet you're very popular on campus."

He looked amused by that. "Why?"

"Because you're cute! And you're nice. And you're smart. That's a home run, Max. And if you're rich, it's a bases loaded home run. You're going to the Super Bowl."

"I think you mean World Series. And I'm not rich." He stretched his legs in front of him and folded his arms across his chest. "But it's nice to know you think I'm cute."

His gaze was on her mouth, and it had the effect of making her heart skip around in her chest. "Is that what I said?" She had to be more careful with her loose lips.

"Pretty sure I heard it with my perfect hearing."

"Then I must have. Well? I do think you're cute, Max."

"For the record, I think you're cute, too." His eyes met hers. "Amazingly, astoundingly, drop-dead cute."

The fluttery thing turned liquid and warm and left Carly feeling slightly dizzy. She tried to think of what to say, something like, *Then maybe we should date*, or *Am I reading too much into this*, or *Do you like to kiss me as much as I want to kiss you? Or Can I crawl inside your shirt and just smell you?* Just something light and breezy, something clever and witty, but all she could do was smile like a loon. "Why, thank you, Dr. Sheffington. I'm suddenly feeling a little floofy."

His gaze drifted lower. "Floofy. I'll take it."

The fluttering in Carly got a little more intense. "But you didn't actually say if there was anyone special?"

"There's one."

Figured. She turned away from him, propping her elbows on the table behind her so that she could better contemplate how ridiculous she could be. What, she was going to meet a great guy through a dog mix-up and suddenly find happiness? Only in the movies, girlfriend.

"It's a little odd."

"Kinky odd?" she asked with a little too much hope in her voice.

"Just a little one-sided. Her name is Hazel and she's awesome."

"Oh *man*," Carly said with a groan of laughter. "You had me, professor."

Max sat up and took her hand. "That's the kind of smooth operator I am," he said, and pressed her hand to his very broad chest. He glanced around them, then leaned close. "I don't want to dispel any illusions you might have about me, especially since you think I'm cute, but I am horrible at dating. I'm horrible at reading women. I honestly can't tell when someone is flirting with me. I'm terrible at drinks or happy hours—"

Carly gasped and shoved his shoulder. "*I'm* like that! I'm *horrible* at happy hours!"

"Right?" he said. "If I ever see a girl I would like to talk to, I can't think of any sort of opening line. And if she talks to me first, forget it— my small talk game really sucks."

"Same!" She laughed with delight. "And I never see the right movies—like I never see Oscar movies because I spend my time at superhero movies—"

"*Really?*"

"Swear. I have a younger brother who used to make me get him comic books."

"And I have this job that puts people to sleep, or they want to know how much the brain weighs or why they can't remember their phone number from first grade, and the next thing I know, I'm in full professor mode." He laughed. "It's a real nerd bonanza over here," he said, gesturing to himself.

"You and me both."

His grin was dazzling. "Superheroes, huh? DC Comics? Or Marvel?"

"Dude . . . DC of course."

Max's grin broadened. Carly could have walked into his smile, never to be seen again, but she was jolted by a dog jumping up onto her lap and panting his bad breath into her face.

"Baxter!"

Max faded back from her, laughing. "They must be hungry," he said. "It's getting late."

She hadn't noticed, but the sun was sliding down into the horizon. Even the young musician was packing up her things. Carly didn't want this afternoon to end. She wanted to sit right here and stare into Max's eyes forever.

He obviously had different ideas. He was picking things up.

They cleaned up, gathered their dogs. On their way to the gate, Carly stopped by to put a couple of dollars into the woman's guitar case. "You're so good," she said.

The young woman grinned. "Thank you!"

"Do you have a card or something? I'd love to catch you in town."

"Oh." The woman patted herself down, then began to dig through her purse. "I don't have a card, but I can give you my name."

"That's okay. What's your website?"

The woman looked up. "I don't have a website." She had found a receipt and a pen, and dashed off her name on the back of it, then handed it to Carly. "I'm playing at Scholz Garten's chili cook-off next weekend."

Carly looked at the piece of paper. *Suzanna Harper*. "Great. Thank you!" Appalled by Suzanna Harper's publicity game, Carly stuffed the paper into her pocket. That woman had some real talent and all she had was the back of a receipt? She resisted shaking her head and hurried to catch up to Max.

Max had hooked the dogs to their leashes and opened the gate for her. They walked out to the parking lot and paused so that he could give her Baxter's leash. "This has been great, Max."

"Yes, it has, and I'm so glad you think so, too. I can't remember the last time I talked so much about myself. I was a little worried."

She had really enjoyed it. She glanced at the parking lot. "I was thinking . . ." She looked down at the dogs.

"That we should totally do this again?"

The flutter in her began to beat like a flock of hummingbirds. "I mean, you know, Baxter obviously really, *really* needs this. And I don't think I'm getting another dog walker."

"Absolutely. It's clear that Baxter's neurotransmitters are not firing on all cylinders."

"I was just going to say that."

"And as I have not had the time to find another dog walker, Hazel needs it, too."

"You have to look out for her. She's your girl."

"Red Bud Isle Park?" Max suggested, his gaze on her mouth again. "Tuesday?"

"Perfect." He put his hand on her elbow.

"I don't know how Baxter will survive until then."

"That's the great thing about dog brains. They have no concept of time." He pulled her close. "Thank you for today, Carly. I hadn't realized how much I needed to talk."

Her gaze went to his mouth, too. Full, plump, kissable lips. *Very* kissable lips. "I hadn't realized how much I wanted to listen. I particularly liked the part where you confessed to being bad at dating."

"I don't mean to brag, but there is so much more where that came from." He dipped his head, slipped two fingers under her chin, and tilted her face up to his. "I'm probably going about this all wrong, but . . ." He touched his mouth to hers. His lips moved on hers, shaping them to his. It was a simple kiss, not overly sexual, but somehow that made it so hot that Carly was surprised she was still standing. And when he did lift his head, he ran the pad of his thumb over her bottom lip. "Hazel and I can't wait for Tuesday."

"Baxter and I . . . are trying to breathe," she stammered.

He chuckled softly, let go of her elbow, and walked across the parking lot, Hazel trotting alongside. Carly wanted to move but her legs felt as buzzy as her head, and Baxter didn't seem to care.

Oh, but Tuesday would not come fast enough.

Twelve

Max had turned into a chatterbox. He shook his head as he pulled out of the parking lot, annoyed with himself. He hadn't meant to talk so much. Jesus, he'd even brought up tenure. "Man, what a nap magnet I've turned into," he muttered.

And that kiss! It had felt the thing to do, and she'd been looking at his mouth, kicking up all kinds of dust in him. So he'd kissed her. He was aroused and her lips were as soft as butter, and she tasted good, and he could have been a goner.

He still couldn't say what exactly was happening with them, but whatever it was, he liked it. A lot.

Hazel surged forward onto the front seat console and lashed her tongue across his face. "Cut that out," he said, but then pulled her forward a little so he could scratch her behind the ears.

He wished he hadn't brought up the tenure thing. It sounded defeatist, and mostly it was fear talking. But it was weighing on him and, he'd discovered belatedly that once he started talking, he couldn't stop. Maybe because he really didn't have that many people in his life he could talk to about things like that. But there had sat Carly, looking interested and cute, and she was listening and engaged, and, wow, he'd felt so comfortable he'd let it all out. He had felt like he could say almost anything to her. He pretty much had—what had he left unsaid today?

He supposed there was some biological basis for that sort of trust to explode out of nowhere, some unemotional delineation between sexual and romantic attraction. But he didn't want to think about that now. For once, he did not want a scientific explanation, he just wanted to experience this heady sensation of attraction and this need to be near her, to talk to her, and the overwhelming desire to touch her . . .

It had been a very long time since he'd experienced anything like this.

On his way to his father's house, he thought back over the serious girlfriends he'd had. There hadn't been so many. His first love came when he was a high school senior and had ended when they went off to different colleges.

In graduate school, he'd met Flavia. The Argentinean beauty was the most significant girlfriend he'd had. He'd once believed she would be his wife. They'd lived together in a tiny studio apartment west of campus. She'd met his family, and she liked Jamie. Max had assumed they would marry. He'd assumed they would research together, teach together, coauthor papers together, and be together for the rest of their lives. Six months after cohabitating, they were through. The fire that had burned so brightly from the moment they'd met flamed out. A couple of years ago, he'd heard that Flavia had returned to Argentina and had a job at a university there.

Since Flavia, there had been other women, but the relationships never lasted more than a couple of months. He never felt ready to get into a relationship, like he didn't have the right mindset. He was too absorbed in his work and the path to tenure. His research had consumed him, and whatever was left of him after that was devoted to his family or laundry or the occasional trip to the gym. He could reasonably deduce that the recent lack of physical contact with a woman was the reason he'd been so eager to jump into bed with Alanna Friedman that night.

He rolled his eyes. Great decision, that.

Nevertheless, it was nice to be in the company of a woman who had nothing to do with work or family for a change. It was surprisingly nice to enjoy a lazy afternoon with dogs and Carly, laughing and talking about everything while some very lovely music played lightly in the background. It was nice to feel so comfortable with a woman who had lips that looked pillowy and soft and silky hair his fingers burned to touch. It was arousing to look into those shining blue eyes and imagine.

Oh, yeah, he imagined. He imagined a lot. He'd wanted more, so much more . . . especially now, after that kiss.

He couldn't wait to see her again.

Max arrived at his father's house with no memory of the actual drive over, given his distraction. He pulled into the drive, let Hazel out, and followed her to the door. They walked into the smell of something delicious. "Hello?" Max called.

"In here!" his dad shouted from the kitchen.

Sometimes, when Max walked into this kitchen, he was struck with a wave of nostalgia so strong that it made him want to sink to his knees with grief. The space looked exactly as it had when Mom had been alive. There were the pair of roosters that hung next to the fridge—her own handiwork, he thought—needle art, cross-stitch, needlepoint, something like that. She would sit at the kitchen table working on it while she waited for the evening meal to cook.

A plastic green plant that she'd picked up at some flea market was on the windowsill where it had always been. It was covered with dust—no one touched it. A porcelain tea set she'd purchased at a museum in Virginia on a family vacation sat in the middle of the kitchen table. Max could never recall his mother using that tea set. It was as if she was perpetually ready for fancy company that never dropped by.

"Hey, Maxey," his dad said cheerfully. He was behind the kitchen bar using the vacuum seal to seal muffins in a bag. He loved that thing.

"Dude," Max said. "Something smells awesome. What is it?"

"Chili," his dad said proudly. "I have perfected the recipe. It's taken some years, but you won't find better in Austin."

Max walked over to the pot and lifted the lid. Hazel, having already hoovered the floor, trotted past him and headed down the hall toward Jamie's room. "That's enough to feed an army, Dad. Are you expecting company?"

"Nope. Sandy is here for a couple of days," he said, referring to his sister. "She's lying down in the back."

Max slid onto a barstool and watched his dad puttering around. His father's skills in the kitchen had vastly improved since his mother's death. In the weeks after she died, her friends dropped by frequently, bearing casseroles and cakes, pies and sandwich trays. Good food, stick-to-your-ribs kind of food. This continued for a few weeks without fail until one night a pair of ladies had dropped by. Max couldn't remember their names now, but they'd stood where Max was sitting now and had howled at some joke his dad had told.

One of the ladies kept stroking Dad's arm in a manner that could be construed to be comforting, or perhaps something more. Max could remember sitting at the table, curious as to what exactly that caress of the arm meant. He'd been so surprised by it that he hadn't even thought of Jamie noticing. But Jamie did notice. He'd become so agitated that he had one of his more volcanic episodes. That's what Dad and Max called them—*episodes*. It was an inadequate word to describe those rare times that Jamie's frustration at being unable to communicate his feelings boiled over into a ferocious caw. When that happened, the sounds he made didn't sound human, and he could get physical, banging his fist on breakable things or throwing them.

Needless to say, his outburst had scared the ladies.

The casseroles and cakes died off after that. Max's dad had re-treated into his new reality, still grieving his wife, still trying to wrap his head around the fact that he was the primary caregiver to a grown autistic son.

Max had been living at home at the time, a newly minted profes-sor. The Sheffington family was small, and Max understood that one day, the responsibility for Jamie's care would fall to him. For that reason, he'd wanted to stay close, to help out his father where he could. But Max's dad wouldn't hear of it. "Either you're going to move out on your own, or I'm going to kick you out," he'd announced after one of their arguments. "I can handle this," he'd said. "That's my son, and I'll deal with him." And to Jamie, who didn't want Max to go, he'd said, "Jamie, Max is entitled to his own life just as you are to yours. I won't hear any more about it from either of you."

"How, Dad?" Max had demanded. "How are you going to manage?"

"I'm going to retire, that's how."

Max had been alarmed, but his father had refused to listen. "Look here, Max, I don't need your approval or your acceptance. I'm still your dad, and you will do as I say in my house. You're a young man and you have your whole life in front of you. I won't have you wasting it worrying about me and Jamie, got that? Just . . . just get out of here and live your own life."

It was around that same time that Max's Aunt Sandy had moved to San Antonio and the opportunity to buy her house had presented itself. Honestly? Between himself and God, Max had wanted to go. He'd been so tired of the sadness and the never-ending attention Ja-mie required.

So it happened that the universe lined things up when Max and his family needed it most. Aunt Sandy moved. Max moved around the corner. His father quite ably handled Jamie's supervision. He also seemed happy to be retired. He liked to putter around his workbench in the garage and build things he thought were useful. He liked to drive Jamie to work at the ACC and back again, stopping off to have coffee with his friends. That he had no life for himself didn't seem to bother him much. Or if it did, he never mentioned it.

Once, Max had asked him if he had any regrets. His father had looked confused. "Regrets? Now why would I have any regrets?" he'd said in a curt tone that suggested he thought his son was an idiot. "I was married to the best woman who ever lived. I have two wonderful sons. I'm healthy and I'm fortunate enough that I can put a roof over their heads and food on the table. What the hell would I have to regret?"

Max didn't ask again.

He looked at his dad now as he finished up sealing his muffins. "How long is Aunty Sandy in town?"

"Hmm? A couple of days. I've got a few plans. Got tickets to that new Broadway musical that's come through town."

That was surprising—Max had never known his dad to be a Broadway kind of guy. "What . . . *Hamilton?*"

"That's the one."

"I didn't know you were into musical theater."

His father laughed. "Well, I'm not, really. But"—he looked up, and there was a twinkle in his eye—"let's just say I've got a new friend who is."

Max's first thought was that the friend was a fishing buddy, which he quickly discarded due to the gleam in his father's eye. It reminded him of the ray of sunshine he'd been feeling in himself today. "Oh. This is news."

His father leaned backward so he could see down the hall, and when he was sure they were alone, he said low, "I've got a new friend, Maxey, and I'm sort of feeling my way through it right now. Not sure what it's all about or where it's going. But I'd like to explore it a little." He grinned.

Max gaped. "You're *dating?*"

"I'm doing something." The old man laughed. He was beaming.

"That's . . . that's *great*, Dad," Max said, and he meant it. And yet, he was so caught off guard he didn't know what to think.

"Well, I hope so. Like I said, we're just friends and I like her a lot. Now Jamie, he's not quite on board with it, so, you know . . ."

"Yeah," Max said.

Hazel's bark interrupted the many questions he wanted to ask—like how and where did he meet her, and how long had this been going on. He slid off his stool and walked into the hall just as Jamie came out of his room, wearing his PUGS, NOT DRUGS T-shirt. "Dad," Jamie said.

"He's in the kitchen. Where's Hazel?"

"Max! Is that you?" Aunt Sandy appeared from one of the bedrooms. She had short gray hair in perfect looped curls all over her head, and wore a red and white striped sweater that stretched over her ample frame. She smiled and tousled his hair like he was a kid. "Your dog came to announce herself with a lick to my face."

The guilty party trotted out of Max's old room. "I'm so sorry. She has some very bad habits."

"Loyal Dad," Jamie said.

"He is, buddy," Max agreed.

"Do you smell that chili?" Aunt Sandy asked. "I'm starving. Are you hungry, Jamie? Toby! Do you need some help?" she called, and continued on down the hall toward the kitchen, yawning.

Hazel barked again. Jamie looked at the dog and clucked his tongue. Hazel sat.

"Let's go check out the chili," Max said to his brother, and turned in the direction of the kitchen.

But Jamie caught his arm and squeezed it. "Loyal Dad," he said. "*Loyal.*"

"He is, Jamie," Max said. "Of course he is." He put his arm around his brother's shoulders. "Loyal Dad," he said, and led his brother down the hall.

Dad was putting bowls around the kitchen table. He'd also made cornbread and salad, apparently, as they were in the center of the table next to the tea set. "It looks like you're feeding the masses," Max joked.

"You're sure going to make someone a good husband, Toby," Aunt Sandy said as she took down some glasses from a cabinet and began to fill them from the fridge. "I always told Melissa that you were the best catch."

"Loyal Dad," Jamie muttered under his breath.

"What's that, Jamie?" Dad asked cheerfully, and spooned chili into his bowl. "Hey, Max, did you hear? Jamie's getting a dog!"

"I did hear that—Aunt Sandy told me. I didn't think you were up for that."

"Why wouldn't I be? Jamie is the best with dogs, aren't you, Jamie? There's a black Lab out there at the ACC that follows him around. He's already adopted Jamie."

Hazel had made her way under the table and pushed between their legs to Jamie. She nudged his hand. Jamie responded with a caress of her head.

"Duke is his name," his dad added as he continued putting chili in bowls.

Aunt Sandy handed glasses of water around, then slid into her seat. "When's Duke coming home?"

"He has to be neutered first, so a couple of weeks after that."

"Labrador. Loyal dog," Jamie said. "Intelligent and loyal."

"Oh, that is so true," Aunt Sandy said. "And such happy dogs, too."

"Loyal dog. Loyal Dad," Jamie muttered.

Max looked at his father, but he didn't seem to notice Jamie's muttering. Jamie wasn't usually so talkative.

"That's what I've always heard," Aunt Sandy agreed. "Labs are the number one dog of choice in American households, did you know that?"

Jamie started to rock in his seat. "*Loyal, loyal, loyal, loyal.*"

Max's dad finally looked up. "What's the matter, Jamie? You don't like the chili?"

Jamie suddenly pushed back from the table and went down on one knee to the floor. He wrapped his arms around Hazel and laid his cheek against the top of her head.

Max exchanged a look with his dad. His dad shrugged.

"Jamie, your supper is going to get cold," Aunt Sandy said.

Jamie did not let go of Hazel, and Hazel seemed happy to let him hang on.

"Yep, we're going to be shopping for a dog bed and some food bowls this week, aren't we, Jamie," his father said as he sprinkled cheese on top of his chili.

Jamie said nothing.

"Jamie? Hop up here and eat your chili," Aunt Sandy said again.

Jamie reluctantly stood up and resumed his seat. He picked up his spoon and stuck it into the bowl. "Loyal dog, loyal Dad."

"Very true," Aunt Sandy said. "Intelligent and loyal."

"Loyal. Loyal. Loyal Dad. Loyal Dad," Jamie repeated, and looked at his father, then at his chili. He began to rock back and forth again.

It was not unusual for him to rock, and the repeating of words, the echolalia, was often seen in people with autism. But still, Max knew his brother well enough to know that something was bothering him. But the hell if he could figure out what. "I have an idea," he said. "I don't have to be on campus before ten tomorrow. What if Jamie came to my house to hang out with me and Hazel? I can take him to work in the morning."

"Oh, that's a great idea, isn't it, Jamie?" Aunt Sandy chirped.

"You want to go with Max?" Dad asked.

Jamie glanced up and glared at his father, startling Max. "Loyal Dad, loyal dog."

"I'm going to take that as a yes," Max said. "Jamie." He waited for his brother to turn and look at him. "Loyal brother. Are you coming with me? We can watch an Air Bud movie," he said, suggesting a series of movies that featured a dog.

Jamie's eyes widened slightly. "Yes," he said. And then he attacked his chili with gusto that made Aunt Sandy happy.

I t was nothing, Max decided later. Something had aggravated Jamie. Dad had probably done something that had annoyed Jamie, but whatever it was, Jamie had clearly forgotten by the time they arrived at Max's house. He sat on the living room floor with Hazel's head on his lap, his attention glued to the Air Bud movie.

Max decided it was a good time to attack his kitchen on the chance that Carly might grace his house with her presence again. He was happily imagining that as he worked, sort of smiling to himself, when Jamie appeared at the end of the kitchen bar. "Dog show."

Max looked up. "Yeah. The DVDs haven't come in yet."

"Loyal dog, Max. Loyal Dad. Dog show."

Jamie was clearly trying to tell him something, but Max couldn't understand what. "You want some popcorn?" he asked.

Jamie clapped his hands and made a high-pitched sound of delight.

Max spent the rest of the evening on the couch on his phone while Jamie watched the Air Bud movie two times through.

He kept thinking about Carly.

He plucked absently at the arm of the couch, and finally, when he couldn't take it any longer, he picked up his phone.

Bad news. Hazel just watched Air Bud and I think she's in love with a golden. How will we explain this to Baxter?

Dr. Sheffington, what were you thinking, letting her watch Air Bud? He's so much hotter than Baxter. His heart will be broken.

Max's phone pinged again—Carly had sent him a picture of Baxter in his current state. He was racked out on his dog bed, with his head firmly in the corner.

If I may offer my professional opinion here, I believe that Baxter's hippocampal volumes are severely reduced.

> I don't really know what that is, but I think it's impossible all the same. Have you seen the size of his skull? It's enormous and I can imagine all kinds of hippos swimming in there. I think he really misses Hazel. And I don't mind telling you that we are both looking forward to Tuesday.

I don't mind telling you that Hazel and I are, too. Very much.

> Are we flirting? Because neither of us knows when that is happening, remember?

I'm not sure, but I think so. I will consult my textbooks.

> I am oddly charmed by your scientific approach. It's surprisingly sexy and makes me want to know more about you. Like, how nerdy are you?

You are in for some dry and tedious detail. I want to know more about you, too. Like, how did you decide on public relations, and who thinks circles of wood are fine art, and what is your favorite ice cream, and what was your second grade teacher's name.

> That is so weird! I was going to ask you if you prefer red or white, and where is the one place you would go if you could leave tomorrow, and how many brains did you have to dissect

to be a qualified brain genius, and when did you first learn to ride a bike.

Ladies first. Start with ice cream.

I ALWAYS start with ice cream. ☺

As Jamie started the Air Bud movie for the third time, one hand flapping with pleasure, Max scooched down on the couch next to Hazel.

He and Carly texted until two in the morning.

He could not wait for Tuesday.

Thirteen

One of the worst Mondays to visit Carly in a very long time—remarkable in and of itself, given her luck recently—arrived with a bang. First, she was late getting up—she and Max had texted every last thought in their heads until the wee hours. When she woke, it was to several text messages left by her sister, complete with exclamation marks, exploding head emojis, and capital letters, complaining that their mother was not answering her phone calls and was probably dead in the ditch, but that Mia couldn't check on her because Will was gone again and she was stuck home with the kids.

Carly thought about pointing out to her sister that their mother might not be answering because she was tired of being tracked like a common criminal, and who texted anyone at six o'clock in the goddamn morning, *Mia*. But this time, Carly was a little curious, too. Usually, her mother called her several times a week, but Carly realized she hadn't heard from her mom at all in the last week. So she began her day driving by her mother's house to check on her.

Her mother was safe and sound and doing yoga in the backyard.

"Since when do you do yoga?" Carly asked as she pulled her jacket around her. The day had not yet warmed.

"Hello, my love!" her mother chirped.

Her mother had never, in all of Carly's life, called her "my love" until a couple of months ago . . . come to think of it, around the same time she started her sexual revolution.

"I began my yoga practice two weeks ago. Penny told me it was the best thing for you, and she was absolutely right. You should try it! It would release all the stress you carry in your face," she said, fluttering her fingers at Carly's face.

"Gee, thanks, Mom."

Her mother pinched her cheek. "You're a beautiful woman, Carly, but you do seem stressed. I worry about you."

Carly couldn't argue. "I'm fine, Mom. Have you been practicing yoga all week and that's why you won't answer Mia's texts? She's worried."

"Don't listen to your sister. I called her back and she didn't answer. And we both know that Mia would worry if she lost a sock in the dryer. It's just her nature. Yours is to be very determined in all that you do, which I love about you, and hers is to worry. And my nature is to look for light. Oh, Carly, I've been having the time of my life!" She began to roll up her yoga mat.

"We all know, Mom." Carly's phone pinged. She pulled it out of her pocket and saw a text from June on her screen. Need you right away! Lord, what now? She texted back: What's going on? And to her mother, she said, "I know you're having this great time and all, but if you could just check in with Mia from time to time, you'd be doing me a huge favor. She blows up my phone when she can't reach you. She's counting on you to watch the kids this Friday so she can go to lunch with her friends."

"And I can't wait to see my little darlings. I'm taking them to Zilker Park to fly kites. When was the last time you flew a kite? It's very free-ing." She breezed past Carly into her house.

"What? You know how to fly a kite?" Carly asked, looking up from her phone. She twirled about and followed her mother into the house.

Her mother was bent over, putting her yoga mat away. She stood up, turned around, and smiled very broadly at Carly. So broadly that she looked younger than her years. So broadly that Carly had a sick little feeling in the pit of her stomach that somewhere, a big fat shoe was about to drop, and probably right on her head.

"Carly? Something *wonderful* has happened."

"What is it?" she asked warily.

Impossibly, her mother's smile got bigger and brighter. "I met someone *extraordinary*."

Okay, no need to panic just yet. Her mother had met several extraordinary people since her divorce. If Carly wasn't mistaken, everyone she met was extraordinary. But she'd never smiled quite like this when talking of those extraordinary people. "Okay," Carly said carefully. "Like . . . how extraordinary?"

"*Very*," her mother said, and Carly's stomach knotted a little tighter. "We're . . . well, I wasn't going to tell you just yet, but here you are, and I think you should know that we're thinking of getting married."

Carly's phone pinged at the same moment she cried out with alarm. "You're *what*?"

"Nothing *big*, of course. Probably a Vegas wedding. You know, pop in, do the deed, pop out."

"Mom? What are you—"

"I mean, we've both been married before, so it wouldn't make sense to have a big wedding. But I would like a dress. I don't care how old one is, or how many times one has been married, which is only one for me, but Shelby Case was wearing a fancy dress on her third wedding. Her third! And it was *white*, can you imagine? Oh! I've got a great idea! We'll make a mother-daughter day and the three of us shop for one!"

Carly's panic burst into full bloom. "Mother! You can't be serious!"

"I am very serious, Carly, and I would like your support. Oh dear, I feared you'd react this way. You're very much like your father sometimes, you know. Very practical." She turned around and went into the kitchen.

Carly was quick on her heels. "I'm reacting this way because it's crazy, Mother. You've been—"

"I want you to be happy for me, sweetie!"

Happy for her? This was the first Carly was hearing of anything serious, and it was already at marriage? "It's a little hard to be happy for you when you're doing something so impetuous, Mom. You've been sleeping your way through half of Austin, and suddenly you're planning a wedding? It doesn't make sense."

Her mother pointed a finger at her. "*That* was the release of pent-up anxiety after forty years of sleeping with your father. And *that* was before I realized my friend's feelings are the same." She grinned.

"Who is he? Who is this guy? Where did you meet him? How long have you actually known him?"

"Don't be so nervous, honey. Really, it wouldn't hurt *you* to live it up a little, too. It's fun. It's invigorating!"

How in the hell could Carly live it up a little when her world was cracking and bits and pieces were falling off? "I'm not nervous. This is so . . ." She had to pause and think of a word that could sum up her utter despair and alarm and disbelief.

"This is my decision," her mother said with a flick of her wrist. "I may be your mother, but I am also a grown woman and I can do as I please."

"How long have you known him?" Carly insisted.

"What does it matter?"

Her mother had a tendency to get defensive when she knew she was wrong. "How *long*, Mom?"

Her mother sighed as if Carly were being unreasonable. "A couple of weeks."

"Oh my *God*!" Carly cried, and turned a complete circle, blindly searching for something that made sense, or at least something to kick.

"Now look. I know it was hard for you to accept that I divorced your father, and it was for him, too. But you have to look at it from my perspective. I gave my best years to that man, and this is . . . well, sometimes you just know. And I know." She laughed, pleased with herself.

"No, Mom. *No*. You can't do this. We have to at least *meet* him before you do anything."

"That can certainly be arranged," she said agreeably. "Just out of curiosity, do you question your father this way?"

Carly snorted. "Dad isn't dating all over town and threatening to run off to Vegas to marry a girl he's known *two* weeks."

"Really? When was the last time you saw him?"

"I don't know. Why?"

Her mother shrugged. "Maybe you should check in."

"Stop it, Mom. I know what you're doing. You're trying to imply something about him so I'll stop asking you questions. Tell me the truth—do you really think it is okay to spring on one of your kids that you're thinking of running off to Vegas without ever having mentioned you were seeing someone? Or letting us meet him? Is that what you would want me to do to you?"

"That's different. You are young and at the beginning of your life, and of course I want to be at your wedding. But I am older and wiser and this isn't my first rodeo. Trust me, you'll feel better about it once you meet him." She gave Carly's cheek a little pat.

The blood was draining from Carly's face. She could feel it leaking out of her, along with everything she ever thought she knew about her parents, about dating, about life. "I can't believe this," she whispered.

"Believe it!" her mother sang happily. "I think you will really like him. Don't look so down, sweetie—you're worried over nothing. Oh!

Will you look at the time? I've got to get dressed and go. Love you!"
she said and disappeared down the hall toward the bedrooms.

Carly's phone pinged again. She glanced down to see June's message: 9-1-1.

On the way to the studio, Carly plugged into *Big Girl Panties* and
hoped Megan had some advice for a mother who was off the
rails. But today's podcast was about self-affirmation. "If *you* don't
believe in you, who will?" she chirped sunnily.

At the studio, Carly discovered that Victor had gotten off the
couch. In fact, he was a hive of activity, cutting and draping that awful aquamarine fabric on the table and onto a new dress form that was
three sizes larger than the average dress form. Even worse, there was
a bolt of shiny lime green fabric propped against the table.

Carly turned with alarm to June. June looked a little sick.

Okay, this was where years of hard work and training kicked in.
Carly pasted a smile on her face and turned to Victor. "Hey!" she said
breezily. "Whatcha got going here?"

"Can't talk," Victor said. "I've got too much to do."

Carly turned back to June. She said, "He's decided he's not going
to show the white pieces." She pointed to a corner of the studio and a
pile of white fabric. When Carly looked a little closer, she noticed that
the pieces were cut up. The white pieces were no longer clothes, they
were a pile of rags. Her gut twisted uncomfortably. She turned back
to Victor.

He didn't bother to look up or offer any sort of explanation. Carly
didn't know what made her more furious—that he'd tossed the white
after all her work to get it into the fashion media? Or that she'd worn
that shit for two solid weeks? "We're doing a YouTube podcast this
week, Victor, remember? The Fashion Divas are going to be discuss-
ing your pieces. Which means your *white* pieces because you pulled
the red. I mean, you do realize that the New Designer Showcase is

right around the corner, right? And that Ramona McNeil is waiting for us to send her something new?"

"I know. I'm starting over."

"But why?" She asked this in a voice louder than was necessary, but she felt herself on the verge of a full-throated, primal scream. "After all that hard work? Why would you do that? Do you really have *time* to start over?"

Victor stopped what he was doing. He pointed his scissors at her. "I'm not showing that collection, Carly. Not now, not ever. I don't feel good about it. Have you seen what people are saying about me?"

"What people?" Carly asked, looking wildly around the studio.

June stepped forward and handed Carly her phone.

It was his Instagram page again. Last night, while she'd been text-flirting with Max, Victor had posted one of the white pieces and the trolls had leapt on the opportunity to trash his design. And then Victor had responded to each and every piece of criticism. "Oh hell," Carly breathed.

"He won't stop," June said. "Just can't keep his fat mouth shut."

"I'm not going to let them walk all over me, Mom!" Victor said.

"Victor, listen to me. You have to stop responding," Carly said. "These posts should be strategically scheduled. That's what *I* do. You make clothes. The reason you pay me is so that I can create a positive impression of you. I can't do that if you are fighting with nameless trolls. And that's all they are. You know that, right? They are nameless trolls and this is nothing but sport to them."

"Yeah, well, it's also my life. Look, I'm sorry. Mom, I'm sorry. But I can't show anything I don't feel one hundred percent."

In the end, there was no reasoning with him—Victor was starting from scratch with the most garish colors he could possibly choose.

Carly called the podcast producer and asked if they could postpone. The answer was no. They were booked all the way through New York Fashion Week.

She left the studio feeling dejected. As if all her hard work was being destroyed. She felt terrible for Victor—she couldn't imagine how difficult it must be to show the world something you had created and watch as people tossed out negative opinions with no compassion and no understanding of the amount of work it required.

Her day did not improve from there. She drove home to think how she could repair the damage Victor had done, to salvage something of the campaign before the New Designer Showcase, and to call Ramona McNeil for the last time.

She could not wait for Red Bud Isle. She couldn't wait to sit on a park bench and stare into the cool gray eyes of Max Sheffington while Hazel and Baxter romped. The trips to the dog park had been the highlight of her life these last couple of weeks. They were the bright spot in a universe that was getting bleaker. And if she needed any reminder of just how bleak, Conrad was on hand to remind her.

He popped up next to the drive so suddenly that Carly first thought he'd been waiting in the bushes. There he was, stumbling and lurching up the incline to the drive when she came through the gate, waving his hand at her. She stopped and rolled down the window, and waited for Conrad to bring the clouds rolling in. "Hello, Conrad. You don't have to try and catch me pulling in, you know. You can call me."

"Oh, that's okay. It's good for me," he said through a wheeze. He braced himself with his arms against the window frame of her car door. She watched a trickle of sweat trace a path down his temple. "How are you?" he asked.

"Good! You?"

"Doing great. We had a Nobel Prize winner of Physics over for dinner last night. Fascinating stuff!"

"I bet." She resisted a roll of her eyes. Conrad was always entertaining the most interesting people on the planet. It seemed impossible that one person could know so many interesting people. The odds had to be stacked against it.

"So, hey, the lease? I need you to drop by and sign it sometime soon. Definitely by the end of the month."

"Oh yeah, of course," she said. "I've been so busy! I'm going to do that this week, but right now, I have to rush." She glanced at her wrist. She was not wearing a watch.

"Sure, sure," Conrad said. "No worries. Just come by this week. Oh, and, by the way, we're going to need a pet deposit." He winced sympathetically.

Carly froze. She looked at him again. "What?"

"You said Baxter was temporary, remember? But it's been a few weeks now, so . . . I mean, unless you're going to surrender him?"

Her throat clenched. She tried to clear it. "Ah," she said, but it came out garbled.

Conrad waited.

"Not surrendering him," she croaked. "How much is the deposit?"

"Five hundred per pet."

Carly must have gasped, or who knows, maybe she fainted and quickly came to, because Conrad threw up both hands and stepped back like he thought she was about to projectile vomit. "Hey, it was Petra's idea. I mean, don't get us wrong, we *love* dogs," he said, tapping his heart with his palm. "But Petra had a problem with an investment property in Santa Monica and said the cleaning bill when you move out could be *horrendous*."

"Horrendous! Have you seen my house? I am very clean."

"Sure, but the dog," he said again.

"Baxter doesn't do anything but sleep all day. In *one* corner of the house."

"Well . . . we think he's been in the herb garden. So, yeah . . . we're going to need that pet deposit."

It was a good thing Carly was in her car, because she might have launched at Conrad, White Walker style, and chewed his head off. But she said, "Okay. Will do!" She put her car in gear. Conrad stumbled a little in his Jesus sandals. She gave him a jaunty wave and drove on to her cottage. "Will *not* do," she muttered as she got out and slammed the car door.

When she walked into her house, Baxter was there in the entry, waiting for her. His tail was swishing across the floor back and forth, and his enormous paws were together in a vee. He looked very excited and impossibly sad at once.

Carly dropped her bag. "I'm sorry." She fell to her knees and wrapped her arms around his neck. "I'm so sorry, Baxter! I'm sorry I *ever* thought about rehoming you. I would never, and I need you to know that. I would *never* give you away, not unless we found a utopia where bassets live freely in a commune. A basset dog ranch with plenty of stuff to smell and organic dog food and couches. *Lots* of couches." She buried her face in his fur.

When she finally sat up, and Baxter had managed to drool on her silk blouse, she thought at least one decision had been made. She was keeping this dog. Or Baxter was keeping her—she wasn't quite sure which way that went. But it was clear that the feeling was entirely mutual.

That evening, while Baxter snored contentedly beside her on her bed, Carly worked on her bills again, trying to find the secret method of squeezing blood from a turnip. She could not find it.

Then she worked on the publicity schedule for the next three weeks, considering Victor had nothing to show. When she'd finished that, she emailed Ramona McNeil.

Dear Ramona,

Once again, thank you so much for the opportunity to put Victor Allen in front of you. I am so excited about his design aesthetic, and I think when you meet him, you will be, too. Unfortunately, sometimes artists reassess their creative vision. Victor has done just that. He is busy creating a completely new show, and it's going to be amazing. But that means I have nothing to show you right now. I am so sorry about that. I know you are frightfully busy, and his spot will likely go to some other deserving designer. I would like to leave you with the suggestion to keep an eye out for Victor. He's going to be a huge talent.

Sincerely, Carly Kennedy, Carly Kennedy Public Relations

She fell asleep on her laptop.

When the light dawned the next morning, Carly felt much better because today was Red Bud Isle.

As they weren't meeting until later in the afternoon, Carly tried to remain focused on work. But the day crawled by. At last, it was time to head in that direction. She just had something she had to do first. Something she didn't want to do, but had decided she had no choice. She was going to swing by her dad's house on the way to Red Bud Isle.

She'd made the painful decision last night to ask him for a loan. Just enough to get her through the next few months so that she could feel more confident about signing a lease. She spent the morning rehearsing her speech. She'd never had to borrow money from her parents before, and she was not asking for a small sum. But she intended to pay every cent back, with interest.

Her father's car was parked in the drive. His yard, unlike her mother's, was neatly manicured. His house was neat, too, and he'd boasted recently that he'd painted the window trim himself.

Carly and Baxter walked up to his door. She tried to open it, but it was locked. That was weird—he always left the door open. She rang the bell.

It seemed to take a little bit of time before her father opened the door. He stood in the doorway, one hand on the door. "Hello, Peach!"

He was a trim man, a little on the small side. His salt-and-pepper hair was mussed, and his shirt, usually ironed within an inch of its life, was buttoned crooked. "Did you fall asleep in your chair again?" she asked with a laugh, and moved forward, intending to step inside.

But her father didn't move. "Peach? Now is not a good time."

Carly laughed a little. "A good time for what?"

His smile was a funny, almost guilty smile.

"Why is this not a good time? Are you sick?"

"No, no, I'm fine. But I'm kind of busy with something." His smile got weirder. The sort of smile a person wears when they think they know you but can't place you.

"Another project, or . . . ?"

"Kind of."

Baxter tried to enter, too, his tail wagging, his attention clearly on something in the house.

"Is it my Christmas present?" she asked, only half joking.

He laughed, too, but really loud and long. "Maybe you could come back later?"

"Come on, Dad, what's going on? I won't stay long, but I need to talk to you."

He glanced over his shoulder.

"Is there someone else here?" Carly asked, trying to see past him.

"No."

She didn't believe him. "If there is no one here, then there must be a ham on the floor, because Baxter is dying to get to something in there."

Her father sighed and he sounded very guilty. "I was going to tell you."

"Tell me what?" Carly stepped up then, pushed the door out of her dad's hand, and walked inside. She immediately saw the woman sitting at the kitchen table in her dad's shirt, her legs long and sleek and very youthful and stretched out to the chair beside her. She looked as surprised as Carly.

Carly had inadvertently dropped the leash, because Baxter was hustling forward, his tail wagging furiously. The woman—or girl?—said, "Puppy!" and bent over to scratch his ears and the scruff of his neck. "*Who's a good boy. Who's a good boy*," she said, petting Baxter. Then she looked up and smiled. "You must be Carla! Because of the black hair. Mia is blond, right?"

"It's . . . it's Carly, baby," her father said.

Baby? Everything around Carly began to swim. She put her hand out, expecting to find the wall, but finding nothing but air. She left her hand in midair and watched, dumbfounded, as the girl stood up and walked to the door in a shirt that hardly covered a thing. She extended her hand. "I'm Hannah."

What was she, sixteen, seventeen? Carly looked at her dad.

"Hannah is my dental hygienist."

"*Was*," Hannah corrected him, and slid her arm around his waist and rested her head on his shoulder.

Carly could not absorb this development. It was like a gong clanging in her head that she couldn't make stop.

"I was going to tell you," her father said weakly.

That was exactly what her mother had said. Everyone was going to tell her something and no one ever did. "That would have been nice," Carly managed to choke out. "Okay. Well!" She looked around her, trying to grasp a way out of this. "I guess I'll talk to you later? So nice to meet you . . ."

"Hannah!" she chirped.

"Hannah," Carly said. She looked around for Baxter, but he was right there, at her feet, staring up at her and clearly wanting to know what was next. At least Baxter wasn't going to do anything to upset her applecart. She bent down and grabbed his leash.

"Don't run off, Peach," her father said.

"I really can't stay. Places to go and all that."

"But . . . you came by for something."

"Did I?" She laughed, and it sounded a little hysterical, and she kept looking at Hannah from the corner of her eye because she did not want to ogle her, but then again, she couldn't believe what she was seeing. Hannah was beautiful. "It was no big deal. Carry on!" she said like a drill sergeant, and with a yank on Baxter's collar, she scurried down the sidewalk to her car.

She loaded Baxter in, and as she pulled away from the curb, she waved at her father with far more enthusiasm than he deserved and sped down the street to the main road.

By the time she reached Red Bud Isle Dog Park, she had worked herself up into a full head of steam. Her father had texted her. I'll call you later, Peach. Don't be upset.

She wasn't *upset*. She was . . . God, she didn't know what she was. Confused? Unnerved? Drifting in and out of reality because everything was suddenly upside down? She tossed her phone onto the passenger seat. She didn't understand how to pick up all the pieces that seemed to be flaking off of her life. Maybe her mother was right—she still hadn't really processed the divorce of her parents, two people who had never spoken to each other in anger in all the years they were married. Carly had been completely blindsided by their split. Maybe she still hadn't really processed losing a job she was really good at. Maybe it was losing one bad client and on the verge of losing another.

And maybe, just maybe, it was simply that everyone in the world was having sex but her. That did not seem remotely fair.

She got out of her car and released Baxter. He raced away from her before she could snap a leash on him—he'd spotted Max and Hazel. Hazel was barking and straining at the end of her lead, eager to see Baxter. Max was leaning up against his car, one leg crossed casually over the other, his hands in his pockets. He smiled at her across the lot, and Carly felt a swirl of so many emotions that she thought she might swoon.

She was suddenly marching across the parking lot before she knew that she was. What did Megan Monroe say? *Be bold. Don't not ask for something because you're a woman. Because you are a woman, learn to ask for what you want in life.*

Okay, well, there was something she wanted.

Max stood up as she neared him. His smile dazzled her, and this was her sun right now, and she was going to bask in it. But his smile turned a little tentative as she got closer. By the time she reached him, he was frowning. He put a hand on her arm. "Is everything okay? You look like you want to punch me."

"Yes. Well, not really. But I don't want to punch you," she said, and a kaleidoscope of butterflies released into her belly and into her bloodstream.

"What is it?" he asked, concerned.

"Everyone—and I do mean everyone, including both parents, my sister, and even Gross Gordon—Gross Gordon! *Everyone* but me is having sex, Max. I am playing the spinster in the sitcom of my life, and that is *not* the part I auditioned for."

Max appeared startled and maybe even a little alarmed and she thought maybe she'd gone too far. But then his gaze slid down her body and back up, and when his eyes met hers, she saw so much heat in them that she began to tingle.

"What part did you audition for?"

"Seductress. Hot chick number one. Sex goddess."

His smile turned sultry. "Then you have been horribly miscast, Miss Kennedy, and that's a problem. I am happy to help, if you think I'm up to it."

Carly was hoping he would say that. She put her hand on his chest. "Oh, I think you're up to the challenge, buddy. How soon can you start?"

He pulled her close to him. "We'll need to work out a few details first," he said, his gaze on her mouth. "But I think I can start immediately." He lowered his head. Her arms slid up around his neck, and Max hugged her tightly to him and kissed her.

He didn't press into her or shove his tongue down her throat like she thought she wanted him to do. His kiss was so easy and ethereal that she had to hang on to his neck lest she melt into a pool at his feet. This was a prelude, a promise of things to come. He casually slipped his tongue into her mouth, like he'd been there all along, and she could feel some very potent sexual desire beginning to bubble, thick as molasses, gooey and warm and sticking to every part of her.

He continued to kiss her so reverently, and yet with so much passion, that every bit of female in her was kindled, ready and willing to explode into a rainbow of pleasure. His hand moved down her hip, his fingers squeezing into her flesh, pressing her into his body. It felt as if the clouds parted and the sun beamed down, and a team of angels gathered their harps and lutes and played the music of lust above their heads.

And then one of the bassets stuck his nose in her butt.

Carly let out a yelp.

Max didn't seem fazed. He grinned, brushed his palm across her cheek to move her hair from her face, and said, in a voice so deep and sexy that she felt in danger of orgasming, "But first, we need to walk the dogs."

Fourteen

There was some discussion about whose house they would go to as they walked along the path. They decided on Max's place, although Carly was at first reluctant. "What if something crawls out of your kitchen while we're not looking?"

"Is that a libido killer?"

"And future grounds for divorce."

"That bad, huh?"

"Pretty bad."

"Well . . ." He brought her hand to his lips and kissed her knuckles like a proper Jane Austen character, then whispered, "I cleaned the kitchen. I even mopped."

"Oh. *Oh*." Her heart sprouted wings. "Max . . . you have no idea how turned on I am right now."

"I'm hoping you'll show me later."

They strolled dopily behind the dogs, hand in hand, smiling at each other like they were in a Cialis commercial. "How long do we have to walk these dogs?" she asked.

"Just long enough to trick them into thinking they've had their walk."

"And then?"

"And then I've got a few tricks up my sleeve."

"Okay. But seriously, it's a little hard to meander along now that I've thrown down the gauntlet."

He laughed. "Then, madam, allow me to pick up the gauntlet and hurry things along." He whistled at the dogs, and they both obediently loped back. Max bent down to attach their leashes, then with a smile that shot right into her groin, held out his hand for her. "Come on. You've got a sitcom to star in."

She slipped her hand into his. "Did I really say that?"

"You really did." He squeezed her hand. "And it was a huge turn-on."

Her blood couldn't run any hotter. It was a good thing that they were leaving the dog park, because Carly was on the verge of asking Max to talk about the hippocampal region or something like it to bring her back to earth.

Max was standing in the open door of his house when she arrived just a few minutes behind him. She quickly checked herself out in the rearview mirror, took a deep breath, and opened the car door. She was not the sort of person to brazenly propose sex like she had, so this was all new territory for her. Was she supposed to take the lead now? Maybe it was her mother's insistence on regaling her with tales of her sexual liberation. Or maybe because she was just that horny. She had a real thing for this guy, and she felt empowered and ready. Tomorrow, she could wonder about the new person inhabiting her skin. At present, she was too tingly to think straight.

She let Baxter out of the back seat, and he raced for the door like he lived here. She followed like she did not live here. Max smiled and opened the door wider. She ducked under his arm and walked into the living room.

He hadn't been kidding—the kitchen was sparkling clean. So was the rest of the house. She put her bag aside and looked at Max.

"Shall I make something to eat?" he suggested.

"Maybe later."

One dark brow rose. "Okay, then. Let me, ah . . . let me just take care of those two."

She nodded. A thought suddenly occurred to her—what if he was bad at this? What if she'd made this grand show of wanting sex with him and he left her unsatisfied? What if *she* was bad at this?

"If you want, you can freshen up. My room is just down the hall."

Did she need to freshen up? Did *he* think she needed to freshen up? *Okay, stop. Stooooppp.* One could not be sexually liberated and then suddenly worry about her hygiene.

"It's clean," he said, as if that was the cause of her hesitation. He smiled and toggled his hand from side to side. "Mostly." And then he turned and walked into the kitchen, whistling for the dogs. Like this was no big deal. Like it was perfectly natural for a woman to ask him to have sex with her.

Well, here went nothing. Carly turned on her heel and walked down the hall.

There were three bedrooms, two of them connected by a bathroom. But at the end of the hall she could see a queen-size bed, covered neatly with a dark blue spread. On a dresser was a tray that held a lot of guy things: loose change, a wristwatch, some receipts. There was a picture on the wall, too, an impressionist painting of a sunset over an ocean. She leaned over to have a look at the artist's name. *Jamie.* The painting was gorgeous. He really was very talented. A stray thought popped into her head—she could get these paintings noticed, unlike Gordon's dumb circles. There was definitely a market for this kind of art.

She moved to the windows and looked through the blinds. Max's view was of a lush backyard with raised beds. It faced east, and she imagined how the morning sun streamed in through the windows.

Carly turned back to the room. She wasn't quite sure what to do with herself. She shrugged out of her jacket and tossed it on top of some joggers he'd draped across a chair. She kicked off her shoes, then climbed on top of the bed.

Her instinct told her to arrange herself to look appealing. She tried a couple of poses, but she didn't have the skill or the personality to pull off a wanton look. Knowing her luck, she would probably appear to have indigestion rather than sex appeal. So she ended up cross-legged, her hands digging into her thighs to quell her nerves.

She heard him walking down the hall toward her and her heart began to pound in time to his footfalls.

Max walked into the room and paused at the threshold, looking at her on the bed.

"I'm supposed to look sexy," she said, gesturing to herself.

"Mission accomplished." He shoved his hand through his hair. "You're kind of gorgeous, actually."

The heat of his compliment scorched her cheeks. "That's flattery," she said, pointing at him. "And it works *great*."

He grinned. "Not flattery. Just truth." He shut the door behind him.

"What about the dogs?"

"They are comfortably arranged on the couch with Dog TV and some peanut butter bones," he said as he moved to the foot of the bed.

"Treats on the couch?" She gave a playful grimace.

"Let it go, Carly," he said with a grin.

"Can I ask you something?" she asked as he leaned over and braced both hands against the foot of the bed.

"I have protection." His eyes moved over her body.

Carly hadn't even gotten that far—that's how awkward she was with this sort of thing, her initial proposition notwithstanding. "I . . . I was going to ask if you're nervous."

Max lifted his gaze to consider her. "A little. Are you?"

"I am. But not because I'm not raring to go." She smiled but realized that sounded like she wanted it fast and furious. She didn't want it fast and furious, she wanted it all. "I mean, after a suitable buildup." And that sounded like she was going to judge his buildup. "Wait. This is coming out all wrong. I mean, I am not usually asking guys to, um . . ." Fuck her? Because that was exactly what she'd asked. But this felt so different from that. This felt like it could truly be the beginning of something. Like it went beyond a physical need. "I mean, you know, building to the big . . ." She tried frantically to think of how to end that sentence without making this less sexy than she already had.

"O," Max mercifully finished for her.

"Something like that," she muttered.

He crawled on all fours onto the end of the bed, his gaze locked on hers. "I have to thank you for working yourself into a lather about this, Carly. It's made me less nervous." He grinned. "If you were superconfident, I'd probably be a wreck."

"Right?" she said, nodding fervently. "I'm really bad at this. I mean, not this," she said, patting the bed. "But this," she said, gesturing between them.

"Are you sure? Because you seem pretty damn good at this to me," he said, gesturing between them, and crawled over her, forcing her back against the pillows. "Would you like to set some ground rules?" he asked as his gaze skimmed over her and settled on her mouth.

"Do we need ground rules?" she asked.

"I don't know. I just want to make sure you're comfortable."

"I'm comfortable," Carly assured him. "I'm more than comfortable. I'm totally into—"

Max suddenly kissed her, silencing her before she could spiral into some long-winded explanation of how she never did this sort of thing, but if she was going to do this sort of thing, she wanted to do it with him. Right now. But Max kissed her back into the headspace she'd occupied when she'd stepped out of her car and had seen him, and she was suddenly back to wanting him in the worst way.

When he lifted his head, he kissed the bridge of her nose and said, "Okay?"

"Let's do this," she said, maybe a little too sternly. She took his head in her hands and pulled him down and kissed him and decided, the moment her lips touched his, that she was going for broke. She was going to enjoy the hell out of this, because it had been a minute since she'd had sex, and she was not going to overthink it, she was not going to burden herself with rules. She was *liberated*.

Eew! Too much like Mom!

Okay, she was a modern woman who asked for what she wanted! Much better.

She was going to go for it, all right, but first, she had to figure out which way was up and which way was down, because Max's hands and lips were all over her and she'd lost touch with where she was in space. His touch was warm and heavy and very arousing. She felt glittery and weightless. She pushed against him, trying to roll him onto his back. Max grunted and resisted her, but Carly leveraged him with her knee and managed to push him onto his back and crawled on top of him.

Max opened his eyes. "Okay," he said, as if trying to figure out the road map.

"I'm going for it," Carly announced.

"Great. So am I." He resumed his caress of her, kissing her in that way that sent her tumbling through some intoxicating space before sinking down into a cloud of sensation and pleasure.

At one point, she tried to remove her sweater, so anxious was she to feel his hands on her skin. But her efforts knocked her off-balance, and she had to catch herself with a palm to his chest.

Max grunted, reached for her sweater, and yanked it over her head. He tossed it aside and cupped her breasts, then kissed her neck at the point where it curved into her shoulder.

It felt as if thousands of fireflies flared through her blood. She shoved at his chest and forced him to lie down, crawled on top of him, and pressed her body the full length of him.

"Look," Max said, and reached behind her and unhooked her bra. "We have to remove some of this clothing if we're going to really go for it." He suddenly surged upward and flipped her on her back again. "If you don't mind, I'm going to take a moment to move things along here."

She realized, even as he spoke, he was kicking out of his pants.

"Agreed," she said, and kicked out of hers, too. And then he was kissing her again, and somehow, they managed to remove their clothes while he kissed her in all the spots that made her sizzle.

And then he slipped his hand into her panties.

Carly closed her eyes. "*Wow.* Okay. This is amazing."

He whispered in her ear, "*You're* amazing."

And that was it, all the talking that was going to happen for the next several minutes, because Carly was floating above the earth on some pleasurable little raft, being pushed and pulled, following the trail of his hands and his lips, spinning faster and faster toward release. His attention to her was a bubbling concoction of warm bare skin and soft lips, and it was all mixing in her, building into a surreal little eddy. This would live with her forever and, holy cow, how had she gone so long without this delicious, earthy activity in her life?

They floated along, kissing and stroking and sliding and sighing. It was twinkly and fiery, it was tender and rough—it was magic. It was all the physical sensations and emotions wrapped into a frothy peak miles high.

Max suddenly sat up and groped around the nightstand next to the bed, producing a condom. Carly sat up, too, and dragged her fingers through his hair, then nibbled his shoulder. "Hurry," she murmured.

A moment later, he pulled her into his body as he slipped in between her legs. He paused, braced above her, and brushed away a strand of hair that draped across her face, and without a word, he entered her.

Carly pitched forward into the sensation, pressing into him, moving with him, losing herself in the sensations he was arousing in her. He caressed her as he moved, slow and fluid, his mouth on hers. Her heart beat at a clip that left her breathless. Her body strained for his, and she caressed his arms and his back, urging him to quicken his stroke. The blur of pure sensation—of touch and smell, of length and breadth—made her wild beneath him, rocking against him, striving for release. Max muttered something and grabbed one of her hands and laced his fingers with hers. He was moving quickly now, pushing her off the cliff. And when she fell, Carly went with a cry of release and gratification, the desire she'd contained for months and months finally spilling out of her.

Max gave in, too, thrusting powerfully into her one last time with a moan against her shoulder.

She didn't know how long she lay there, panting like she'd run a marathon, but Max's voice woke her from the fog. "Way to go for it," he said.

She giggled. "Way to bring it home."

Max lifted his head and gazed at her with an expression that made Carly's heart skip. The regard reflected in his lovely expressive eyes seemed fathoms deep. She was pretty sure there was some sexual liberation shining in there, too. And maybe a hint of surprise and romantic desire, as well.

Oh, but she was feeling all the same things in her. That had felt good. It was the best she'd felt in weeks. Months! A very long time.

He grinned and rolled onto his back, then took her hand into his. "You know what? I never liked Brant so much as I do right now."

She laughed. "I was going to kill him, but now I think we should invite him to dinner."

Max stroked her cheek, his gaze soft and adoring.

Carly felt vibrant and sexy and she could stay in this bed for the rest of her life as long as this drop-dead gorgeous man continued to look at her as he was at this very moment. How had she gotten so lucky? How had her yin fit so well with his yang? How had . . .

"Wait," she said. "What is that noise?"

Max kissed her temple. "That is the sound of two dogs sniffing after us."

Carly sat up. At the bottom of the closed door she could see the shadows of a lot of paws.

"They aren't going to let up," Max said. "Should we let them in?"

"I don't think we have a choice," Carly said.

Max slid off the bed and walked in his gloriously naked form to the door. When he opened it, two basset hounds raced as best they could for the bed. With a squeal, Carly dug in under the covers. Hazel made it up onto the bed in one leap. Max had to help Baxter. After they painted her face with doggie kisses, the two dogs settled at the end of the bed as if it was theirs.

Max pulled on a pair of sweats. "Want some cold pizza?" he asked.

Carly looked at the dogs. Then at him. There were so many emotions swirling in her, filling her up. She smiled.

Max smiled back, and there were a thousand different shades of wonder and happiness in his smile.

"Hell, yes, I want some pizza," she said, and began to fluff the pillows at her back.

Fifteen

Max and Carly were snug in a pillow fort, eating leftover pizza straight out of the fridge, and every so often, pushing a curious dog away. They talked about everything. Carly told him about her last job and how she was laid off. She told him about her parents' divorce and how crazy they were acting now, and how her sister had some unsubstantiated theory that their parents were still totally into each other.

For his part, Max told her about losing his mother and how he'd lucked into his house. How he'd taken Hazel from a professor who was transferring and didn't have room for a dog.

They talked about trips they'd taken. Close friends. Sports they loved. Places they wanted to see. It felt good. It felt natural. Max was pretty sure there was no one else he would rather eat cold pizza with while naked in bed. One day, he would have a son, and his son would ask him what was life, and Max would tell him this. *This* was life. This is what made every day worth getting up for.

"This thing with you has been a very pleasant surprise," he said, after they'd exhausted all the important topics.

"It's fantastic," she said, through a mouthful of pizza. "This must be what winning the Mega Millions lottery feels like." She tossed down the end crust. "What's that?" she asked, and indicated with her chin as she picked up another slice.

Max looked across his room. On the wall next to a chair, he'd tacked some of the calculations and lab results he'd run as part of his research. "That," he said, "is my rehearsal for my presentation of my tenure dossier to the committee."

"Oh," she said, looking at him with bright eyes. "Like, in an auditorium?"

"In a conference room. It's not a lot of people—the committee members, the department head, and . . . well, the other professor up for tenure."

"The professor with the amazing research?"

"Yep, the one with the amazing research." He sighed. "She'll be there to see my presentation. And I'll see hers."

Carly chewed thoughtfully a moment. "That seems kind of brutal, to be honest. If it were me, I'd be obsessing more over what my competition thought of my presentation than the actual committee."

"You have no idea," Max muttered, his gaze still on his graphs and charts.

Carly giggled. "Really? Why?"

Funny, but there was no hesitation in him to tell her the truth. "My situation is particularly awkward. I didn't know I had any competition until recently, and I only found out because of a unique situation."

"What, did she fly a plane with one of those message banners across the sky?"

"Not quite." Max laced his fingers with hers. "The thing is . . . we sort of hooked up one night."

Carly stilled. Her brows rose, and for a moment he thought he'd blown it. But then she burst into laughter. He didn't know what he was expecting, but it wasn't gales of laughter. "What's so funny?"

"I don't know. It's just that you don't seem the type, Max. Like, not at *all*."

"I'm not. I'm not for all the reasons I'm not great at dating. But, you know, it was one of those things—we had a couple of drinks, *too* many drinks, and she said we were being too scientisty, which I took to mean we were overthinking it, and one thing led to another, and, okay, yeah, it happened. And it was . . . it got the job done," he said, and felt himself blush a little. "But the next morning?" He shook his head. "It was obvious that neither of us was going to use the occasion as a jumping-off point to anything else, and I was hungover and miserable, and I didn't know how to get out of it, but then she said that it was really a bad idea because she was up for tenure. That was the first I knew there was anyone else up for tenure this year. She didn't know, either."

Carly gasped. "No! Oh my God, Max—that's unbelievable!" She laughed again. "I'm so sorry! I'm not being insensitive, I swear it, but . . . but that is the *worst*."

"Tell me about it," he said, chuckling a little, too. "I probably shouldn't have told you, but at least you'll know the truth about my rocky path to being denied tenure."

She settled in next to him. "You haven't been denied yet, pal. You should listen to my favorite podcast, *Big Girl Panties*. Megan would tell you to pull them up and believe in yourself, and until the door is shut, it's still open. I've never done it, by the way," she said. "The one-night thing."

"I wouldn't advise it," he said, putting his arm around her. "It's fun in the moment, but afterward, in my experience, you definitely have to face some feelings about yourself you'd rather avoid."

"Oh, *interesting*," she said. "What feelings did you have to face?"

"I'll just say I'm not that guy, and in the light of day, I didn't like that I'd been that guy. But it happened, and life goes on, and I'm going to present my findings to the full departmental committee and Alanna and hope for the best."

"I think you're amazing, no matter what," she said. "I mean, you literally know how the brain works. I don't think I could ever understand it."

"Sure you could." Max pushed aside the pizza box. "Give me your hand."

She put her hand into his, and he turned it palm up. Carly laughed. "Are you going to read my palm now? Please tell me if I'm going to get a job soon."

"The fascinating thing about the brain is how it takes in and processes information. The strongest pathways are your senses. Like, the smell of apple pie may remind you of your grandmother's house."

"The smell of anything being deep fried reminds me of Grandma," she said.

He traced a line across her palm. "What do you feel?"

"A really smart guy tracing a line across my palm, and my brain is wondering if it's a joke."

He changed direction and moved his finger up her palm and to the inside of her wrist. Her lips parted a little.

He moved a little farther up, to the inside of her elbow. "Still feeling a guy tracing a line across your palm?"

"No." She looked into his eyes. "I feel an ocean. And there are waves and peaks and valleys, and I feel a little unsteady."

"How interesting. Because my gonadal hormones are taking a dip in that same ocean." He lifted her hand and kissed the inside of her wrist. "When you experience something, as opposed to reading or hearing, you tend to remember it longer."

"So neuroscience is about experience?"

"In a way."

"I'm going to remember this night for the rest of my life."

"Me, too. It's indelibly imprinted right here," he said, tapping a finger to his temple. He leaned over and kissed her again. And then he got up, shooed the dogs out, and leapt onto the bed. "And now I'm going to give you something spectacular to remember."

Carly squealed with delight. "I can't wait!"

Max was happy. And in his bed, with this woman, he really could believe there was nothing that could derail them. This felt meant to be.

Carly woke up the next morning in Max's bed feeling like something big and wonderful had happened to her, and it wasn't a dream. It was real. They had started something really great last night, she could feel it in her bones.

She dressed quickly so she could dash home and change for work. Max had propped himself up on one arm to watch her. "How are you this morning?" he asked.

She pulled on a sneaker. "I'm pretty damn good, Max Sheffington. I rarely make it this far in most relationships I attempt. How are *you* this morning?"

His gaze languidly moved over her. "Fucking fantastic."

"No morning-after regrets? No facing any feelings you've avoided?"

"Not at all. I am very much looking forward to all the feelings."

Carly grinned. She stood up and brushed her fingers through his hair, then trailed them down his cheek to his chin. "So . . . we're doing this? We're going to be a thing?"

Max got off the bed. He pulled her into his arms. "We are *so* going to be a thing." He kissed her, then put his arm around her shoulders and opened the door to the bedroom.

Baxter and Hazel were waiting for them like two little sentries. They both instantly turned and trotted down the hall as if they knew where they were all off to.

Max walked with Carly to the front door. As he opened the door, her phone rang. "When will I see you?" he asked as she dug around in her bag for the phone. When she didn't find it, she turned from the door to prop her bag on a brick planter so she could better search for her phone. "Tomorrow?" She found her phone and looked at him. "Maybe we could try out Barkin' Springs?"

"Perfect."

Carly looked at her phone. It was a message from her mother. You may meet your future stepfather tomorrow. Jesus. She'd managed to forget that looming disaster in the last twenty-four hours.

"Dinner after?" Max asked. "I know a couple of places that take dogs."

"Wait," Carly said. "Something just came up. I can't do tomorrow." She would deal with this when she got home. "How about Friday?"

"Friday," Max agreed. "Barkin' Springs and then dinner?"

"Yes! And then . . . my house?"

"I thought you'd never ask."

"I'm excited." Carly rose up on her toes and kissed him. He kissed her back, anchoring her to him with one arm. And when he lifted his head, he kissed the tip of her nose and said, "Are you forgetting something?"

"I couldn't find them," she said, assuming he meant her panties.

He looked at her funny. "I meant your dog."

"Baxter!" she cried and scooped down to give him some love. "I'd be lost without you."

She stood up and kissed Max once more, then she and Baxter trotted off together to her car. Halfway there, she turned and walked backward, unable to take her eyes from this man. Unable to believe this had actually happened to her, the unluckiest person she knew. Maybe this was her reward for having done everything right. Maybe at long last, she'd found the right guy. "Hey," she said. "This?" She gestured between them. "It's really awesome."

Max leaned against the post. "It really fucking is."

She beamed with delight. "This is really happening, isn't it?"

"Happened, baby. It's already embedded in your hippocampus."

Carly laughed. She got in her car, waved once more, and drove away. She was on top of the world. She was flying over everything, looking down at all the poor schlubs who hadn't had their dogs mixed up with Hazel and a gorgeous scientist. This was what it felt like to fall in love, wasn't it? She was falling in love. She was in love with life.

This she decided, was going to be a gorgeous, beautiful day.

Sixteen

After Carly left, Max picked up his mail. He hadn't looked at it in a few days, and as he was sorting through, he found the DVDs of previous years of the National Dog Show he'd ordered for Jamie when they were in Chicago. He decided he would drop them off at his dad's house on his way to work. Jamie would already be at work, and his dad would probably be off having coffee with the guys.

At his dad's house, he parked in the street and jogged up to the side door they always used when the garage door was closed. Predictably, his father had left it unlocked. Max carried the mailer with the DVDs into the kitchen and was looking around for something to write a note with when he heard what he thought was someone in the throes of sex.

Stunned, he paused a moment, listening. That was definitely the sound of sexual escapades. He put the package down on the bar and wondered what he should do. Was it a party of one? Jesus, was his dad into *porn*?

A woman cried out, and Max jumped. *That* was a living, breathing, moaning woman behind the closed door of his father's bedroom.

Max backed up so quickly that he hit the wall, and with alarm and adrenaline shooting through him, he vacated his dad's house so quickly that he forgot to leave a note.

In his car, he sat in the driver's seat, staring blindly through the windshield, his heart pumping with adrenaline. Who *was* she? His dad said he had a friend, but . . . but this was highly unexpected.

He put the car into gear and drove away from his father's house, surprised and unsettled by this sudden turn of events.

His mind was still racing when he reached his office, and he sat down behind his desk and put his head in his hands. It wasn't that he didn't want this for his father. He very much wanted his dad to be happy. But what about Jamie? What about . . . what about the picture of Mom in Dad's room? And the pillows on Dad's bed that Mom had embroidered? And shouldn't they at least have Jamie in a group home before something like this happened? Shouldn't that be the natural order of things?

Max's computer pinged, yanking him back to the moment. He glanced at his screen. It was an email from Dr. O'Malley.

Dr. Sheffington:

Please consider this to be your formal invitation to present a summary of your tenure dossier to the Department of Natural Sciences Tenure Committee for consideration. The committee will determine whether or not your request for tenure and the supporting work should be forwarded to the dean and the campus tenure committee for further review. You will have thirty minutes to summarize and take questions from seven committee members. Time and date to follow in a separate email.

Yours, Dr. O'Malley, Department Chair

This was the last thing he wanted to think about right now. What he needed was days of preparation, to ask Drake to workshop the presentation with him so that it was as concise and informative as he could get it. But he'd just started this amazing thing with Carly, and his dad had obviously started something, too, and there was Jamie to consider in the middle of it all, and his mind was a million miles away from his research.

Max's thoughts continued to race as he taught his introductory class on the body's nervous system. Fortunately, he'd taught this particular unit so many times he could do it by rote. While his mouth formed words, his mind went over his upcoming presentation, about all he needed to do. About the veil of disappointment that was starting to settle in over him.

He also thought about Carly. Or rather, she was there, perched like a bird above his thoughts, all colors and shapes and sparkling things, whereas his thoughts were generally algorithms and equations and lists.

He thought about his dad, about how this could be the opportunity to speak seriously about moving Jamie to an adult home. Maybe he could at last convince his father that he and Jamie both needed their own lives, especially now since his father appeared to actually have one. Or was this merely recreation for his dad?

Max was so lost in thought that when he dismissed class and was headed back to his office, he didn't see Alanna until she waved her hand in his face right before he might have bowled her over. "Sorry!" he said. "I didn't see you."

She smiled sympathetically. "You must have gotten the email from O'Malley, too."

He shoved his fingers through his hair. "Yep. So. I guess it's me and you."

"Look, Max . . ." Alanna paused, looking around her. "I don't want this to be weird. I have always admired you and your work. I want to wish you the best of luck."

He was grateful for that. "I don't want it to be weird, either, Alanna. You've done some really amazing work. I wish the best of luck to you, too, but I don't think you're going to need it. They'd be idiots not to put you forward."

"Thank you, but I think the same about you. You're an excellent teacher, you know that? You have a knack for making some pretty complex concepts seem simple. And, really, who knows, right? So many factors go into this decision, right?"

She was being modest. "I guess."

"Well . . . good luck," she said.

"Good luck to you, too."

Alanna smiled and walked on.

He watched her go. Intuition was a phenomenon that was not well understood, as it couldn't really be quantified. But studies had shown that people who trusted their gut instincts were right more often than not. Max's gut instinct told him Alanna Friedman would be a tenured professor in the next few months. Seeing her had somehow confirmed the inevitability to him—he was going to have to wait for tenure. Again. Which meant grants and other sources of funding for his research would be harder to get. It was just the nature of the beast.

The realization dampened his mood even more.

His mood did not improve as the day wore on, and that night, exhausted by his emotions and dilemmas, he wanted to talk to Carly.

Hazel presented me with a gift today. Would you like to see what it is?

That looks strangely familiar.

Thank goodness. Because all my underwear is accounted for.

What is Hazel doing with them, if I may ask?!?

Sleeping with them. I would take them from her—for safekeeping, of course—but I don't want to upset my awesome dog and I don't want to come off as creepy and scare you away. So let's pretend I never said that.

It would take something weirder than that to scare me away. Speaking of things that don't belong to us, I found this stuffed in my bag along with my sweater. My plan is to bedazzle it and leave it in your mailbox. It's called *dress for success.*

Carly included a photo of his favorite knit cap.

Did you steal my beanie? Because if you did, you are definitely the kind of girl I've been wanting to meet for a very long time. Pretty, unafraid to wear big shoulders or lock herself into a skirt, and with her own beanie BeDazzler. I'm falling hard.

☺ ☺ ☺ Just wait until I dress *you.* I think I'm falling hard, too. I wish it was Friday.

Me, too

Baxter says good night and kisses to Hazel

Hazel says good night and that she really misses you, which is kind of crazy. Everything is kind of crazy right now.

Max's mood was somewhat improved the next morning because he got to pick up Bonnie, the Australian shepherd with the missing back leg. Miranda Hastings, the Austin Canine Coalition manager, led Max through the kennels—where dogs of all shapes and sizes, of all ages and breeds, and all with eager, wagging tails—were waiting for volunteers to come walk them.

"This is Bonnie," Miranda said when she reached one of the larger kennels. The dog was dancing with delight on her three legs, happy to be noticed. Happy to be picked. Miranda opened the kennel door, and Max went down on one knee. Bonnie planted one front paw on his shoulder.

"She was hit by a car and the owner surrendered her. Couldn't afford her medical care."

If Bonnie held a grudge, she didn't show it. "Anything I need to know?" Max asked. "Any special instructions?"

"Nope. She's very agile even with the missing leg and supersmart. Aren't you, Bonnie?" she said, ruffling the dog's fur. "Aren't you a good girl?"

Max quickly discovered that Bonnie was so eager to please, it was a little heartbreaking. At least she would get a lot of love in his lab—the students and his two research subjects flocked around her, cooing to her and petting her.

Like Clarence, Bonnie would be joining his labs until she was adopted out or the semester ended. "You can probably count on having her around awhile," Miranda had said. "Disabled dogs, old dogs, and black dogs are always the last to go."

After Bonnie was picked up by an ACC volunteer that afternoon, Max went home to collect Hazel, then headed to his father's house. He'd thought about it, and he'd decided that he was going to talk seriously to his dad about finding a place where Jamie might be comfortable and could live a little more independently.

When Max opened the side door, Hazel raced ahead, running for Jamie's room like she did every time she was in this house.

Max found his father in the kitchen. He had the oven door open and was checking on something inside. "Oh, hey, buddy!" he said cheerfully when he glanced up to see Max.

"Hi, Dad."

"I'm glad you're here. I made some chicken Parmesan tonight. It's a new recipe."

"Smells delicious," Max said. He went to the fridge and opened it and grabbed a beer.

"Max!"

He turned toward the hall as Jamie came barreling in, grinning. "Dog show," he said, and held up the case for the DVD.

"Great, you got it," Max said.

"Got it," Jamie said. He turned around and went back down the hall.

"He's been building one of those ships in a bottle," his father said. "He's obsessed with it. It's good! A very painstaking process, too—I wouldn't have the patience for it, but Jamie? He spends all evening back there working on that and watching dog shows."

"Yeah, he's pretty self-sufficient in a lot of ways," Max said. "I've actually been meaning to talk to you about that."

"Me, too, son," his father said, and pulled out some lettuce and vegetables from the refrigerator. "I've got some ideas."

That was unexpected. "Oh. Great. So do I. I, ah . . . I stopped by—"

"*Yoo-hoo!*"

The woman's voice startled Max so badly that he knocked his beer bottle against the counter. Hazel, hearing the intruder, came racing out of Jamie's room, barking wildly. She tried to negotiate a turn toward the front door but missed and slammed into a barstool. But she bounced back up and carried on with her mission.

"Well, aren't *you* a cutie," the woman said, presumably to Hazel, and then Max heard the unmistakable sound of heels coming down the hall from the front door . . . the front door they never used. Max looked at his dad.

His dad was beaming just like he had been the day he told Max he had a date. Beaming like he'd bought a Maserati. "Hey, could you put Hazel in the yard?" he asked Max. He was moving, wiping his hands

on the apron Max's mother used to wear and striding toward the front
door that no one ever used.

Max put down his beer bottle. He whistled at Hazel, walked to
the back door, opened it, and sent her out. When he stepped back into
the kitchen he heard the whispering and the giggling and then, with a
wince, he realized he was hearing the definite sounds of kissing. He
turned toward the stove so that he could get his shit together. And
when he turned around, his dad was walking into the kitchen with a
woman on his arm.

The woman was attractive, petite, with a neat blond bob and a
slender figure. She was so tanned that he instantly thought of a tan-
ning bed.

"Oh my! Who is *this* tall drink of water?" she asked, boldly looking Max up and down.

"This is my son Max," his dad said. "Dr. Sheffington on campus."

"You weren't kidding when you said he was *handsome*," she said
appreciatively. "If I'd known that, I might have asked *him* out for a
drink!"

Max flinched at the idea, but his father laughed. "Max, this is
Evelyn. She's the reason I'm glad you stopped by this evening."

Max was stunned, but he managed to walk around the end of the
kitchen bar and offer his hand. "Hello, Evelyn. Very nice to meet you."

She took his hand in both of hers and squeezed it warmly. Max
realized, dumbly, that she was speaking, but he hadn't heard a word
she said because he was still trying to wrap his head around this idea
that his dad was dating. That there was another woman in his dad's
life who wasn't Mom. That this wasn't a recreational thing, this was
a *real* thing. He couldn't get over how happy his dad looked. Ridiculously happy. Besotted.

"Wine, Evelyn? I am making my specialty—chicken Parmesan! It's
a new recipe."

"Well, that sounds lovely. And, yes, Toby, I would very much like
a glass of wine."

Max stood firmly rooted to his spot, amazed once more. His dad didn't drink wine. He'd never seen a bottle of wine in this house in all his life.

"Would you like me to get it?" Evelyn offered.

And she'd been around enough that she knew where this phantom bottle of wine was?

"No, no, you sit. You are our guest. Max can get it," he said, and gave Max a look as he disappeared around the corner to the pantry. He returned with the bottle, which he thrust at Max.

"Ah . . . corkscrew?"

"Right there, Son."

Max picked up the corkscrew from the counter and set to opening the wine. He glanced at Evelyn. She was smiling at him sympathetically, as if she knew he was uncomfortable. And, boy, was he uncomfortable. He wanted to leave, to let his dad have his date. He needed time to process this shift in their family universe. But what about Jamie? What would Jamie do when he saw this woman in their kitchen? Had Dad thought of that? Had Jamie already *seen* this woman in the kitchen?

His dad handed him a wineglass, also a new development. Max poured the wine and handed it to Evelyn, then stood back, not unlike a bartender.

"I'll have one," his father said.

Max looked at his dad. "You will?"

"Maxey," his dad said. "Glasses are up there."

Max obediently poured his dad a glass. As he handed the stemware to him, a door closed from somewhere down the hall. Max steeled himself—Jamie was about to discover Evelyn. He could be very unnerving when he was surprised, and Max worried there'd be some sort of episode. But when Jamie walked into the kitchen, he looked around, his gaze landing on Evelyn, and said, "Dog show," and ran his hands down the T-shirt he'd bought in Chicago.

"Very nice," Evelyn said.

Jamie studied her a moment, then turned on his heel and headed back down the hallway.

Max stared after his brother. And then at Evelyn. "Sooo . . . you've met Jamie?"

"I have!" she said cheerfully.

Max turned back to his dad in shock, but his dad was busy with the salad.

"So, Max, you're the *brain scientist*," Evelyn said.

Funny, she said it the same way Carly had in the beginning. "Ah . . . yes."

"I heard we only use ten percent of our brain. Is that true?"

He really didn't want to talk about brains right now because there were too many questions rumbling around in his. "No," he said, and tried to smile. "Not true. Where did you and Dad meet?"

"Tinder."

Max's mouth dropped.

"We did not meet on Tinder," his dad said with a laugh. "Evelyn likes to joke around."

"You like it when I joke around, Toby."

"I like it when you do a lot of things." His dad winked.

"Okay," Max muttered, and looked around for an escape hatch.

"Toby! Your son is standing right there!" Evelyn said with a girlish giggle.

"He's a grown man," his dad said jovially. "He knows how these things go. Max, will you set another place? You're staying for dinner, right?"

"I wasn't—"

"I insist, Max!" Evelyn said. "Toby, tell him he has to stay. Please, Max. I've so wanted to meet you."

"You have to stay, Max," his dad said.

His father was smiling, but his eyes were narrowed slightly, just enough that Max got the message. "Sure," he said tightly. He went to the cabinet to get another place setting. He took it to the table while his dad and Evelyn continued to flirt.

The table was set for four. He would be adding the fifth setting. But . . . there were only four of them here for dinner. "You already set it," Max pointed out.

"Hmm?" his dad said and had to work to turn his attention from his date. "Oh. Yes. Evelyn has invited her daughter to join us."

"My *daughter*," Evelyn said heavily. "I'll explain to you, Max, just as I explained to Toby, that my daughter isn't quite on board with her mother having a boyfriend."

Boyfriend? So it was that official? How could his dad have a girl-friend and not have told him? How was he just hearing about this? And moreover, why was he so disturbed by it? He couldn't make sense of his own emotions.

"I don't know this for certain, but I think she doesn't like the idea that I have a boyfriend when she doesn't. You know how that is," Evelyn said. "I mean, not *you*, obviously, because I imagine you are dating all the time. Just look at you—very handsome! But in general. What do you call that? Do you call it jealousy?"

"I'm not a psychologist," Max said. His dad shot him a look.

"Yes, but isn't it all the same, the brain sciences?" she asked, as if Max wasn't certain what sort of brain scientist he was.

"Oh, this came out perfect," his dad said as he pulled a dish from the oven. "I'm going to put in the popovers now. They won't be as good as yours, though, Evie."

Another stunning development. Max had never known his dad to bake. And she had a nickname. Yeah, okay, this was fucking *official*.

"I've been making them a really long time. Can I help you, Toby? Do you want me to do something?"

"Could you toss the salad?"

"I'd be delighted!" She took her wine around to the other side of the bar and picked up the salad tongs.

They were puttering around like they'd done this a million times and Max wanted to demand an explanation. How long had this been going on? Why was it a secret? Where was it going?

He might have demanded, too, had the knock not sounded on the front door. In the backyard, Hazel began to bark.

"I'll get it," Max said, and walked out of the kitchen. He made his way to the front door, still the door they never used. Were they going to start using it now? Even that irritated him.

Max opened the door. And stood, paralyzed, unable to speak.

He couldn't say which of them was more shocked—Him? Or Carly?

Seventeen

For the second time in her life, Carly's mind could not process what her eyes were seeing. She could not comprehend why Max was standing at the door of her mother's new boyfriend's house. He should not be here. He didn't know her mother. Oh hell—was she at the wrong house? Had she been thinking about him so much that she'd accidentally driven to his house? She leaned back and looked at the house.

This was not Max's house.

She heard a dog barking, and she knew that bark instantly. That was Hazel. The barking dog was Hazel, and this was Max, and this was definitely the address her mother had given her to meet her new boyfriend. What were Max and Hazel *doing* here?

Max wasn't smiling. He looked stricken. Sick, almost. Stunned. Like a man who had been caught red-handed. Like a man who had seen something awful or had done something awful.

And then it hit her—Max didn't look that way because he'd murdered anyone. He looked that way because he'd been caught with *their parents.*

Carly's mind said no, but when she tried to say it, it came out in a shriek. She whirled around—to do what, she didn't know—but Max caught her by the hand before she could run screaming into the street.

"Carly," he whisper-shouted. "Wait. *Wait.*" He made her turn around, then quietly shut the door behind him.

"Did you *know*?" she whisper shouted back at him.

"No, of course I didn't," he said, frowning. "I didn't even know my dad was seeing someone until yesterday. And this?" he said, gesturing wildly to the house at his back. "Tonight? I had no fucking clue. I'm as shocked as you are."

She began to shake her head. "This can't be happening, Max. It *can't.* This is a freaking disaster!" She shook her hands as if she'd burned them, trying to shake this off. She tried to see around Max, certain her mother would come barreling out that door at any moment. "What are the odds?" She lunged for him, grabbed his shirt in both fists, and shook him. "*What are the odds?*"

"I would say infinite." He covered her hands with his and gently pried them from their grip of his shirt.

"What are we going to do?"

"I don't know," he said. "I don't know how long or how serious—"

"Oh God," Carly said, and slapped a hand to her forehead. "Oh my *God.*"

"What?"

"It's *serious*, Max!" She was almost levitating with anxiety. "That's why I'm here! Because my mother very casually announced to me a couple of days ago that she and some guy were going to run off to Vegas to get married!"

"*What*?" Max looked back at the house. He suddenly grabbed Carly's elbow and marched her out to the drive, away from the house and any ears. "What did you just say? Why didn't you tell me? Seems like something you might have mentioned when you were telling me about your family."

"Because you don't know her, and, honestly, my mother says crazy things all the time. She's a little out there." She covered her face with her hands. "I can't believe this is happening."

"*Fuck*." Max groaned. He looked back at the door.

"We have to make them promise they won't," Carly said. "That's the best thing to do, isn't it? We just go in there and tell them this isn't happening, and—"

"We can't," Max said. "Jamie is in there and he's already met your mother. I can't do anything to cause a scene and set him off. We need to think about this."

Carly could feel the blood draining from her. "My mother has met your *brother*?"

"Apparently," he said. "We need to talk to them about this . . . but preferably away from Jamie and this house."

"What are we going to do, just sit there and act like everything is okay?" she asked, gesturing wildly to the house, bouncing up and down on her toes in distress. "This can't happen, Max! I mean for so many reasons, right? *Right*?"

"I know, babe," he said softly, and squeezed her shoulder.

Shoulder squeeze notwithstanding, he did not sound confident. How could he be? This was insane, and of course it would happen just when this relationship between her and Max had started. This really wonderful relationship that was so good and pure and so full of hope and wonder. The real deal. The falling in love. All of it. Her mother really had a knack for ruining everything. "What are we going to do?"

He rubbed the stubble on his chin as he thought for several long moments, then announced, "I got nothing."

"How can you have nothing? You're a scientist!"

"You can't expect me to know what to do about this," he said. "I study the brain, not the heart, and besides, it is my *father*, and I had no idea, and I am a little freaked out right now!"

"This is a disaster—"

Max took her hands in his before she corkscrewed herself right into the ground. "Okay, take a breath. How about this—we get through this evening and see how much we can learn about their plans. Let's see how serious it really is. Then we'll figure out what to do next."

"But . . ." Carly wanted to ask what happened if this was really serious between their parents. But she couldn't even bring herself to ask because the answer, whatever it was, would be devastating.

Max seemed to understand. He glanced over his shoulder, then put his arm around her and kissed her quickly. "We'll figure it out. But let's just get through tonight and then see what's up."

There really was no other option at that moment, and Carly couldn't deny she wanted to know what was up with those two. She nodded. "Okay."

"Ready?"

"No! But let's go," she said. She pulled a bottle of wine from her tote bag and hitched it under her arm, then walked with Max to the door.

Max led her inside, and she walked past dated furniture, through a living room where the drapes had been pulled closed, and into the kitchen. There was her mother, bustling around as if she already lived there. Her mother looked up and smiled. "Ah, there you are, Carly! You're only a few minutes late."

Carly looked at Max sidelong. Their relationship was so new that she hadn't yet explained her mother to him.

Her boyfriend—*Max's father*, God save him—put down his oven mitt, wiped his hands on his apron, and walked around the bar to greet her. His smile was as warm and charming as his son's, and she instantly liked him. He was shorter than Max. He had a kind face, a thick head of gray hair, and curiously, a missing forefinger on his left hand. "Hello, Carly. Welcome."

"Hi. Thank you. Very nice to meet you."

"Toby Sheffington," he said, shaking her hand. "And this is my son—"

"Yeah, funny thing," Max said, interrupting his dad before he made the introduction. "Carly and I have actually met."

"*What*?" her mother trilled. "Well isn't this *wonderful*! It's already a family affair! I want to hear how you two met, but first, Carly, would you like some wine?"

Carly held out the wine she'd brought. "Yes, please. A bucket of it if you have it."

Everyone in the room looked at her with surprise.

"Just kidding," she muttered. But *so* not kidding. She was going to need a new kind of fortitude to get through this evening.

"So," Max said, and put his hand to the small of Carly's back, giving her a nudge toward the barstools. Mr. Sheffington took her offering around the kitchen bar, poured her a glass from an open bottle, and slid it across the top to her. Carly picked it up and took a slug, and as she did, she caught her mother's disapproving look. She carefully put the glass down.

"So, umm . . . where did you two meet?" Carly asked with as much enthusiasm as she could possibly muster. Which was none.

"At the Austin Canine Coalition," Mr. Sheffington said. "We're volunteers there."

Carly laughed at a pitch that was way too high for her. "My mom went to the ACC and came back with a dog and a boyfriend and all I got was this lousy T-shirt."

Mr. Sheffington laughed. "That's one way of looking at it."

Her mother did not laugh. One of Max's brows arched in the silent question of what exactly she was doing. How was she supposed to know? She couldn't think right now.

Carly's mother looked at Max and asked, "And how did the two of you meet?"

Oh no. Her mother was going to have to deal with her. "Well," Carly said, before Max could answer. She picked up her wineglass again. "You remember the dog you came back with that I had to take? He got mixed up with Max's dog."

"Oh! Max, does that mean *your* delightful pup is the same pup someone left at Carly's house?"

"That's her," Max said.

"And did you get Carly's sad dog?"

"For a time," Max said.

"This is so much fun!" her mother declared. "Who would think we'd all *four* meet! This only happens in those Nora Ephron movies, but here we are, and really, doesn't it make everything so much easier that we're all acquainted?"

This was no Nora Ephron movie. This was not easier in any shape or form. This was horrible.

"Carly, I understand you're in fashion," Mr. Sheffington said.

"Not exactly," she said. "I'm a publicist for a fashion designer who will be showing in the New Designer Showcase in New York."

"Max is a *brain* scientist," her mother said. "That's a job that requires a very high intelligence." Her mother waggled her brows at Carly, which, knowing her mother, was an indication that she thought Carly ought to be impressed with this fact.

"Yes, he, ah . . . he mentioned it." She glanced at Max for help. He looked terribly ill at ease.

"I hope you like chicken Parmesan and popovers," Mr. Sheffington said to Carly, and held out a pan so that she could admire the dish.

"That looks delicious," Carly said. "Thank you for, um, agreeing to meet me, Mr. Sheffington."

"Call me Toby," he said genially. "And of course! I am very happy to finally meet you. I know you're just looking out for your mamma."

She was not looking out for her mother. She was looking out for the rest of her family, because none of them could trust Mom to not do something head-scratching and crazy. She could have been running off to Vegas with a circus clown for all Carly knew.

"Carly is very attached to her father," her mother said, apropos of nothing.

"What?" Carly's laugh was strangled. "That's not true, Mom."

"Oh, I think it is, my love."

And what was it with this *my love* business? Where had that come from? What ever happened to *Carly Jane*, or just *you*?

"Food's ready. Go ahead and take a seat at the table," Mr. Sheffington said. "Jamie!"

Carly heard a commotion, and a man came hurrying down the hallway in a manner that reminded Carly of the rabbit in *Alice in Wonderland*. She was taken aback by how much he looked like Max. His hair was lighter than Max's and his chin covered in the stubble of a healthy beard.

When he saw Carly, he stopped in his tracks and stared.

"Jamie, this is our friend Carly," Max said.

"Oh, hey!" Carly said, and pointed at his shirt. "The dog show!"

Jamie looked down at his shirt. Then up at her. "Dog show," he agreed. And then he abruptly turned, went to the back door, and opened it. Hazel bounded in and made a beeline for Carly.

"Hello, Hazel." She was glad for something familiar, and she slid off her stool to greet her old friend properly, grateful for the opportunity to hold on to something for a moment.

"Loyal dog," Jamie said. "Intelligent and loyal."

"Oh, she *is*, she is, she's such a *good* girl," Carly cooed to Hazel.

"You'll need to wash your hands now," her mother said. "Bathroom is just there." She gestured to a door.

As if she was twelve. Carly shot her mother a look and went to wash her hands.

When she returned, they gathered around the table and passed their plates so Mr. Sheffington could heap chicken Parmesan onto them. Carly noticed Max wasn't eating much, but picking at his food. He was laser focused on their parents. He looked as serious as she'd seen him yet—like he was assessing Evelyn and Toby together, trying to make sense of it. Jamie, on the other hand, dug right in, with no regard for anyone else or any table manners. He ate loudly. Max smiled sheepishly at Carly.

"Slow down, there, Jamie," Mr. Sheffington said. "This isn't a race and it's not good for your tummy to eat so fast."

"Loyal dog, loyal Dad," Jamie said through a mouthful of salad.

"You know it," Mr. Sheffington said cheerfully.

Carly wondered what that meant, but neither Max nor his father seemed curious.

"So, umm . . . Mom said things are . . . progressing with the two of you?" Carly asked carefully.

Her mother laughed. "Things are *more* than progressing, aren't they, Toby?"

Mr. Sheffington chuckled, and for some reason, he picked up his wineglass and tried to toast Max's beer. When Max didn't take the bait, he did it anyway, reaching long to tap his wineglass against the bottle sitting on the table.

"This is all really new to me," Max said. "Mind if I ask what progressing means?"

"The thing is, Max," his father suddenly interjected, "you've been really busy with your work and your research and all, and I thought, well, I'll tell him when the time is right."

"Oh." Max put his fork down. "Is the time right? Because I don't know if you would have told me if I hadn't stopped by."

"I think the time is definitely right, don't you, Toby?" Carly's mother asked.

Max and Carly exchanged a look of dread.

Mr. Sheffington was looking at his plate. "Toby?" Carly's mother said, and leaned forward so that she could look him directly in the eye.

Mr. Sheffington suddenly sat up. He smiled at Evelyn, grasped her hand, and then turned to Max. "We're in love."

"Loyal Dad," Jamie said. "Intelligent and loyal. Loyal Dad."

Mr. Sheffington didn't seem to notice Jamie, but Max did. He put his hand on Jamie's arm and gave it a soft squeeze, then let his hand drop. "Congratulations," he said quietly to his father.

"Thank you." Mr. Sheffington was beaming so hard that Carly's heart began to pound in her chest.

"We are so happy," her mother said, and then, to Carly's horror, she leaned over to Mr. Sheffington and kissed him on the lips.

"Loyal Dad!" Jamie said, his voice rising.

Mr. Sheffington laughed sheepishly. "It's okay, Jamie," he said. "We're just fooling around."

"I'll say," Carly's mother murmured, and blushed.

"*Jesus*," Carly whispered. She wished she could crawl under the table and curl up next to Hazel.

Her mother said to Max, "I know this is all very sudden. But, as I explained to Carly, sometimes you just know things. Wouldn't you say that is true from a brain perspective?"

"Mom," Carly said. "What does that even mean, 'from a brain perspective'?"

"I think Max can tell us, sweetie."

Max looked at Carly. She didn't know what she would call that look in his eye, but she felt it reverberate through her. It was a mix of horror and defiance and a little *are we being punked* confusion. He shifted his gaze to her mother. "I'm not sure I follow, Evelyn. What I can tell you is that the biology of love is basically a lot of neurochemicals moving around in you."

Her mother laughed as if she thought Max was joking.

"There are dopamine pathways that mediate your preferences, and then, of course, vasopressin and oxytocin kick in and release into your hypothalamic nucleus," he said, fluttering his fingers at his head. "That's a very generalized statement, and, of course, it's a little more complicated than that, but you could say love is merely a chemical reaction. Think of it like . . . an allergy."

Carly nearly choked on the large sip of wine she'd just taken. Under the table, Max put his hand on her knee and squeezed.

Her mother stared coolly at Max. She didn't like that explanation, which, Carly guessed, was why Max had given it to her like that. She'd wanted Max to back her up, to agree that, yes, sometimes you just *know*, and since a brain scientist said it, it made it all right. But Max wasn't going to hand this to her, and Carly thought she might possibly love him for it.

Her mother pursed her lips. "Well, I'm sure there is something to what you say, but what *I* mean is that sometimes you meet someone, and you just know he is your person. Toby is my person."

Oof. Her mother was watching *The Bachelor* again.

"And Evelyn is mine," Mr. Sheffington added, clearly delighted by the notion. Mr. Sheffington had been watching *The Bachelor*, too, apparently.

"I thought Mom was your person," Max said calmly.

"Well, she was, Max," his father said. "But she's gone and life moves on and I've got more to give."

Max put down his fork, folded his arms against the table, and asked, "So . . . what exactly are we saying, here?"

"We are *saying* that we are going to Vegas to tie the knot," Carly's mother announced grandly, and beamed at Toby.

"Loyal Dad. Intelligent and loyal Dad," Jamie said. He was beginning to rock a little in his seat.

"Loyal Jamie," Max said, and Jamie looked at him as if finally someone was speaking his language.

"That seems a little rash," Carly said. "Is there any reason you can't get to know each other a little longer before making it until death do you part?"

"*Rash*?" her mother said, slicing a warning look at Carly. "It's not *rash*, not at our age."

"But you hardly know each other," Carly pointed out.

"Well, we think we know what we need to know, Carly," her mother said.

"Dad?" Max asked, looking for confirmation.

Mr. Sheffington looked at Evelyn. He smiled. "We're not going tomorrow, Max."

"But you're going," Max said flatly.

"We need to settle a few things first."

Carly's mother grinned. She'd won this round.

Mr. Sheffington picked up his fork. "Tell me about the fashion guy, Carly. I hear he's very odd."

Who knew what her mother had said? "He's a creative genius, actually," she said, and grudgingly did her best to talk about Victor's design work, when that was the furthest thing from her mind.

She didn't know how she got through the rest of that evening. Her head was spinning with disbelief, and every time she looked at Max, her heart ached. He was subdued, his expression unusually dark. When Jamie disappeared to his room with Hazel, she stood and said, "Thank you for dinner, Mr. Sheffington. I've got an early start tomorrow so I should probably go."

"Oh good, you can give me a ride," her mother trilled.

Her mother lived well out of Carly's way, which would add thirty minutes to her drive home. "Oh. How'd you get here?"

"I took a Lyft, my love! That's what everyone is doing now. No one wants to drive in Austin traffic." Except that she was happy to make Carly do it.

The worst of it was she didn't get to say goodbye to Max. She could only give him a meaningful look and a tense smile, and he touched her hand and smiled in a way that if she hadn't known better, she would have thought he'd just suffered a great loss.

Her mother talked incessantly all the way home and would not allow Carly to squeeze more than a word or two in edgewise. Carly knew that trick—her mother was filling all the available space and air with her words to avoid Carly's questions.

After she'd dropped her mother off, she called Mia. "Mom is getting married," she blurted.

"So I heard."

"You *heard* and you didn't tell me?"

"I just found out."

"What are we going to do, Mia?" Carly exclaimed.

"Will said it's her life to live as she wants."

"Yes, it's her life, and she is free to ruin Mr. Sheffington's life, too, I guess, because you know that's what she'll do. I don't know why she is so hell-bent on getting married, but she will make that poor man as miserable as she made Dad."

"Don't say that!" Mia cried. "Dad loved her, and, if you ask me, he still does. Frankly, I am a little surprised by this. I thought they would get back together. I mean, they still talk all the time—"

"They talk to jerk each other's chains."

"I know, but I thought that was like, you know, their love language. If you ask me, Dad started dating that girl just to make Mom crazy."

"Mom *is* crazy, Mia."

"Carly." Mia suddenly sounded calm and collected. Motherly. "I can't explain it, but Mom seems happy with this man. And there is nothing we can do about it, is there? You just have to accept it."

Mia was right, of course. Carly could not stop the crazy train of her mother's life. And honestly? A few weeks ago she would have said great, Mom, have at it. She would have been delighted if some gentleman had come along and taken her mother off the market. But did it have to be *that* one? Did it have to be Max's father?

She finished her phone call with Mia just as she reached her house. When she pulled into the drive, it was dark, but she could see Conrad on his back porch, could see him rise and wave at her. She gassed it a little and hurried down the drive and bolted into the house. Once she was safely inside, she dropped her bag on the floor and walked into her living room. She felt heavy. Weighed down. She kicked off her shoes and fell onto the couch, facedown. She heard the click of dog nails against the wood floors and a moment later, Baxter appeared, having come out of his corner in the kitchen. "Hi, Baxter," she said sadly, and rolled onto her side. After a couple of starts, Baxter climbed onto the couch, and even though there was no room for him, he draped his body over Carly.

"Oof," she said. "You're too fat, Baxter." But she turned to her side and wrapped her arms around his warm, stinky body and buried her face in his fur. "I love you, too."

She and Baxter lay like that for some time, her eyes closed as she mindlessly stroked Baxter's fur, her thoughts drifting over the events of the last few weeks, of the strange space she found herself now. Baxter was content to lie like a sack of potatoes, sighing occasionally, and once almost knocking them both off the couch when he had a sudden itch that required the vigorous use of his back leg.

But then someone knocked at the door and Baxter, in his haste to be both guard dog and welcome mat, launched off Carly with a paw to her belly. She cried out as he slid down the hall, barking at the door. She rolled onto her back and looked at a mantel clock. It was half past ten. She guessed Conrad had run out of patience. With a weary sigh, she made herself get up and go to the door.

Eighteen

Carly's expression went from weary resignation to a winsome smile, and it waved through Max in a rush of desire. He stood there like a dolt with his hands in his pockets while Baxter and Hazel did their usual greeting, rolling and tripping over each other.

Carly didn't seem to notice the dogs at all. She grabbed his arms and stared up at him in wonder, and he imagined that all the same thoughts were slamming through her head like they were slamming through his. "I'm sorry, it's late," he said. "I texted you—"

"You did? I was on the phone with my sister—"

"If you want me to come back—"

"No!" She grabbed his hand. "No, no, please come in." She tugged on his hand. "*Please*. I need you."

He stepped inside and Carly threw her arms around his neck and hugged him tight. "I'm so glad you're *here*. That was crazy, Max. Wasn't that *crazy*?"

"It was so crazy," he agreed. He put his hands on her waist and pushed her back a little. He wanted to see her face. He wanted to see her dark brows and the way they arched over her eyes. Her slightly upturned nose. Her tempting, plush lips. In this light, she looked almost dreamlike. He kissed her. He lingered, his kiss reverent in a way it probably wouldn't have been had this night not happened.

She kissed him back, sinking into him, her arms tightly around him. But then she sighed, and it sounded weary and sad, and he felt weary and sad. "Let's talk," he said.

"Yeah."

Max whistled for the dogs. They came romping into the house, their paws covered in dirt. They'd been digging. "Great," he said. "I'll go see what they—"

"No, no, I'll look tomorrow. It's the herb garden, I'm sure. Once Baxter tasted basil, there was no turning back. Come on," she said, and took his hand, pulling him into her living room, all the way to the couch. They fell on it together like they'd just run a race. Hazel trotted off to explore, and Baxter trotted after her.

"Do you want something to drink?" Carly asked.

He shook his head. He had an early start tomorrow. He was meeting with Drake to go over his presentation. He'd meant to work on it tonight, but he'd stayed behind after Carly and Evelyn had left to have a talk with his dad.

"Max? I'm so sorry," Carly said.

He frowned with confusion. "For what?"

"For what," she said with a roll of her eyes. "My mother, for starters. And everything that happens from here on out."

He didn't understand her, exactly, but he shook his head. "You have nothing to apologize for. This is just . . . wild." He took in her face and stroked her hair. "I had a long talk with my dad about it."

"You did?" She twisted around on the couch to face him. She looked so hopeful, like he would fix this thing for them. He couldn't fix it. No matter how badly he wanted to fix it for her. For *them*. He wanted to do whatever Carly needed. He wanted to be the one to do it all for her. He really liked Carly. He might even be falling in love with her. Whatever it was, he didn't want to lose her.

Maybe her mother was right. Maybe you could meet someone and just know.

"Oh no. I can tell by the way you're looking at me that it's bad. It's bad, isn't it? Are they already married?"

"No," he said with a bitter laugh. "But he really loves her, Carly. And I don't know how to feel about it. My dad has been lonely for a long time, and devoted to Jamie, and I . . . I can't help but be grateful he's found someone to love."

"I know, I understand," Carly said. "But not my mom, Max. Anyone but her."

He snorted.

"I'm serious. You don't know her. She's going to . . ." Carly looked off a moment as if trying to find the right word. "She's going to ruin it. Not intentionally. But she's really impetuous." She groaned and rubbed her eyes with her fingers. "This is hard to explain." She dropped her hands. "I love my mother. I do. But loving her doesn't mean I don't *see* her. She makes emotional decisions and acts quickly, and then . . . everyone around her pays the consequences."

"What, you think this is a whim for her?"

Carly shrugged. "Maybe. Probably. I don't know, I just . . . I know how she is."

"I know my dad, too, and he's a good judge of character. I can't believe he'd be so head over heels for someone who wasn't . . . totally into him?" he said, looking for the right word.

"Right," she muttered. "My mother *is* totally into him. At least for right now." She picked at the fringe of a pillow that looked like it had been chewed on. "So you think this is really happening with them?"

Max sighed. "Dad seems pretty determined."

"Did you try and talk him out of it?"

The temptation to talk him out of it had been strong, but Max couldn't and wouldn't tell his father how to live his life. And his father did not ask for his opinion, which spoke volumes, really. His dad always asked for Max's opinion. But not in this. "I cautioned him, but honestly? He didn't want to hear it. My dad has been carrying the burden for a long time and he wants to be happy. I *want* him to be happy. And . . . apparently, your mother makes him happy. He was smiling at me like a little kid, Carly."

Carly twisted around and fell back against the couch with a groan. "Did he say when they are going to Vegas?"

"He didn't say and I couldn't bring myself to ask." He pushed his arm behind her and pulled her into his side. "The one thing we agreed is that it's probably time to get Jamie into a living situation where he can have his own space." *That's* how Max knew his dad was serious. He finally agreed that Jamie needed a place of his own.

Hazel and Baxter returned to the living room and lay down together in front of the fireplace. Baxter put his head on top of Hazel's body and sighed contentedly. That simple canine gesture tugged at Max's heart. That's what he wanted—to curl up next to Carly and sigh with contentment. "Maybe we could just . . . continue on. Let what happens with them happen in a world outside of us," he suggested. Like Hazel and Baxter.

"We'll be stepsiblings, Max. Isn't that weird?"

"We'll be stepsiblings in name only."

"But in real life," she said. "I mean, think about it. We go out to family dinners and my mom says, and this is my daughter and her boyfriend, my stepson Max."

He winced a little. "We're adults. It's not like we grew up together. It is completely doable."

"It's completely kinky."

"If we tell people."

"So we never mention our parents are married?"

He knew what she was saying. It *was* weird. It wasn't exactly wrong, but it still left a bad taste in his mouth. "Okay. We just found out about this. Let's . . . let's just take it a day at a time for now. Who knows what will happen?"

"So true," she agreed.

"It may be over as quickly as it started."

"Or we may be over as quickly as we started," she murmured.

"Hey," he said, nudging her. "Be optimistic, for my sake."

She smiled. "I will try and be optimistic. For your sake. And mine." She turned in his arms so that she could see him. "What about Jamie? Is he going to be okay with this new reality?"

Max wondered the same. "I don't know. I hope so."

"Hey," she said, brightening a little. "Here's an idea. What if you told your dad about us?"

"I thought about it. But I know him, and I know what he'd do—he'd end things with Evelyn. He would never stand in the way of my happiness, no matter what sacrifice he has to make in his personal life." He scratched his chin. "What if we told your mother?"

Carly snorted. "She would think it was just grand. She would not think of it as standing in the way of my happiness, she would think of it as a party."

Max kissed Carly's forehead. "It's been a draining night. Maybe we don't think about it at all right now."

"I can't *stop* thinking about it. Do you ever feel like the universe is conspiring against you?"

"What happened to your big girl panties?"

"Hazel has them, remember?"

He kissed her lips. "I have an idea how to cheer us up."

"Really?" She kissed him back. "It better be good. It better involve sex because I don't think anything else will work."

"If it will make you stop thinking about it, I am willing to donate my body to the cause."

"And I am willing to take it. You're not my stepbrother yet."

Max didn't know what was going to happen in this strange weird universe they found themselves in, but suddenly, the only thing he cared about was making love to her. She pushed him down on the couch, and with every stroke of her hands, he floated a little further away from caring and a little closer to the edge of losing control. It was odd how the desire for her blazed in him each time they were together. Every touch of her lips, every caress of her fingers, stoked the flames. He couldn't think of anything else, and he couldn't lose this moment, not after tonight, because the little bird of intuition that fluttered around his gut was chirping that this could be the last time.

Carly suddenly gripped his head between her hands. "This is crazy!" she said breathlessly.

"No, no, not yet. It's not crazy yet."

"I mean, what are we doing on the couch with an audience of two when I have a perfectly fine bed?" She hopped up, grabbed his hand, and pulled him up off the couch. Both dogs lifted their heads in anticipation.

"Stay," he said firmly, which, of course, never worked, and in this case, enticed the two lazy hounds to get on their feet, too. With a shriek of delight, Carly ran down the hall, trying to outrun them. Max followed her, looking back as the dogs pursued them, and crashing into the door when he turned to see how close they were. He managed to slam it shut just as the dogs reached them.

Carly pressed her ear to the door. "They're right there," she said, panting a little. "I can hear Baxter sniffing."

Max laughed. He suddenly caught her by the waist and lifted her up off her feet, swinging her around and away from the door, then marching her backward to her bed. They fell together, laughing at their silliness. On the other side of the door, one of the dogs barked.

Max sat up. "Do you have a bone or something I could give them?"

"No! Baxter snacks on carrots—"

"My God, woman, when will you learn? A dog needs his treats." With a growl, Max launched himself at her.

She pulled his shirt from the waist of his pants, then pushed him and rolled on top of him. From this vantage point, he could see her room—the overstuffed closet. The sheer curtains. The Post-its and pictures taped to her vanity mirror.

She undid the buckle of his belt.

Max came up on his elbows and watched her unfasten the button and unzip the fly.

"Do you have a condom?"

Her gaze flicked up. She suddenly hopped off him and the bed, went to her vanity, and reached down next to it. She held up a plastic sack, then tossed it onto the bed.

Max opened the bag and looked inside. There was a box of tampons, a new tube of toothpaste, and a box of condoms. He pulled out the box and looked at it. "*Economy* size," he said appreciatively.

"I was getting prepared for a long and happy relationship." She pulled her dress over her head, then shimmied out of the tights she was wearing. She reached behind her and unhooked her bra. "Any more questions?"

Max kicked off his shoes and began to push his jeans down his hips. "Yeah . . . what are we waiting for?"

Carly climbed onto the bed. And then his hands were on her, moving over her body, tweaking her, caressing her, biting her. She wrapped her fingers around his erection, and everything disappeared for Max. They moved like this for a time, rolling one way, and the other, so that no part of their bodies were left untouched. And then he groped for that giant box of condoms.

Carly's release was long and slow, and he took great pleasure in it, aroused beyond reason. When he looked at her, he could feel the flow between them, the silent communication, the mutual expectations and regard. He had never felt that sort of connection with anyone else, and he wondered again, was this love? Forget the chemical reaction— was this *love*, that thing that pushed all rational thought aside and drove men to do things they might never do? Was it love that made this feel momentous and slightly desperate and unworldly? It wasn't just corporeal—it was more transcendent than that. It was weird, this thing called love—you didn't see it, you didn't hear it, but suddenly, you just were.

If he didn't believe it, all he had to do was look at her and the way she gazed at him now. She made him believe.

When they had both found their release, neither of them spoke for a very long time. He felt like they were tumbling back down the mountain, a free fall into reality. But eventually, she moved. She stroked his back, then kissed his shoulder. "What was *that*?"

Love. That was love, Carly.

"Whatever it was, it was fantastic," she said, and kissed his shoulder blade.

But everything was not fantastic.

Max woke up in a cold sweat in the early morning hours to the sound of two snoring dogs. He vaguely remembered Carly letting them in the room.

She was curled on her side, her back pressed against him, her skin warm and surprisingly fragrant.

He stroked her arm, then heard someone in his head say, "You're dating your stepsister?"

It sounded like cheesy porn.

Nineteen

Max left Carly's house before dawn, smothering her with kisses and whispering that she should meet him at Barkin' Springs as they'd planned. She got up, showered, and dressed for the day, and sat down to check her email.

Carly gasped—there was a message from Ramona McNeil. Carly hadn't heard a peep since sending her the Bad News email.

> Ms. Kennedy, please call my office to set a meeting in advance of the
> New Designer Showcase. If you have anything to show me, please
> bring it at that time. I am sending a photographer to Austin next week.
> His information is attached. Please arrange some time in the studio
> for him. Thank you, RM

Carly stared at her screen. "Really?" she whispered. She was sure Ramona had written her off when Victor had nothing to show by her deadline. She fired off a response.

Thank you so much! I am looking forward to showing you the next
great point of view in fashion. I know it has been a rocky road, but you
won't be disappointed. Victor Allen will be a household name.

"This is amazing," she said to Baxter, who was lying pressed
against her leg. "Do you know what this means?"

Baxter thumped his tail.

"This means I might pull this rabbit out of the hat after all!" She
picked up her phone and dialed Victor. It rolled to voice mail. "Ugh,"
she said. They had a phone interview with *Entertainment Weekly*
early this afternoon, one she'd worked really hard to get. She'd sent a
video of all the positive press Victor had received for his red-carpet
design, a swatch of the red fabric (she would explain that later), and
some gifts for the publicity department that she hoped would grab
their attention. It had worked—she'd gotten the call a couple of
weeks ago.

Victor had confirmed the interview call yesterday. Between *EW*
and *Couture*, Carly was convinced she could turn this thing around.
That's what she loved about this career—it was so satisfying to fix
difficult situations and show the world true talent. She did a little
dance move on her bedroom floor but tripped over a dog toy and
stumbled into her vanity.

"It's okay," she said to Baxter, who barely even lifted his head.
"I'm good."

She was so excited that she donned a Victor Allen original—navy
pants with enormously wide legs and a white jacket with pointed
shoulders that reached her ears. She gathered her things, leashed Baxter up to ride along with her this morning, and opened her front
door—and stifled a shout of alarm.

Conrad was standing on her porch.

Carly laughed nervously. "You scared me!" This was creepy—how
long had he been standing here? She wondered if she ought to grab

something to defend herself with. Like what, her very cute Kate Spade clutch?

"Good morning, Carly," Conrad said coolly. He paused to lean down and give Baxter a proper greeting, then rose. "You haven't come by to sign the lease yet."

"I know," she said apologetically. "Honestly, Conrad, it's quite a hike in the rent, and I'm still working things out."

He looked confused. "What are you working out?"

"Like . . . where I'm going to get the money."

"*Oh.*" He was clearly surprised by this. As if he couldn't grasp even the idea of not having money. His eyes moved over her face, as if he was double-checking to make sure she was who he thought she was. "Well . . . when will you know if you can work it out?"

That was the ten-thousand-dollar question. But she couldn't keep dodging him like this. "Can you give me a couple of weeks? I've got Victor Allen's fashion show in New York coming up, and when I get back, I should have some answers." She didn't know how she would possibly have any more answers then than she did right now, but at least it would buy her some time to figure this out.

Conrad frowned. He looked at Baxter and hitched up his giant cargo shorts. "I guess," he said. "But if you can't afford this place, we've gotta get you out and someone else in. It's just business, you know."

"Sure. Business." And so much for loyalty and paying on time and taking immaculate care of this cottage. She could feel her frustration building like a bad case of heartburn. She really loved this cottage and the thought of living someplace else made her immeasurably sad. "Umm . . ." She looked at her watch. Except once again, she wasn't wearing one. She stepped out onto the porch, pulled the door shut, and stuck her key in it as Conrad stood there, looking confused.

When she turned to go, she said, "So we're good for now?"

"For now," he said, and scratched at his ponytail. He looked as if he wanted to say more, but whatever it was, she really didn't want to hear it. She smiled and said, "I better go or I'll be late."

"Yep." He stepped out of the way. He watched as she and Baxter walked to her car, rubbing his nape like he didn't quite know what to do with this plot twist.

He was still standing there when Carly pulled out of the gate.

She dialed her dad as soon as she was out of the neighborhood. "Good morning, Peach!"

"Hi—"

"No, sweetie, not there. The other cabinet."

Carly winced at the thought of her father starting his day with Hannah. She pictured the long legs, the skimpy T-shirt.

"Sorry," her dad said. "So good to hear from you, Peach! I thought maybe I upset you. But you know, Carly, I'm still very much a man with needs, and I—"

"Dad!" she said before he could explain his needs. "You didn't upset me. I was surprised, that's all."

"Well, I can understand that. I guess between my relationship and your mother's ridiculous idea to fly off to Vegas—"

"How do you know that?" she asked, then shook her head. "Never mind. I'm kind of in a rush, and, Dad, I need to ask you something."

"Sure! What do you need?"

"A loan," she said. "My business, my life, such that it is, is not going well, and I could lose my house."

"Oh no. I'm sorry to hear that. But what about that kid you're working for?"

"That kid by himself is not enough to pay the new rent that starts next month. And Gordon Romero and I parted company."

"Who?"

"The guy with the circles."

"Oh. Right. Well, how much are we talking?"

Carly had always made her own way. She had never had to borrow a dime, and to have to start now made her feel ill. "I'm thinking . . . five?"

There was silence on the other end for a moment. "Five hundred?"

"Five thousand," she said softly. "I know it's a lot, but until I get another client, I need some help. I'll pay you back as soon as I can. With interest."

"Oh. Well," he said. "I don't know about that, Peach. I put a lot of money into the time-shares. And Hannah wants to go to the beach for Thanksgiving."

Carly held the phone away from her ear. "*Shit*," she said. She put the phone back to her ear. Her dad was still talking. "Maybe a thousand? I could spare that. And, you know, you could make some calls for me."

"Calls?"

"To friends and family. Maybe a few cold calls, but let's exhaust who we know first. You were always very persuasive. I think you'd do a great job selling time-shares. And for every time-share you sell, you're paid a percentage."

Carly was so dumbstruck that she had to swerve to miss the bumper of the car that stopped suddenly in front of her. "Dad, please don't take this the wrong way. But I am not going to sell time-shares. I'm in public relations. Not sales."

He chuckled. "You're the one calling and asking for money, Carly. I'm just trying to help out."

"I appreciate it. But . . ." But what? Was she going to just give up and die and sell time-shares? "But I'll figure something out."

"Have you asked your mother? She got quite a lot of money in the divorce, and if she hasn't flitted it all away, there might be something left. Better get it before she gives it to this new guy. Who knows with her? She was never very thrifty, but somehow, her spending habits are my fault because I didn't make enough—"

"Can I call you later?" Carly asked.

"Sure, Carly. And, listen, for every valley, there is a peak."

"Right. Thanks." She hung up and swallowed back the heartburn that had climbed into the back of her eyes.

She tried to figure out another way to get by as she drove to Victor's studio. Sell her car? She could Uber around town. But with the rush hour traffic around here, the surge pricing would eat through what she thought she could save in gas and insurance in no time. There were the ubiquitous electric scooters on every corner for rent. But really? When temperatures in the summer sat at the century mark?

She could put some of her handbags on a consignment site to sell. But she had no idea how long that would take. Would she be waiting six months for a sale?

When she hit the crush of traffic on Congress Avenue, her phone began to ping. As she was stuck at a light, she picked it up. There was an entire string of messages she hadn't noticed.

Mom: Good morning, my darling girls! I did a little online shopping last night. What do you think of this as a wedding dress for your dear old mother?

Her mother had attached a snowy white wedding dress, completely blinged out.

Mia: Mom, you're nearly sixty. Take it down a notch.

Mom: Well, thank you, Mia. Just because I am nearly sixty doesn't mean I have to take it down a notch. I am as vibrant as I ever was and frankly a lot sexier. You sound just like your father. What about this one?

The next picture her mother attached was a sleeveless dress with a sweetheart neckline and mermaid skirt. That one was followed by several more pictures of bridal gowns, none of them suitable for a second wedding or frankly, anyone who wasn't twenty-four and planning a big church wedding with twelve attendants.

Mia: Pretty!

Carly guessed with that text, Mia was trying to put an end to the conversation, because this was utter insanity. The light turned. Carly tossed her phone into the passenger seat and drove to the studio. When she pulled into the parking lot, she picked up her phone and fired off a text message:

Carly: Mom—these gowns look like the type someone would wear to a first-time church wedding. I thought you were going to Vegas. Vegas says cocktail to me, not blushing bride.

Mom: Who cares where the wedding takes place? Why shouldn't I have the gown I want?

Carly threw her phone in her bag. But her mother wasn't done yet. She heard the ping and with a growl of frustration, she pulled her phone out of her bag.

Mom: Toby and I would like to have you all come to my house Sunday afternoon. His kids will be here and Trace is coming for the weekend. We would like everyone to meet.

Carly did not answer right away—she needed some time to adjust to that idea.

She got Baxter out of the car and went into the studio. The moment she stepped into the door, her gaze instantly landed on one blue and one lime green dress hanging on the wall. The blue one had some hand-sewn fabric flowers on a single shoulder strap. The green one had an asymmetrical hem. Both of them looked hideous.

Baxter trotted to the couch, where Victor was lying on his back, his feet stacked on one arm, his attention on his phone. He absently put his hand down to stroke Baxter's head. There was something else about Victor, Carly noticed. He'd shaved his head. The rainbow was gone.

"You got a haircut!"

"Yep," Victor said, without taking his eyes off the screen.

Great. He was in a bad mood. Carly looked around. "Where's June?"

"Don't know, don't care," Victor said. "I'm tired of her riding my ass."

While it was true that June could ride his ass, Carly was nonetheless alarmed. She rarely saw Victor without June. "Okay. So, you want to get ready for the interview with *Entertainment Weekly*?"

"Nope. Don't need to."

She put down her bag and folded her arms. She really wanted to kick something right now. Maybe Victor, maybe a nice karate kick to his gut. She didn't know what had happened, what exactly had turned, but Victor was clearly suffering from some sort of depression and a stunning lack of confidence. She didn't know what to do for it. She walked to the dresses on the wall, trying to think of anything that might draw him out of his funk. "Want to talk about the inspiration behind these designs?"

Victor turned his head and looked at the dresses. "Yeah. They are inspired by being pressured to create." He turned his attention back to his phone.

"Are you going to make more?"

"I don't know, Carly. I don't want to talk about it right now. Everyone just needs to let me breathe."

Carly had to bite back everything she wanted to say to him. "I would love nothing more than that. But it would help me to help you if I knew what you were planning for the New Designer Showcase. We leave next Wednesday."

"Now you sound like my mom. I've got time."

He didn't have time, at least none that she could see, but Carly wasn't going to argue with him. She had one huge goal today—to get him through the interview with *Entertainment Weekly*. Maybe that would do it. Maybe enthusiasm for his designs from a major publication would turn his mood around.

Her second goal today was to find more jobs to apply for, because this clearly was not going to be her meal ticket.

And the third goal . . . well, she didn't know what the third goal was, exactly, other than she was going to be at the dog park, come hell or high water.

Since Victor refused to talk or get off the couch, Carly made some calls and scoured the job sites until it was time for the phone call with *Entertainment Weekly*. When she told him it was time, he wouldn't look at her.

"Come on, Victor, please," Carly said. "I worked so hard to get you this interview."

With a heavy sigh, Victor hauled himself up off the couch and joined her at the worktable so they could Skype the reporter.

Kristie Anderson was a cheery blonde with heavy eye makeup and a sunny smile. She seemed genuinely thrilled to meet Victor Allen and gushed about the red-carpet design he'd done for the actress Taryn Parker. Victor was polite and responsive. He said he got into fashion at a very early age, fascinated by the ladies that attended a church in his neighborhood. They wore lots of pastels and creative hats. He said his mother had taught him to sew. He said he attended an arts high school and learned the basics of design there, and was self-taught after that, studying the great designers.

Carly was thrilled. This interview was going better than she possibly could have hoped, given his recent attitude.

And then Kristie said, "Your red-carpet look was really spectacular. I read that Taryn Parker said it was the most comfortable dress she'd ever worn. I thought it was one of the most flattering dresses she's ever worn. What inspired you for that red carpet and what did you think of the outcome?"

Victor pressed his lips together and stared at the screen. He ran his hand over the top of his head then said, "What inspired me was a paycheck. What I thought of the outcome? Stupid and lame. Frivolous."

"Whoa!" Carly said, and laughed. "Victor is kidding, Kristie—"

"I'm being real with you," Victor said, and looked at Carly. "Look, I know that disappoints you. You think I'm not disappointed in myself? But when I look back, all I can see is someone who has been inspired by a paycheck instead of art. I need to be inspired by *art*." And with that, he stood up and walked out of sight of the camera.

Carly looked at Kristie. Kristie was staring back, wide-eyed with surprise and a bit of delight. "Wow. Is someone having a bad day?"

"Can I call you back in a few minutes?" Carly asked.

"Sure!" Kristie said. She was grinning, as if she was thoroughly enjoying the story she'd just stumbled into.

Unfortunately, there was no talking to Victor. He told Carly he'd thought a lot about it, about what was wrong with him, why he couldn't create, and he didn't want to talk about it. Carly told him he was making art, that every piece he sewed was art, but Victor didn't want to hear it. He said if she was going to "run her mouth," she could leave. Carly was going to run her mouth, so she left.

She and Baxter sat on a bench outside and she called Kristie back. Kristie took her call, but it was clear she was not going to leave out a single detail in her story. "I hear the pressure can really get to these young designers once they reach fame."

Oh really? Did you hear that, Kristie? "Victor is working really hard for the New Designer Showcase, and it's a lot of stress. As you can imagine, there is a lot of interest in him, and these interviews are added pressure. You know, the artist likes to create and doesn't want to waste time talking about it."

"Uh-huh," Christie said. "Well, thanks, Carly, for setting this up!" she chirped, and hung up the phone.

"Damn it damn it *damn it*," Carly groaned. She fell back against the bench.

Baxter hoisted his front paws onto the bench and licked her arm, then laid his head in her lap. She sighed and bent over to hug him. "You always know the right thing to say. *Who's a good dog?* You're the best dog, Baxter."

The day had turned overcast, and the air was damp and cold when Carly met Max at the dog park. They sat on a bench in contemplative silence as Baxter and Hazel explored. Max looked as tired as Carly felt, as if he, too, had been aged in a single day. She felt weary to the bone, really. Her life continued to collapse around her and now, her buoyant little raft with Max had sprung a leak. She tried to assess his mood. He smiled, but it seemed like he had to make himself do it.

He took her hand in his. "So this thing on Sunday."

"Yeah," Carly said. "Should be interesting." She picked at some lint on the sleeve of his professorial sweater. "My mom has been texting photos of wedding gowns all day."

"Wedding gowns. Wow." He squeezed her hand. "Honestly, Carly? Last night, I thought sure, we can weather this. Today, I can't wrap my head around any of it."

"You and me both." She leaned her head against his shoulder.

"Is it weird that I'm not prepared to see my dad with anyone but my mother?"

"Not at all. Is it weird that I wish my parents were still together?"

"Nope. Should we just . . . I don't know . . . take the dogs and run away to Costa Rica or something?"

"Live on the beach?"

"Eat coconuts for breakfast."

"Fish for our supper."

"Start a fire to cook the fish and talk about maybe building a tree house. With a dog elevator, of course."

"*Yes,*" Carly said. "We should go right now, this very minute, before things get crazier. Or, maybe, we hold off until after Sunday so we see for ourselves just how crazy this is."

"Sure, why not," he said wryly. "Jamie is coming over tomorrow so Dad can"—he flicked his wrist—"go on a date."

"Shoot me," she muttered.

"No way." He put his arm around her shoulders. "You're my only ally right now and I would miss you so bad."

"Same," she said softly. "What are you and Jamie going to do?"

"I'm going to plug in one of the dog show DVDs and work on my presentation. I got an email today. It's next Thursday."

"But I leave for New York on Wednesday. I won't be here!"

He chuckled. "Don't worry about it. I'm probably going to want to drown my sorrows in a few beers and, since I can't hold my liquor, I'll probably be sorry company."

"Max, you never know—"

He stopped her before she could give him a speech. "But I do know. I'm not being fatalistic, I just know how these things work, and the bottom line is that she is the stronger candidate. Hey, don't be sad for me," he said, and playfully pinched her chin. "I'll buck up. It's not like I'm losing a job. It's a setback, that's all. Anyway—how is your boy wonder?"

"Where do I begin?" Carly asked. "He shaved off his rainbow hair. And he was wearing a *polo* shirt."

"My God," Max said, and pressed his hand to his heart. "What malign influence has befallen him?"

"Hilarious, professor. It may not seem like a lot to you, but for a guy like Victor to shave his head and put on a polo shirt? Instead of something he's made to express himself? I'm really worried about him. The showcase is next Friday, and if he doesn't make some clothes now, he's going to have nothing to show."

Max frowned. "Can he make clothes in a week?"

"No! I mean, I don't know, but it seems impossible to me. He says he can. He said he created a beautiful red collection in, like, four days, but he worked around the clock to do it. I don't know if he will do that now." She stared up at the gray of the early evening sky. "All the press and publicity I have lined up is flitting out the window, one by one. I've had to cancel so much because he has nothing to show. And then, today, he did a Skype interview with *Entertainment Weekly* and told them he thought his red-carpet looks were frivolous and he was in it for the money. The kid is a train wreck right now, and I get it, I do, and I feel bad for him. But at the same time, I am so angry, because I have worked really, really hard."

"I'm sorry, Carly," Max said softly. He pulled her tighter into his side. "Man, did we stumble into a regular *Peyton Place* or what?"

"No kidding." Carly sighed.

They returned to staring into space. Carly thought of herself in his house, lying in his bed, staring out the window into that pretty backyard, thinking that for once, something spectacular was happening for her. That it was finally *her* turn.

It wasn't her turn at all. She wondered if it would ever be her turn. "We are, like, the two most unlucky people on the planet, aren't we?"

He chuckled darkly. "If we're not, we've got to be running a close second or third."

They didn't say any more than that.

There didn't seem to be anything more to say.

Twenty

When Sunday afternoon rolled around, and Max and Jamie arrived at Evelyn's home, Max could not deny that Dad and Evelyn looked like a couple in love. Their happiness had taken years off his dad's face and Max was happy for him. But, like Carly, he was also a bit resentful. Why this now?

He and Jamie had come with flowers. Jamie thrust the bouquet at his dad, but his dad said, "I think you meant those for Evelyn, didn't you, Jamie?"

"Loyal Dad," Jamie said, and thrust them at his dad again.

"That's okay," Evelyn said, and took the bouquet. "Aren't they lovely! That was so considerate of you!" She suddenly surged forward and kissed Max on the cheek as if she'd known him for ages instead of days. And then she made the mistake of trying to do the same with Jamie. Jamie made a sound of alarm and ducked out of the way.

"Oh. I beg your pardon," Evelyn said. She twirled around and disappeared into her house with her flowers.

"It's all right, Jamie," his dad said, his voice full of warning. "Come in, you two."

Evelyn's house, just around the corner from a shopping center with a Target as the anchor, was much bigger than the Sheffington house. The yard was filled with bird feeders and fountains. It occurred to Max that he didn't know where his dad and Evelyn were going to live. He had a hard time picturing his father here. He was an old Austin kind of guy. North Austin seemed like the land of PTA and retail sales and neighborhood restrictions.

The house had a sunken living room and an expansive view of the yard. Evelyn's tastes were definitely antique and formal. Far too formal for the Sheffington boys. His mother used to say the one thing she would never have on this earth was fine furniture, because why would she pay all that money on something her boys were going to break?

He could hear that somewhere in the house there were children, and then suddenly, they burst forth, three of them streaking by, one of them screaming at the other two. Jamie caught Max's arm. He was humming to himself, a technique he'd been taught along the way to calm his nerves.

A woman, blond and petite like Evelyn, but who resembled Carly in her features, emerged from the kitchen in the company of a tall, athletic Asian American man. "Hi!" she said, striding forward, her hand outstretched. "I'm Mia. Soon to be your new sister!" She laughed. "My husband, Will, and those three hellions are Finn, Bo, and Millie."

"Very nice to meet you," Max said, and shook Will's hand. "This is my brother, Jamie."

Jamie turned the other way, avoiding eye contact.

"Who's here?" a male voice shouted from the hallway.

"That's Trace, my brother," Mia said as a man walked into the living room. He was dark haired, like Carly, with a stocky frame. "But don't worry about remembering him. He only comes at Christmas."

"It's not Christmas now, and I'm here, aren't I?" Trace looked at Max, sizing him up. "So you're Toby's son?"

"Sons," Max said, indicating Jamie. He wondered if any of them had noticed Jamie's humming. He sure did—it was getting louder.

Trace studied Jamie for a moment, then seemed to remember himself. "Good to meet you." He shook Max's hand, then tried to shake Jamie's. Jamie ducked behind Max.

"He'll warm up to you," Max said apologetically. "New things take some time."

"Max, darling, would you like something to drink?" Evelyn trilled from the doorway to the kitchen.

So he was a darling now. *Congratulations, your stepmother thinks you're darling.* "No, thank you," Max said.

Trace's phone rang, and he took the call, moving away from them to the windows.

"Are you sure?" Evelyn asked. "This is a celebration! Gin and tonic?"

"Max isn't much of a drinker," his dad said, appearing at Evelyn's side. "But he'll take a beer. Won't you, Max?"

"Sure," Max said. He didn't want a damn beer.

"I'll get it," his dad said. He kissed Evelyn, and she tousled his gray hair, and Max thought he was going to have to sit down before he passed out.

"Guys, there is a *lot* of PDA going on in here," Mia said.

"Well? We're in love," Evelyn said dreamily.

The front door opened just then, and Carly banged in with Baxter. Her hair was mussed like she'd run all the way here, and she was wearing a shiny aquamarine dress with little flower appliques that looked . . . different. As usual, when it came to Victor Allen's clothing, he had questions.

"There you are!" Evelyn said.

"Sorry. I got caught up with Victor."

"Obviously," Evelyn said, looking at her outfit.

One of the kids appeared and ran straight for Carly, throwing himself at her legs and almost knocking her over and causing her to drop Baxter's leash. "Oof," she said, catching herself on the kid. "Hello, Bobo."

"Good boy," Jamie said, and went down on one knee. Baxter eagerly trotted to him.

The child who was wrapped around Carly's legs apparently spotted his sister with something that belonged to him and shrieked, "*That's mine*!" and took off again.

Carly straightened. She tried to smooth out the thing she was wearing and smiled warmly at Max. "Hi, Max. Hi, Jamie."

Jamie had taken a seat on the floor and didn't look at Carly. Baxter had arranged himself across Jamie's lap to take full advantage of the attention.

"Hey, Sis."

Trace was still holding the phone to his ear, but he sauntered across the room, put one arm around her, and hugged her. He looked at her dress. "Hold on, Jerry." He pulled the phone from his ear and gestured to Carly's dress. "What the hell is that?"

"It's call art, Trace."

Trace snorted. "Don't think so," he said, and put the phone back to his ear. "Go on, Jerry."

"So! Now that everyone is here, Will and I have some news!" Mia said brightly. She put her arm around her husband's waist. He was grinning widely. "We're pregnant!"

Someone screamed and Baxter leapt off Jamie's lap and began to bark in response. It took Max a moment to realize it was one of the kids, who had somehow found their way into Evelyn's backyard.

"I'll take this one," Will said, and walked outside.

Jamie scrambled to his feet and began to rock back and forth. "Too much noise," he muttered. "Too much noise from all the boys."

"Oh, you made a rhyme," Evelyn said cheerfully.

"It's cool, Jamie," Max said softly.

"Hello?" Mia demanded. "Is no one going to congratulate me?"

"Mia, seriously?" Carly said. "You can hardly handle the three you have. You complain you have too many kids all the time."

"Carly! I had a couple of bad days, that's all."

"Well I, for one, am thrilled," Evelyn said. She picked up a tray of appetizers and began to swan around the room in her caftan. "You can't have too many grandchildren."

"Congratulations, Mia," Max's dad said.

"*Thank* you, Toby," Mia said, and glared at Carly. "See, Carly? It's not that hard."

"Congratulations," Carly said. "I'm just a little taken aback is all. Four is a lot."

"Congratulations," Max added, just as Will returned to the room.

"Thanks, man," Will said. He was still beaming, clearly happy about this turn of events.

Evelyn brought the tray of cocktail weenies speared with toothpicks to chunks of pineapples around to Max and Jamie. It looked like something right out of a dusty old 1950s cookbook. Jamie grabbed several and Max had to ask him to slow down. Max, on the other hand, could hardly look at the appetizers.

The kids raced through again, Millie shrieking at Finn for taking her doll and Finn laughing maniacally.

"I rest my case," Carly said, gesturing to Mia's children. Mia shrugged.

"Too much noise," Jamie said.

"Toby, when did you plan to grill the burgers?" Evelyn asked.

"In about thirty minutes," he said, and sipped from a cocktail glass. Another new development—his dad was drinking cocktails now.

"Well, now is a good time, isn't it?" Evelyn asked, and put down her tray.

"Oh no. *No no no.*"

Carly spoke so softly that no one else but Max heard it. He had to agree with her—there was never going to be a good time for whatever was about to happen.

Evelyn took Dad's hand and pulled him into the middle of the room. "Trace? Could you please put the phone down?"

Trace looked up to everyone's attention on him. "Gotta bounce, Jer. I'll call you in a few." He clicked off and gestured to his mother to continue.

"Will? Could you summon your children, please?" Evelyn asked.

"*Kids!*" he shouted.

Jamie put his hands over his ears. "Too much noise from all the boys," he muttered.

The kids came running, Millie still crying, and took seats on the floor before their parents.

Evelyn, apparently pleased with all the undivided attention, wrapped both arms around Max's father's waist, leaned her head on his shoulder, and said, "Toby and I would like you all to know that we have set a date!"

"I thought you said we didn't have to go," Trace said instantly.

Evelyn lifted her head and glowered at her son. "No, Trace, you don't have to go, but I thought you'd at least want to know when your mother is getting married."

"Oh. Sure." He glanced down at his phone.

"When, Mom?" Carly asked.

The two lovebirds exchanged a look. "Next weekend."

"*Next* weekend? Like, seven days from now?"

Max knew that Carly was the one who had shouted that question, but he shouted it just as loudly in his head. He and Carly exchanged a look of panic. He said, "Dad, why the race to the altar?"

"Good question, dude," Trace said to his phone.

"Too much noise from all the boys," Jamie muttered. He was rocking back and forth, and Max wanted nothing more than for this to be over so he could get his brother out of here.

"I have to agree," Mia said. "This weekend seems *really* soon. Does Dad know?"

"What?" Evelyn said. "What on earth, Mia?"

"Dad," Max said, "can you postpone this?"

"Why are you all so against this?" Evelyn asked. "We are two grown adults who know what we want. We are eager to get on with our lives together, so why would we delay it?"

"If you're worried about your brother, Aunt Sandy is going to come and stay," his father said. "Now listen, all of you. We know this is sudden. But we are happy and in love and, like Evie says, we want to get on with it. We want us to be a family. We'd like to propose a Thanksgiving feast to celebrate our marriage and our new family."

"Jesus," Max muttered.

"We're having Thanksgiving with Will's family," Mia said.

"Mia! Can't you just once come to my house?" Evelyn asked.

"We can probably arrange something," Will said helpfully, and seemed surprised by the dark look he got from his wife.

"Can we get up now?" Finn asked. His father shook his head. Finn pushed his little brother.

"No can do," Trace said. "I'm working."

"Really, Trace?" Mia said. "Are you selling a lot of pharmaceuticals on Thanksgiving?" She turned back to her mother. "What about Dad?"

"What about him?" Evelyn said sternly.

"He said he and his new girlfriend are going to the coast," Carly said.

"Don't think so," Trace said to his phone. "He broke up with that chick."

Evelyn jerked her gaze to her son. "Excuse me?"

"It's okay, Evelyn," Max's father said, and patted her arm.

Evelyn did not look like she thought it was okay. But she pinned her gaze on Carly. "Carly, you'll be here, won't you?" she asked. "And you, Max. We all need to bond as a family!"

Max could almost feel Carly stiffen. "I, umm . . ."

Evelyn suddenly broke away from Max's father and marched to where Carly stood. "I know this is hard for you, sweetie. But it's going to be okay." She abruptly threw her arms around her daughter and hugged her tight.

The sudden movement startled Jamie, and he gave a small shriek of alarm, as if he feared he was next.

The kids laughed. Finn got up and came over to look at Jamie, who was rocking quickly now and flapping one hand. "Dad," Finn said, "what's wrong with him?" That question caught the attention of his brother and sister, who hurried over to look.

"Hey," Max said, and tried to draw Finn away from Jamie.

"Jamie!" Evelyn said. "Please don't be afraid. I'm sorry if I startled you."

"Evelyn, don't—" his father tried, but it was too late. Max didn't know what Evelyn intended to do, but she moved toward Jamie, and Jamie mistook her intentions. He shrieked and pushed her away. But he was a big guy, and when he pushed her, he sent her tumbling backward.

That's when everyone started shouting.

Twenty-One

The aftermath of Evelyn Kennedy's fall was pure chaos. The adults were shouting, the children were crying, Baxter was barking, and Carly's mother was looking a little dazed. Carly helped Max get an inconsolable Jamie out to his car. The only thing that kept Jamie from curling into a ball was Baxter, who hopped into the seat beside him like they were all going on a big adventure and let Jamie wrap himself around him, happy to help.

"I'll come for Baxter later," Carly said, looking back at her mother's house.

"I'm so sorry, Carly," Max said.

"Don't be." She pressed her hand against his cheek, and then remembered the reality of their situation—not to mention many nosy eyeballs—and jerked it away. "I'll see you later?"

He nodded and walked around to the driver's side.

Carly hurried back into the house as he drove away. Her mother was sitting on the couch. When Jamie pushed her, she'd fallen backward, landing halfway onto the couch. The couch had prevented her from hitting her head.

Everyone was gathered around her, and Millie was in her lap, sucking her thumb.

"Are you all right, Mom?" Carly asked.

"Yes, I'm fine," she said. She gave Carly a shaky smile. "I'm more startled than anything."

"I'm so sorry, Evie," Mr. Sheffington said.

"No, don't apologize. It was my fault—I wasn't thinking. I didn't mean to scare him, Toby. I hope he's okay."

"He's fine. It just takes time," Mr. Sheffington said, wincing slightly.

Her mother nodded. She swallowed. "All right, the circus is over," she said, and put Millie down so she could come to her feet. "Let's get those burgers on. There's no reason we can't continue our celebration, is there? We'll come together as a family at Thanksgiving."

No one spoke of the incident again, except for Finn, who asked his father once more, "What was wrong with that guy, Dad?" Will pulled him away to talk about it.

When the burgers had been eaten, Mia and Will gathered their brood and went home. "So much for my announcement," Mia said accusingly to her family as Will shepherded the children out the door.

"I am sure we'll all be more excited when Mom isn't blowing up the world with this wedding thing," Trace said.

He was the next to leave. "Going to stay downtown, Mom," he announced.

"Downtown? Why? You have a perfectly nice and free room here."

"Because *here* is boring. And I haven't been to Sixth Street in a long time."

"Haven't you outgrown the frat boy party thing by now?" Carly asked.

"Outgrown having a good time?" He shook his head. "Never." He punched Carly in the shoulder. "See you, squirt."

Carly and her mother watched him go. "What is the matter with him?" her mother asked. "Why won't he settle down?"

"Because he's a bro, Mom."

"A what?"

Carly shook her head. "Might as well face it—Trace is probably going to party until he drops."

"Well, girls, I'm going to go check in with my sons," Mr. Sheffington announced. He had gathered up an enormous bag that looked to be stuffed with cooking gear, judging by the handle of a grill spatula that stuck out the top.

"I'm sorry, Toby," Carly's mother said. "I wish things had gone better."

"Growing pains," he said kindly, and gave her a kiss. Carly's mother grabbed Mr. Sheffington's shirt when it looked like he was going to pull away and held on, kissing him harder.

"Ohmigod," Carly whispered, and stepped around the couple and went into the living room.

It was a full five minutes before her mother let Mr. Sheffington go and returned to the living room, too, looking glassy-eyed and sheepish. "Well!" she said. "What do you think?"

"I think it's all really fast."

"Oh, Carly," she said with a sigh. "You're young. Just wait until you're my age. You'll move fast, too. I haven't got all the time in the world."

"You're not even sixty, Mom. You make it sound like you've got one foot in the grave."

"Come help me clean up," she said, and walked into the kitchen. "I'm so happy that Toby is such an excellent cook. I never was, you know. I never had the interest or the imagination to be a *good* cook. That was one of your father's ongoing complaints, I'm sure you remember. He always said I didn't take the time to learn to cook better for the family."

"Dad has learned to cook pretty well," Carly said absently.

"Hmm," her mother said.

Carly had to talk to her about something else, and her stomach was churning with it. "So listen, Mom . . ." If there was one thing she'd learned in her life, it was to not ask her mother for anything. There were always consequences for asking. But she was an adult now, which she had to remind herself when her mother looked at her curiously. Megan Monroe said, *Don't take no for an answer just to be good.*

"I need a huge favor."

"Oh." Her mother put down a pot she'd picked up. "I hope it's not money, sweetie. I have to buy a wedding dress. Your father nickeled-and-dimed me in the divorce—"

Her father had said she got a lot of money from it. Whatever. "I need to stay in your house for a little while."

Her mother blinked.

"For just a little while, I swear it, until I get back on my feet."

"You're not on your feet? What do you mean? I thought you loved that little house."

"I do, but they are going up on rent, and I lost Gordon Romero—"

"What? Why?"

"It was just a bad fit. Mother, listen—Conrad is going up on the rent, and he wants a year lease, *and* he wants a pet deposit, and right now I can only cover about five months of bare-bones expenses, so unless you can loan me five thousand dollars, I need to find some place to go."

"Oh dear," her mother said, and looked genuinely distressed. "I can't loan you five thousand dollars."

"I didn't think so."

"This is unfortunate timing."

Carly actually snorted. Her mother was the one with unfortunate timing. "But you're going to get married, and you're going to live with Mr. Sheffington and Jamie, aren't you?"

"No, he's going to live here and Jamie is going to live with his brother."

Carly mentally stumbled. "Jamie is going to live with Max?" Why hadn't Max mentioned it?

"Toby's house is small and dated. We'd be much more comfortable here, starting our new life together. Oh dear, the timing is just not good," she said, her brows furrowing into a frown as she thought about it. "Have you asked your father?"

"Oh, believe me, Mom, I know all about bad timing. And guess what? Timing isn't good for Dad, either." She picked up her bag. "May I have the extra room or not?"

"Of course, sweetie. Of *course*." Her mother smiled and stepped forward and wrapped her arms around Carly. "The timing may be bad, but I am always here for you." She laughed. "I know it may not always seem that way, but my children are always first and foremost in my mind. If you need to stay here, we will figure it out." She let Carly go.

"Thanks, Mom."

"But please, sweetie, not before Toby and I get married. There's just too much going on right now."

"Sure," she said. She hoisted her bag onto her shoulder. "I'm going to take off now."

"Call me later!" her mother trilled.

Carly walked outside into a fine mist that had started to drench the town. She could feel that the temperature was dropping and remembered the first real cold snap of the season was supposed to arrive later this evening. She got in her car and sat a moment. That burn behind her eyes was there again, but Carly was not going to be defeated in this. She was *not*. She swiped angrily at the single tear that slid down her cheek and drove to Max's house.

Max answered the door and opened his arms to Carly. She walked into them and let him wrap his arms around her, holding her tightly as she rested her cheek against his chest. "What a fucking disaster," he said.

"The worst." She lifted her head. "Can I ask a huge favor?"

"Anything."

"Do you have some sweats I could borrow? I can't wear this stupid ugly dress another minute."

He smiled with surprise. "I do. Come on in."

Hazel and Baxter were on the couch, of course, one on either side of Jamie. He was leaning forward, watching a dog show competition on TV. "How is he?" she whispered.

Max shrugged. "I think he's okay now. He has to be eased into new situations and the kids . . . I think they threw him a little. Come in," he said, and with his hands on her shoulders, he nudged her in the direction of his room.

In his room, Max went into his closet and Carly asked, "What does it mean, 'loyal Dad'?"

"Jamie?" he asked from somewhere inside. "I can't say for sure, but I think he's expressing his uncertainty about Dad's new arrangement." Carly could hear him rummaging around until he appeared again, holding a hoodie and some sweatpants.

"You know how he says, 'loyal dogs, intelligent and loyal,' right?" She nodded.

"That's what he admires about dogs. They're loyal to you, no matter what. I think he's trying to tell Dad he wants him to be loyal, too. And I think he feels like Dad isn't being loyal right now." He shrugged. "That's my best guess. Will these do?" he asked, holding up the sweats.

"Yes. Thank you so much." She reached for the sweats. "It must be really confusing for him."

"It is," Max said. "I think it will help when his dog is ready and he doesn't feel as if he's being abandoned."

Carly presented her back to Max to be unzipped. "When is he getting his dog?"

"The next week or so," he said. "Hey, I may be way off base here, but you don't seem as enthusiastic about this piece of wearable art as you have been about others," Max said.

"Very astute of you, professor. This dress is hideous. It isn't art— this is Victor phoning it in. The only reason I put it on today was to try and inspire him because he hadn't seen it on a model yet. He's been in the studio, half-heartedly working and trying to understand the universe and looking for clues on Instagram of all places."

She quickly changed as Max watched, but the vibe between them was not a sexy one. It was a resigned one. When she'd finished, they stood staring at each other.

"How is your mom?" he asked.

"She's fine. She felt bad about it."

Max looked at his feet.

It felt to Carly a little like her nerves were curling and twisting together in her. She didn't know what to say and turned away, pushing her hair from her face. She noticed several shirts and jackets laid out on his bed. "What's this?"

"Oh . . . I was trying to find something to wear to my presentation Thursday."

This was something Carly could do. Something productive, something she could control, something she could help with. She picked several shirts and held them up, discarding those that were definite noes—denim, of course—and those that were acceptable. "I have something to tell you," she said as she sorted through the clothes.

"I don't know if I can take any more good news, but go ahead, lay it on me."

"My landlord is going up on the rent. Two hundred a month. And he wants another five hundred for Baxter."

"What? Why?"

"Pet deposit. Right now, I don't have enough work to keep my house. And until something breaks for me, I think I'm going to have to move out."

"Move, like . . . where? Are you okay?"

She laughed, a little bitterly. "I'm not a pauper yet. But I have to find a job. And this thing with Victor . . . it's not giving me a lot of confidence that he's going to be a client I can build. Without clients, I can't create an effective social media presence, and without social media, I'm pretty much unknown in this line of work. I'm going to have to step back and reassess. So . . . I decided this morning that I definitely can't sign a lease. There's just too much uncertainty in my future right now."

"This is sounding pretty bleak," Max said, and sat on the bed.

"No kidding. So, today, after everything, I asked Mom if I could stay in her house after she got married. I just assumed she'd be living with your dad and Jamie. But she informed me that she and your dad would be living there, and that . . ." She looked at Max as she laid one shirt out at the end of the bed. "Jamie would be living with you."

Max stared at her as if she'd just slapped him.

"You haven't heard that plan?"

"No." He dragged both sets of fingers through his hair and looked away. "Was he even going to talk to me about it?"

"Before you say anything to your dad, it's entirely possible my mom is doing some wishful thinking." Carly walked into his closet and began to go through his pants. "She does that, you know—she just says what she wants to be true like that will make it true."

"Maybe so, but it's clear that something has to happen with Jamie. I don't know if he can live with your mother and my dad without making it difficult."

Carly came out of the closet with a pair of slim brown chinos. She added them to the shirt at the end of the bed. And then she added a sport coat. "There. Wear this to your presentation."

Max looked at the bed. And then at her. "Carly," he murmured.

She glanced down, trying to keep the heartburn in her eyes and chest from turning to actual tears. "I cannot believe we are being cockblocked by our *parents*."

Max stood up. They stared at each other across the bed. As if they both wanted to speak. As if they both wanted the other to fix it. As if they had no idea what to say to any of this.

They stood there until Jamie laughed at something in the living room.

Max looked at the closed door, and then at her, and Carly felt everything in her well up to a sudden burst of despair. The tears fell before she could stop them.

"Oh, baby," he said, and walked around the bed to fold her into his embrace.

"I'm so sorry, Max. My love chemicals are all out of whack. You know what's worse than being cockblocked by your mother? The *worst* thing is to meet the right person at the wrong time."

He cupped her head against his chest.

"How are we going to make this work?" she asked tearfully. "Even if we could get over the weird stepbrother-stepsister thing, there is Jamie, and me living with my mother and your dad, and, my God, that just sounds worse every time I say it." More tears leaked from her, and she hiccupped with a sob she tried to suppress. "I can't cry," she moaned. "I am such an ugly crier."

"You're always beautiful."

"Nope. You haven't seen me full-on cry. I look like one of those horrible creatures they find on the bottom of the ocean."

Max sputtered a laugh.

"This is going to sound crazy, Max, but . . ." She rubbed her hand under her nose and looked up. "I've never met anyone like you. And I don't think I ever will again. I just . . . I just want to be happy. I want to be with you, and I don't know if we can and I'm breaking inside." She choked on another sob and let her head fall forward against his chest.

Jamie began to call for Max.

Later, Carly wouldn't remember actually leaving Max's house. But she would remember how she and Baxter dragged into her house, with a garish aquamarine prom dress thing draped over her arm. She would remember how Baxter solemnly followed her into her bedroom, and the two of them sat on her bed while she typed out an email to Conrad on her laptop telling him she'd be out by the end of the month.

Twenty-Two

On Monday, Max confronted his dad about his new living arrangements.

His dad claimed confusion. "I don't know what you're talking about," he said, scratching his head. "We haven't discussed Jamie's living situation."

This did not alleviate Max's annoyance—it just made it worse. "Are you kidding, Dad? You're planning on marrying this woman this weekend, and you haven't discussed where you and Jamie would live?"

"I didn't say that," his father said with a frown for Max's tone. "Evelyn and I haven't decided where *we* will live, but she knows Jamie will be with us until we can get him situated in a group home. He's been part of this deal all along." He patted Max on the arm. "I think Carly misunderstood."

"So . . . you're moving to her house with Jamie?" Max was incredulous.

"We haven't actually decided anything. But . . . I'd say it's a good possibility."

Max couldn't believe what he was hearing. "You've lived in this house thirty-five years, Dad. This is where we grew up." Max's objection now had less to do with Jamie and more to do with his own feelings. About his mother, about his parents, about his childhood. His dad was about to obliterate it all with one whirlwind romance.

"Max, come on now," his dad said patiently. "This house is old and needs repairs, you know that. I could get good money for it. Or, if you feel that strongly, I'll rent it out."

"But what about Jamie, Dad? This is a lot of change for him."

His father sighed. "You are the one who's been advocating for him to move to a supervised home. That's a big change, too, isn't it? Is that sort of change less disruptive than this change? I don't think so. I've put a lot of thought into the situation, and you know damn well I will do what is best for him. I always have and I always will."

Max didn't like the dismissive way his father spoke to him, as if his concerns were not valid. A memory abruptly popped into his head—he and Jamie were boys, walking home from school. Max was maybe twelve or thirteen, completely caught up with his friends, Jamie trailing behind them. One of Max's friends alerted him to the fact that a couple of older kids were bullying Jamie. They'd seemingly come out of nowhere and were taunting Jamie, calling him retarded. Max had flown into a blind rage and had attacked them. Jamie had followed suit, swinging wildly and connecting with Max by accident. In the end, Max and Jamie had limped home.

The impotent rage he'd felt that day was the same as the rage he was feeling now. But this time, his rage was directed at his own father. "Have you at least talked to Evelyn about autism? About Jamie in particular?"

His father frowned darkly at him. "What the hell do you take me for? Of course I have talked to her about him. She ordered some books about it so she could learn. But she's new to the disorder, Max. She hasn't studied it like you have, and you've got to cut her some slack. There's going to be a learning curve. You need to have patience."

"*I'm* the one who needs patience? That's rich, Dad. You're the one rushing off to Vegas for no good reason."

"Mind your own business about that," his father snapped. He walked into the kitchen and started pulling dishes out of the drain tray to put away. "So, hey, you have a big presentation this week, right?"

Max wasn't going to let him change the subject. "Why not put your wedding on hold a couple of weeks so we can get Jamie into a place he can live on his own? With people who understand the disorder and don't have a learning curve. Let's put him somewhere he can take his dog, someplace where he can get on a bus and go to work and come home and paint and get him settled first. Can you not wait that long?"

His father started to shake his head.

"Come on," Max said impatiently. "You know she doesn't want Jamie there. And honestly, I don't think Jamie wants to be there."

"You don't know what either one of them want," his father snapped. "You pop in and out of here a couple of times a week, and you think you know what Jamie wants?"

The truth in that stung, but Max pressed on. "What I know is that we coddle him. We do everything for him. And because we have, this change is going to be harder for him to navigate."

His father's face began to mottle with anger. "We do not *coddle* him." He turned his back to Max and walked to the window, his hands shoved in his pockets, staring out. "I'm not going to talk about this now. I have enough to do as it is. Jamie will be fine."

He meant what he said—he refused to talk further about it, changing the subject when Max tried. So Max left. He had a meeting with Drake to go over his presentation one last time.

Drake watched as Max walked through the various elements of his research, the same thing he'd done a couple of times now. But Drake had a curious look on his face. "What?" Max asked.

"I don't know—you're usually stoked about your research. You look and sound like your dog died."

"Yeah," Max admitted. "Family stuff. And, you know . . . Alanna's got me beat."

Drake looked down at his paper, which Max took to mean he thought so, too.

"I don't know. Just a lot of stuff bubbling up at once," Max muttered. "Can we walk through this again?"

"Sure," Drake said. "But this time, at least *look* like you're interested in your work."

Max looked this way because life had kicked him in the ass. Carly was right—nothing sucked worse than meeting the right person at the wrong time.

He had plenty to worry about and sort through with his dad and brother. But he had his job to think about, too. He loved this campus. He loved his job. There was so much he wanted to accomplish, so many things he wanted to study, and the University of Texas had deep pockets for it and a willingness to go the extra distance. But without tenure, he couldn't bring in the sort of money he needed to really dig into his research.

There was so much weighing on him, but it was really Carly who wouldn't vacate his thoughts for even a second. He was talking about neural pathways and thinking of her. He couldn't believe that a woman who dressed like she did, who questioned his dog-keeping abilities, who listened to inspirational podcasts and had an idea for every situation, would be the one to worm her way into his heart. He'd always assumed it would be another academic. He'd never envisioned a woman who showed up with a dog in a tutu and gave it Evian water to drink. But it *was* that woman, and he missed her so much already even though they were still together.

He didn't know where they went from here. Where *he* went from here.

When he'd finished his second run-through, Drake sat up. "Max, listen to me. Your dossier defense is in a couple of days. You need to keep your head in the game here. I know Alanna is a strong candidate, but so are you. You are not out of the running, no matter what you think."

Max nodded. He appreciated Drake's friendship, and he'd do no less for Drake. But that gut feeling wouldn't leave him. It was over. All of it. Tenure, his family, Carly . . .

Nevertheless, Max spent the rest of the day prepping for his research defense. He and Carly had mutually agreed they both had too much to do before she left for New York and he made his presentation. She'd texted him, said her client was coming around, and she was tied up with him until she left.

He texted her and said he had to spend every moment preparing for his presentation. She asked if Baxter could hang out with him for a few days while she was out of town. He said of course. She dropped Baxter off with a box of his things Tuesday morning. From the note she'd left, it looked like she'd just missed him.

They hadn't said it, but it seemed to Max as if they'd both decided that whatever was going to happen was going to happen. Life rolled on. Max just needed for his parasympathetic nervous system to kick into gear sometime soon and bring him down off the ledge so he could fight for the thing he'd worked so hard to achieve. He had to place the rest of his life on hold for a couple of days.

Somehow, he was able to do it by sheer force of determination. But Wednesday morning, his phone pinged bright and early.

Hey, you! Go kick some ass tomorrow!

Max smiled at his phone. He was extremely happy to hear from her.

Wish me luck.

LUCK. Anyway, you won't need it. I am sure there is some biological explanation for what is really happening when people feel they need luck, but you'll do great. You're a rock star, Max Sheffington!

"Thanks, Carly," he muttered.

Thanks again for keeping Bax. No couch! (just kidding) But for real, no mac and cheese. I mean, unless he won't eat. Anyway, let me know how your presentation goes?

Will do. You do the same. When is your flight to New York?

I'm on the plane now. So, hey, Tobias Sheffington III . . .

He waited. Three undulating dots appeared on his screen. Then disappeared. He pulled on a jacket, looked again. Still nothing. Maybe the text had dropped.

He was combing his hair when the three dots popped up again.

Megan Monroe of *Big Girl Panties* podcast says that you should accept disappointment and not lose hope, and use the disappointment as a stepping-stone to greater things. I totally hate her right now. Who can be that Pollyanna all the time? Anyway, I don't want to use you as a stepping-stone to anything. I just need you to know that you are the greatest love I will never have. Sorry if that's too much, but I had to say it.

Max stared at the message, his heart racing. That was the way he felt, too.

Good luck tomorrow. Good luck good luck good luck. You deserve
the best. Oh, the flight attendant told me to put my phone in
airplane mode . . .

She ended the text with a picture of a little airplane. And then she
was gone.

Max texted back, *I love you, too, Carly.* But he deleted it as his
heart fissured right in his chest.

Twenty-Three

Carly arrived in New York at noon on Wednesday, utterly exhausted. She'd spent two full days with Victor, working into the night, helping in any way she could while he patched together what could be salvaged from his red and white collection.

Late Sunday night, Victor's mother had texted with an SOS. She said Victor was so lost, but at least recognized that he was too much in his own head.

Carly arrived at his studio the next morning with the red suit he'd tried to throw away and she'd tried to wear. She hung it next to the awful blue and green pieces he'd been making. When Victor saw it, he'd paused and had stepped back to study it, as if seeing it for the first time. He picked up a piece of the white fabric and fashioned a bandeau and held it up beneath the jacket.

"Looks great," Carly had said instantly, although she couldn't tell what he was doing.

"It does," June had agreed, just as quickly. Carly looked at June. June looked at Carly. They knew what they had to do here.

"You can still do this, you know," Carly had said softly.

Victor had stood for a long moment, rubbing his hand back and forth over his head. "Yeah," he'd said at last. "But I cut up most of the white." He dropped his hand. "I've ruined everything. I don't know, Mom. I'm so sorry. I didn't mean to ruin everything."

"Oh, Victor," June said, and put her arms around her son.

Carly laid her hand on his back. "We can fix this, you know. You work really well under pressure, Victor. And we can get more white fabric."

"I'm still pretty handy with a sewing machine," his mother added.

Victor sighed. "Yeah," he said slowly. "Okay. Okay."

He went to work immediately and removed the blue and green cabana wear and had begun to piece together what he could. With June on a sewing machine—the woman had mad skills—and Carly doing cleanup or whatever could be managed with a thread and needle, Victor worked around the clock to cobble as much of his original collection together as he could.

When Carly left for home very late Tuesday night, he had seven pieces. His original collection had ten, but seven would work. His models were all still booked. All he had to do was get on the plane for New York.

When he didn't show up for the seven A.M. flight, Carly didn't allow herself to panic. As long as he was in New York by four, in time for the photo shoot at *Couture*, all was well. It was quite possible he'd overslept—she nearly did. She kept telling herself that all the way to New York.

In New York, she made her way to Naomi's, buzzed in with the code, and used the key Naomi had given her the last time she'd been in town. She called Victor. There was no answer. She thought that meant he was on a flight.

But Victor didn't show up to New York by four. Carly canceled the *Couture* photo shoot and emailed Ramona her sincerest apologies.

Not surprisingly, she couldn't get Victor on the phone after that, either. Or June, for that matter.

Carly looked at the cute green pants she'd brought to wear out tonight. She'd been looking forward to this girl's night out for the last two weeks.

Naomi was late from work and flew in. "We have to do a quick change. Tandy and Juliette are already at this great new restaurant we discovered in Chelsea. Cuban and Japanese fusion. Isn't that crazy? Anyway, it's going to take us forever to get there." She'd grabbed Carly in a bear hug. "I'm so glad you're *here*," she said. "We are going to have so much fun when you move to the city. I can't *wait*."

Carly tried to smile as Naomi peeled off her work clothes. "What?" Naomi asked as she shimmied into a skintight silver dress. "Why are you looking like that? Why aren't you dressed?"

"I can't go."

"What? Why not?" Naomi cried. She rushed to the mirror in her room and began to fluff her dark hair. "You're in New York, Carly. You *have* to come."

"I *want* to come. You have no idea how much I want to come. But I can't, Naomi. My client is . . . not cooperating."

Naomi paused and glanced back. "What does that mean?"

"He hasn't actually made it to the city yet." Just saying it made her feel like a failure.

Naomi looked confused. "What, is he in Jersey or something?"

"No, he's still in Austin," Carly admitted. "I mean, I think. All I know is that he was supposed to be here today and he didn't show."

Naomi gasped. She shook her head. "I don't know why you are keeping him around, honestly, Carly. It's like one thing after another with him."

"Well, for one, he is the only one who is paying me right now. And two, Victor Allen is truly a remarkable designer." She still believed that. Watching him work like he had the last two days, and how quickly he could take a piece of cloth and turn it into art, had astounded her. She leaned across the bed and took out some photos she'd brought to show Ramona McNeil—the photos Phil had taken with Hazel, including some of the pieces Victor had salvaged from that original shoot. "He's remarkable, but he's young. Sometimes I forget how young he is. But so undeniably talented. And, you know, sometimes we all lose our way. He just needs a little help."

Naomi looked at the photos. "These are cool. Except this one is a little weird. That dog is adorable."

"That's the thing about creative geniuses," Carly said, tucking the photos away. "Not everything they make is a home run, you know? There has to be trial and error, because that's how they evolve."

Naomi shrugged. "Maybe. All I know is that this jerk is keeping you from going out tonight. Okay, sweets, gotta run. Don't wait up." She was out the door in a flash.

Carly ordered in Chinese and tried Victor two more times. At eleven o'clock, she was ready to throw in the towel. She had done all she could do. But first, she was going to call him and tell him what an asshole he was.

She expected the call to roll to voice mail like all the other calls, but this time, Victor actually picked up. "Don't hate me," he said.

Carly was stunned. It took her a moment to gather herself. "What the hell, Victor? You've been ghosting me all day. This is twice I've had to cancel a *free* photographer for you! What happened?"

"I don't know," he said softly. "I don't know if I can do it. I keep thinking I'm going to throw up."

This, Carly thought, was the difference between twenty and twenty-eight. "But, Victor . . . you've worked so hard. The pieces look great. You were happy with your work. What changed between yesterday and today?"

"I'm just not feeling it."

Carly closed her eyes and prayed for providence. She did not wait to get it. "With all due respect, if you tell me you are not *feeling* something one more time, I am going to totally kick your ass and trust me, you will feel it. What is the matter with you? I mean, *really*? Do you think some divine light is going to shine on you and make you *feel* it? *None* of us knows what is going to happen. There is not a single person on this planet who walks out their door every day and really knows what is going to happen." She thought of Max, who would march off to his presentation tomorrow, certain he'd be denied this shot at tenure. She thought of herself, on her way to New York this week, trying to convince herself that Victor wasn't going to ruin this for both of them. "Not feeling it is part of life."

"Yeah, but you don't have trolls," he said quietly.

"You know what? You did that to yourself. I'm not saying the Internet is fair or there aren't evil beings parading as humans online, but you responded. You fed them red meat. And now you have to forget them, Victor. You know why? Because in six weeks, they will have moved on to the next victim and won't remember your name. But where are *you* going to be then? Nowhere! Because you are too chicken to show your work."

"Don't yell at me," he complained. "I know I let you down."

He sounded like a kid. Carly drew a deep breath. "Okay. I'm about to say something in the kindest way I know how right now. You need to grow the fuck up. Life is a lot of hard work and sometimes all that hard work pays off and sometimes it doesn't. But that doesn't mean you don't try." She was suddenly reminded of a poster that hung in her high school gym. She and her cross-country teammates saw it every time they went out to the track. "Victory belongs to those who believe it the most and the longest," she said now, repeating the poster. "Your mom and I believe it. Don't you? Haven't you believed the longest of anyone? Are you going to stop now because some nameless cretins got under your skin? You have a great collection and you're so talented, and there are hundreds, *thousands*, who would kill to be in your shoes, and who are never going to have an opportunity like this, and you are throwing it away because you're scared. You know who would really love an opportunity like this? *Me.* Me, Victor! I have worked so hard to get this for you! So get your ass on a plane and get to New York. Because if you don't, there is no helping you. This is your shot at victory!"

She sounded like her old cross-country coach. She hung up before Victor could utter one more whine at her. And then she buried her face in Naomi's pillow and cried. With regret, with exhaustion, with loss. This was it for her. She had nothing—no job, no clients. She had done everything right, and she had nothing to show for it.

Carly apparently cried herself to sleep. She never heard Naomi come in. She never heard her leave for work. She was awakened by the ping of a text. Her eyes were puffy, and she groggily groped for her phone. The text was from Victor.

Like . . . where are we supposed to go.

With a shout, she sat up. Victor was in New York.

Later, when Naomi and her roommates asked how Victor's show went, Carly said it was great, but in truth, it was all a big blur.

They had worked all day Thursday and through the night. Friday morning, the place was a madhouse. There were models and makeup artists, hairstylists and seamstresses. People were ironing, people were rushing around looking for shoes or bags or the little bows that were supposed to go in someone's hair.

Victor had found an inner well of strength. He was everywhere, perfecting the garments up to the last minute. There was a glitch with the sound, and Carly thought that was it, finally the death knell to this thing. But the sound guy got it up and running just in time. The show started fifteen minutes late, but the room was full, and the lights went down, and on a big screen at the back of the runway, a summer sky appeared with birds flying across.

When the music started, the first model appeared wearing the red suit. She had stark red eye shadow and a stick of hair about a foot long that stood straight up from her crown. The next piece was white, with the long sleeves Carly had worn.

Carly was impressed and relieved and happy, and also numb as Victor came out for the last walk down the runway when all seven pieces had been shown. She knew that for him, it wasn't as much a fashion victory as it was a personal accomplishment, and he was beaming. He was proud of himself.

There was a lot of applause when the show was over, and then a crush of people waiting for a chance to tell Victor he was great. Some of his old cast members for *Project Runway* had come, and she watched him laugh and talk with them. He seemed like a different person. As if the weight of his show had been lifted from him at last.

After the show, Carly and June stood propped up against the same wall, June looking as exhausted as Carly felt. "I can't believe you did it," June said.

"What? *I* didn't do it. *You* did it. Victor did it."

"No, you did this, Carly. You got that boy off his ass. I don't know how you did it, but that was all you. Let's just hope it takes." She pushed away and walked to where Victor was now talking to reporters. When he saw his mother, he threw his arms around her and hugged her tightly.

Carly smiled. She supposed she ought to be in there, spinning the story just right. But she was too tired to think. She didn't know where she went from here with Victor, or if she wanted to go with him at all. He didn't pay her much, and even if he was her only client, she wasn't sure it was worth the anxiety.

She wanted to call Max and tell him about her Calvin Klein. She wanted to tell him about this entire awful week. She wanted to know how his presentation went. She took her phone out and was remembering that he'd be in class just now when she became aware of someone sidling up to her. When she glanced to her left, she started. Carly would know that face anywhere—Ramona McNeil was as formidable in person as she was on the phone. She had a folder and a phone in one hand, a large coffee in the other, and a pair of eyeglasses perched on top of her head. Carly shoved away from the wall. "Oh my God, Ms. McNeil," she said, and extended her hand.

"My hands are full."

"Right," Carly said, and dropped her hand. "It's such a pleasure to meet you."

"So you're Carly Kennedy of Carly Kennedy Public Relations?"

"Yes!" Carly said, smiling.

Ramona slipped a folder under her arm then yanked her glasses down to her nose to give Carly a good once-over. She looked to be around sixty-five or maybe seventy. She was impeccably dressed in a Chanel suit and flawless makeup, including the eyeliner that swooped out from the corners of her eyes. And she'd had so much Botox that her expression was completely unreadable.

"What did you think of the show?" Carly asked.

Ramona looked across the room to Victor.

"His aesthetic is very avant-garde, wouldn't you say?" Carly asked. "The thing about Victor is that whatever he comes up with will be editorial. And you have to admit that no one is doing work quite like him, besides, maybe, Christian Siriano, which is why, frankly, I think Victor is so interesting. He has this fantastic, unique ability to take something ordinary and turn it into very high fashion. This could be a great opportunity for you."

Ramona snorted and looked at Carly again. "For *me*?" she drawled.

"Well, sure. After the show today, everyone is going to want a piece of what he's got."

Ramona chuckled. "Carly, you have an annoying tendency to

oversell things. His show was good, but it wasn't *that* good. I'm surprised you got him here, frankly."

"He's had a small crisis of faith. But he's back on track."

"Hmm," Ramona said, looking Carly over. "Must be hard to work with an artist who doesn't believe in himself."

That sounded very much like Megan Monroe. *First and foremost, believe in yourself!* "I'm a big fan of his work. I really am. And he is so stupidly young that I couldn't let him blow this opportunity. He doesn't know yet that it would be something he'd regret all his life."

Ramona leaned forward. "Nevertheless, I ought to kick you out of here for wasting so much of my time with him. And yet, I like you, Carly Kennedy. You've got some grit."

Was that what she had? All she knew was that she liked solving problems like Victor. "Yeah, I guess maybe I do." She smiled as she hoisted her bag onto her shoulder. "I am so very sorry for wasting your time. That was never my intent."

"Don't waste more of it now. You have an application in our publicity department."

Carly sighed. "I do. I'll withdraw it as soon as I get to a computer."

"I don't want you to withdraw it. I want to talk to you about it. Can you be in my office by four today?"

Carly was certain she'd misunderstood. "What?"

"You don't give up, and I like that. We could use someone like you. Someone who would go out and find the young talent for us. But talent that will deliver," she said, pointing her coffee cup at her.

Carly's brain couldn't compute. Was Ramona McNeil offering her a job? "But . . . but I live in Austin."

"You can't move to New York? You applied, so I assumed you'd be interested in moving here. What have you got to lose by talking, Carly Kennedy? Four o'clock. My office. And, for the love of God, do not be late." She walked away.

Carly stared after her, her mouth agape. Was this really happening? Was her dream really going to come true? She couldn't even absorb it—she'd been working so long and hard toward this, and here it was, on a silver platter. She was . . . flabbergasted. *Stunned*. And . . . and something felt a little off in her chest.

She was walking without realizing it, trying to make sense of it all. "Carly!"

She paused at the sound of Victor's voice and turned around. "Hey! Great show, Victor! See? I knew you could do it." A lie, but it seemed appropriate in the moment.

"Thank you," he said and smiled sheepishly. "Hey . . . I've been a jerk. I'm sorry. But I wouldn't have made it if you hadn't, like, hounded me every day. I owe you, man."

Carly blinked. Something else she hadn't expected and couldn't quite grasp. "Oh. Wow!" She grinned. "You're welcome, but you were the one who overcame your fears and put on this amazing show. It must feel fantastic."

He nodded. "It does. I'm really glad I came."

She smiled. "Me, too."

"See you in Austin," he said, backing away. "We'll grab a Whataburger." He turned and jogged back to where people were waiting for him.

Carly was not late to meet Ramona in her office. Ramona was not kidding about the job, either. The pay was decent—actually, at this point in her life, it sounded like a king's ransom. After they discussed arrangements and start dates, Carly headed back to Naomi's, her head spinning.

It was happening. After all these years of working hard to make it in Austin, she had absolutely nothing left to show for it or to lose. There was nothing keeping her in Austin except a dog and a couple of hearts she did not want to break. Hers, for one. And Max's.

Twenty-Four

Late Saturday afternoon, Max received a text from Carly. She'd landed in Austin and asked if she could pick up Baxter. Max was happy to hear from her, eager to hear about her trip to New York, and eager to share his news, too.

Baxter and Hazel heard her before Max and Jamie did, and the two dogs raced to the door, barking and tails wagging. Max had to reach over them to open the door.

Carly was on his porch in a puffy jacket, jeans, and Uggs. Baxter launched himself at her legs with verve and missed. Hazel managed to plant her paws on Carly's thigh.

"Hey," Max said, and had to lean awkwardly forward, over the dogs, to hug her. He kissed her cheek. "You smell so good."

"Thank you!"

Jamie appeared, wearing a paint-spattered apron and holding a paintbrush. "Duke," he said. "Loyal and obedient. Likes dogs."

Carly looked at Max.

"Jamie is getting his dog today," Max said. "It's a big deal in the Sheffington household. His name is Duke, he is loyal and obedient, and we have an appointment to pick him up in an hour."

"Labrador," Jamie added, then turned and disappeared into the house with Baxter and Hazel hurrying along behind him.

Max grinned at Carly and brushed hair from her face. "Hey, gorgeous. How are you?"

"Good! *Tired*. By the way, have you heard from our parents?"

"You mean apart from the dozens of wedding photos last night? Not a peep. You?"

"Nothing," Carly said.

"I guess they are having a good time."

"*Eew*, don't," she said with a playful grimace. "Mia has been blowing up my phone. She's convinced there is some big conspiracy underfoot, because she can't get hold of Mom *or* Dad. But forget them—I'm dying to know how your presentation went," she said as they walked into the living room.

"It went well," he said. "It went very well, better than I expected." He was waiting for the right moment to tell her that it was him. By some miracle, he was the one being put forward for tenure. He sat on the couch and pulled Carly down beside him.

"And the other professor? How did she do?" Carly asked.

"She was good," he said. "Very interesting." She'd been so good that he'd felt himself sinking during her presentation. Alanna was impressive. When Max was summoned to a meeting with Dr. O'Malley yesterday, he'd assumed it was the meeting where the department chair would explain to Max that he was a good scientist but not ready to be put forward for tenure. Max had come to terms with it. So he'd stopped by O'Malley's office on his way to teach an undergraduate class and walked in, reached across the desk to shake O'Malley's hand, and said, "I want to thank you for the consideration. I understand that it's a difficult decision, but I was grateful just for the opportunity to present."

"Don't thank me," Dr. O'Malley said. "You did the work to get there."

"Yep. Well, again, thank you."

Dr. O'Malley looked at him strangely. "Don't you want to know the next steps?"

"For . . . ?"

"Dr. Sheffington . . . I called you here to inform you that the committee has recommended you for tenure. Your dossier will go to the dean, and if he agrees, you will next present to the university tenure committee."

Max had been so dumbfounded, he could only stare at him.

Dr. O'Malley graced him with a rare smile. "Did you hear what I said? We're putting you through for tenure."

It was odd how the brain worked, how cognitive distortion could take a very logical thing and make it illogical. Because this all seemed illogical to Max. He said, "Alanna . . ."

"Yes, Dr. Friedman is very good. But she doesn't quite have the breadth of research to support her work that you do." He reached his hand across his desk. "Congratulations, Dr. Sheffington. It is well deserved."

Max had been so stunned that he'd almost missed Alanna walking in to O'Malley's office as he was walking out.

"But, hey, I want to hear about your trip," he said. "How did things go?"

"*Horrible*, to start," Carly said. "Victor was a no-show on Wednesday."

"No way," Max said. "What happened?"

"He read his social media feed again and freaked out. But I trotted out some of the motivational things my high school cross-country coach used to say, and you know what? It worked like a boss. Better than it ever worked on me! Victor showed up on Thursday, and somehow he pulled a show together, and all things considered, it was actually pretty damn good."

Max grinned. "I'm not surprised. You seemed pretty determined to make it happen. But I have to know, did you wear one of his designs to the show? Please tell me you did and describe it in detail."

She playfully punched his arm. "You loved those sleeves, admit it. However, I did *not* wear them. Victor ended up showing the red and white pieces. Remember those?"

"Like I could ever forget?"

She laughed. "See? You will never forget the name Victor Allen. But since he'd cut up so many, he needed every extra piece and I had to wear regular clothes and Max? I *love* regular clothes." She laughed and laced her fingers through his. "Something else happened."

Her eyes were shining. She was happy. "What?" he asked.

"You know how I wanted a job in New York? In fashion publicity, or at least in publicity?"

He nodded.

"Well . . . I was offered one. One that I'd applied for, the one I really wanted. At one of the biggest fashion magazines in the country."

Max's breath hitched in his chest. "What's the job?"

"Working in the publicity department and scouting new talent. Oh my *God*," she said with a squeeze of his hand. "It's my dream job, Max!"

He tried, he really did try, to be ecstatic for her. "And it's in New York?" Dumb question, but he needed to hear her say it.

Her smile dimmed. "Well . . . yes."

"But what about . . ."

She knew the question he couldn't quite voice. *What about us?*

"It's what I've wanted to do for so long," she said. "I've worked really hard to get this opportunity."

"I know." Max didn't know if he was angry or resigned or what. He felt suddenly empty. Of course he knew that was her goal, but he hadn't expected this, not after the kind of luck she'd been having. He damn sure wasn't ready for this.

"And . . . it's the only solution I have to my job situation. I mean, I can live with Mom and your dad, but I don't have work, especially now. And I—"

"You don't have to explain it, Carly," he said, interrupting her before she twisted herself into an explanation she did not need to give. "I understand."

"But wait, Max, wait," she said and caught his hand between both of hers. "What if you came to New York, too?"

He gave a quiet laugh.

"I'm serious! If you're not getting tenure here, can't you get a job there? NYU, maybe?"

"Well, that's my news—I'm being put forward for tenure."

Her mouth fell open.

"Yep," he said with a sorrowful smile. "It's me. They picked me."

"*Max*," she whispered.

"I know, right?"

She suddenly threw her arms around his neck and squeezed him, then cupped his face. "I am so proud of you."

"And I am so proud of you," he said.

Her hands slid away from his face. "Oh my *God*, we are so snake-bitten."

He stroked her hair. "We're definitely something. We are—shit, I have to take Jamie to get his dog," he said, noticing the clock on the mantel behind her. "Can I call you later?"

"Sure," she said.

He stood up and took a jacket from the back of the couch. "When do you start your new job?"

Her face flushed. "In a week."

He dropped his arm. His heart began to crumble. "A *week*?"

"I don't have income," she said quietly. "I need to start work. So I'm going back Monday to look for a place to live."

"Jesus," he said helplessly. "So soon? What about Baxter?"

"I'm going to ask Mia to keep him until Mom and your dad have settled—"

"No," Max said, and pulled on his jacket before holding out a hand to pull her to her feet. "I'll keep him."

"I can't ask you to do that, Max."

"You're not asking—I'm demanding. I love that dog. Besides, it will give me an excuse to talk to you whenever I want." He kissed her. But only briefly. He was feeling a little sick.

"I want to bring him to New York," Carly said. "I love him, too, and I hate being without him—"

"Loyal and obedient. Lab."

They both turned as Jamie entered the room. He'd removed his apron. "His name is Duke."

"I can't wait to meet him," Carly said. "Baxter, come."

The dog came forward, his tail wagging with anticipation, happy to be called.

"He's missed you," Max said. "We've all missed you."

"Loyal and obedient. Duke," Jamie said.

"Carly, I have to go," Max said. "Can we talk later?"

"Sure. Yes. I just . . ." She dragged her fingers through her hair. "My love to all the dogs, okay? Send me a picture, will you?"

"His name is Duke," Jamie said. "He's good with dogs." He walked out of the house before them. Baxter ran behind him, and Max tossed Hazel a biscuit as he followed Carly and Jamie out.

Carly put Baxter into her car, then waved at Max before slipping into the driver's seat. Max waved back. But even from that distance, he could see the look in her eye. She knew. Just like he knew. This thing between them, this beautiful, unexpected, wonderful thing, could not overcome the forces in their lives. It couldn't knock them off the roads they'd labored to pave for themselves.

"Loyal and obedient," Jamie said.

"That's right," Max said. "His name is Duke."

Duke's arrival in his new home was not without incident. He was overexcited and couldn't stop jumping and drooling on everything. Hazel took exception for some reason, and there was an immediate issue over who would be the alpha and who would not. Duke, a happy Lab, quickly acquiesced, but the first day was tense.

Jamie was beside himself with joy. He'd bought Duke a neon green collar, and because Duke was a black Lab, at night, when the lights were off, it looked a little like a disembodied collar moving around the house.

Max tried more than once to FaceTime his dad so that he could see Duke and be here for Jamie's big day. But he couldn't get the old man on the phone. He assumed that his father was honeymooning.

He texted Carly, but she said that her sister was having trouble, sick with her pregnancy and no one to watch the kids. Plus, they were worried that they couldn't get ahold of either parent.

It felt as if everything was moving so fast. The weekend had rushed past before Max could catch a breath. Carly arrived Sunday night to meet Duke and to drop Baxter off again. Baxter raced into the house toward Hazel, but Duke hadn't seen him coming and was startled. A lot of barking and shouting ensued, Jamie shrieking that Duke was loyal and obedient. Duke hadn't gotten the memo.

When they got the dogs calmed down, Carly asked Max once more if he was certain he was okay keeping her dog.

"I'm certain. Baxter is part of the family."

Carly couldn't stay. She had to pack and then go check on her parents' houses, as Mia was still feeling ill and they still hadn't heard a word. "My family," she said with a shake of her head.

"Are you worried?"

"Nope. I know where Mom is, and my guess is Dad is back with his very young girlfriend. What about your dad?"

He shook his head. "I have no doubt he's living his best life right now."

Carly nodded, but she was looking over her shoulder at her car. Max took the opportunity to impress this image of her on his hippocampus. He wanted to remember every freckle, every loose strand of hair. He didn't want to forget her like this, wrapped in a wool coat, the tip of her nose pink from the cool air, her lashes long, her hair silky on her shoulder.

When she turned back to him she said, "I guess I better go."

"So this is it?"

"*No,*" she said. "But sort of. And if you make a thing out of it, I will cry."

"I will join you," he said, and wrapped his arms around her.

"I'm so sorry, Max," she said into his coat.

"Don't be. The worst thing would be for you to give up this opportunity and then one day wake up and resent the hell out of the fact that you stayed."

"I know," she whispered. "I wish it was different. I so wish it was different."

"Me, too," he said sadly. "Carly, I—"

"Nope. No," she said, and lifted her head from his chest. "I am not going to do whatever you are about to do."

He stroked her cheek. "I wasn't going to do anything. You deserve this shot, and I wish you—"

"Yep, okay, enough of that." She pushed out of his embrace, her eyes glistening. She popped up, kissed him on the cheek. "Bye, Baxter!" she shouted over his shoulder, and then fled to her car. "I'll call you! Remember, dogs don't belong on the couch!"

He lifted his hand and waved. He was not offended by her abrupt departure. He completely understood—neither of them wanted to say goodbye, because when they did, they both knew that would be the end.

Twenty-Five

If Max had been a betting man, he would have lost, because the end came faster than he ever would have guessed. Not him and Carly, although that end came much faster than he wanted. But twelve days after his father eloped to Las Vegas, it was over. Just long enough for Jamie and Duke to move in with Max. Just long enough for Jamie to create a new painting of three dogs, with two men in the background who were not Jamie and his father, but Jamie and his brother.

Just long enough that Max managed to take a day off from work to take Jamie around to check out some group homes. One of them was next to a park and on a bus line, and would accept Jamie's "service" dog. The home was expensive, but Max thought that he and his dad could make it work.

On a crisp and cool Thursday afternoon, Max was finishing up his last class when he got a call from Jamie. When he answered, Jamie shrieked, *"Too much noise!"*

Max couldn't get Jamie to say more. In the background, he could hear Duke barking. He dropped Bonnie at the lab and then he ran. He thought his father had died. He thought there had been a heart attack or a stroke, and he raced to his car, his arms pumping and his legs churning.

But when he got to his father's house, he found his father very much alive and on his feet. Jamie had been with Max the last week while his father slowly packed and got ready to move to Evelyn's. He was busily gathering things that clearly belonged to Evelyn—quite a lot, Max thought, in such a short time—and piling them on the kitchen table.

"What's going on?" Max asked.

His father paused in his almost maniacal gathering. "I'm only going to say this once, Tobias Maxwell. You were right—it was all too fast. I didn't know her well enough. Fuck that—I didn't know her at *all*. But it's done, and I never want to lay eyes on the woman again. *Never*. I don't care if she drops dead tomorrow, I won't be at her funeral."

"Whoa," Max said, holding up both hands. "What happened?"

"Don't ask," his father said, and tossed a bra onto the pile. "Just get her shit out of here." He jerked around to where Jamie was rocking back and forth. "Jamie, stop the caterwauling! You saw a heated argument, so what!" And with that he stomped down the hall. They heard the door to his room slam shut.

Max looked at Jamie. He was breathing hard, his chest rising and falling. "Too much *noise*," he insisted again.

"I know, buddy." Max glanced at Duke, who was supposed to be soothing Jamie. But Duke was on his belly on the tile floor, his head between his paws, as if it were a lazy summer afternoon.

His dad returned a moment later, marching down the hall and unceremoniously dumping clothing onto a pile at the back door. "Take those things to her and get my things, Max. If I see her, I'm telling you, I may kill her."

"You *just* married her, so maybe take the murder talk down a notch or two."

"I'll get it annulled and then I'll kill her." He turned again, and they listened to him mutter under his breath all the way down the hall. And then his door slammed shut.

Max found a couple of grocery bags, stuffed Evelyn's things into them, told Jamie to work on his painting and take care of his dog, and that everything was okay. No more noise.

When he pulled into Evelyn's drive twenty minutes later, he instantly knew that the neatly stacked boxes on the porch were his father's things. From what he could see, there was the handle of a skillet poking out the top of one and a sunhat he recognized. Max thought he'd place his two bags of her things on the porch, grab his dad's stuff, and make a quick getaway. But the moment he put the bags on the porch and picked up the first box, Evelyn came striding out in a silk caftan that flowed around her.

"Hello, Max," she said.

"Evelyn." He took the box to his car.

She folded her arms and watched him come back for the next one. "Did he tell you what happened?"

Max grimaced. The last thing he wanted was to get dragged into the middle of this. He shook his head.

"Well, I'm sorry. I owe you all an apology and you have it. My *sincerest* apologies. But I couldn't have predicted what happened. I thought I knew—"

A man suddenly appeared behind Evelyn. He stepped around her and came off the porch. "You must be Max." He offered his hand.

Max stared at him, trying to work out who he was, ignoring his hand.

The man dropped his hand. "I'm Paul Kennedy."

Carly's dad? What the hell was happening right now?

"We sincerely apologize for—"

"Don't apologize for true love, Paul," Evelyn interrupted. "That's what we always had and we still do. We just lost our way a little bit." This, she directed at Max.

"I don't . . . understand," Max said.

"I'm sorry, Son," Mr. Kennedy said. "Evelyn and I have been dancing around this thing."

"This *thing*?" Max said angrily. "My dad hasn't been dancing around. How long has this been a thing?"

"Forty years is all," Evelyn said defensively.

"Great. You've been dancing around this *thing*, but you got us all in the middle of it, and you took my dad on this roller coaster and married him," Max reminded her.

"I know, and I feel very bad about that," she said quickly. "Unfortunately, that's what it took for Paul and me to realize that what we were doing was *crazy*—"

"I tried to stop them," Carly's father said. "I wasn't able to, and then things got messy, and, well, the bottom line is, here we are. Evelyn and I are back together and committed to resolving our issues."

Max stared at them, both of them looking back with such sheepish expressions. "You are standing on the ruins of two families," he said. "I hope you can live with that." He picked up the last box and walked to his car. He didn't look back. He drove to the strip mall with the Target and parked in the lot. He closed his eyes for a long moment. His poor dad. And, sheesh, poor Carly with parents like that.

Carly.

He texted her for the first time in days. He'd intentionally tried to stay away, to make a clean break. But this, she needed to know.

Hi, Carly. Checking in to see if you're okay. I guess you heard?

Max! So happy it's you! Heard what?

She didn't know. Max dialed her number.

Twenty-Six

Carly had managed to shove her suitcase onto the one shelf she had in her tiny little closet. Now rose the question of what to do with her handbags. She was studying her dire situation when her phone rang. She backed away from the closet, huffing with the exertion of unpacking, blew her hair out of her face, and glanced down. "Max!" she said with delight and answered the phone. "Hey!" She bounced onto her bed.

"Hi, Carly."

They had texted sporadically since Carly had taken the job in New York. Sporadically, because even though they hadn't declared it so, she thought they were both trying to ease out of what could never be. But this thing between them was hard to end—there was true affection there. True *love*. Carly was clinging to a fantasy that he might actually come to New York. She'd created the whole thing in her head—they would be away from her crazy family. He would visit Jamie every month. Baxter and Hazel would learn to potty on the patches of green around the trees in the sidewalks, and they would walk them through parks, and order in, and go out, and host supper parties with fabulous friends.

"How are you?" he asked.

"I am . . ." She had to stop and think about it. *Life begins at the end of your comfort zone!* Megan Monroe had shouted on her podcast yesterday. "I'm good, I think. I'm discovering New York." She was discovering a shabby corner of New Jersey, actually. She was not living with Naomi—it was too small for four women, and Naomi said no dogs and Carly really wanted Baxter. Funny how that dog had worked its way into her membrane. Hazel, too, for that matter.

"Did you get moved in?" he asked.

"Today, actually. I went with the one in New Jersey. You know, the one with only the hour commute." She laughed. "It's actually not horrible."

"Oh, well, then, not horrible," he said with a chuckle. "What's the place like?"

She looked around at the space. A tiny sink and an electric cooktop stove were two feet from her bed. Her bed—purchased at one of the big-box discount furniture places—left hardly any room for anything else other than a chair. There was a small space in the corner where she hoped she could stuff a dog bed. "It is teeny tiny," she said. "I have a view of an air-conditioning thing and the bathroom has a shower and sink all in one, and I have a major closet situation working, as in no place for my handbags."

"That sounds ridiculously unworkable, Carly."

"It is! I looked at another apartment that would have accommodated the handbags, but rent is astronomically high around here." And she'd thought Conrad's rent was out of line. She laughed again, but the truth was that she was worried if she could really afford New York, even with her new salary. She'd signed a six-month lease in a building that catered to short-term rentals. That was all she could afford to commit to right now, and she sincerely hoped that she wouldn't have to stay in this dreadful box any longer than that.

She missed her cottage. She missed Max and the dogs and everything about Austin. It was cold in New York. It was loud and crowded and there wasn't a lot of green. Plus, there was not a decent breakfast taco to be found.

"How's the job?" Max asked.

"Interesting," she said. She still hadn't figured out what she was doing there.

"Do you like it?"

Did she? She wasn't sure. "I've only been on the job three days, so I'm not quite sure what I think. There's so much to learn," she said. "And my coworkers are . . . confused." *Confused* was actually kind— her coworkers seemed mostly resentful of Carly.

"Why?" Max asked.

"Well, for starters, Ramona didn't tell anyone she'd hired me. On my first day, when no one knew I was coming, they had to make room for me. Which meant moving a couple of people." She shook her head. "It was horrible, Max. One guy quit and walked out into a rainstorm. My boss said he was always unhappy, but I don't know, I think it was because of me. Still, it's a *great* opportunity." That was her mantra. She didn't like the job right now, but she would. She had to give it time, she had to work hard. Everything new required a process of growth and she had to be patient. As Megan exhorted daily on her podcast, she had to pull on her big girl panties. "The magazine is doing a feature on Victor in April. And guess what? He's in Los Angeles right now, working on a wedding collection for *Lovely Bride*."

"Okay, *that* I cannot picture."

She laughed. "So, hey, how's my pup? Have you found that kangaroo food I told you about? He really likes it. And he really should have bottled water, Max. You don't know what's in the tap water sometimes."

"Don't you worry about Baxter. He's living the life. I have a new dog walker who, insofar as I know, is not dealing drugs next to Stevie Ray. Fabian takes the creek path behind my house, and they love him."

"They love everyone. But he sounds perfect. How's school?"

"Good. The dean approved my tenure and sent it forward, so the ball is rolling. I should have a final decision in a month. So, hey, have you talked to your mom recently?" he asked.

Carly had been too busy to keep up with the family dramas. Mia had texted her, worried that neither parent answered her calls, or if they did, they were always too busy to talk. *Something is not right, Carly, I'm telling you*, she'd texted. And then she'd invariably launch into her complaints about morning sickness or the newest household catastrophe—Finn's broken arm, earned when he climbed a ladder he found in the garage and tried to fly like Superman from it. *I miss you so much*, Mia had texted. *I never realized how much I need you.*

Carly had never realized how much she needed Mia, either.

"Not for a few days," Carly said. "Why?"

"Then you don't know that they ended things."

Carly frowned. "Who ended what?"

"My dad and your mother have ended their marriage. They split up."

Carly's breath caught. That was impossible. They'd been married less than two weeks! She suddenly laughed. "If that's your idea of a joke, it's not funny, Dr. Sheffington, because that sounds too close to something my mother would do. Last I heard, your dad was packing up things and moving in."

"I wish I was kidding, but I'm not. It's over."

The news caught Carly off guard, but part of her was not surprised—her mother was unpredictable. "*Why?*" she asked. "What happened?"

"That's the thing I think you should know. Seems like your dad is, umm . . . he's back in the picture."

Carly gasped. All of Mia's warnings began to clang in her head. "Oh my God," she whispered. "You're absolutely sure?"

"Oh yeah," he said. "He apologized to me for everything they put us through."

Carly didn't know what she was supposed to feel, but fury leapt right to the top. "I *knew* something would happen. I told you—didn't I tell you?"

"You told me," he agreed.

"So now what? I mean, my mother and your dad got married, right?"

"Yep," Max said. "My dad says he's filing for a dissolution. I guess what happens in Vegas . . ."

"Stays in Vegas," she muttered. "Oh my God, Max, your poor dad! How is he?"

"He's pretty fucking furious, to be honest. Apparently, your parents were chatting it up all along."

"Mia was right," she muttered. "What about Jamie?"

"He's great," Max said. "He wasn't a fan of the arrangement."

"Me and Jamie both." She fell back on her bed and closed her eyes. Somewhere above her, a couple was fighting, and down the hall, someone was singing off-key.

"Sorry to be the bearer of bad news," he said. "You're doing okay?"

"Me? Doing *great*. New York is so exciting."

"Is it me, or does that sound a little like a line from a podcast?"

Carly and Max had not known each other very long, but he was good at reading her. He seemed to know when she was substituting enthusiasm for her true feelings.

She sighed. "Busted. Honestly, it's hard. I don't know anyone and my apartment is far from work. But, you know, I signed a lease, and I've got health care, and it's a job in my field which I am super excited about, and it's a job that I never would get in Austin."

Max didn't say anything for a moment. When he did, he sounded hoarse and weary. "That's great. I'm so happy for you."

"You're going to have to come visit," she said eagerly.

"Maybe someday," he said vaguely.

Another moment of silence passed. "Our timing sucks, doesn't it?" Carly said softly.

"Massively." He sounded very far away to her. Like he was already fading from her life. "You should probably call your mom."

"I'm really looking forward to that. Hey . . . I'm coming for Baxter, you know."

He said nothing for a very long moment. "Hazel will be heartbroken."

"Hey, Max? I sincerely . . ." She swallowed, trying to find the right word.

"You don't have to thank me, Carly. I love Baxter, too."

"No, I wasn't . . . I was going to say that I sincerely *love* you." She said it in a near whisper. "I do. So much. I wish I was there, to tell you in person. But I want you to know." She closed her eyes, waiting for him to speak.

He groaned. "I love you, too, Carly. You will always be my right person at the wrong time."

That did not make her feel better, it made her feel that much sadder. "I'll call you later?"

There was another long silence, and she heard Max draw a shaky breath. "I think it's best if we don't."

Carly's heart stopped. She slowly sat up. Panic began to fill in at her edges. "Why?"

"Because this is too hard. Don't you find this too hard?" he asked. "I walk around miserable half the time, with you up there and me down here, and just wanting to be with you. What are we even doing? We are the two unluckiest people in the world, but if this is it, we need to let it go."

"You mean like never speak?" she asked him. "We can't just . . . check in?"

"Baby . . . it's a breakup. That's the way these things go. I don't know about you, but I need a minute. Do you understand? My heart . . . my heart is broken."

Carly couldn't respond to that because her throat was thick with grief. She had no idea his heart was broken. She had no idea he was longing for her like that. He'd been nothing but supportive and . . . and she was such an *idiot*. What was she doing? Living in a box trying to be someone in a big pond when a guy like that was longing for her? But what was she supposed to do, give up everything she'd made of herself and all the goals she'd set because a man was into her?

"Listen, you need to go live your life and I need to live mine. If we can't make this work, then we need to let go."

"You are making this sound so final, Max."

"Carly . . . it *is* final. It's been final. It was final the day you took a job in New York and I got the green light from my department's tenure committee. We're going in opposite directions."

There was no argument she could give him to make that any less true or this conversation any better. He was right—it wasn't practical, and there was nothing that she could say to make it so. "But can't we at least be friends?" she asked tearfully.

"Of course we can. Always. I just need some time."

So that was that.

When Carly clicked off the phone and looked around at her box of an apartment, she felt so sick that all she could do was curl around a pillow and listen to the fighting upstairs.

She picked up one of her ridiculously expensive handbags to throw at the wall. It was a soft bag and wafted through the air. A piece of paper fluttered out of it and fell on her bed. She picked it up. It was the name of the singer from the Yard Bar. The girl with the beautiful voice and haunting music and absolutely no online presence.

Carly tacked the paper to her wall, then grabbed her things and went out in search of a bar.

Twenty-Seven

Two Months Later
New York City

It was sleeting, and traffic was snarled, and Carly was going to be late. She kept leaning forward to peer out the front window of the cab.

"That ain't going to help," the cabbie said.

"You're killing me," she muttered, and dug her phone out. She'd been at a photo shoot on the Upper East Side today. She'd discovered a woman who made fascinators of iconic New York sights. The little shop was adjoined to an art gallery that was currently featuring impressionist art that reminded her of Jamie's paintings.

The fascinators were delightful, and Ramona loved them. She loved everything Carly was doing. Priyana, who shared cube space with Carly, had the most luxurious thick hair Carly had ever seen and the worst scowl. She rolled her eyes when Ramona stopped by one day to tell Carly to keep up the good work. "She likes you now, but just wait. When she turns, she turns."

She hadn't turned yet, and had given Carly the green light to get some professional photos of the fascinators. The only day the designer

could do it was today. *Today.* The day she was going to see Max
again.

It had been a very pleasant surprise to receive his text. They'd been
texting a little here and there, mostly about the dogs. She'd assumed,
when he'd finally texted her out of the blue with a hi, how are you, a few
weeks after their breakup, that he'd gotten over it. She'd done an ad-
mirable job of restraining herself and not bombarding him with questions. She wanted to know everything, but more than that, she
desperately wanted him in her life. She still loved him. She missed him
desperately.

And then he'd made her day, her week, her month and sent her a
picture of Baxter and Hazel side by side, looking up.

> OMG! They are adorable! However, B is looking a little chonky.
> What's our rule about mac and cheese?

> Your rule is that he doesn't get any. My rule is he does if H does
> because it's only fair. I'm wondering if you're up for dinner next
> Wednesday? I'm in town to make a speech. Quick trip, in and
> out, but I'd love to see you if you are available.

Was he kidding? She would leap tall buildings in a single bound if
he asked.

> Not only am I available, I am so excited to see you. I know a great
> restaurant. Cuban Japanese fusion! I haven't actually been there,
> but I've heard it's great. I'll make a reservation and text you the
> addy. 7?

> Perfect. Looking forward to it.

Not as much as she was! She'd brought clothes with her to the
photo shoot, and used a back room to change. The shoot had run late,

because of course it did, and it had taken forever to get a cab. But at last, the cab pulled up outside the restaurant and she dashed inside.

She spotted him instantly. He was standing at the hostess desk in a long trench coat and a knit cap—a new one, she noted. He had a scruff of a beard and he was wearing his glasses. Carly's heart began to race. She was astonishingly nervous. Max was the most gorgeous thing—did she know that about him? Had she appreciated just how gorgeous he was? And it wasn't just her—the hostess was all googly-eyed as she chatted him up.

"Max," Carly said.

He turned, and his eyes went all soft and light. "Carly." He opened his arms, and she walked right into them, like she'd never left Austin. He kissed her like a friend, a quick peck, and then smiled down at her. "You cut your hair."

"I did! It's a lob now."

"Nice hat," he said, smiling with amusement.

She put her hand to her head. She'd forgotten she was wearing a fascinator shaped like a blue Tiffany box. "Oh. Well, that's a story."

Max grinned. "I can't wait to hear it."

The suddenly pouty hostess took their coats and Max's hat, and Carly swore his hair tumbled out of it like a shampoo commercial, except that it wasn't that long. He was wearing the outfit she'd put together for him when he'd made his presentation for tenure.

At the table, they ordered drinks and Max started by asking about her job. They never stopped talking. They hardly stopped long enough to order. But Carly wasn't interested in food. She told him about the fascinators, how Ramona really liked her work. He told her that he was getting an endowment that would be more money for research and more money for him.

She asked about Jamie. Max said he was doing great. He was in a home that housed six adults with special needs, run by a retired couple whose daughter had Down syndrome. The adults shared a kitchen, but Jamie had his own room, and there was a yard for Duke. Another resident had a collie for a service dog, and Duke and Molly had quickly become inseparable. Jamie's artwork was already appearing on the walls of the house. He rode the bus every day to the ACC and came home to his dad's house on weekends. He still had never missed a shift of work.

"There is an art gallery on the Upper East Side where I could see his work," Carly said. "He could make a fortune."

Max smiled and looked at the food on his plate.

"What about your dad?" Carly asked. "How is he after . . . you know."

"Now there is a man who knows how to bounce back," Max said with a wink. He reported that their parents' annulment was on a court docket in Vegas next month, and that his dad and some of his buddies were flying out to make a weekend out of it. He said his dad was back to his old self and joking about the time he'd lost his damn mind. Carly told him that her parents were planning on remarrying, but that they were going to do it in private, and none of the children were invited. "I don't think they want a peanut gallery," she said.

Max said there had been a feature about Victor Allen in the *Austin American-Statesman* recently, and a picture of him standing next to a bridal gown, and that he was wearing a long skirt himself.

Carly laughed. "He's someone else who can bounce back very fast and very high. He's been trying to talk me into doing some work for him, but I already have a crazy job." She told him Mia had finally found a nanny, which was good, because this pregnancy was a hard one for her.

Max said Baxter and Hazel loved the new dog walker. He asked if she still planned to come and get Baxter.

The question made her infinitely sad. "I don't know," she said, and it hurt so much to say that. It hurt so much to admit that what was best for Baxter was not best for her. "He seems very happy with you. I don't think he'd be happy in my tiny apartment, and me gone all day."

Max smiled sympathetically. "It would be hard on you both."

When they had finished what they were going to eat of their meal, Carly put her fork down and said, "May I ask you a personal question? A nosy one?"

"What, you didn't google beforehand?" he teased her.

"Of course I did. But you are notoriously bad about posting news."

"That, I am. What do you want to know?"

"Are you dating the other professor?" she blurted. It had been a worry since he'd popped back up in her texts. The idea that he was over their breakup because he'd moved on.

He looked confused. "What other professor?"

"You know . . . the one who was up for tenure."

Max blinked. "Alanna?" He suddenly grinned. "No. First of all, she is transferring to Rutgers. And second, that was definitely a one-night kind of thing." His eyes moved over her face. "What about you? Are you dating anyone?"

She shook her head. "No. I haven't met anyone who comes close to measuring up to the last guy."

Max said nothing. He held her gaze for one very interminable moment. He reached across the table for her hand. She slipped it into his palm and it felt as if everything they hadn't said the day they broke up was churning between them.

But then Max looked at his watch.

"Need to go?" Carly asked as her heart plummeted.

"I have a super early flight in the morning and a class tomorrow afternoon." He glanced up and smiled. He pulled his hand free of hers. "This has been great. It's so good to see you."

Carly tried to smile, but she felt a little sick. "Are we friends now?"

"Always, Carly."

He paid the check and they got their coats and he put on his beanie, and they stood at the window looking out at the icy sleet coming down. Carly was shivering. Max put his arm around her. She closed her eyes a moment, relishing the feel of him. Missing it so terribly.

"I'm going to get a cab. Can I drop you somewhere?" he asked.

"No, I'm going to walk up the block and get a train home."

"Ready?" he asked. "You're shivering."

She wasn't shivering because of the cold. Because she couldn't bear this goodbye, either. "Ready," she said.

They stepped out onto the street. Max went to the curb and put up his hand. At a stoplight up the street, a cab put on its blinker and turned off its taxi light, indicating it was coming for Max.

Max looked back at Carly. "Carly, I . . ." The light turned green and the traffic started rolling through the intersection.

"I miss you," he said.

"What?"

"I just miss you so much," he said. "Me and the dogs. We think about you all the time."

The cab pulled up to the curb. Max opened the car door. But he looked back at Carly and he looked panicked.

"Max, I—"

"Listen," he said, and grabbed her hand. "I should have said this earlier. Or maybe I shouldn't say anything, I don't know. But if anything ever changes . . . Jesus, I am bad at this." He took both her hands. Someone behind the cab honked. "I miss you so damn much. I love you. It's not over for me, it's never going to be over, and I knew you got your hair cut and you wear buildings and boxes on your head because I google you, and I just can't stop and I need you to tell me to stop."

"Max!" she cried, and cupped his face with her mittened hands. "Why didn't you say so?"

"Because you have your job here, and nothing has changed, and I would never ask you to give up your life for me. It's just wishful thinking, but I can't stop wishing, and I . . . I wish for you all the fucking time."

Carly's heart swelled in her chest, pushing against her ribs. She put her arms around him and kissed him. Max threw his arm around her waist and moaned into her mouth and kissed her back. It was a lovely kiss. A beautiful kiss. It was the best kiss of her life.

And then, just like that, he faded away from her and got in the cab and drove away.

L ater, when she was back in her apartment, staring at the piece of paper with the songwriter's name on it, he texted her.

> Sorry about that. Emotions got the best of me and I really can't read a room.

>> You read the room right. I didn't have the chance to tell you that I miss you, too. I wish for you all the time too, Max.

>> I hope you'll call me when you're in town. I promise, no more awkward declarations.

>>> ♥

Twenty-Eight

Two Months After That
Austin, Texas

It was another dull Friday at work. Max had Bonnie the Wonder Dog in the lab today, and the students were working with her while he supposedly entered data. But in truth he was staring out the window at another dreary rainy day.

It seemed to him like every day felt dreary of late. He'd given his dossier presentation to the campus tenure committee in a torrential rain. That group had enthusiastically recommended him forward and now his application was with the university provost. According to O'Malley, it was a done deal.

On a day that was bitterly cold, O'Malley told Max about the endowment that would allow him to significantly increase the scope of his work. Not to mention give him a fat pay raise. And on a day where the clouds hung low over campus, he got word that some German scientists planned to visit in a month, intrigued by what he was doing.

Everything was working out in spite of weather doldrums. So why did he feel so glum?

When the lab was over, and the ACC volunteer had picked up Bonnie, and the students wandered out talking excitedly about the work they were doing, Max gathered up his things and headed home.

Baxter and Hazel were waiting for him at the door. They always seemed to know just when to position themselves there. Max sighed at the sight of their bright brown eyes and tails wagging in perfect unison. Today was not a Fabian day, and they were eager to go out. He supposed he ought to be grateful they would make him walk. Otherwise, he suspected he'd end up on his couch with a couple of beers and a bag of chips. Again.

The thing was, Max had ended relationships before, and after a couple of weeks, he generally bounced back from them. He'd even bounced back from Flavia fairly quickly. But he couldn't seem to bounce back from Carly. It had been what, three or four months? And with the exception of his outburst in New York, he'd worked hard to put it behind him. From a scientist's perspective, he thought his emotional state was weird—they hadn't been together that long. But they had connected in every way and in some dusty corner of his mind, he knew that she was the one who got away. He couldn't explain it. His brain was a bunch of sluggish neurons, whatever. It could be the unscientific, indescribable broken heart. But he lacked all motivation to figure it out.

He stuffed a knit cap on his head, leashed up the dogs, and said, "Come on. Let's get this over with."

They didn't care if he was happy or sad. They eagerly pulled him down the street to the entrance to the path along the creek.

Everyone's life was rolling along, but Max was stuck in a rut. He'd lost his footing and had slid off into this ditch and now he couldn't get out. He thought about Carly too much. He'd finally logged on Instagram just to see what she was doing. She posted a lot. She looked happy and beautiful and living her best life in New York. He saw pictures of her at a party. Pictures of her with her friends, always laughing, always out and about. There were pictures of her workspace and the food she ate. As much as he hated to admit it, she looked like she belonged there.

Not here. Not with him.

He had to figure out how to accept that.

He'd done a complete circuit with his hounds and was letting them lead him home. They were nearing the entrance to the street where the trees cast a long shadow in the gray light. There was a park bench there, next to a posted warning about entering the greenbelt during a flood. Someone was sitting on the park bench, tying a shoe. One of the dogs started to whimper as they walked past.

"Well, hel-*lo*, Handsome."

Max's heart seized. He stopped walking. He turned back to the woman on the park bench. She was not speaking to him, but to Baxter. Both dogs leapt up at her, and she leaned over them, laughing with delight and accepting their kisses.

"Carly?"

She stood up. Her eyes sparkling. She had on a knit cap, too, and her hair spilled around her face, and she looked . . . she looked glorious. His heart began to thud in his chest. He had trouble finding his tongue.

"Oh! Did I catch you coming back from your mountain hibernation?" She touched the beard he had now because he couldn't be bothered to shave. "*Nice*. Full and fluffy and may I say, *very* sexy."

"What are you doing here?" he managed to ask.

She held out an arm and pushed her way through two excited bassets to hug him. "Hi, Max. It is *so good* to see you." She put her arms around him and held him tight.

He stiffened at first, but then he smelled her perfume, and he felt her hair on his face, and her warmth, and he closed his eyes and hoped this wasn't a dream.

She let go and took a step back.

Something in Max, which had been moored and had sprouted barnacles and had grown into a reef, broke free and began to drift. "You should have let me know you'd be in town. I didn't know you were coming."

"I had to come. You have my dog, and I'm going to need him."

Max's heart fell. "You've come for Baxter?"

"Sort of," she said cheerfully. She slipped her hand into his and pulled him until he had to walk beside her. "Hey, remember that singer we heard at the Yard Bar?"

"What?"

"She had such a pretty voice and her music was so haunting."

"I mean . . . yes, but—"

"Well, she has a *horrible* online presence. I'm talking caveman level social media."

"I don't—"

"I couldn't get her out of my mind! I mean, can you imagine having that kind of talent and no one knowing about it? Her name is Suzanna Harper, by the way. Anyway, I called her up and told her that her publicity sucks, and at first, she was not appreciative of my frank assessment, but after we talked, she agreed that she could use some help. So I'm here. Helping her."

"Wait, are you—"

"And Deja Brew," she said, squeezing his hand. "Have you heard of them? They are opening six new stores in Austin with a flagship on Congress, and they put out a request for bids for a publicity campaign because they know they are going to need help to compete with Starbucks, right? Well, they thought my ideas were great, which they totally are, and I told them, the great thing about me, is that I never give up. I told them what Megan Monroe says, that if you want something, you need to ask for it, and I was asking for it, and they were, like, yeah, no, you're pretty annoying in this—I'm paraphrasing of course—and I was, like, right, so think how effective I would be getting the word out. Oh! I almost forgot! I'm even doing some work for Victor. I'm doing all of his social media. He's sworn it off. *Finally*, oh my God."

Max stopped walking and made her look at him. "What's going on? What are you telling me?"

"That I have two new clients!" she said happily. "The pay is not great—actually, it's pretty awful, so I will not be able to drape you in diamonds. But for now, it's enough to get by."

Max became aware of a reverberation around him. It was the sound of his heart, thrumming away in his ears. "You may move back to Austin?"

She laughed. "*Am* moving back to Austin. Just as soon as you help me get out of New York. Will you help me? I'm going to live in my dad's house for a couple of months while he gets it ready to put it on the market. Because, you know . . . he's living with Mom. Oh! And I should definitely stress that I will be completely broke for a few weeks because I figure it's going to cost me everything I have left in the bank to break my lease if I can't sublet it. And, trust me, it is going to be tough to sublet because, man, is it a tiny little hellhole. There is not enough Megan Monroe in the world to get me to see that place as having any potential."

All the things Max thought he'd lost were cropping up like rain lilies all around him. Little rain lily possibilities—he and Carly, their dogs. Their lives. "What about your job? It was the one you wanted."

"Funny, it turns out that I didn't want it. I mean, Ramona will never speak to me again, but I figured out that what I like is solving problems. I don't like sitting at a desk. And between you and me, living in Jersey was not what it was cracked up to be. Plus, I couldn't *breathe*."

"Too crowded?"

"Yes, but I couldn't breathe because I didn't have you, Max. Have you ever felt that way? Like something is weighing on you and you aren't sure what, you only know that you can't breathe? I can't breathe without you."

Baxter barked to gain her attention.

"I know! I'm coming home for you, too, you lucky dog. Look at you, living here with treats and Hazel and mac and cheese!"

Max was stunned. After all the hours he'd spent thinking about her, wishing for her, and here she was, appearing out of thin air to save him from himself.

She squeezed his hand, brought it to her mouth, and kissed his knuckles. "I know it's a lot to take in. And maybe you've finally moved on, and maybe there is a new Carly coming over later. But if there is, I am ready to fight her for you. Except that I'm not a fighter, so it will be ugly, and I'll probably hurt myself, but, Max, you are the best thing. You *are*. You are worth fighting for, and I have missed you *so much*. And if there isn't another Carly, I am here to tell you that I love you, and I've loved you from the moment you got me out of that skirt. And I am never going to love anyone like I love you, so if you still love me, I thought—"

"There is no other Carly. There could never be another Carly— are you crazy?"

"Are you sure? Because—"

"Carly. Stop talking," he said, and grabbed her up and kissed her. He kissed her with all the despair and desire and the longing he'd felt in the several months, wishing for something he thought could never be. He pressed his forehead to hers. "I've been wrecked since you left. But . . . but I don't want you to give up what you've worked for."

"But that's the best part, Max—I'm not giving up anything. There is more than one way to achieve what I want, and, trust me, I've worked just as hard for this, because *this* is what I want. So do you think . . ."

"Yes," he said instantly. "I need you here. I love you."

"And it's not like a histamine thing?"

He laughed. He took her head in his hands. "There is no scientific explanation for how much I love you and I don't care. I don't even want to know. I've missed you madly, Carly, you have no idea." He kissed her again and kept kissing her until one of the dogs tried to crawl in between them and the other barked at someone passing by.

"We're causing a scene," Carly muttered.

"Don't care. But, yeah, maybe the house would be a better place for you to tell me why I am just finding out about this." He wrapped an arm tightly around Carly and took her home.

Later, when he and Carly had exhausted everything they wanted to say, and had reconnected in his bed in a way that he would be corny enough to describe as transcendental, he would feel his happiness mushrooming in him, and his relief and his anticipation, and he would muse that Baxter was indeed a lucky dog—but for Max. He was the luckiest charm Max had ever come across, because he had brought Carly into his life.

He would be forever grateful to Baxter and a pothead named Brant.

Epilogue

It was an early spring day when Suzanna Harper played in the expansive backyard garden of the brand-new Deja Brew Coffeehouse on South Congress Avenue. Carly, Max, and Jamie and Duke were guests of honor, as Carly had arranged the event for her new client, Suzanna Harper.

In the window of the Deja Brew was a fancy, artistic poster proclaiming Suzanna Harper would be playing by special engagement. The fine print informed guests that she had also secured a spot in the annual South by Southwest Music Festival, and a list of dates for her appearances at the festival. Suzanna had a new website, too, done for a song by one of Max's undergraduates looking for extra money.

In the window on the other side of the door was a smaller poster:

KING MUTT!

COMING IN JUNE

VOTE WITH YOUR DOLLARS FOR YOUR FAVORITE DOG
AT ALL PARTICIPATING LOCATIONS!

ALL PROCEEDS WILL GO TO BENEFIT THE
AUSTIN CANINE COALITION

KEEP AUSTIN WEIRD!

Carly's other new client, the Deja Brew coffeehouses, had agreed to participate in the annual fundraiser. "Nothing will get people in the door faster than a cute baby or a dog," she'd said confidently.

Carly and Max and Jamie and Duke made their way through the coffee shop, pausing to admire Jamie's three paintings hung on the walls, all for purchase. Originally, there had been four. One had sold for enough that Jamie was able to buy a state-of-the-art doghouse for Duke. Jamie was Carly's newest client. He didn't pay her anything, and sometimes, she didn't know if he understood his work was selling. He just wanted to paint.

"Isn't it cool, Jamie?" Carly asked. "People love your work."

"Busy work for busy hands," Jamie said.

In the back garden, beneath glittering bulbs and Chinese lanterns that hung from the live oaks, Suzanna was already on stage, tuning her guitar. The place was packed because, Carly whispered to Max, "of excellent publicity."

He squeezed her hand.

They chose a table in the back so that Jamie and Duke were not in the middle of all the people going in and out of the shop.

Mia and Will were to join them, and as they watched the door for them, a man stepped out. He had a rotund figure and wore a thick black sweater over a white T-shirt and tiny wire-rimmed glasses.

"Wow, I feel like I know him," Carly said. "He looks *so* familiar." She studied him a moment as he picked his way through the crowd, then gasped. She turned to Max. "I've got it!"

"The Penguin," Max said.

Carly laughed, and they high-fived each other. They hadn't missed a *Batman* reference yet.

Carly was crazy happy in her new life—crazy, crazy happy.

She and Max were in love, and that's all she needed to know. They had not talked about the future, not yet—neither of them were ready to do anything that would necessitate parental involvement, like a wedding. That was definitely going to require some finessing. But it didn't matter right now. They knew where they were going, and it was into the future together.

"There they are," Max said.

The kids were out first, the three of them running into the garden setting as if they lived there. Millie pulled up to one table and stared at the grown-ups. That table thought the little girl was cute. For the moment.

"Too much noise," Jamie said as Finn and Bo raced toward them.

Duke pressed his head against Jamie's thigh and licked his hand. Jamie looked down, put his hand on Duke's head. "Too much noise," he said again, but he didn't seem overly agitated.

"You brought the kids?" Carly asked as Mia waddled over in her eighth month of pregnancy and fell into a chair. Will and Max greeted each other, and Will said hello to Jamie and told Finn to stop staring at him.

"Was I supposed to abandon them?" Mia snapped.

"Not *abandon* them, but maybe a sitter? Where is your nanny?"

"Quit! Got a job in West Lake Hills. Those people pay some *bucks*, Carly. I'm so glad you're back. I'm going to need all the help I can get. *Millie!* Millie, come here!" she hissed loudly.

"Thanks everyone for coming," Suzanna said into her mic. She strummed her guitar. "It's a beautiful day, isn't it? This first song is one I wrote for all the lovers out there. You know who you are." She started to play.

Carly glanced at Max. He smiled at her. He put his arm around her and drew her into his side as Mia admonished Millie for running off and Jamie muttered under his breath and Will pretended not to hear the fight that had broken out between his sons. "Well, this has disaster written all over it. Any regrets?" he whispered.

She didn't know if he was asking about this outing in particular or life in general. But she had not a single regret about anything. Certainly not about leaving New York. She loved what she was doing now. And just as Megan Monroe had promised, when one door closed, you pulled on your big girl panties and walked through the next open door.

Carly looked forward to each day, and amazingly, it just got better and better.

She was one lucky dog.

Acknowledgments

I've written several books now, and sometimes I forget to say out loud how thankful I am to all the people who bring my books into the world. My part is the easy part—I tell myself a story and write it down. Getting it into your hands takes an army with skills I could never possess. That army has my undying gratitude, even if I haven't said it. Let me say it now:

First and foremost, I have to thank my agent, Jenny Bent. We've been together a long time and she is still my biggest cheerleader, sounding board, and reality check. I adore her. To Kate Seaver, who brought me to Berkley Publishing, and who has a very keen editorial eye. Plus, she's so bloody charming that you realize you've done a big dose of revisions and forgot to get mad about it. Thanks to Mary, Brittanie, and Jessica, and probably a host of others whose names I don't know, who make sure my books get to production and then get noticed in this crazy, noisy world. It's a superhuman feat. To whoever designed this cover, you are a genius and I love you. Thanks to my copy editor, the nameless, faceless person who pulls at all the loose threads until the manuscript is spic and span.

A big thanks to Linda, who keeps the social media machine humming when I'm writing, and is so cool that she actually sent me some of her Clorox wipes recently when I couldn't find any anywhere. My one regret after working with her all these years is that she doesn't live closer.

To my bestie writer friends, who I need in my life every single day, because no one but another writer ever gets how weird this industry is, and no one but another writer agrees it's "not too much, it never gets old" when you schedule another video happy hour with wine to talk about writing books. Thanks Teri, Sasha, Sherry, Tracy, Laura, Marnie, Beckie, Janene, Connie, Christina, Julie, Dee, and Sherri. You have been the village that has raised this child through the years. Love you, man!

Thanks one thousand times over to my family, every single one of you. You're so proud of me! Even though I think we all know you've created a bit of a J-Lo monster. For that, I'm sorry-not sorry. Love you all so much.

Photo by Kathy Whittaker Photography

Julia London is the *New York Times*, *USA Today*, and *Publishers Weekly* bestselling author of numerous romance and women's fiction novels. She is also the recipient of the RT Bookclub Award for Best Historical Romance and a six-time finalist for the prestigious RITA Award for excellence in romantic fiction.